Forget Me Not

SAVANNAH SHEETS

Content Warning

This book contains mentions of suicidal ideation, child abuse, self harm, and rape. If you are struggling, remember that you are not alone. There is help, there is hope, and there are people willing to listen. Take care, and please be kind to yourself.

To Mrs. Morgan, who inspired me. To Miss Smith, who encouraged me. And to Professor Flowers, who told me that my real-life story mattered and deserved to be shared.

Thank you for shaping me into the person I am today. <3

Prologue:

C ole

Headlights sliced through the darkness, tearing across the cracked road. Somewhere ahead, an owl cried out—like it was waiting for me.

Calling me.

The wind shifted, biting through my t-shirt and stealing what little warmth my body had left. But I didn't stop. I couldn't.

This was my way out.

The cry of the owl came again, closer this time, the sound burrowing under my skin, twisting through my thoughts, and pulling me forward. My heart pounded harder with every step, my chest burning with something hot, electric, *alive.*

Almost there. Then I could be done.

That's when the light came.

It exploded through the night, swallowing everything—blinding, searing, too bright to even be real. I froze, every nerve in my body locking up as panic surged like ice through my veins.

Every instinct in me screamed to move, but I couldn't.

The light wrapped around me, digging into my skin like it wanted to peel me apart. My breath caught, and for the first time, I thought, *Maybe I made a mistake*.

The impact came—no, it *should have* come.

But it didn't.

Chapter One:

AUGUST 2ND

G racie
    I had gotten really good at pretending.

Pretending I wasn't about to be late for work (again), pretending I didn't mind the kitchen being so quiet on Saturday mornings, and pretending I actually enjoyed making smoothies for my little brother, Bear.

Yeah, I was really nailing this life thing.

The blender whirled, crunching together the last of the frozen berries we had in the house as I tapped a finger against my black glasses frames. The habit was barely noticeable now, just the faint click of my fingernail against plastic, but it used to drive Mom crazy.

"Gracie, stop doing that. You'll scratch the lenses,"

Her voice trailed off as she wiped down the windows in this same kitchen, humming softly while sunlight poured through the glass.

Those first months after the move had been straight out of a Hallmark movie. Everything seemed brighter—the house, the town, the promise of something better.

Bear had been eleven at the time, darting between boxes and disassembled furniture as he practiced his stickhandling for middle school hockey tryouts later that month.

Dad was arguing with the movers about where the couch should go.

Mom paused mid-swipe, her gaze fixed on the backyard. *"Look at this view,"* she breathed in awe. *"It's so green here, nothing like Vegas."*

I hadn't thought much of it at the time. I was too busy sneaking another handful of marshmallows from the bag on the counter. But now, years later, the window was smudged, and the sunlight that streamed in had dulled, muddled by the clouds that seemed to hang over everything these days.

The blender sputtered and stopped, snapping me back to the present.

I grabbed a glass, mechanically pouring the smoothie into it and sliding it across the counter to Bear, who was hunched over his tablet listening to some recap of a hockey game from last season.

So many things had changed since we moved to Utah, but at least I could always count on quiet moments like this.

For now, at least.

"You don't have to make me breakfast every morning, you know," Bear said, his eyes flicking up briefly before returning to the screen.

"Yeah, well, someone has to," I muttered, turning my attention back to the sink.

Bear's blonde curls fell over his eyes, and he blew at them in frustration.

His frame was smaller than it should've been, and honestly, it wasn't fair. Fourteen-year-olds weren't supposed to look that skinny. They weren't supposed to struggle with things like walking across the kitchen or eating solid foods.

But life didn't ask what was fair, did it?

I turned the faucet on and plunged my hands into the warm, soapy water. The pile of dishes felt endless—kind of like my life these days. Some mornings, I could convince myself this was just how things were supposed to be. Taking care of Bear. Being the responsible one. Juggling school and work like all normal sixteen-year-olds did.

But other days, like today, it was harder to gaslight myself into thinking that I hadn't been dealt a shitty hand.

"Have you heard from Dad?" Bear asked suddenly, pausing his game.

I shook my head as I dried my hands on a dish towel. "Not since Thursday. He said he'd try to call, but, you know…"

"Yeah, I know."

Bear didn't say anything else, and neither did I. Because what was there to say? Dad was always working, and Mom—well, she was gone. Not in the "out of town" way, but in the "she's not coming back" way.

I picked up a sponge and started scrubbing at a stubborn spot on a plate, trying to swallow the lump in my throat.

Over the years, I had learned a hard lesson: I wasn't a princess. Prince Charming wasn't coming for me. And no matter how hard I tried, I'd always be the girl stuck babysitting my little brother.

I looked up from the sink, just in time to see the clock ticking on the wall.

8:02 AM

8:03 AM

Congratulations, Gracie… and now you're late for work!

"Shoot," I said, setting down the sponge and shutting off the water. "Are you going to be okay by yourself for the next couple hours?"

He nodded. "Yep,"

"And you're not going to 'forget' to take your meds this time?" I asked, raising an eyebrow as I grabbed my bag from the back of one of the kitchen chairs.

"I won't forget," Bear sighed. "You don't have to remind me every five minutes."

I didn't mean for it to sound nagging. I just worried. A *lot*.

And lately, I had more to worry about. His doctors were pushing him to switch to a new medication—something experimental that might help more with his Juvenile Myasthenia Gravis. But of course, it came with a whole list of side effects longer than my arm.

Which was why we had to get through his current prescription. Because maybe then, things would finally start looking up. Maybe, if we just kept pushing forward, he'd wake up one morning and magically be cured.

Stupid, I know.

But my whole *life* had been stupid since Bear had gotten sick.

I slung my bag over my shoulder and tugged on my boots, the soles scuffing against the worn linoleum floors underneath me.

"Bye, Bear," I called over my shoulder as I headed toward the door.

"Later, Gracie," he mumbled, already lost in his hockey game again.

I paused with my hand on the doorknob, the words "I love you" resting on the tip of my tongue. They were right there—so close I could almost taste them.

But like always, I left them unsaid.

Old habits die hard, I guess.

Chapter Two:

"Sorry I'm late, Mary Anne," I panted, clutching my sides as I tried to catch my breath. Sprinting from my car to the barn hadn't been the brightest idea in the world, but I still shot her a grin, holding up a bag of horse treats. "Would you do me the honor of accepting this very thoughtful, definitely-not-last-minute bribe?"

My boss chuckled, shaking her head as she glanced at the treats with a raised brow. "You're lucky we ran out this morning. Set those over there and come help me finish mucking these stalls."

"You sure know how to make a girl feel welcome." I laughed, placing the bag with the rest of the feed before following her.

Deep down, though, I didn't really mind. Working here wasn't just about the money (although that was a bonus); it was about the experience. It was about feeling like I belonged somewhere. And Mary Anne had this incredible ability to do just that.

It was the reason I had stuck around so long in the first place, because Heaven knows I wasn't in it for the horse shit.

I grabbed a shovel and started working on the manure, pushing the wheelbarrow as we went along. The heat from it rose in waves, and I had to physically stop myself from gagging.

It wasn't glamorous by any means, but it was mine. It was where I could lose myself for a little while. The one place where I didn't have to think about school, or my messed-up home life, or even what people thought about me.

The only thing that mattered was that I fed the horses on time.

"Are you excited for school to start back up soon?" Mary Anne asked, breaking the silence.

I shrugged, lifting another load. "To be honest, I haven't really thought about going back."

She leaned on her shovel, sighing as she watched me. "I remember junior year. Full of fun, school dances, *boys*... You'll see."

I snorted, giving her a look. "Yeah, because boys my age are so mature."

She laughed. "They grow up. Some of them, anyway."

"Not holding my breath," I muttered, turning back to the pile of feces before me.

Mary Anne smirked. "When the right one comes along, you won't be so cynical."

"Sure," I scoffed, wrinkling my nose. "My Prince Charming's bound to come riding up on a white horse to whisk me away. Should be any day now."

"Well," she said with a wink, "we've got plenty of horses."

I stuck my tongue out at her, and she laughed, wiping her hands on her jeans. "I better grab Apollo for his checkup. Why don't you see if Cole needs help? He's been at it since dawn."

8

I groaned. "Great. Nothing like an early morning bonding session with the spawn of Satan."

Mary Anne just smiled as she walked off. "He's not so bad."

"Sure," I muttered, giving the wheelbarrow a shove. "He grows on you... like a fungus."

Cole Brown: If you've ever seen a movie in your entire life, he's the stereotypical jock. The kind of guy who thought he was the greatest thing since sliced bread, the type of person who could benefit from being knocked down a peg... or two.

Or seven.

I wasn't in a hurry to find him. In fact, I was more than happy to delay the inevitable. So instead of heading toward the hay barn where he probably was, I veered off toward the pasture because if I was going to suffer through another morning with *him*, I needed a little me time first.

Y'know, so he didn't make me commit a felony against him or something.

My favorite horse, Painted Lady, was grazing lazily in the field when I walked up, her black-and-white coat catching the dewy sunlight. She was Mary Anne's miracle "child," one that she'd rescued from a slaughterhouse a few years back.

At first, Painted Lady had been skittish around everyone. But it was for a good reason. When she arrived at the ranch, she was malnourished and *visibly* abused. But over time, Mary Anne's patience worked its magic (as it always did), and slowly, the beautiful mare became more of "herself" around her.

And for whatever reason, I'd even grown on her too.

I whistled softly as I approached the pasture fence, my fingertips grazing the weathered wood. Painted Lady's ears flicked back, her head lifting to see me.

The second we made eye contact, she took off in my direction. I grinned, quickly pulling myself up one rung of the fence to hop over it and meet her halfway.

She skidded to a stop just before she could barrel into me, and I reached out, stroking her neck with my fingers.

"Between you and me," I whispered to the horse, "I'm not looking forward to seeing any big, scary meanies named Cole today. How about you?"

Painted Lady snorted softly, nudging me with her nose, as if agreeing. I smiled and leaned my forehead against hers for a second.

Being with her was easy—no words, no judgments, just peace.

But naturally, it didn't last. Because of course it didn't. Not when *he* was around.

"Yo, Princess!"

My hand froze on Painted Lady's neck, and I sighed, already bracing myself as I turned. *Cole*.

He was by the hay barn, tossing bales into the bed of his idling two-toned brown Ford truck—the picture of *effortlessly rugged* confidence.

He always looked like that, though, like he *belonged*. Like he knew exactly what he was doing and exactly how to irritate me. And okay, fine, I guess I could see why half the school thought he was good-looking.

He was (annoyingly) tall, broad-shouldered, with shaggy light brown hair. And those gray eyes of his... they weren't the kind you could ignore easily.

But I wasn't one of those girls who swooned over him. Not even close.

It wasn't because I thought that I *couldn't* fall for him. Before everything, I'd even wanted to be friends with him. But Cole, being the *charming soul he was*, had made it his personal mission to hate me for no reason since middle school.

I'd barely said two words to him since I was just the new girl from Vegas back then, but that didn't stop him from treating me like a disease. And it wasn't just your average schoolyard bullying either. He went out of his way to find and exploit your insecurities like it was the only thing that got him out of bed in the morning.

"You gonna stand there all day, or are you actually going to help?" Cole called out as he tossed another bale of hay into his truck.

I patted Painted Lady one last time and climbed back over the fence, my boots crunching against the gravel as I reluctantly made my way towards him. "Hello to you too, Cole."

"You were supposed to help me *ten minutes ago*, Princess."

I sucked in a sharp breath at the nickname. He always said it like he was trying to remind me that to him, I was just some spoiled city brat who couldn't possibly understand what real work was. It didn't matter that I'd been at Mary Anne's longer than he had. To Cole, I'd always be the outsider.

And then there was that stupid accent he had...

I still wasn't sure if it was real or just part of his ongoing campaign to irritate the hell out of me. Especially since I was pretty sure he'd never been south of Utah in his *life*. But that didn't stop him from talking like he'd just strolled out of an old Western movie.

I reached for a bale of hay, ignoring the way his smirk deepened as I struggled to get a good grip on it. "Trust me, Cole," I grunted, gripping the bale tighter than necessary, "if I had a choice, I wouldn't be here."

And just to clarify, by *here*, I didn't mean Mary Anne's ranch—I meant anywhere around *him*. Because if there was one thing Cole excelled at (besides being a complete moron), it was making sure I regretted every second of our proximity.

I heaved the bale off the stack, the rough twine biting into my palms immediately. It wasn't even that heavy, but the awkward shape made it nearly impossible to hold it right.

My arms screamed in protest as I hauled it toward the truck, but I kept my mouth shut and face neutral. I wasn't about to give Cole the satisfaction of thinking I couldn't handle myself.

Out of the corner of my eye, I saw him pick up another bale like it weighed nothing, slinging it over his shoulder with ease. He didn't even bother to glance my way as he walked past, humming loudly—*too* loudly.

Wait, no. He wasn't humming. He was *singing*.

My jaw clenched as recognition of the song hit me. "*Seriously*, Cole?"

He raised an eyebrow. "Not a fan of Chris LeDoux songs, Princess?"

"Not when *you're* the one singing them," I shot back, adjusting my grip on the bale as I stumbled forward another step. "And really? *This Cowboy's Hat*? Again? Don't you know any other songs?"

He grinned, tipping an imaginary hat in my direction. "Why would I, when this one's your favorite?"

I groaned, dragging my bale the last few feet and practically shoving it onto the truck bed. "It's *not*."

"Right," he laughed, shaking his head like I'd just proven his point. "Because city girls like you probably think that Luke Combs and I dunno... *Taylor Swift* are the pinnacle of country. Let me guess, you've never heard of Chris LeDoux, have you?"

"I've heard of Chris LeDoux," I snapped, crossing my arms hard against my chest. "Just because I don't have *your* musical taste, doesn't mean I'm stupid."

He shrugged. "Debatable..."

"And for your information," I shot back, glaring as he strolled around the truck to grab some ties, "Luke Combs is amazing. And if you can't appreciate Taylor Swift, that's just proof you've got the emotional range of a teaspoon."

Cole stopped, leaning his elbows lazily on the truck's bed as he gave me a long, almost bored look. "I'm not even gonna argue with the Swift thing because the last thing I need is you turning into some unhinged Swiftie on me. But let's not pretend you're actually a Luke Combs fan. I bet you can't even name one of his songs."

I laughed dryly, holding out my fingers as I started counting. "Let's see... there's *All Over Again, When it Rains it Pours, Beer Never Broke My Heart, Does to Me...* oh, and my personal favorite, *Beautiful Crazy*—"

"I said *one* song."

I shrugged. "What can I say? I'm an overachiever. Unlike *you*."

Cole grabbed a tie and looped it around one of the bales. "Overachiever, huh? Is that why you spent fifteen minutes trying to lift a bale of hay?"

"I got it in the truck, didn't I?" I fired back. "*Ugh.* I'd rather be back talking to the horses. Or, better yet, maybe a rock—at least that's got a better personality than you do."

His jaw ticked, but that stupid smirk stayed firmly in place. "Cute. I'll be sure to get you a pet rock for Christmas."

"Oh, good," I said, matching his sarcasm level. "I'll name it Cole, so I have something else completely useless lying around."

"*Funny,*" he said dryly.

I clenched my fists, my nails biting into my palms as I fought the urge to throw something at his head. "*Are we done here?*"

Cole didn't answer, just gave me one last look as if to say *duh,* before climbing into the truck and slamming the door harder than necessary. The engine growled as he peeled off toward the pasture, leaving a cloud of dust in his wake.

I stood there, my chest heaving with pent-up frustration. It didn't matter how many times I told myself not to let him get to me—he always did. Cole Brown wasn't just a thorn in my side; he was the whole damn briar patch.

Chapter Three:

Cole

I slammed the truck door harder than I'd meant to. The old Ford rattled as the engine coughed to life, and I gripped the wheel like it was the only thing keeping me from losing it completely.

My eyes flicked to the rearview mirror, catching sight of Gracie still standing by the barn. That stupid, shiny hair of hers was blowing in the wind like she belonged in some damn movie scene.

I quickly tore my gaze away from her and slammed my foot on the gas. Gravel kicked up under the tires, rattling the truck as it bounced down the dirt road toward the pasture. My chest felt tight, like something was squeezing the air out of me.

It wasn't her fault. I knew that. But hell, if she didn't make me feel like everything I did didn't matter. Like all the time I put in at the ranch, all the sweat, all the work—none of it counted the second she showed up. Like

Mary Anne and everyone else would choose her over me in a heartbeat if given the chance.

I hated how much she got under my skin. Hated the way I fought her on everything every time she opened her mouth. But mostly, I hated how easy she made it all seem. Like she could just waltz into this life and fit right in. Like she belonged here. Like she'd earned it.

But me? I didn't belong. And I couldn't leave. Not even if I wanted to. *Just imagine what Dad would think if he could see me now...*

I bit down hard on the inside of my cheek, gripping the wheel even tighter. The wind whipped through the windows, but it didn't cool the fire burning in my gut. I kept driving, the pasture finally coming into view, but the pit in my stomach only got heavier.

Every time I had to go back home—pretend to "play family" with my little sister, Mom, and that idiot she married—I felt like a damn ghost. We'd sit around the dinner table, passing mashed potatoes like we were some picture-perfect family. Like Dad hadn't left a hole the size of the Grand Canyon in our lives.

My mom wanted to pretend, keep acting like everything was fine because she'd found herself a replacement. But I knew better. *Nothing was fine. Nothing was ever gonna be fine.*

I swallowed down the knot in my throat as I pulled up to the fence. The horses were already there, waiting. At least *someone* was happy to see me.

Killing the engine, I stepped out of the cab, the smell of hay and dirt filling the air. *There was work to do.* That was something I could control, at least.

I grabbed a bale of hay from the truck and tossed it over the fence, the weight barely registering. Just another chore that wouldn't change a damn thing.

Another bale hit the ground, and the horses were already pushing forward to feed. I ran my hand through my hair, my arms tingling with exhaustion, my whole body feeling like it usually did after a long football practice.

But nothing came close to the anger bubbling under the surface.

Gracie didn't know what it was like to watch your whole life fall apart and be the one who had to piece it back together. She didn't know what it was like to wake up every day and feel the weight of everything pressing down around you, reminding you that no matter how hard you tried, you'd never escape. You'd never be good enough.

She didn't know what it was like to lose someone. Not the way I had.

I grabbed another bale, throwing it harder than I needed to.

The horses didn't care, though. They just kept eating, oblivious to everything. Oblivious to the fact that the only thing keeping me from falling apart completely was hating her.

Because at least hating her felt better than everything else I couldn't fix.

August 3rd

Gracie

I pushed open the heavy barn doors, expecting to see Mary Anne at her usual spot by the stalls, greeting me with her cheerful, "Morning, Sunshine!" But the barn was unusually quiet. Something was... off.

Where's Mary Anne?

17

I shrugged it off at first, figuring she must be in her office or outside somewhere. Still, it felt weird that she hadn't popped in to say good morning.

But maybe she had lost track of time. Maybe she was running errands in town.

Maybe something horrible had happened to her.

Way to think the worst out of every situation you're in, Gracie. I thought as anxiety fluttered around in my stomach like rabid dogs attacking a little lamb.

My feet shuffled automatically to the place she probably (*hopefully*) was: her office, and to my relief, I heard her voice as I approached the door. But it was low and serious, and not at all like the tone of hers I was used to.

I knew I probably shouldn't, but I just couldn't help myself. With all the stealth of a cartoon character sneaking through a hallway, I tiptoed closer, my boots making the faintest creaks on the floorboards.

I pressed myself against the wall just outside the office door, heart pounding like I was about to get caught with my hand in the metaphorical cookie jar.

"Yes, Officer Walker, I understand," Mary Anne said, her voice carrying through the slightly ajar door.

Officer? I leaned in closer, careful not to bump into anything that would give me away.

"No, no, Cole's doing fine here," she continued, "He's kept up with his work, and there haven't been any major issues." There was a long pause. "Well, he's got a bit of a temper, but nothing I can't handle. It's just... you know how hard this is for him, given everything."

My mind raced. *Wait. Cole?* I frowned, shifting to get a better angle without making any noise. *What's she talking about?*

"No, everything's been fine. I promise," Mary Anne reassured the person on the other line, "He's been careful not to mess up since the whole... well, since the last incident."

My heart skipped a beat. *What incident?*

I heard the scrape of a chair against the floor, and I quickly pressed myself back against the wall, biting my lip in an effort to stay silent. I knew eavesdropping was wrong, (like, *really* wrong) but my brain wouldn't let me pull away.

I have to know what's going on.

"Yes, I'll continue to send you updates." Another pause, "Of course, I'll call if there are any problems. He's doing fine with the community service, though. Working here at the ranch has been good for him. He's learning some responsibility..."

Wait... *Community service?*

Cole—Mr. "I'm-so-perfect-with-my-fake-southern-charm"—was doing *community service*?

I didn't need to stick around for anything else.

I bolted out of the barn, heart racing, my boots slipping slightly in the gravel as I made my way back to the horses. I couldn't believe it—Cole was doing *community service*.

All this time, he acted like he was better than me, like he owned this place, when really, he was nothing but a criminal working off a punishment.

The fact that he'd gone out of his way to make my life miserable, and now I knew his stupid, little secret? It was almost too perfect.

He had it coming.

I could use this—no, I *would* use this.

He couldn't look down on me or *tease* me anymore, not after this.

Maybe now he'd shut his mouth and leave me alone. After all, he had no choice. He wouldn't risk his precious reputation as captain of the football team just to spite me.

I grabbed a pitchfork, half-heartedly mucking the pasture as my mind spun, feeding on the possibilities. Cole was about to find out what it was like to be the one with no power.

It was going to be so satisfying seeing him sweat. To see him squirm in the way he'd made me squirm for years. *This was it*—my chance to turn things around, to *redeem* myself... to finally put him in his place.

This was my Christmas morning.

As the sky turned to early afternoon, my heart started beating in double-time while heading back to the barn. I knew he'd be in there, and I also knew that this would be as good of a time as ever to enact my slightly evil but totally deserved plan.

I pushed open the door, my eyes scanning the dim space until they landed on him. He was over by the tack room, wiping down some gear like he didn't have a care in the world.

Just you wait, Cole Brown.

"Nice day for community service, isn't it?" I said, keeping my voice light as it dripped with fake sugary sweetness.

But surprisingly, he didn't look up at me. He didn't even flinch. He just kept working—although his jaw grew noticeably tighter.

"What's wrong?" I pressed. "Cat got your tongue, or are you just too embarrassed to talk to me now that I know?"

Still nothing. Just the sound of the rag dragging over the leather.

"Come on, Cole. Aren't you even a little worried about what people might think? What do you think the football team would say when they hear that their precious captain—"

20

"At this point," he interrupted flatly, "everyone knows about my 'little secret'. So, if you want to get something on me... I suggest you try a little harder."

My cheeks burned. "You think you're so untouchable, don't you?" I shot back. "But you're not. Not even close."

I was about to keep going, to say something about his dad—which would've been horrible, I know, but it was all I could think of. Only, something about the way his expression shifted stopped me cold.

His smirk was gone, replaced by something darker, *harder*, like he already knew what I was thinking.

"Don't finish that sentence, Princess,"

I should've stopped. I *knew* I should've. But it felt like he was baiting me, so before I could think it through, I blurted out. "Your dad wouldn't have liked you always bullying me, you *ass*. I bet he'd be seriously disappointed in how you turned out if he was still here."

Cole turned to face me fully now, the rag hanging limply between his fingers.

For a second, I thought he was going to break the silence by throwing some stupid insult back at me like he always did. But after a heavy minute of silence, he gritted his teeth and mumbled. "Don't talk about things you don't understand, Gracie."

Gracie. Not *Princess*.

He never called me that. *Ever*. It was always "princess". Hearing him say my name now, my *actual* name, sent the temperature in the barn plummeting.

It was like a line had been crossed, like whatever invisible wall stood between us had shattered, and now I was standing in the path of something I didn't really know how to come back from.

I took a small step away from him, but instead of embracing the silence that had settled on us again like I should have, my mouth ran ahead of my brain. "Look, I get it. I understand more than anyone what it's like to have daddy issues. I—"

"I *don't* have daddy issues."

"I just thought since…"

Before I could finish, Cole snapped, his whole body going rigid. "Stop acting like you know anything about me or my dad!" he roared, his voice louder than I'd ever heard it before.

I took another mini step back, panic creeping in, but before I could even think about apologizing—*hell, what was I even apologizing for?*—he grabbed my arm and dragged me toward the nearest stall. I stumbled, my breath catching in my throat.

"Cole, what are you—" I started, but his grip tightened, and he shoved me into the stall anyway.

"You want me to be the bully?" he growled as he blocked the exit. "Fine. I'll be the bully."

I scrambled back as he stalked his way closer to me. The barn suddenly felt suffocating as my heart pounded so hard it echoed in my ears.

Here's what I knew: Cole was a loose cannon with *CLEAR MENTAL ISSUES* who had been sentenced to juvie. For what? I didn't know. But upstanding citizens didn't just *get juvie*. And right then, all I could think about was we were alone *together*, and while again, I kind of deserved this…

Never mind. No matter what I had done, I didn't deserve to die alone in a barn.

"You have no idea what it's like to be treated like a fucking monster." His voice cracked as he closed in on me.

I barely knew how to respond to that, but somehow, I managed to say, "No one's treating you like a monster..."

"Oh, yeah?" Cole's voice was low, the words clipped. He leaned in closer, his hands pressing against the wooden frame about me, caging me in. "Then why do you look like I'm about to kill you, Princess?"

His breath was too close and hot against my skin. I almost wanted to laugh, but I couldn't find the humor.

"Back to the nickname, huh?" I forced the words out, trying to sound more confident than I felt. "Guess that means we can... move past this little hiccup?"

For a second, something shifted in his expression. He stepped back just enough for me to breathe, his posture less hostile, at least. And for the first time since this whole nightmare had started, I thought *maybe* we could actually have a normal, adult conversation.

"You're tough, Princess," he muttered, almost to himself, "Tougher than I gave you credit for."

I blinked up at him, caught off guard. *Is that... an olive branch?*

"Look, I..." I swallowed the lump in my throat, trying to gather my thoughts. "I shouldn't have implied that you have daddy issues or anything." The words tasted weird on my tongue. Apologizing wasn't something I was used to, especially to someone like him. "But you haven't exactly been a saint either."

His eyes softened for a second. Then he let out a humorless laugh. "I probably *do* have daddy issues. Guess I'm just as fucked up as you, Gracie."

Coming from anyone else, it probably would've been an insult, but if Cole was saying it. Well... I'd take it as a half-assed attempt at a compliment.

He rubbed a hand across the back of his neck, looking somewhere off to the side like he was trying to figure out how to say whatever was on his mind.

Then, finally, he let out a long, heavy sigh. "You're right. My dad... he wouldn't be proud of me. In fact, he'd be disappointed to see how I turned out, no question. But just because your mistakes aren't listed on some criminal record doesn't mean you're perfect."

His words hung in the air between us, heavier than I expected. I wanted to argue, to defend myself. But there was the slightest bit of truth in what he was saying that made me think twice.

"You're right too. I'm *not* perfect." I muttered, surprising myself with the admission. "Far from it. My parents are barely around. It's just me and Bear most of the time, and I have to figure it out. Alone."

Cole watched me, his expression unreadable, but there was a shift, a crack in his usual disregard for human life. "I get that," he said softly, "My dad... he's gone. And I have to live with that. It's fucking lonely sometimes."

"Guess we're more alike than I thought," I said, offering a small smile.

Cole shrugged. "Maybe."

For a small, fleeting moment, it was almost like we were getting somewhere. Not as friends, *definitely not as friends*—but not enemies either. Like there was this tiny bridge between us that was starting to form. Almost like we could understand each other for just a second.

And then *it* happened.

As he shifted his weight, his hand brushed against my thigh. The touch was light, barely even there, but it sent a shockwave through my body, freezing me in place. And suddenly, I couldn't breathe again, my head swimming as the barn closed in around me.

I was thrown back into the fire of a place I didn't want to go.

My memories.

My body moved before my mind could catch up—some kind of instinct taking over, and I reached for the first thing I could grab: a plastic pitchfork, swinging it with everything I had.

The prongs hit his (*Cole's*) chest and then bounced off like a rubber ball hitting a brick wall. He didn't even flinch. He just blinked at me, unimpressed, his brow furrowing in confusion more than anything.

"What the *hell*, Gracie?" His voice wasn't angry, just... baffled.

I looked at the rake in my hand, completely useless. Great. *Note to self: next time I'm fighting the ghost of my past, grab something with a little more impact.*

My hands shook as I dropped the rake, the reality of the situation came rushing back to me. "I... I'm sorry. I didn't mean to—"

But I couldn't even finish the jumbled mess of that sentence. I felt exposed, raw, and ugly, like everything I had worked so hard to keep buried was now out in the open for all to see and prey on.

That moment we had shared was now completely obliterated. *Gone.* And probably forever, too, because Cole was right. I *was* fucked up.

His face hardened again, his walls slamming up just as quickly as mine had. "So that's how it is, huh?" His voice was low, but there was a hint of disappointment in it. "I try to have an honest fucking conversation with you for one second, and you *hit me with a pitchfork*?"

I backed up, feeling the wall pressing against me again, my body still vibrating from the swing. "You touched me," I whispered, the words coming out in a breathless rush, unsure if he could even hear me over the pounding in my ears.

"I *barely* touched you," he shot back, shaking his head, "Are you insane? You—"

"I don't care what you have to say right now!" The words slipped out harsher than I'd meant for them to, but I didn't apologize. I just pulled my arms around myself, like somehow that would protect me from it all. "Just *stay away* from me."

Cole's jaw tightened, his hands curling into fists at his sides. For a minute, he didn't say anything, like he was trying to make sense of everything that had just happened. I could see the wheels turning in his head, but I didn't know if he was coming to any conclusions.

And then without warning, his expression turned to stone, like something inside him just clicked into place. Before I could even react, he was already charging toward the exit.

He reached the door, his hand gripping the latch in one fluid motion. The sound of metal sliding into place echoed through the barn.

I blinked before what had just happened finally sank in. Panic shot up my spine as I ran to the bars, shaking them with everything I had. "*Hey*! Let me out!" I begged, "You can't just lock me in here!"

"Mary Anne will let you out at dinnertime... probably," Cole replied coldly. I could hear him and his stupid boots walking away from me as he made his way down the breezeway. "Have fun with the rats, Princess!"

The door to the barn clanged shut behind him, the sound deafening in the silence that followed. I stared at the bars in front of me, my fingers still gripping the metal, but it felt like the world had shifted, and I wasn't part of it anymore.

"Cole!" I shouted, my voice cracking, hands trembling as I yanked at the bars again.

My breath came in short gasps, and I turned to the stall, the air thick with the fresh dust I had accidentally kicked up. My heart raced as I scanned the space, desperate for something... *anything* to get me out.

In the corner, a loose wire tangled in the straw caught my eye. I yanked it free, the metal digging into my palm, but the pain barely registered. I pressed the wire against the lock, trying to maneuver it into place.

Sweat stung my eyes as I fought to stay focused. My breath was ragged, and all I could hear was the pounding of my heart and the sound of me desperately twisting the wire.

It wouldn't work, though. Every move I made, the lock fought back, and my fingers kept slipping, slick with sweat.

I let out a strangled sob. "This can't be happening right now," I muttered, sinking against the wall. Tears fell down my face, but I quickly wiped them away. I was furious at myself for getting upset, but I was even more furious for letting him win.

As I sat there, I tried to remember that Mary Anne would be looking for me. But in the silence of the stall, with Cole's words still echoing in my mind, it felt like hope was slipping through my fingers, just as unsuccessfully as the wire slipping from the lock.

Just as Cole had predicted, Mary Anne noticed that I was locked inside the horse stall around dinnertime. But by then, I was beyond angry.

"I can't believe you hit him, Gracie." Mary Anne said as soon as she let me out.

I brushed past her, fuming. "I was *defending* myself."

Mary Anne sighed, following me as I stormed toward the office. "Defending yourself isn't the same as hitting someone with a rake."

I whipped back around. "I'm glad he had a chance to tell you his side of the story while I was *locked in a stall*, but he was the one who backed me into a corner! What else was I supposed to do? Just stand there and let him—"

"He wasn't going to hurt you," she cut in, her voice calm but stern, "He's got a temper, yes, but you... you overreacted, Gracie."

"Are you seriously taking his side right now?"

"I'm not taking *anyone's* side." She rubbed her temples as if I were giving her a headache. "I'm just trying to understand what's going on with you... Is something happening at home? You know you can always come to me if—"

"*Nothing* is going on at home!" I snapped, "And you know *why*? Because my parents are never there so anything *can* happen! Don't you get it? You're the only family I have left, and you don't care about me. You're not even listening!"

She fell silent, watching me, her eyes softening with pity. *Pity.* I hated that look.

"Okay, Gracie," she said after a moment, her voice gentler, "I'm listening. Tell me your side of the story."

"I don't want him here!" I shouted, my frustration spilling over before I could stop it. "He's nothing but a narcissistic jerk, and you're acting like it's my fault. I was just defending myself, and now *I'm* the bad guy?"

Mary Anne's eyes darkened, "No, Gracie. You were *pushing* him. You knew exactly what you were doing."

I froze. "You think this is *my* fault?" I asked, blinking with disbelief.

Mary Anne crossed her arms. "I think you heard that conversation with his parole officer this morning, didn't you?"

I opened my mouth to argue, but nothing came out. *She knew*. I turned my gaze downward, only confirming it for her.

"You took that information, and you used it against Cole. You went after him on purpose. Right after you found out how much trouble he's in, you started pushing his buttons. You knew he'd snap. You wanted a reaction."

I scoffed. She made it sound like I'd planned this whole thing out, like I was some kind of psychotic manipulator. But she wasn't there. She didn't see how he'd tossed me into that stall, *cornered me*. How he'd made it so there was no choice but *to* fight back.

"I was just trying to stand up for myself!"

"By mocking his situation?"

My fingernails dug into my palms as I tried not to cry. "He's done the same thing to me a *million* times. How come he can get away with it, but I can't?"

Mary Anne's eyes flashed with frustration. "Because you're not him, Gracie. You don't have to sink to his level just because he chooses to lash out. It's not an excuse for you to act the same way."

I threw my hands up in exasperation. "So, what? I'm just supposed to sit there and take it? I'm supposed to let him treat me like crap?"

"No," she said firmly, but her tone was quieter now, "But there's a difference between standing up for yourself and deliberately provoking someone."

"I didn't provoke him!" I shot back, my voice cracking again. But even as the words left my mouth, I knew they weren't entirely true. I *had* provoked him. She was right. I knew what I was doing. I wanted him to hurt. I wanted him to *feel* it.

Like I had to.

Because of him.

But that didn't make me as bad as him. Did it?

"I know you're hurting. I know you're angry, and I understand. There's a lot going on in your life right now between your brother and your parents' divorce... I can't imagine. But lashing out like that, using someone else's pain to make you feel better—that's not who you are."

"I—"

"I'm not finished." Mary Anne cut in. Her shoulders sagged as she let out a deep, weary breath, her gaze drifting toward the window. Cole's truck was disappearing down the road, a laughable reminder of the mess I was stuck in and how he was getting off scot-free, like always. "I didn't want to make this decision, Gracie. Really, I didn't... but I have this deal with the State right now. Ten hours of community service a week for a year. I can't go back on it."

I blinked, trying to process the cold, hard truth of her words. "No. You're not saying what I think you're saying. Are you?"

"I'm going to ask my nephew to help out during the week. Cole can take the weekends."

Bile rose in my throat as the realization sank in. She wasn't taking my side. She was taking *his*. I'd fought so hard to make this place feel like home, to make it work. And now, it was slipping away. *Everything was slipping away.*

"I'm so sorry, Gracie," Mary Anne said, her voice breaking, "But I can't keep you here if it's causing this much trouble. You know I care about you, but..."

I care about you, but...

Yeah, those four words were all too familiar in my vocabulary.

I care about you, but I'm at the doctor's office with your brother right now.

I care about you, but I just can't afford that for you right now. Not with all your brother's medical bills...

I care about you, but... your mom and I are getting a divorce.

It never mattered how much someone *cared*. It was always conditional. Always followed by a *but*.

I only half-listened to the rest of what she was saying—something about lawyers, giving Cole a second chance—until the words that shattered my whole world finally reached my ears.

"You're fired."

The finality of it hit me like a punch to the gut, and all I could do was stare at her. I couldn't breathe. I couldn't think. *This cannot be happening to me right now.*

"Wait..." I swallowed hard, fighting to keep it together. "Mary Anne, please. I'll—I'll never do it again, I promise." My words tumbled out in a rush, desperation clawing at my throat. "Just give me another chance. Please. I can fix this. I'll... I'll apologize to Cole. I'll do anything."

She looked away, her jaw tight, like she didn't want to see me like this. Like it hurt her to watch me fall apart. But I couldn't stop. I had to make her understand. I couldn't lose this—*her*.

"I *need* this job," I begged, "I need *you*. I'll be better, I swear. I know I screwed up today. Just... don't take this away from me. Please."

Mary Anne's face was unreadable, her eyes dark with something I couldn't place. Pity again? Regret? Whatever it was, it wasn't what I wanted to see. It wasn't forgiveness.

"I think you just need some time to yourself," Mary Anne said gently, "With school starting up again, you don't even need to be here. Go enjoy your life, Gracie. You have so much to live for, so much to do. Cole doesn't have other options."

"Please don't do this to me..."

"You need time, Gracie," Mary Anne said, placing a hand on my shoulder as a single defiant tear slid down my cheek. "Time to figure out who you are, outside of all this. That's why I'm letting you go. It's not a punishment. It's a chance."

"I don't want a chance." I whispered, "I just want things to go back to how they were."

"I know," she said, "But that's not how life works. We can't go back, only forward."

I couldn't respond. There was nothing left to say. I had already lost everything.

Chapter Four:

AUGUST 14TH

The heater whirled to a stop, leaving a sudden silence that made the room feel even colder. I burrowed deeper into my comforter, holding onto the last bit of warmth I had.

But mostly, I was using the cold as an excuse to stall. Because I *really* didn't want to face today.

Not when today, the first day of school, gave the popular kids like Cole a chance to let everything they'd been holding back over the summer out onto the people they hated. And I could only imagine how that conversation with him would go having *spent* the summer with him.

"Hey, Princess! How's the job treating you? Oh, wait. You were fired, weren't you? Damn, guess I forgot."

No sense in delaying the inevitable then...

I shoved my blankets off me and glared at them as they fell to the floor. The bedspread was a Christmas gift from what felt like a lifetime ago—back when I still *enjoyed* Christmas. Back before the divorce. Before Bear got sick. Before everything got complicated.

Christmas used to be my favorite time of the year... now, it wasn't.

Eventually, I found some clothes buried in the never-ending pile at the foot of my bed and headed across the hall to Bear's room. A faint glow leaked out from under his door, and I knocked softly.

"Bear? You up yet?"

There was a muffled groan, then the sound of shifting blankets. I pushed the door open a little, letting the hallway light spill in.

His room was a mix of things that used to be his life and the things that filled the gaps now. Shelves of hockey trophies sat next to video games and books. He used to be this amazing goalie—everyone thought he'd go into the NHL someday. But then his muscles started giving out, and Juvenile Myasthenia Gravis took all that away.

Now, he was stuck watching hockey instead of playing it.

Bear was sprawled out on his bed, a pillow over his face. "Five more minutes?" He mumbled.

"*Absolutely not,*" I said, leaning against the doorframe. "C'mon, this will be your best year yet."

He peeked out from under the pillow just enough to give me a skeptical look. "You said that last year."

A laugh escaped me, but it didn't land how I wanted it to. "Yeah, well... this time I mean it."

Last year had been rough. Actually, *all* of them had been rough lately.

Mom and Dad were always there for Bear when it came to setting up doctor appointments and finding new treatments, but beyond that, they were like ghosts—just... gone. They only showed up when they absolutely had to.

34

I glanced over at his nightstand, where an old family photo sat in a cheap frame. It was from one of his hockey tournaments, back when everything was still normal. Mom was in the front row of the stands, bundled up in her giant puffy jacket, screaming louder than all the other parents combined. She'd never missed a game.

And now? She was halfway across the country in Chicago. Too busy, too far away for anything but the occasional phone call.

I picked up the photo, running my thumb over the glass.

She cared about us. But never enough to stay. Even for Bear.

That's when my brother shifted in his bed, catching me with a sideways glance. "You okay?"

I put the picture back quickly and forced myself to smile again. "Yeah. Just thinking... *Anyway*, I'll be in the car. Don't make me late."

Bear let out a dramatic sigh but pulled himself up anyway, stretching his arms out as far as they could go. His body moved slower than it used to, like his bones were carrying something heavier than just sleep.

Before I shut the door behind him, I took one last look at the old hockey gear gathering dust in the corner. The doctors had warned us that his muscles would weaken as time went on... but now, it was starting to feel *real*.

It was funny—you don't realize how much something will change your life completely until you're right in the thick of it. Before Bear, I didn't even know what Juvenile Myasthenia Gravis was, and now... I was an expert.

And I hated it.

I hated what it did to him.

I shook the thoughts away as I headed for my car. Today would be better. It *had* to be. Even if nothing else in my life was going the way I had planned. It was only fair.

Cole

"Good to have you back, buddy!"

There was nothing like the first day of school. Hillview High was my kingdom, and it felt damn good to be back where I belonged. The high fives, the laughter—it was as if the universe had finally righted itself, and I was at the center of it again.

I wouldn't admit it out loud, but I'd missed these idiots.

"Max! You're still ugly as ever," I said, grinning as I slapped him on the back. Max, dark-skinned and built like a tank, just rolled his eyes and shoved me in the shoulder, barely moving me. I laughed it off.

Max had been my rock since forever—the chillest guy in the world and the perfect center to me as the quarterback. We'd led Hillview High to more victories than we could count, and this year? It'd be no different. We were unstoppable.

As Gracie kept telling me, *this* was the year college scouts would take notice. Junior year was important—I knew because she never shut up about it. Even now, I could still hear her voice in my head, droning on about how "this was it" and "my BS won't fly in college."

The worst part, though? She wasn't wrong.

It wasn't like I had stellar grades to fall back on, and I didn't have a backup plan—for good reason, though. Football was my ticket and my only shot at making it out of this place. No scholarship, no future. That was the reality.

My dad had been a legend back in the day. Everyone in town still talked about him like he was a superhero, like he could've gone all the way to the pros if life hadn't gotten in the way.

I mean, he played in college, had scouts for the pros watching him and everything, but then... he let it all slip through his fingers. He threw it away—to start a family with the bitch who moved on to another guy so quickly after he died, his body probably wasn't even fucking cold yet.

But that wasn't going to happen to me. No girl, *no one* was gonna mess up my shot. I was better than that. Better than *him*, even. Football was in my blood, and I wasn't just going to be remembered as some small-town hero who *could've* been great. I already *was* great. And I was going all the way.

Max glanced at me. "Coach's gonna be on your ass at practice today. You missed every team meeting this summer."

I shrugged. So what if Williams made me run a few laps? It was a small price to pay for not having to be stuck at school all summer. Besides, it wasn't like I needed the extra help anyways. Playing football was just like riding a bike. At least for *me*.

I steered Max toward the cafeteria. The place had gotten a facelift over the summer, courtesy of the state championship money—*in other words, thanks to me*. I was the guy who had gotten us the win, after all.

"This is going to be a great season; I can feel it, man," Max grinned.

As we passed the first set of trashcans, I glanced down at the floor, searching for the place where I'd scratched my name into one of the tiles my freshman year.

It was a stupid little thing I did whenever I walked past, yeah. But it was a reminder that my name represented the mark I had on the school. It was my *legacy*. And years from now, when people told their kids about me, they could take them back to where it all started. Right here in this lunchroom.

My foot hovered over the spot, pride settling in like it always did when I kicked at it... but I came up empty.

That's weird.

My eyes shot to the ground, only to find that the tile had been replaced. *Gone*, just like that.

For a split second, something weird twisted in my chest. *Could I really be erased that easily?* Like I never mattered?

Stop. I corrected myself quickly. *No need to fucking spiral.*

And what did it matter, anyways? They could replace a tile, but they couldn't replace me. I was *the* Cole Brown, quarterback and king of this school. Everyone knew it. No one was gonna forget me.

"And with me as your captain..." I started, flashing Max a grin.

"You're not captain yet, buddy."

"Well, yeah." I admitted with a shrug. "But do you think that there's really any other competition?"

"I mean... *I* might have a shot..."

I raised an eyebrow, waiting for the punchline. When nothing came, I burst into laughter. *Was he serious?*

I had been the team captain since freshman year. *I* had led my team to State. *I* was the one Williams was gonna pick. No questions asked.

"Max, buddy," I started, sifting through the irritation bubbling up in my chest as I clapped him on the back. "I appreciate the sentiment, but there's no way Williams is gonna pick you over me."

Max's smile faded a bit.

If I had been that kind of emotional, touchy-feely person—you know, like *girls* were, I might have considered asking what his problem was.

Thank God I wasn't.

Either he had to man up and deal with whatever shit he was going through in his head, *or* he could try taking a shot at my title as team captain. And in that case, bring it on. I was the better athlete, better leader, better *everything*.

I spotted a group of girls at the far end of the cafeteria and caught the brunette's eyes, giving her a quick nod as she walked past. She giggled like I had just blessed her existence, tossing her hair over her shoulder as she attempted to play it cool.

It was always the same reaction—girls fell over themselves for a shot at even standing near me. All except...

Gracie.

My eyes locked onto her like a heat-seeking missile as she wandered into the cafeteria. Some nervous-looking blonde kid was behind her, and my eyebrows furrowed in confusion the longer I stared at them.

I knew him from somewhere... but where?

"How's working with her at Mary Anne's been?" Max asked, following my gaze.

"She got fired a couple of days ago. Doesn't matter." I mumbled, still trying to place where I knew the kid from.

"Fired? *Gracie?*" His surprise was obvious, but I wasn't in the mood to entertain whatever he was thinking.

He'd always had this weird thing for Gracie, and couldn't help bringing her up every time he had a chance. Maybe he liked her, maybe not. I didn't know and honestly, didn't care. She was just another pretty face to most of the guys here.

It clicked for me then. *The kid*. I'd seen him before, a couple of years ago. Back in middle school.

It was right after I had lost my dad. I'd been walking out of school (I'd gotten detention for something stupid—I couldn't even remember what for now), and I'd seen them: Gracie and the kid—her brother, probably, walking hand in hand with their parents in the parking lot.

They were laughing like everything was perfect, like they didn't have a care in the world. That image had been burned into my mind—their happiness while *I* was in pain.

And that was bullshit.

But something must have happened to the kid between then and now because now, he shuffled weirdly behind his crazy sister, and his hoodie hung loosely on him like he hadn't eaten... *ever*.

"Fuck, he looks malnourished or something."

Max didn't comment, but he didn't have to. We were both thinking the same thing, even if he was too soft to say anything.

I kept watching as the Princess, in her full "reigning glory," gestured animatedly, explaining the cafeteria line to her brother as if he were stupid. Even from fifty feet away, surrounded by a hundred other people, I could still hear her irritatingly perky voice.

"Okay, Bear, see that line over there? That's where you grab your tray, and don't forget milk—Dad would kill me if you don't get enough calcium."

The kid's face flushed as he glanced around, clearly praying no one was paying attention to him. Too bad I was.

I smirked, nudging for Max to follow. "Hey, Shrimpy!" I called, striding over. Max trailed behind, muttering something about leaving them alone, but I ignored him.

The kid tensed up, trying his best to avoid eye contact with me, but Gracie wasn't one to ignore anything *grace*fully (haha, see what I did there?).

Instead, she whipped around, her glare practically burning a hole through me.

Perfect.

"Looks like someone's a little lost on his first day of school," I said, grinning down at him. "Need your sister to hold your hand? Maybe wipe your ass when you use the bathroom too?"

"Leave him alone, Cole," Gracie snapped, stepping in front of Bear. "You really got nothing better to do with your time than pick on a freshman?"

I laughed. "Don't get your panties in a bunch, Princess. I'm just welcoming your brother to high school. You know, showing him the ropes—like you were trying to do... only less condescending."

Her jaw tightened, and I couldn't resist pushing further. "Hey, Shrimpy, are you gonna contaminate the rest of us?"

That's when Gracie shoved me square in the chest. *Hard.* "Back. Off."

"*What?*" I spread my arms wide, feigning innocence. "I'm just asking a question. Is he even supposed to be at this school? Like, medically?"

Bear flinched, mumbling something I didn't catch while Gracie's fists clenched even tighter. "You're disgusting."

"Disgusting?" I snorted. "I'm just saying what everyone else is thinking."

Her shove hit harder this time, and I grinned as I let it happen.

"You're a jerk," she spat.

"And you're a control freak, Princess," I fired back. "What's it like dragging him around everywhere? Bet it's exhausting being his babysitter."

When she tried to shove me again, I caught her wrists mid-air. The momentum sent her crashing into me, her chest flush against mine, and for a split second, the heat radiating off her made my head spin.

My heart thudded against my ribs, as I shoved her back, pushing her away like she was nothing.

"I am *not* your fucking princess."

She looked like she was about to take a swing at me, before Max awkwardly stepped between us, throwing up his hands like a human barrier. "Okay, okay, let's chill. This is getting way out of hand."

"*Shut up, Max!*" we both snapped in perfect unison.

Gracie glared at me, her face flushed. "I hope you know how much I hate you."

"I hate you too, *Princess*."

We stood there, glaring at each other like the world had disappeared, both breathing hard as we dared the other to make the next move.

But before either of us could speak, Bear quickly piped up. "Can we please stop? Gracie, let's just go."

"Yeah, guys, seriously. This is insane." Max agreed.

"You hear that, Cole? You're *insane*."

"And you're just a slutty bitch." I fired back, "In fact, let's fill your brother in on everything you've kept under wraps over the years, shall we? I wonder how long he'll look up to you after he hears..."

That did it.

Before I could react, her fist connected with my jaw. Stars exploded behind my eyes as I stumbled back, clutching my face.

She stared at me wide-eyed as the color drained from her face with the realization of what she had just done.

But weirdly enough, I couldn't help but grin through the throbbing pain, slightly impressed with her. "Not bad, Princess."

"I—" she started, still looking down at her hands in disbelief. But before she could say anything else, someone gasped sharply behind us.

"You two! Office. *Now.*"

We both turned to see Ms. Newman, the history teacher, glaring at us with her hands on her hips.

Gracie's breath hitched, and without a word, she stormed off in the direction of the front office. I followed behind, still rubbing my jaw as I watched her go.

She threw punches like she was on a prison yard, and for a second, I almost admired her for it.

Don't get me wrong, I still hated her. But watching her crack was satisfying to watch in a way I couldn't explain.

And the best part? I didn't have to lift a finger. She was already ruining her reputation herself.

Check, Princess. Your move.

Gracie

I sat in the stiff office chair, bouncing my leg up and down as my whole body buzzing with adrenaline.

I'd actually punched him. *Cole fucking Brown.*

My knuckles still stung from where they'd connected with his stupid jaw, but honestly? It was probably nothing compared to what *he* was feeling.

But I had to do it. Or else...

I wonder how long he'll look up to you after he hears...

My little brother would realize just how messed up his big sister was.

The only thing that sucked about my choices in self-preservation was the fact that this was the second time in less than a month that I'd been dragged into an office because of Cole.

First, the whole Mary Anne disaster, and now this.

He's literally ruining my life. I glared at the empty chair next to me, almost wishing he was sitting there so I could punch him all over again.

As I waited, I felt the eyes of a few teachers fall on me, probably wondering why I was even there to begin with. I mean… it wasn't like I was *known* for getting into physical altercations with people.

Cole deserved what I did to him, didn't he, though? He'd been tormenting me since I had known him, and today I decided to be a vigilante instead of a doormat.

But doubt still gnawed at my stomach. What if Principal Hawkins didn't see it that way? What if I got suspended? Or worse? Got sent to jail.

Dammit, I can't afford a lawyer.

Ironically, that's when the door to the principal's office creaked open, and Cole, the devil himself, walked out. Even with half of his face swelling, he still grinning like the cocky jerk he was. "You're next, *Princess*."

I swallowed hard, forcing myself to stand. At least I'd have the satisfaction of knowing I messed up his pretty face—one small victory before I got expelled for assault or whatever.

"Gracie Lewis, please come in," Principal Hawkins called from inside.

I took a deep breath and walked through the threshold, trying to ignore the hammering of my heart in my chest. As calmly as I could, I slid into the chair across from his desk, attempting to look composed. But every part of me was screaming to get out of there.

"*Look*, before you get mad, Cole was saying stuff. About my brother…" I blurted out quickly. "And I know I shouldn't have hit him, but Cole…

he's just so *infuriating*, you have no idea. And I just—" I stopped myself, biting my lip hard.

No amount of explanation would make this look better. I was doomed.

Principal Hawkins leaned back in his chair, thoughtfulness pulling at the corners of his eyes. "Gracie, I've known you since you started at this school. This isn't like you."

Now, where did *that* sound familiar? Oh, right... Mary Anne said the same damn thing before I'd gotten fired.

"...you're an honor roll student. You're also respectful and hardworking." he paused, glancing toward the door. "And then, there's Cole."

I blinked, suddenly thrown off by the way this was going. "I... I still punched him, though."

"I know," he said with a small sigh, "but I like to think I know my students. And when a kid like you ends up in my office with a kid like him, I think I can put two and two together."

"What are you trying to say?"

Principal Hawkins gave me a small, understanding smile. "You're getting a warning this time. But I expect you to stay out of situations like this from now on. I don't want to see you in my office again, unless it's for something *good*."

I stood up from my chair before he could change his mind, my legs still a little wobbly. "Thank you. Seriously. I mean it. It won't happen again."

"Gracie," he called gently, stopping me in my tracks as I reached for the doorhandle.

I turned back to face him, and his expression softened. "I just hope that when the time comes, you'll be able to forgive him... and maybe even help him forgive himself."

Chapter Five:

I t was safe to say that my first day of junior year was *not* like the movies. But after you end up going to the principal's office, even if you *did* get off with just a warning, can it really ever be a *great* day?

Surprisingly, Cole wasn't even the worst part.

To start, I missed my entire first-period class because, again, I was in the *principal's office*. Then, I found out Cole and I shared the same third-period science class. The *only* upside? He sat as far away from me as possible, and I got to enjoy the sight of his face looking like a bruised eggplant.

Small victories, am I right?

But the true cherry on top of this disaster of a day? Ms. Newman. Yeah, the *same* Ms. Newman who witnessed me literally attack Cole, was my new fourth-period history teacher. Let's just say... I did *not* make a great first impression.

By the time I'd dragged Bear to my Future Farmers of America (also known as FFA) meeting after school, I was still slightly homicidal.

It wasn't the first time I'd let my temper get the better of me, and knowing Cole, it definitely wouldn't be the last.

But at least I had my happy place to look forward to.

"Seriously, Gracie, you don't have to babysit me." Bear said as we walked down the emptied hall.

"I'm *not* babysitting you. Just humor me for like... twelve minutes?"

Bear shrugged, shoving his hands deep into his hoodie pockets. "Yeah, okay."

We reached the classroom just as Emma, my better half and best friend of almost four years, was stepping out.

"I heard *you* had a fun day." she teased, raising an eyebrow as she hugged me. Her tone was light, but the curiosity in her watercolor-green eyes was unmistakable. She wanted details about the incident with Cole but was trying not to push.

Not yet, anyway.

I rolled my eyes. "Fun isn't the word I'd use, but sure."

Bear smirked, glancing sideways at me. "That's not what you said to me earlier. Pretty sure your exact words were, *'I swear, if I could punch his smug, perfect face again, I would.'*"

Emma stifled a laugh as she pulled back from the hug, still holding onto me just enough to give me one of her signature *are-you-serious?* looks. "Gracie-girl, I swear, you're going to be the first one out of us to end up in jail."

"Yeah, yeah, just bail me out when it happens," I muttered sarcastically.

"At least you're learning to be nice, though!" Emma shot back, her voice dripping with mock encouragement. "Calling his face *perfect*, huh? That's a start!"

I groaned. "Oh, don't *even*. You know what I meant."

Emma's giggle bubbled into a full-blown laugh, and even Bear cracked up beside us. That was Emma for you—she could find the light and brightness in any situation. That's why we got along so well because I...

Well, I was the complete opposite.

"You know," Bear said, still grinning, "I think I like her better when she's angry. It's way more entertaining."

Emma giggled. "She's *always* angry, Bear-Bear."

"*Rude*," I muttered, but I couldn't help but smile back.

Emma rolled her eyes, still laughing as she ushered us into the agriculture science room, the second-floor classroom where we held Vet Science meetings every week.

It had these wide windows that framed the mountains in the distance, letting the afternoon sunlight bathe the room in a warm, golden glow.

I pulled up a seat next to me for Bear while Emma sat her stuff next to us, taking her spot at the front of the room.

But instead of starting the meeting on time like usual, she fiddled with the hem of her baby pink cardigan, eyes fixed on the door.

Which meant only one thing: she was waiting for more people to show up.

We'd always had enough for a decent sized group, even if FFA wasn't the biggest thing at our school. But as the minutes ticked by, with no one else walking through the door, a bad feeling settled in the pit of my stomach.

Meanwhile, Emma's phone buzzed on the table for the umpteenth time in a row. She bit her lip, glanced at the door one last time, before reluctantly making her way over to her desk.

She quickly skimmed the notification, her face tightening slightly before setting it down.

A few seconds later, it buzzed again, then again. And every time, she glanced at it with the same tense expression.

When it went off again, I couldn't help but lean over, curiosity piqued. By the way she was reacting, it *had* to be some creepy guy sliding into her DMs or something. Knowing Emma, she'd be way too polite to tell him to fuck off, so I figured I might as well do it for her.

After all, I'd already decked Cole for less.

"Want me to handle it?" I asked, half-joking, as I reached for her phone.

We'd done this same routine with about a million guys before—I was the mean one and she was the saint.

But this time, instead of letting me fix it, her hand darted out to grab the phone before I could.

"It's nothing," she said quickly, slipping it into the pocket of her cardigan. She gave me a big, easy smile. "Just my dad checking in."

I clicked my tongue as I leaned back in my chair and let it go.

Of course, her dad was checking in. He was *always* checking in. It'd been that way since Emma's mom had died when she was eight. And since she was the only child, her dad prioritized her.

It was sweet.

And something I'd probably kill for since my *own* parents didn't give a damn about me.

Her phone buzzed again in her pocket, and she silenced it without pulling it out. "He's probably just bored," she added with a laugh, brushing a loose strand of honey-blonde hair from her face.

The movement tugged her sleeve down a little, revealing a faint bruise on her forearm before she pushed the fabric back into place.

Emma had worn long sleeves every day for as long as I'd known her. Even when it was well above ninety degrees outside because she was *always* tripping or bumping into things and getting bruises.

I used to tease her about it and ask why she didn't just embrace the "battle wounds." That's when she told me that she hid them so no one would think her dad was secretly abusing her or something.

He was the only family she really had left, so I guess I understood. But it took the fun out of joking with her about it after that.

She finally stopped pacing and sat down next to me.

I guess whatever had been floating around her head had finally started to settle. But that didn't mean that *I* wasn't beginning to freak out at the fact that we were the only three people here still.

"Em…" I said finally. "Shouldn't we have started the meeting already?"

A nervous laugh escaped her as she wrung her hands underneath the table. "See… that's the thing."

"The *thing*? What thing?"

She hesitated, biting her lip. "I was hoping the rumors weren't true…"

My stomach tightened. "What rumors?"

"Gracie, I'm so sorry… but it's just us this year."

"*Excuse me?*"

She sighed. "There's been some cuts to the school's budget this year," she said slowly. "I mean, we all know that."

"Yeah, no kidding," I scoffed. "The football team gets a shiny, new cafeteria while the rest of us are completely forgotten about."

It didn't take a genius to see how things worked around here.

The clubs dedicated to sports got everything handed to them, while the rest of us (especially FFA) were shoved into *literal* closets that were affectionately referred to as a "classrooms" instead.

And yet Cole had the audacity to call *me* a princess.

"Exactly," Emma said, back to fidgeting with her cardigan again. "But because of the cuts, we didn't have enough people sign up for FFA." She tried to lighten the mood with a halfhearted smile, throwing in some jazz hands for dramatic effect. "So, *surprise...* it's just the three of us for the Vet Science competition."

"You've *got* to be kidding me."

She shook her head, her smile fading. "I wish I was. To compete at State, we need four people. And right now... we only have three."

I glanced around the room again, hoping someone might magically show up. No luck, though. Still just the three of us—one of whom, Bear, wasn't even officially part of the team yet.

This meeting was supposed to convince him to join. Now we needed him *and* someone else.

"There's no one else who wants to join?" I asked, quietly, already figuring (and dreading) the answer.

Emma shook her head. "Unfortunately not."

I bit my lip, frustration rising. "How long do we have to get our numbers up?"

"December." she mumbled softly.

I slumped back in my chair. *Great.* Just a few months to pull off a miracle.

Her phone buzzed again, and she glanced at it, her expression flickering. I almost asked if she was okay—if her dad was texting because something bad had happened.

But this was Emma's dad we were talking about. He was probably just checking on when she'd be back home so he knew when to start dinner.

I wished *mine* cared half as much.

"Well," I said, forcing a smile. "Guess we'd better start recruiting."

Chapter Six:

C ole

"What do you *mean* I'm not the captain this year?"

I shifted in my chair, the torn cushion scratching against my palms. Across the desk, Williams looked up from his dinosaur of a computer and gave me a sympathetic, almost apologetic look that made my stomach churn.

His office, like him, hadn't aged well.

The oak desk was cluttered with old sports magazines and VHS tapes like something out of a relic museum. Behind him, a corkboard displayed last season's stats, strung together with red string like he was solving a murder instead of coaching football.

My name was up there, though. Front and center, right where it belonged.

I had the best stats on the team. *Period*. Fastest speed. Farthest throw... I wasn't just qualified to be captain—I was *the* captain. Everyone knew it.

Hell, Coach knew it too. So why was he sitting there, acting like there was even a discussion to be had?

"Cole," Williams started carefully. "You're a good player..."

"I *KNOW*!" I cut him off, my voice rising as I dropped the loose thread I'd been picking at. "I'm the best person to lead this team. Who the hell else would you put in charge?"

Williams sighed, pulling off his glasses to clean them with the hem of his shirt. "This—" he gestured vaguely at me, "this is exactly why you're not captain this year. You're too arrogant for your own good."

Arrogant? Seriously? "You've gotta be kidding me."

"This decision is what's best for the team. Maybe next year, if you get your grades up and keep that attitude of yours in check, then..."

I slammed my fists on the desk, making his mug of cold coffee rattle. The chair scraped loudly across the floor as I shot to my feet. "You're benching me because of my *grades* and *attitude*? Are you fucking high right now?"

"No one is benching anyone right now, Cole," Williams said, motioning for me to sit back down. "But I won't tolerate that kind of language—not in my office and not on my field. And if you keep this up, you'll be lucky if I don't suspend you right here and now."

My fists clenched, but I forced myself back into the chair. "Suspend me for calling you out on a bullshit decision?"

"For disrespecting your coach *and* your team," he shot back. "This isn't just about your stats, Cole. It's about being someone the team can actually look up to."

"I *am* someone they can look up to!" I snapped, leaning forward in my seat. "I've led this team to State, for fuck's sake. The guys trust me. They follow me. You know that."

He shook his head slowly, as if he were disappointed but not surprised. "They follow your talent. But leadership isn't just about talent. It's about accountability. Responsibility. Respect. And right now, you're batting zero in all three."

I scoffed, my nails digging into the armrests. "Who'd you pick over me?"

"Cole..."

"*Who was it?*"

"Max."

One word. That was all it took to obliterate my entire world.

Max? A *center*? After everything I'd done—every drill I ran, every victory I delivered, every touchdown I scored. And he gave *my* spot to him?

"*Max* showed up to the summer practices," Williams continued. "Maybe next time, think ahead. Your actions have consequences. When you show me that you can lead yourself, we can see about you leading a team."

"This is bullshit," I spat, shoving the chair back again with a loud screech against the linoleum.

Williams leaned back, crossing his arms. "Maybe it is. But it's my call. If you want that 'C' on your jersey again, you're going to have to earn it."

I didn't say another word. Instead, I turned towards the door, my hands pushing it open with more force than necessary.

"See you at practice tomorrow, Brown," his voice echoed behind me.

The door slammed shut before I could tell him there wasn't a chance in hell I'd be there. Not until he realized what he'd lost.

August 31st:

Gracie

I used to have the worst nightmares as a kid.

Horror movies and true crime documentaries didn't scare me, but the things I saw in my sleep?

That was a completely different story.

In my dreams, the world always felt... wrong. The colors bled out, leaving everything in this dead, soulless gray. Things would crawl out from the shadows and wrap around me, tightening their invisible hands around my neck until I couldn't breathe.

Sometimes, I knew I was dreaming, but it didn't help. Because I couldn't force myself to wake up even though I so desperately wanted to. Something held me there—a dark, heavy pull, forcing me to face whatever was lurking.

That night was no different.

I was in a misty forest, the kind where the trees felt alive, closing in on you, and a serial killer was on the loose.

I'd just finished washing the dishes from dinner when the air shattered with a scream so sharp it pierced my lungs.

My brother's scream.

My heart froze for a split second before taking off like a racehorse. I called for my parents, but the house swallowed my words. No one answered.

I was alone.

I reached for the door, my hands trembling as they touched the handle. But my feet refused to move any further.

He's your brother. Don't you love him?

Guilt wrapped around my neck like a noose as hot tears began to burn my cheeks. *Open the door, open the door, open the door.*

But I wasn't strong enough to try. I was too selfish. I was too scared.

He's going to die.

Somehow, I managed to find the courage to throw open the door. But by then, it was already too late.

There he was—my brother—lying limp on the ground, his blonde curls streaked with blood. Standing over him was a man in a twisted, wooden tiki mask.

He didn't speak. Didn't move. He just stared at me.

We were only a few feet apart—a few feet. I could've saved him. I could've saved my brother.

But I didn't.

Because I was a selfish monster.

That's when I woke up gasping for air, my face slick with sweat.

When I was younger, I'd scream after nightmares like that. Not just because they scared me, but because I wanted someone to hear me. Someone to care.

I used to imagine my parents rushing in, sitting by my bed with hugs and cookies, telling me it was all just a bad dream. But that never happened. No one ever came.

Now, I didn't bother screaming.

I curled into myself, shaking uncontrollably, but the fear didn't let up.

My stomach twisted, knowing that I needed to check on Bear otherwise I'd never sleep again.

So, even though my legs felt like lead, I forced myself to move, and crept down the hall to his room.

I cracked the door open, and there he was, asleep in bed, messy blonde hair spilling over his pillow.

No blood.

Relief hit me so hard I nearly collapsed.

He was okay. My brother was okay.

Quietly, I shut his door and dragged myself back to my room. My hands shook as I flickered on the overhead light—and my emergency nightlight.

I climbed back into bed, pulling the blankets tight around me like armor.

It was just a dream, it was just a dream, it was just a dream...

But as I stared up at my ceiling, there was only one thing I knew for sure: this was going to be a long Labor Day weekend.

Cole

"What the—"

My little sister, Chloe, covered her ears in the kitchen, blocking out the "no-no" word, her hands useless against our house's paper-thin walls.

"...is wrong with you? Are you *kidding* me right now?"

I paced near the fireplace, not necessarily trying to control my anger, but rather trying not to involve the neighbors as my mother sat on the couch, dabbing at her eyes, draped in one of her beige cardigans that perfectly matched our beige life.

The living room screamed "contemporary farmhouse" (my mother's words, not mine) with spotless white furniture and perfectly placed trendy décor. A picture-perfect home for a picture-perfect family.

It was like we were living in a fucking display case.

And maybe that's why the idea of my stepdad tagging along on our annual family trip pissed me off. My mother didn't like the "look" of going without him, as if it somehow made her "family" seem incomplete, so we just had to go along with it.

Her insecurities were her problem—but dragging him along just to keep up appearances? That wasn't what this trip was supposed to be about.

"I know you don't like Peter, but..." she started.

I scraped my hand over my stubbled jawline, my anger coiling tighter. *Of course* I didn't like the guy. She hadn't even waited for Dad's casket to be lowered before parading him into our lives.

Now, four years later, they were married, and she wanted me to treat him like some kind of replacement? Hell no.

Chloe, at least, didn't know any better. She'd been too young to remember Dad. Peter was just "fun Uncle Peter" who built her a swing set and gave her candy. But I remembered everything. Every Labor Day trip to Red Cliffs, just me and Dad—no humoring anyone, no pretending.

Now, she was dragging Mr. Right along to ruin the one place I still had with Dad.

I didn't have time to think before reacting and flipping her stupid glass coffee table over, sending magazines and puzzle pieces scattering. Chloe, who had at that point ventured out into the living room to see what was going on, yelped and ducked behind my mother's arm.

"Of all people! Of all places! You take *him* to Dad's campground! Are you *insane*?"

"That's enough!" my mother's voice snapped. She gently placed Chloe on the couch and wrapped her in a geometric abomination of a blanket. "Peter is your stepfather, and you *will* respect him. My decision is final. Clean this up."

Without waiting for a response, she stormed out, probably to the garden Peter had built for her. She used to hate plants when Dad was alive. Now she was practically married to a damn fern.

I sucked in a sharp breath, crouching to gather the wreckage around me. My hands moved fast, snatching up torn papers, pens that had rolled under the coffee table, and the edge of some puzzle box the "happy family" had been working on earlier.

Behind me, Chloe cleared her throat. "I could help you clean..."

I froze mid-motion, looking over my shoulder. She was still on the couch, bundled in that stupid blanket.

Her face was half-hidden behind it like she thought I might explode again, and her gaze darted toward the floor, avoiding me, like eye contact alone might set me off.

Why did women always have that reaction around me?

For a second, I thought about saying yes. Better to let her help than to have her grow up thinking I was just her scary, older brother who had anger issues. But then my eyes landed on it.

The picture.

It was lying face-up on the floor like some smug reminder of everything I hated. My mother, Peter, Chloe. Smiling. A perfectly curated image of happiness that didn't include me.

That wasn't to say they hadn't wanted me in it, they'd begged me to come. But I'd refused. It wasn't a family picture without my dad.

And now, it stared back at me, fucking making fun of me.

The puzzle piece in my hand pressed against my palm as my fist tightened around it, and before I even realized what I was doing, I was grabbing the frame and throwing it across the room.

The crack of shattering glass echoed through the house like a gunshot, and I stared at the broken frame lying on the floor in satisfaction.

The faces in the photo were fractured, the glass splintering into jagged lines across their perfect smiles.

I didn't stick around for Chloe's reaction, and instead, I stormed upstairs, slamming the door hard enough to shake the house.

The rage inside my chest burned, but it couldn't fill the hollow ache that was suddenly seeping into my veins as the adrenaline wore off. I dropped onto my bed, staring at the ceiling as my hands trembled.

Dad would've hated this. He would've hated *me* for what I'd become. But he wasn't here. And now, the one place we'd shared—the one memory I had left of him, one that was just for *me* to keep—was being trampled on by my mother's need to move on.

How could she do this to me? How could she just move on like Dad never existed?

I rolled over, burying my face in the pillow, wishing I could scream loud enough to drown out the pain. But no amount of rage or destruction could change what had happened.

And that was the hardest part—accepting that this was my reality now.

Chapter Seven:

M y plan to skip out on the "family fun trip" had backfired spectacularly, and now I was crammed into the backseat of Peter's SUV, sandwiched between a squirmy third-grader and my mom's oversized duffle bag, which she'd packed like we were trekking into the damn Amazon instead of spending the weekend at a campsite.

Chloe was narrating everything she saw outside the window, her voice three pitches too high for the cramped car.

"Another cow! Look!" she squealed, shoving her face against the glass like the cows were actually doing something interesting instead of just fucking standing there.

I ignored her, arms crossed, glaring out at the blur of open fields.

My mother sat up front, twisted slightly in her seat, trying to convince Chloe to play the license plate game while Peter was driving, humming along to Kidz Bop, which Chloe had somehow won the right to play on repeat.

This was not camping. Not even close.

Dad and I used to throw our gear into the back of his truck (before we'd fixed my Ford up), pull out his old Chris LeDoux CDs, and head for the Red Hills Campsite.

By now, we'd already be at the riverbank, setting up camp with just the basics: a tent, a cooler, and two fishing rods.

He'd taught me how to cast properly, how to wait, how to be patient. "Fishing isn't about the catch, bud," he'd say, leaning back in his folding chair like he didn't have a care in the world. "It's about the quiet."

That quiet was everything.

Now, Chloe's sticky hands were getting over everything as the sound from one of her dumb games blared from her iPad, and my mother kept commenting on the "dry air" and "how a cute little AirBnB would be nice for next time."

I glanced back at Peter.

If he'd been put off by the mess from earlier, he didn't say a word about it, which somehow made me even angrier.

In his mind, I was just "acting out." A lost kid who needed the right "love and support" or some other patronizing bullshit. Fuck that, though. I didn't need love *or* support from him. I just needed him to take the nearest bus the hell away from me.

By the time Peter pulled into the gravel parking lot, I was ready to launch myself out of the car. And the second the engine stopped, I did just that.

I shoved the door open and hit the ground running, ignoring Chloe's "Cole! Wait for me!"

The crunch of gravel under my boots felt like freedom, even if it was short-lived. I'd barely made it to the edge of the parking area before I heard Peter's footsteps behind me.

"Want to help pick out where we set up the tent, Brown?" he asked, irritatingly cheerful.

I cringed at the name. It was my last name. *Dad's* last name. As soon as my mother had gotten married, she'd opted to take Peter's last name instead, Curtis, replacing yet another pivotal piece of my dad.

But I kept it. *I* still loved him.

I didn't bother turning around. "Not really."

"Come on," he said, trying to keep up with me. "We're a team here. Let's make it fun."

I spun around to face him. "Why do you care what I want? We're only doing this for you, anyways."

"Now, Brown—" He reached out to grab my arm, and I jerked away from him like his touch burned.

"Don't," I snapped. "Go play family with someone who actually wants you."

He didn't flinch. Didn't get angry. He just stood there, his expression calm in that infuriating way that looked like he thought he could outlast me. "Look," he said, "I'm not trying to replace your dad in any way. I just thought this could be something good for us. For all of us."

That almost got me. It's not like I didn't w*ant* a family... I just didn't want it with *him*.

Not as quickly as I would have liked, but still in a blink-and-you-miss-it kind of thing, I shoved the rawness in my throat back down and shook my head as I turned away, stalking toward the trees without another word.

Behind me, I could hear my mom messing with a parasol she clearly had no idea how to open. "Peter, can you help me with this?" she called, her voice bright but with a waver of frustration. "I think I'm doing it wrong."

She was. I knew that without looking.

And for some reason, knowing she'd packed that stupid thing—probably trying to avoid *more* of the sun while being *actively* outside—made the twisting in my gut worse.

If Dad were here, there wouldn't be parasols. There wouldn't be Peter, either.

Chole ended up picking the camping spot because I'd wandered off at the check-in. That's what they told me, anyway. She'd stuck her finger on the map and landed us here—right next to the outhouse and in full view of the camp office.

Fantastic.

If it had been me and my dad, we would've searched for hours until we found *the* spot. Somewhere quiet, far away from everyone else, where you could see the stars stretch across the sky like spilled sugar. Not stuck next to a trash bin that smelled like moldy hot dogs.

But that was the difference, wasn't it? My dad had cared about the details. About getting it *right*. Peter and my mother? They just wanted me to sit down and smile.

The fire was already roaring by the time I got back, and even though I hated to admit it, it was impressive how fast Peter had gotten it going.

My dad had never been great at starting campfires. Some nights, he'd curse under his breath while fiddling with damp kindling, until we finally gave up and bundled ourselves in blankets to keep warm.

I hadn't minded, though. Those nights, shivering in the cold, made me feel alive. After all, I was "roughing it out" with my hero.

Those nights built memories. They built *me*.

"Cole!" Peter grinned when he saw me. "Thought we lost you there for a minute, bud."

"Unfortunately not," I muttered, kicking at a rock near my foot.

He ignored the comment, brushing his hands on his jeans as he stood. "We're just about to start roasting marshmallows. Come grab a stick."

Chloe was already at it, jabbing a marshmallow onto the end of her skewer.

She held it over the fire for only a couple of seconds before it burst into flames. Her eyes widened, as she yanked the stick back, blowing on it like she'd just set off fireworks.

"Careful, sweetie," my mother said, smiling as she passed Chloe a napkin. "Try again. This time, hold it *just* above the flames."

Chloe giggled, already reaching for another marshmallow.

My mother looked at me next, her smile more hesitant. "Why don't you come sit, Cole? We saved you a spot." She patted the empty log beside her.

I shrugged. "I'm fine right here."

Her shoulders dropped slightly, but she kept her smile. "It's a beautiful night. You'll want to see the stars later. Remember how much you loved that?"

Yeah. With *Dad*. Not this bullshit.

I stayed standing, hands shoved deep in my jean pockets, watching Chloe burn through another marshmallow. That one went black almost instantly, but instead of looking upset, she laughed.

"Did you see that?" she squealed. "It *exploded*!"

"Congratulations," I said dryly.

Peter pulled out his guitar after a while, strumming a few off-key notes before breaking into a Willie Nelson song. His voice cracked during half of it, but my mother clapped along anyway, like he was some kind of rock star.

It was pathetic. All of it.

I rolled my eyes, then turned toward my tent, desperate to escape.

At least I had my own space—a small mercy.

I was halfway through unzipping it when Peter's voice stopped me in my tracks.

"Hey, Brown! Why don't you join us for a song?"

I froze, my fingers tightening around the zipper.

The fire crackled behind me, throwing long, flickering shadows across the ground. I could feel everyone's eyes on my back.

"Yes!" my mother chimed in, clasping her hands together. "He used to sing all the time with his dad."

My jaw tightened. How dare she mention that, mention *him* like she actually cared about any of it?

"Not interested," I mumbled.

"Cole," she tried again. "We're just asking you to spend a little time with us. That's all."

"To do what?" I snapped, spinning around. "Pretend we're a happy family? Sing a few songs, roast some marshmallows, and call it a fucking day? Forget it."

"Language!" she gasped, yanking Chloe into her lap and covering her ears.

"And you," I snarled, turning on Peter, "you will never replace my dad. I don't care how many stupid trips you drag us on, I want *nothing* to do with you."

"Now, *son*..."

I heard it. The slip. The one word that stopped everything cold.

The fire popped and hissed in the silence that followed. My mother froze, her hand gripping Chloe's shoulder. Even Chloe seemed to sense that something had shifted, her marshmallow stick hovering in midair.

Peter's face paled as he realized his mistake, but it was too late. The pin had already been pulled on the grenade.

"I am *not* your son."

Before anyone could stop me, I lunged forward, snatching the guitar from Peter's lap. He opened his mouth to protest, but I was already hurling it into the fire.

The flames swallowed it eagerly, curling around the strings and licking up the neck. The varnish cracked and popped, releasing a sharp, bitter smell into the air.

Chloe let out a soft whimper, pressing her face into my mother's chest, while my mother gasped, one hand flying to her mouth as her eyes darted between me and the fire like she didn't know which disaster to handle first.

Peter stood slowly, his face a mask of stunned disbelief. For once, he didn't have anything to say. Good. I didn't want to hear it.

I was done. With all of it.

Gracie

I'd spent half the evening trying to make something edible for Bear that wasn't the usual bland vegetable purée his doctors always insisted on.

Cooking wasn't exactly my strong suit (unless you counted reheating frozen meals in the microwave) so that was why it was midnight before I'd actually gotten something somewhat decent going.

The kitchen smelled faintly of scorched death, (probably from the first two attempts I'd trashed), and the counters were cluttered with measuring cups, cheese wrappers, and my phone, where I'd been squinting at a recipe I was barely following.

Bear sat at the island, his tablet propped up on a leaning tower of old cookbooks so he could watch another old Vegas Golden Knights game from last season.

"Did you pick one where they win?" I asked, half-distracted as I squinted at the recipe on my phone.

He didn't look up, his eyes glued to the screen as the puck streaked across the ice. "It's Vegas. We always win."

I just scoffed, turning my attention back to my workstation and the pot of water that had finally started to boil.

Well, "boiling" was a generous term; the stove was so old it probably took twice as long to heat up than it should have.

Dad used to joke that our kitchen looked like it was sponsored by a thrift store. Now, it just felt... tired.

Kind of like everything else in our house—the sagging couch in the living room, the foldable dining table we kept next to the fridge (if we ever used it), the bare walls where pictures should have been...

One stupid thing at a time, Gracie. I told myself, pushing the thoughts down as I scanned the mess of a countertop in search of the salt. "Where did I put it...?"

Suddenly, my mind flashed with the probable location. I looked up, and sure enough, there it was in the most inconvenient spot imaginable—perched smugly on the top shelf of the highest cabinet.

Impulsively, but not without a dramatic sigh, I kicked off my shoes and hoisted myself onto the counter, the laminate cool beneath my bare feet. My hand braced against the cabinet door for balance as I stretched upward.

"Gracie!" Bear's voice cracked, his tone a mix of alarm and amusement. "What are you doing?"

"Relax," I called over my shoulder, fingers just brushing the shaker. "I've got it."

"You look like a raccoon raiding a trash can," he deadpanned, setting his tablet down to fully enjoy the spectacle.

I shot him a sharp look, clutching the saltshaker triumphantly as I hopped down, landing with a soft thud. "Not exactly the gratitude I expected to hear from someone who's being made a meal fit for a king."

His eyebrow arched skeptically. "Which is?"

"Mac and cheese."

Bear rolled his eyes, but the corners of his mouth twitched into a smile anyway. "You're insane."

"And *you're* welcome." I dumped a heap of salt into the pot with the confidence of someone who had absolutely no idea what they were doing.

Bear rested his chin on his hand, watching me like I had lost my mind. "Are you sure I can eat that? Feels like it's probably a choking hazard."

"Not if I make it right," I shot back. "And if I don't, well... chew slower?"

His smile turned into a quiet laugh, and I counted that as a win.

The water finally boiled, and I tipped the noodles into the pot, stirring them in slow circles with a wooden spoon. As the steam curled lazily upward, Bear slid his tablet closer to the counter's edge, angling it toward me.

"Look," he said, his voice lighting up as the camera zoomed in on the VGK goalie. "That guy's the best in the league. He had, like, a 93% save rate last season."

I grinned, leaning against the counter as Bear launched into a breakdown of the players' stats, his eyes alive with excitement.

And right then is how I knew that life wasn't fair. Because if anyone deserved to have their dreams come true, it was my brother. He had his whole life ahead of him as an NHL goaltender before Juvenile Myasthenia Gravis had taken it from him.

I blinked hard, pushing the lump in my throat back down as the stove timer beeped, snapping me back into action. I drained the noodles, the steam hitting me in a wave and fogging up my glasses.

"Ugh." I groaned, tugging them off and wiping the lenses on my shirt.

"Nice one," Bear teased, grinning like he'd been waiting for this to happen.

"Careful," I shot back, wagging the wooden spoon at him. "Keep it up, and it's back to mushy vegetables for you."

He raised his hands in mock surrender.

Just as I grabbed the cheese, my phone buzzed on the counter, Emma's name lighting up the screen.

"Who's that?" Bear asked, leaning over like he could read the caller ID from his seat.

"Emma," I said, swiping the screen. "Why is she calling me at midnight?"

Bear smirked. "Because she knows you have no life."

I flipped him off without missing a beat and pressed the phone to my ear. "Heyyy, Emma. What's up?"

"You are *not* going to believe this."

Cole

I was lost.

Not just in the physical sense, though I'd definitely screwed that up too. The trail had disappeared a couple of miles back, swallowed by the shadowy underbrush, and my phone had died before I could check where I was. So, now the sliver of moon above was my only guide.

But I couldn't stop. Not until I found it.

I shoved past another cluster of thorny bushes, the barbs slicing at my arms. Warm blood trickled down to my wrist, but the pain barely registered.

Somewhere out here was the perfect spot. *Our* spot. My dad would've known the way—he always did. He'd have said something like, "It's not the destination, son. It's the journey." Whatever the hell that meant.

But the journey sucked. My boots were soaked, my legs ached, and the night air bit through my flimsy t-shirt.

I hated this. But more importantly, I hated how empty everything felt without him.

Nothing around me reminded me of camping with my dad. The scenery had changed too much. Or maybe *I* had changed too much.

I kept walking, the cool night air brushing against my skin. Above me, an owl called out, and I paused mid-step, drawn to the sound. But when I scanned the treetops, nothing was there.

You're going crazy, Cole.

I shoved my hands deep into my jean pockets and tried to brush it off, turning my focus back to the path ahead. But the nagging feeling, like there was something I was missing, stayed.

I walked faster, trying to outrun it.

Then, out of nowhere, my surroundings shifted.

To my right, the shadows peeled away like smoke, and the world exploded in color. The night gave way to a golden haze, like someone had flipped a switch and lit the world on fire.

I stumbled back. The transformation was so sudden, so vivid, that it didn't even feel real. Everything glowed, bathed in the warm, syrupy light of late afternoon. It was a light I hadn't seen in years.

And suddenly, there we were—a smaller me trailing behind Dad as we walked along a well-worn path.

"Cole, you'll scare them away stomping around like that."

"I'm not stomping," younger me protested.

Dad grinned, rolling his eyes before turning his attention back to the path, crouching a few feet ahead, motioning me closer. "C'mere, bud. Look at this."

I watched as younger me knelt beside him, jeans soaking up the dampness of the earth. "What is it?"

Dad pointed at the ground, where faint tracks wove through the mud. "Coyote," he said with a grin, his voice low like he was sharing a secret with me. "You see how they overlap like that? Means it's been running."

My younger self nodded, wide-eyed but distracted, probably thinking about the granola bar stuffed in his pocket.

"Life will always put you on the right path, Cole" he said softly. "You just have to know what signs to look out for."

I stepped forward without thinking, trying to reach out and touch him, touch the memory... and the scene began to dissolve.

The golden light faded, and my dad and the younger me blurred into nothing but shadows on the shrubbery.

"*No*," I whispered as panic shot through me, then louder, "No! Wait!"

I took off running, my boots pounding against the dirt path as the images slipped further away.

The owl, who I'd forgotten about until just now, screeched again, cutting through the air as it guided me in the direction of him, the direction of my dad.

He was supposed to come home that day. We were supposed to fire up the grill, and he was going to show me how he made his famous burgers. We were supposed to watch a movie while we ate. We were supposed to *stay* a family.

"Dad! Wait!" I screamed, my voice breaking as I pushed myself harder. Branches clawed at my arms and face, but I didn't care. I couldn't stop. I couldn't let him go again.

My chest burned, and my legs felt as though they were about to give out. *And then another memory.*

The officers standing at the door that night.

Their stiff uniforms. Their serious faces. They knew us. They worked with Dad—they were his friends.

But that night, they acted like they weren't.

They talked to us like we were strangers, like it was just another job for them. I guess that was easier for them.

It wasn't easier for me.

"We're so sorry," one of them said. Uncle Phil. I used to call him that because he was at our house every Friday for dinner.

My mom screamed before he could finish what he was saying. A sound so raw and guttural that it didn't seem human.

74

And that's when I knew. *He wasn't coming back.*

The owl shrieked for a third time, louder. Closer.

I forced my legs to keep moving, even though every muscle in my body begged me to stop.

I couldn't stop picturing him—his stupid dad jokes, the goofy faces he'd make to cheer me up when I was mad. He wasn't supposed to just be gone like that. He was supposed to still be here.

But he wasn't.

Instead, he was lying in some coffin, cold and lifeless. And everyone just... moved on. My mother remarried. My sister started calling Peter "Dad." The police department brought in new recruits. Uncle Phil never came to another Friday night dinner...

But *I* couldn't do it. I couldn't move on.

And maybe it was because of the last thing I had said to him.

We'd gotten into this stupid fight the night before. I wanted to go to hang out with a friend for Labor Day weekend. He wanted to stick with our camping tradition. He tried to talk me out of it, said that we didn't have many years left to do this stuff before I went off to college.

I didn't care, though. All I wanted was to go water skiing with a friend. A friend that I didn't even talk to anymore.

I hate you, Dad! This is so unfair.

That's what I said to him. That was the *last* thing I said to him.

The next morning, he came into my room to say goodbye before work.

I'll see you when I get back... I love you, son.

I was awake but didn't say anything. I just laid there, stewing in my own anger.

Before he left, he said one more thing.

And if it means that much to you, you can go with your friend on that trip. We can always go camping next year.

He waited a minute, like he was hoping I'd say something, but I didn't. I didn't even look at him. Then he closed the door, and that was it.

Twelve hours later, he was gone.

I should have begged my dad to take me camping with him. I hadn't realized how important time with him was to me—until he was gone.

I hate you.

If I could take it all back, I would. I'd tell him how much I loved him. How fucking sorry I was. But I was too selfish.

He died thinking I didn't care about him. Thinking I wanted nothing to do with him.

I didn't even get to say goodbye.

And as punishment, I was reminded of my dad everywhere I went.

Your father hung that picture for me.

Your father always told the funniest jokes!

You remind me of your father...

The worst part, though? They meant it as a compliment. Like it was supposed to make me smile or something. Instead, it made me want to claw at my skin, rip it off until I didn't "remind" anyone of him anymore.

I didn't want to think about him. I didn't want to think about anything. I just wanted to forget. Forget all the pain, all the regret, all the broken pieces of a life I couldn't fix.

The owl's screech sliced through the air again. I looked up just as it was swooping down onto a branch just ahead. Its huge yellow eyes staring at me like it was waiting for me to catch up.

I skidded to a stop, panting, the sharp, icy air burning my lungs.

For the first time, I got a good look at it. The bird was massive, bigger than any owl I'd ever seen. Its feathers were a mix of whites and grays, like the ash that spilled from the backyard fire pit my dad and I used to sit around.

The pit where we used to talk about everything and nothing at all. The pit that hadn't been lit since he died.

My stomach twisted then, and I had to force myself to look away.

That's when I realized where I was.

The trail was gone, and I was standing in the middle of a one-lane road. The darkness stretched on forever in both directions, like the whole world just dropped off into nothing.

And then, I heard it...

Gravel crunching in the distance.

I spun around. Headlights. Barreling toward me.

Fast. Way too fast.

Move! My brain screamed, but my legs wouldn't listen. They stayed locked in place, frozen like someone had glued them to the pavement.

The car was flying toward me, and all I could do was stand there, staring it down like an idiot, fascinated by it, just like I had been earlier, when I nicked my arm on that branch.

The reminder hit me hard, and my eyes snapped to the cut. The blood had dried by now, crusty and rust-red. But even still, the sight of it... it felt *good*.

I couldn't explain it; it just did.

There was something intoxicating about it—having a battle wound. The sting had felt right, like I was finally in control of something.

Like I deserved it.

Like I deserved *this*.

My chest heaved as the headlights got closer, brighter, hotter.

This was a good thing, right? One hit and I was done for—no more guilt, no more pain. The villain of this story would finally be slain for good.

Forty feet. Thirty feet.

I could just let it happen. No one would blame me. My mother would finally get her picture-perfect family, Max would be able to captain his team in peace... people would be happier without me, *wouldn't they*?

Maybe... maybe this car was a godsend. It could finally take out the guy who made everyone's lives miserable with no strings attached.

It wasn't like I was killing myself exactly. It was more of using my surroundings in my favor.

Twenty feet. The horn blared, but by then, I had made up my mind: I wasn't leaving.

This felt right. It felt *noble*. My brain was finally catching up to what I'd known for a while: I was the problem. I had *always* been the problem. And I always would be... unless I did something about it.

Ten feet. The tires screeched, desperate, and my heart thumped in my chest so hard I thought it might explode. But I didn't move.

They say that in your last moments, your life flashes before your eyes. I couldn't speak for everyone, but I definitely wasn't the exception to the rule.

A barrage of memories hit me all at once: birthday cake smeared across my face for my fifth birthday party, Dad lifting me on his shoulders after my first football win, the disappointment in everyone's eyes every time I messed up after that. Every. Single. Time.

You're making the right decision.

Five feet.

I thought about Gracie and the fear in her eyes anytime I got remotely close to her.

You have no idea what it's like to be treated like a fucking monster...

The car attempted to veer off to the side, but it was too late. I braced myself, expecting to feel the impact.

But it never came.

Gracie was the last thing I thought about before the world went black.

Chapter Eight:

G racie

"Wait, wait, wait! *Slow down*, Emma." I said, pressing the phone tighter against my ear as my free hand fumbled with the wooden spoon I'd been using to stir the noodles.

It slipped from my grip, crashing to the floor with a loud bang.

"Great," I muttered under my breath, scooping it up and flinging it into the sink with a flick of my wrist. My nerves were already coming undone, and Emma wasn't helping.

"TURN ON THE NEWS!"

I flinched, pulling the phone away from me like it might explode. "Okay, okay. Calm down."

Bear paused his hockey game. "What's going on?"

I shrugged, mouthing, *no clue*, while digging through the couch cushions in search of the remote. It took way too long before I finally found it and yanked it out, brushing off the lint and crumbs as I clicked the TV on.

I pressed the phone back to my ear. "What channel?"

"IT DOESN'T MATTER!"

My heart started hammering. Emma didn't freak out like this... ever. Whatever was going on was wrong, *really* wrong.

Bear must have noticed the panic written all over my face because he slid off the stool at the kitchen island and climbed onto the couch beside me.

He tucked himself against my side, resting his head on my shoulder. Instinctively, I smoothed a hand over his curls.

"Emma, you're kind of scaring me," I muttered, flipping through channels faster. "What's going on? Did someone die or—"

And then I saw it.

Cole Brown's enlarged face staring back at me from the TV screen.

They'd used a football picture. Because *of course*, they did. That was probably the only picture his parents had of him. He ate, slept, and breathed football.

Bear immediately sat upright, his body going rigid. The two of us stared at the screen and then back at each other in complete shock.

The news anchor was talking. I mean, *obviously*—her lips were moving, but I couldn't understand a single word she was saying. It was like she was speaking an entirely new and made-up language.

"Gracie?" Emma's digital voice sounded—the first word of hers that I'd actually understood in a while.

My phone. I must've dropped it at some point and scrambled to grab it off the couch cushion. Pressing it to my ear again, I tried to steady my voice. "Yeah, I'm still here."

"They just life-flighted him to St. George," she said. Her voice sounded shaky now, like she was trying not to cry.

I swallowed hard. St. George was forty-five minutes away from us. They hadn't taken him to the hospital in town. They'd *flown* him to another city.

What the hell was going on?

I gripped the phone tighter as the news anchor continued: "The driver in question is currently being interrogated by police..."

I stared at the screen, the image of Cole continuing to burn through my retinas. My fists clenched, nails biting into my palms as anger surged out of nowhere.

Of course, something like this was bound to happen. Cole had always been so incredibly stupid. It was only a matter of time before his face ended up on the fucking *news*.

But under all the anger, there was something else... something I didn't really want to admit.

I was *scared* for him.

Bear shifted beside me, and I felt him looking at me, as if he was waiting for me to say something, to *do* something. But I couldn't.

All I could do was sit there and stare at the TV.

Because no matter how much I hated him, no matter how many times I'd wished he'd disappear from my life completely, I couldn't lie to myself.

I didn't want that asshole to die.

September 6th

???

A sharp light pierced through my eyelids, dragging me out of some dreamless sleep. My head throbbed in time with my heartbeat, making me want to curl back into whatever darkness I had just been in.

I squeezed my eyes shut tighter, hoping the pain would stop, but it didn't.

"Is he... Is he awake?"

"The doctors said..."

"Thank God!"

The voices around me blurred into static as I tried to force myself to focus. But my headache was making it hard to concentrate on much of anything.

Where am I? What's going on?

After much self-motivation, I finally managed to pry my eyes open, but the light stabbed again, making the world go blurry for a minute.

Slowly, though, shapes came into focus—a small, cramped room filled with chaos.

A man with broad shoulders and dark hair slipped out the door, shouting something about a doctor as a petite blonde woman stood in the corner, her voice shaking as she clutched a phone to her ear.

Behind her, a little girl with wide blue eyes stood in silence, watching everything unfold with unnerving stillness.

I tried to speak, but my throat felt like sandpaper. After a few tries though, I managed to croak. "What's going on?"

Nobody answered me.

The little girl continued to stare at me, her eyes locked on mine. She was young (maybe seven or eight), her arms wrapped tightly around herself like she was trying to hold her whole body together.

She looked scared. I mean, *obviously*—hospitals weren't exactly calming. I hadn't gotten a chance to look at myself yet, but I could imagine the sight was a little graphic for an elementary schooler.

My brain felt like a scrambled mess. I tried to think... tried to grab hold of anything that might explain why I was here—but there was nothing. No memory. Just blank space.

"Hey," I croaked again, turning to the little girl this time. Maybe if I got her talking, she'd feel less freaked out.

Although, I wasn't sure why she was here in the first place. Shouldn't she be with her parents? Shouldn't *my* parents be with *me*? "What's your name?"

Her whole body jerked like I'd physically hit her. She shrank back, her fingers digging into the hem of her dress like she was bracing herself.

I blinked, confused by her reaction. "You don't have to be scared," I said, slowly. "I just... I just wanted to know your name. Where's your family?"

The second those words left my lips, everyone's heads whipped toward me.

"What did you just say, honey?" the blonde woman asked slowly.

I swallowed hard. *Why is everyone looking at me like I'm crazy?* "I was just asking..." I coughed, forcing the words out. "Her... name?"

The woman glanced around at the doctors, who looked just as confused as I felt, but the reaction was *insane* because I'd never seen the girl in my entire life.

Now that I thought about it, I'd never seen *any* of these people in my entire life before.

Why does my head hurt so much?

"Cole..." the woman started, her voice faltering. "Sweetheart, that's your sister."

I stared at her, waiting for the punchline. "What?" I asked, a shaky laugh slipping out. "No. That's impossible. I think you guys have the wrong room or something because I think I'd remember—"

Before I could finish, the door flew open, slamming against the wall with a loud *bang*. The man who'd left earlier rushed back in, followed by a flood of nurses.

"Cole," he said, hurrying toward me. His hand clapped down on my shoulder with a firm squeeze that made me wince. "You're awake. Thank you, Jesus."

His grip was warm and weirdly personal, and I flinched, instinctively jerking back as much as the stupid wires and tubes would let me. "Umm, hello to you too?"

The blonde woman quickly stepped forward, her face tight. "Peter, stop for a second."

His eyebrow lifted at the woman in confusion, but he dropped his hand from me.

I looked between them, my heart pounding. "Okay, somebody better start talking," I said, my voice rising uncontrollably. "Who *are* you people? Why am I here? What the hell is going on?"

"Cole, just take a second," the guy (Peter) said, his tone uncomfortably calm, like he was trying not to freak *himself* out. "You've been through a lot..."

"Stop calling me... I don't—I don't know you, man! I don't know who any of you are." I snapped.

The woman's face crumpled like she was about to cry, but she didn't say anything.

"This has to be some kind of mix-up," I continued, shaking my head. "Just get my actual family, and we can clear this whole thing up."

The couple's initial excitement vanished, replaced by unreadable expressions. Doctors continued their work—checking IV bags, recording vitals, checking temperatures—but my focus remained fixed on the couple and the girl they called my sister.

Finally, after what felt like an eternity, Peter spoke, his voice heavy, "*We're* your family, Cole."

September 6th (still)

~~???~~ Cole

"Cole," I repeated under my breath, the name rolling awkwardly off my tongue. "Cole..."

I stared at the handheld mirror one of the nurses had handed me, and the reflection of a stranger glared back at me. Dark hair, pale skin, cuts and bruises everywhere, hollow gray eyes that didn't feel like mine...

The longer I looked into the mirror, the less sense it made. This face, this body—none of it fit. I ran a shaky hand through my hair, wincing as my fingers brushed over a tender spot on my scalp. Even the way my hand moved felt wrong.

I shoved the mirror back into the nurse's hands. "I can't..." I muttered. I couldn't look at that face anymore. It wasn't mine—it couldn't be.

Could it?

"Can someone *please* tell me what's going on with my son?" the woman (*my mom, I guess?*) demanded.

More doctors filed into the room, gawking at me like I was a zoo animal on display. It made my skin crawl, and I wanted more than anything to get out of this hospital bed and take the quickest trip back to reality... wherever reality was.

I turned my attention to the man standing near her, searching his face for answers. "So, that makes you my... dad?"

He hesitated, shifting on his feet before offering a thin smile. "Well *stepdad*, if you want to get technical."

Stepdad. Right. Because, of course, nothing about this could actually be simple. Before I could even *start* unpacking that, an older man with glasses stepped forward and eased himself into a chair by my bedside.

"Next, you're gonna tell me you're my long-lost grandfather." I muttered, sarcasm dripping from my voice as I eyed him.

The man's laughter was warm and genuine, making me pause for a second. And for some reason, I decided then that he didn't bother me as much as everyone else did.

"No relations that I know of my boy!" he said, his tone hearty and light as he extended a gloved hand toward me. "I'm Dr. Andrews. Pleasure to meet you."

I stared at his hand for a second before shaking it. "I'm... Cole," I said, trying out the name again. It still felt wrong, like a label someone else had slapped on me, not quite sticking.

Dr. Andrews nodded thoughtfully. "Can you tell me what you remember about the accident, Cole?"

"The *accident*?"

The words felt strange in my mouth. I searched my mind for any flicker of recognition, but it was like reaching into a black hole. There was nothing. No images, no sounds, no answers. Just a gaping void where answers should have been.

"No," I said finally. "I don't remember anything. I don't even know what's going on, or who these people are, or..." My voice rose with every word, anger spilling out before I could stop it.

Dr. Andrews held up his hand, shutting me down. "Okay, Cole. That's alright. Let's try something simpler... Do you remember anything from *before*?"

Before? I stared at him, the word bouncing around in my head as I tried to make sense of it. *Before what?* My life? My existence? How was I supposed to answer that?

My gaze shifted back to the woman—the one claiming to be my mom. She was sobbing quietly into my supposed stepdad's chest. Something bloomed in my stomach then—guilt, maybe? Or pity?

No. I didn't even *know* her.

"I..." I tried to focus, forcing myself to remember *something*, even if it was as small as my favorite fucking color, but my mind stayed stubbornly blank.

I let out a sharp breath, finally giving in. "No. I don't remember anything."

Chapter Nine

SEPTEMBER 9TH

Gracie

Beep, beep, beep.

Great. My least favorite sound in the world: my alarm clock.

"I'm up, I'm up," I grumbled, reaching out to slap the snooze button.

I laid there for an extra second, cocooned in the tangled sheets, as the slightest early morning chill seeped through the thin fabric of my pajamas.

The scent of stale coffee from the kitchen (probably from my dad before he left for work) wafered into my bedroom, and I let out a sigh as I stared up at my popcorn ceiling, listening to the whirl of the heater overtake my overactive thoughts.

Thoughts that, apparently, couldn't stop circling back to him.

It'd been six days since Cole had been at school, and while, yeah, I was happy I didn't have to see his stupid face, I was still... worried for him, I guess?

Dumb, I know.

Curiosity ended up getting the better of me, and before I could even register what I was doing, I was deep in an Instagram rabbit hole trying to figure out if he was even alive.

Mostly because I had to know if I was a horrible person for wishing it on him or not.

Cole had basically become a celebrity overnight. For the past few days, every corner of the internet had been flooded with posts about him—photos of his hospital room, vague updates on how he was doing... There was even a #ColeStrong and GoFundMe floating around.

But as far as I could tell, the most recent update was that he was still in a coma. The timestamp was four days old.

Honestly, the whole thing felt surreal, like something that only happened in the movies, not at some random high school in Cedar City, Utah.

I scrolled through a few more accounts, but there was nothing new about how he was doing or if he'd even be back to school soon.

It was like Cole had vanished from the virtual world as suddenly as he had from real life.

With a groan, I tossed my phone onto the bed. It landed with a pathetic thud, the screen flickering briefly before settling into darkness. *Why do I care what happens to him? I don't actually want Cole to be okay... do I?*

I mean, he was the reason I'd lost my job. Not to mention that Mary Anne (who was basically my second mom) had taken his side. *His.* Over mine. Like, sure, let's all go rally around Cole Freaking Brown, the town's favorite juvenile delinquent.

A wave of bitterness suddenly washed over me.

Ugh. I wished I had been driving that car myself.

With the peace of the morning finally dissipating the second I turned homicidal, I dragged myself out of bed, and threw on a crumpled shirt from the floor—a black crop top with the Vegas Golden Knights logo on it.

Hopefully, Bear would appreciate the sentiment since he'd gone to bed last night feeling miserable. And that meant he'd probably wake up feeling even worse today.

Just in case, though, I knocked lightly on his door to check if he was feeling up for school.

"Yeah?" he mumbled from his room.

I pushed the door open and found him buried under his comforter. "How are you feeling?"

He didn't skip a beat. "Like garbage."

I sighed, leaning against the doorframe as I pressed my palms to my forehead, willing the start of a headache to go away.

His sick days were happening more and more frequently, and it was starting to affect *me*.

I didn't know what I was doing. Or even how to take care of a sick kid. Hell, I was still a kid *myself*.

I'd called Mom a couple days ago to ask what insurance card I was supposed to use for Bear's next appointment (since all the cards I *did* use kept being declined) but no answer. *Shocker*.

I tried not to take it personally, but it was hard not to.

Sometimes it felt like Mom and Dad just left me with this giant "good luck" with Bear while they did... *whatever it is they did*. And yeah, I knew they were both "working," but at the end of the day, was it too much to ask for a little help?

I bit my bottom lip as I looked back at my brother.

I'd figure out what to do about all the medical stuff... eventually. But until then, there was only one other option: to pretend like I was an adult who knew what I was doing. "Did you want to skip school today?"

Bear peeked the rest of the way out from under the blanket. "Do you think Dad would mind?"

I let out a laugh before I could stop it. "Not if we don't tell him."

My brother cheered sleepily but it didn't land as enthusiastically as I knew he wanted it too.

Guess he'd gotten just as good at pretending as me.

"Do you need anything before I go?"

"To be cured forever?" he suggested with a crooked smile.

I rolled my eyes as he laughed, but none of it felt very funny.

I hated this. I hated seeing him like this. I hated that my parents weren't here. And I hated that Cole was taking up any space in my brain at all when I should've been focused on my brother instead.

I pushed off the doorframe. "I'll get you the next best thing: yogurt. And you better finish it this time," I said, already knowing if he was feeling more like himself, he'd fight me on it.

He was sick of yogurt, yeah. But he was also sick and needed to eat.

Today will be better... I told myself as I headed to the fridge, knowing in just a few seconds, I'd be late for my first class. But then again, maybe today *wouldn't* be.

Maybe hope was the reason we were in this mess to begin with.

Having an assembly in the middle of a Monday morning was weird—even for Hillview High. And *that* was saying something.

As we shuffled into the auditorium like a herd of semi-conscious cattle, I slid into a seat in the back row, hoping to avoid the minefield of forced small talk.

Assemblies were simple like that: show up, sit down, zone out, and pray that it ended before second period did.

That's when a hand clamped down on my shoulder.

I twisted around just in time to see Emma vaulting over the row of chairs behind me as she plopped into the seat next to mine with the kind of energy that should've been illegal this early in the morning.

And that was coming from the ranch hand who got up this early *every* day.

Well... ex-ranch hand. *Thanks, Cole.*

"Of course, you're bright-eyed and bushy-tailed this early, Em," I muttered, slinking further into my uncomfortable seat.

"One word: coffee," she replied, waving a half-empty iced latte in my face. "Splitsies?"

I made a face like she'd just offered me poison. I didn't really *do* sharing. "Absolutely not."

The sound system crackled to life, snapping my attention to the stage, just as a nervous sophomore, who looked like he'd just been thrown into the lion's den, began fumbling with the PA system.

The mic he was messing with screeched like it was being tortured, and everyone collectively winced.

But suddenly, the noise was replaced by Principal Hawkins's booming voice, only confirming my worst fears as he welcomed us all.

"Today, we have a guest speaker joining us, so I expect you all to be on your best behavior," he said. "Let's give a warm welcome to Dr. Andrews!"

The applause was about as enthusiastic as a group of teenagers could muster as the guy, Dr. Andrews, waddled onto the stage.

His leopard-print glasses glinted under the harsh lights, and he gave an awkward wave to the crowd before reaching and almost dropping the microphone.

"Good morning, students. I'm here today to talk to you about your cognitive health!"

Seriously? If this was the school's idea of "education," they might as well have handed out juice boxes and coloring books instead.

And just so we were clear: if this *was* supposed to be about the accident Cole had gotten into, our guest speaker should've been a surgeon. Or, at the very least, a priest. Maybe even a mortician.

Not whoever *this* was.

"Now, can anyone tell me why it's important to prevent head injuries?" Dr. Andrews continued, forcing an awkward smile as he scanned the room for an unfortunate volunteer.

The collective silence was deafening until someone from the front row chose mercy and mumbled. "Because concussions are bad?"

The doctor breathed a sigh of relief at the answer and continued on like we all weren't literally witnessing him drowning right in front of us.

"Exactly! Concussions, traumatic brain injuries—these are all serious consequences that can occur when we don't prioritize brain protection."

I stifled a groan and slouched lower in my seat.

After about forty-five minutes of politely trying to listen, I nudged Emma. "Do you want to just leave? All I've got next is science, but I could skip if we wanted to go somewhere."

Her face lit up at the idea, and we both started to stand.

But just as we were about to make our great escape, Dr. Andrews cleared his throat and said. "As I am sure you've all heard by now, one of your fellow students, Cole Brown, was in an accident a few days ago."

That got us. Nothing like some good, ol' morbid curiosity to sit us right back down.

"What I'm trying to say is... Cole has suffered from a traumatic brain injury and has... amnesia."

The auditorium fell into a stunned silence.

Could that even happen to a person? Lose their memories?

Was someone pulling a prank on us?

Is he okay?

The irony of why I suddenly cared so much was not lost on me. I mean, what did it matter if he *lost his memory*? He was Cole Brown for crying out loud. Nothing was going to change that.

Dr. Andrews cleared his throat. "Anyway, there's only so much that we as adults can do to help ease Cole's transition. So, we are counting on *you* to help make it his best year yet."

I didn't know if it was the insanity of the situation or the idea of *this* group of people being the ones to help *anyone* through a life-altering injury, but before I could stop myself, a laugh ripped out of me.

Dr. Andrews looked up from the stage just as every other head in the auditorium was whipping around toward me.

Emma's mortified stare burned into the side of my face. "Gracie," she hissed, trying not to laugh herself, "stop!"

Am I suffering from shock?

By the time I was finally able to shut up, my cheeks were burning a deep fire-engine red, and I wanted to crawl under my seat and disappear forever. "Oops," I mumbled.

Emma gave me a playful shove, just as (wouldn't you know) Mrs. Newman shot me a glare. "Now you sound like a jerk. Don't worry, though. He is too."

I shot her a slight grin, grateful for her loyalty, even if I *was* a TINY bit in the wrong for laughing... maybe.

"And hey," she added with a smirk, taking a sip of her drink, "by tomorrow, nobody will remember the crazy chick who laughed at a kid with amnesia."

"Crazy Chick and Amnesia Boy... sounds like a superhero comic."

Unfortunately, any plans to skip class with Emma had been scrapped the second Dr. Andrews dropped the bomb about Cole and his so-called amnesia.

So, that's how I ended up storming into science, slamming my bag onto the desk, and pulling out my FFA binder.

Planning always calmed me down, and right then, I needed it.

I flipped through the pages, muttering under my breath. "Okay. What to do, what to do, what to do..."

My pen tapped against a crème-colored schedule of all the competitions for the year.

December. That was the deadline to find our new president. *How am I ever going to pull this off?*

Obviously, what we needed was someone with experience, otherwise we'd flounder at competition.

And Emma? She'd already done it once before.

She was organized, good with people, and genuinely just a *good* leader.

Versus me, who... well, let's just say I wasn't like my best friend.

I didn't have the ability to rally people together like she did. I couldn't make them *care*. Hell, I just laughed at a kid for being hit by a car and getting "amnesia."

Even if it *was* Cole.

It was safer to let Emma have this one and for me to stay in the background where I couldn't mess things up.

Or be a disappointment.

My throat tightened at the thought, but I scribbled her name in bold at the top of the page anyway, feeling a brief sense of control wash over me.

That was the right call. It had to be.

The bell clanged overhead as the last few students shuffled into their seats, and I glanced at the empty chair next to me out of habit. The new kid hadn't shown up today—again. He hadn't been in class in almost a month.

"Hey," I whispered to the girl sitting next to me. "Whatever happened to that new guy—Justin, or something?"

The girl, Sierra, barely looked up, her attention fixed on her phone. Her acrylic nails clinked against the screen as she typed. "Umm... I heard a rumor that Cole bullied him so badly that he moved back to Kansas. Something about his underwear on the flagpole?"

"*Excuse me?*"

Sierra shrugged, scrolling with zero interest. "Hey, don't shoot the messenger,"

Suddenly, Miss Holland clapped her hands, drawing our attention (minus Sierra) to the front. "Class, as you probably know, Cole has been in the hospital for a few days now."

No. Fucking. Way.

Was she about to say what I thought she was going to? Was he really *coming back* today? What moron would let him come back to school this early after getting into a car accident if the amnesia thing was legit?

"Like Dr. Andrews said, if you were paying attention..." Miss Holland shot me a pointed look. My cheeks flamed—I guess my outburst *was* as loud as I thought it was. "I want you all on your best behavior. He should be here any minute."

I leaned toward Sierra, lowering my voice. *Guess I hadn't really learned my lesson.* "Funny how *we're* supposed to be nice to him when he's never bothered to do the same. What'd he forget anyways? His favorite insult? Favorite *victim*?"

Hopefully, he forgot his favorite victim... which was unfortunately me.

"*Gracie,*" Miss Holland warned. My mouth snapped shut. "Just try to be understanding when he arrives."

She let out a tired sigh, sinking back into her chair, and for a split second, guilt tugged at me.

Heaven knows she didn't get paid enough to deal with my B.S. But at the same time, there was a glaringly more important matter at hand: me. (Well, Cole in *regard* to me).

What exactly did Cole having amnesia entail?

Because the chances of him forgetting *everything* were slim, right? So, what *did* he forget?

Was he going to pretend none of... our history had ever happened? Was I supposed to pretend like it hadn't either?

What if he *lying* about having amnesia...?

"Head injury or not, I'm not getting twenty feet near him," Sierra muttered.

Even though I was slightly hyperventilating over the Cole thing, I snorted at that.

Unfortunately for me, I was too loud again and Miss Holland's head shot up from her desk. "Gracie Lewis! That's enough from you!"

My jaw dropped. "But... but I didn't even say anything this time!" I protested, but it didn't matter—she was already pushing her chair back and heading for the door, throwing me a look of *you should know better*.

I sank lower in my seat, my cheeks burning with embarrassment.

But thankfully, I wasn't everyone's main focus for too long because just then, the door creaked open and all eyes shot toward the entrance like we were all a part of the weirdest reality TV show in the world.

Miss Holland straightened her skirt, her careful, bright smile practically screaming *Welcome back, please don't sue us*.

And that's when I caught a glimpse of messy brown hair. *Cole*.

Principal Hawkins was next to him, muttering something before slipping away. But the second he was out of sight, leaving Cole alone in the doorway with Miss Holland, the room buzzed back to life.

Wanting no part in the rumor mill (I'll make my own assumptions of the ass, thank you very much), I couldn't help but zeroing in on Cole as he stepped inside.

He was wearing blue jeans, cowboy boots, and a fitted shirt, like he wanted us to notice the bruises trailing up his arms and face.

Arrogant as ever, I guess. No "accident" could change that.

But something was... different.

His eyes kept sweeping around the room in short, nervous glances like he was searching for someone... someone happy to see him.

No one met his gaze.

Miss Holland made her way to the front of the room, while Cole trailed behind, suddenly opting to keep his head down instead.

"Everyone, say hello to Cole." Miss Holland said, her tone stretched thin with artificial warmth.

She smiled, but it was in a way where it didn't really reach her eyes—like she was just as uncomfortable with this situation as the rest of us were.

A few of the more polite kids managed a weak "hi", though it sounded half-hearted at best. Most of the class avoided eye contact altogether.

I was the only one who kept looking at him.

I didn't even know why I did it, honestly. Curiosity, maybe? Distain? Disbelief? I couldn't tell you.

Up close, I could see the rough, angry patches of road rash covering his arms, and I couldn't imagine how fast a car could've been going to make him skid across the road like that.

Or how it didn't even look like he'd broken a single bone.

He also looked... smaller, somehow. Not physically, obviously—he was still annoying six-foot-something of broad shoulders and dark hair—but something about the way he carried himself was different. Like he didn't know what to do with his body anymore.

Does that mean this amnesia thing is real?

"Uh, hi, everyone." He raised a hand in the saddest little wave I'd ever seen, his mouth twitching into something that might've been a smile if it had tried a little harder. It was *bizarre*.

Our eyes met.

I didn't mean for it to happen. I didn't *want* it to happen. But it was like gravity had shifted, and suddenly, looking anywhere else felt impossible.

There was something off in the way he looked at me—his gaze was soft... *friendly.*

He didn't look at me like I was Gracie Lewis, the girl he had all the history with. He looked at me like I was someone he'd just met.

And somehow, that made it even weirder.

Then, (because the universe hates me) he smiled. At *me.*

My cheeks burned, and I shifted in my seat, finally giving in and looking away.

I hate my life.

"I'll let you pick your seat," Miss Holland said with the kind of over-cheeriness that only made the whole situation worse. "You'll find that this classroom is filled with *nice, amazing* students who are willing to help you if you need anything."

I stole a look at her, only to find her eyes locking onto mine. *You better be on your best behavior, Gracie.*

And to that, I wanted to say: *Ha! Because clearly **I'm** the problem here. Not the guy who's definitely faking amnesia for attention.*

Cole's gaze swept across the room before landing on the empty seat next to me. His brow furrowed then, like he was genuinely debating the decision.

You've got to be kidding me right now.

His hesitation should've been a clue—Cole *never* hesitated. He was the guy who made decisions on impulse, like throwing a basketball at my head in gym class and calling it an "accident."

But no, this absolutely was not a coincidence. Not with him.

When he started walking in my direction, I gritted my teeth, my fingers gripping the edge of my desk like it was the only thing to keep me from bolting out of the room and away from whatever this little plan of his was altogether.

"Shit." I muttered under my breath.

Sierra, who I'd honestly forgotten was even sitting next to me, actually looked up from her phone for once in her life. "Does the school bully have a premature crush on you already?" she whispered, biting back a laugh.

"*No.*" I snapped, more heat rushing to my face. "Shut up."

Suddenly, a shadow (*his* shadow) loomed over my desk.

I tilted my head up, forcing myself to meet his gaze, and I was surprised to find that his expression wasn't smug—it was... neutral. Calm. Almost like he didn't recognize me at all.

What the hell kind of game are you playing, Brown?

"Mind if I sit here?" he asked, almost cautiously.

Cautious? Since when is Cole Brown cautious?

"Actually, I'd rather, umm—" I stumbled over my words, unable to string a coherent sentence together. *Go away, go away, go away.*

"She'd *love* for you to sit next to her!" Sierra chimed in before I could finish.

I whipped around to glare at her, but when I turned back, Cole wasn't paying any attention to her.

His eyes were locked on me. *Only* me.

"You good with that?" he asked, eyebrows raised. His tone was almost gentle—like he actually cared what I thought. *Yeah, right.* "I can sit somewhere else if you want."

Molten lava churned harder in my stomach. *Why does he want to sit here anyways?* Of all the empty seats in this stupid classroom, he chose the one next to *me*.

What if... No. He's lying. He has to be lying.

"Whatever." I mumbled, sliding my chair a few inches away as he lowered himself into the seat.

My heart thudded painfully in my chest. *What in the twilight zone is happening right now?*

Out of the corner of my eye, he gave a polite smile—the kind you'd give a stranger on the street and not someone you've known (and hated) for years.

That's when he pulled out two pencils, placing them neatly on the desk in front of him.

My nose crinkled before I could help it. *Who even was this guy?* The Cole *I* knew wouldn't bother to show up to class, let alone come with actual school supplies.

"Do you need one?" he asked, following my gaze. "I brought extra."

I narrowed my eyes at him. There was no way in hell that this was the same person from *last week* who not even joking, shoved some poor kid into a locker because he "looked at him the wrong way."

The silence stretched uncomfortably long, and I swore I saw him start to sweat (which not going to lie, kind of brought me immense joy).

His gaze flicked down to my shirt, and he quickly blurted out, "Vegas Golden Knights... Hockey, right?"

I stiffened instantly. "I thought you lost your memory. Now you're some sort of sports expert?"

He blinked, like *I* was the crazy one. Then he glanced down at his own shirt and gently pointed to the tiny Knights logo embroidered on the fabric. "It's on my shirt too."

"Oh," I mumbled. "Guess I didn't see that."

He gave a small smile as he leaned back in his chair, completely at ease now that we were "talking." "My mom's a big fan. I guess I was too... before."

The way he said it... *before* hung heavy in the air, and for a minute, I couldn't tell if he was sad or just... blank.

I studied him, half-expecting someone to pop out with a camera and yell, *Gotcha!* But I didn't think he was *that* good of an actor. Let's be real. He wasn't good at *anything*.

"Have you ever been to a game?" he asked like he was trying to coax an actual conversation out of me.

"Once," I mumbled, attempting to turn away from him and end this "little chat" altogether. But suddenly, as we adjusted in our seats at the same time, his knee brushed against mine.

A normal person wouldn't have even felt it, but over the years, I'd learned that I was anything *but* normal.

My stomach twisted violently, and before I could stop myself, I jerked back as if I'd been electrocuted.

"Sorry," he said quickly, leaning back slightly to put some space between us. "That was my bad."

But I wasn't thinking. I *couldn't* think. I shot my chair back as far as it would go, the metal legs screeching against the linoleum like nails on a chalkboard.

The sound echoed through the classroom, and for one horrifying second, the world froze.

Every single head turned toward me. Every. Single. One. My cheeks lit up like someone had cranked the heat on a stove burner, and I could feel it spreading to my ears and neck, my entire face betraying me.

He touched me, he touched me, he touched me...

Miss Holland stopped mid-step, the stack of packets she had been passing out freezing in her arms.

Her eyes narrowed, first on me, then on Cole, as if she was trying to get the full picture.

Then, her gaze softened—not toward me, of course, but towards *Cole*, like she had decided he was the victim in all this.

She pressed her lips into a thin line. "Gracie? Is there a problem?"

My throat tightened as she waited for an answer, my skin still burning where he had made contact with me.

I couldn't get the feeling to *go away*.

I felt sick.

But I'd be damned if I gave anyone at this dumb school something else to make fun of me for, so I put on the most neutral face that I could muster.

"No," I managed to choke out. "I'm fine. Totally fine. Just... dropped my pencil."

Before she could ask anything else, I grabbed the first pencil I could find, (ironically, the pencil Cole had offered me earlier) and held it up to the class.

It was the worst cover in the history of lies, but it was all I had.

Miss Holland's eyebrow arched slightly, skepticism written all over her face. But after a beat, she just sighed and turned back to the stack of packets in her arms. "Alright," she sighed, moving down the row. Not without throwing me one last look that screamed: *Pull yourself together, Gracie.*

I slumped back into my seat, gripping the pencil like it was the only shred of dignity I had left. My pulse refused to settle, and all I wanted was to disappear. Melt to the floor. *Cease to exist.*

Next to me, Cole shifted again, this time, even *further* away from me. "I'm sorry, again. I didn't mean to... you know... whatever that was."

Before I could even think of a response, (because seriously, what could I even say to the first apology I'd ever heard Cole say... ever?) Miss Holland swept by, placing a packet on his desk.

"Let me know if you need any help, okay?" she told him, sweetly.

Then she shot me another glare, like *I* was the one who'd hit him with that car.

Cole gave her a slight nod and a polite, tight-lipped smile. "Thank you." But as soon as she moved on, his face fell, and he sighed, opening the packet with all the enthusiasm of someone about to endure dental surgery.

I turned to my own packet, hoping to move on from my *second* hysteria of the day, but the sound of pages flipping furiously pulled at my attention.

Out of the corner of my eye, I saw him skimming through the packet, his brow furrowing deeper with every page. His fingers tapped an anxious rhythm on the desk, and finally—*slam.*

The sound echoed in the room, making Sierra jump in her seat. She glared at him before going back to scrolling on her phone. Because *priorities.*

I raised an eyebrow at him. "What?"

He ran a hand through his hair, leaving it sticking up in every direction. "I thought I'd at least remember *some* of this," he muttered.

I gave him a look as if to ask if he were serious, and when he *was*, I let out a light laugh.

"Sucks to suck, I guess," I shrugged as I twirled my pencil between my fingers, eyes drifting back to my packet.

Honestly, I expected him to roll his eyes and fire something equally as rude and sarcastic back at me.

Better yet, I expected him to shove the packet aside and give up entirely. Because let's be real—that's *exactly* what he'd do. Create some elaborate excuse just to get out of doing any real work.

But instead of doing any of that, he hunched back over his desk, pencil scratching furiously against the page as he scribbled something down.

Then he paused, stared at it, erased the entire thing, and started over.

I blinked. *What the hell is he doing?*

He was supposed to give up by now, lean back in his chair, and flash that stupid grin of his like none of this mattered, knowing that he'd convince one of the cheerleaders to do it for him later.

But no—he was still going, his brow furrowed like he actually cared.

Finally, his pencil stopped moving, and I couldn't resist leaning over slightly to witness the first homework problem he'd probably ever done in his life.

Well, that's a bummer. "That's wrong," I said flatly.

He didn't even look at me. "*Thank you...* for that."

I shrugged. "Just trying to help."

He let out a dry laugh, then leaned back in his seat and rubbed the back of his neck, clearly annoyed with me.

After a minute, he shifted in his chair, (going *out of his way* to avoid physical contact with me like I was some kind of disease) his eyes scanning the room.

He's looking for someone else to sit by, isn't he?

His gaze landed on Sierra first, who didn't even bother glancing up from her phone.

Then he tired Zach, who immediately avoided eye contact, suddenly becoming very interested in his packet.

I smirked. Unfortunately for him, no one was coming to his rescue. He was stuck here just like I was.

But then again, didn't he know that this little seating arrangement was never going to work? Wasn't this his *own* stupidity backfiring on him?

"Having trouble there, Cole?" I asked, propping my chin in my hand and batting my lashes mockingly.

His jaw tightened, giving up on his little quest, but *not* his packet, for some reason. "Do I have any friends..."

"No." I cut him off before he could finish. "Absolutely not. Y'know, it's an epidemic, really."

He closed his eyes for a long second, as if he were mentally counting to ten. "...in this class?"

"Still no," I said, my grin widening.

He turned his head toward me, his expression somewhere between exasperation and disbelief, as if trying to decide whether I was genuinely *this* annoying or if I was messing with him.

"Would you tell me if I did?"

"You tell *me*." I shot back.

He exhaled sharply, and I could practically see his patience fraying by the second. Honestly, I was just impressed he hadn't lost it already. *Props to him!*

"Do I need to spell out for you what amnesia *is*?" he asked, his voice edging on frustration. "I have no clue what sounds like something you'd do, because I don't even remember *who you are*."

"Sure," I said, dragging out the word with as much sarcasm as humanly possible. "I believe you."

He pinched the bridge of his nose, exhaling as if he were summoning every last ounce of willpower. "Look, I have no clue why you're mad at me, so if you could *please* just—"

"You know what, Cole?" I interrupted, finally sick of the "game" we were playing. "I *am* mad at you. And y'know why? Because you're so wrapped up in yourself that you don't care who you've hurt. So, get used to all the nasty stares and all the whispers, because you're an asshole, and you always will be."

His eyes flickered, but instead of backing down, he gave me a dry, humorless smile. "Is that all?"

"*Dear Lord,*" I muttered, throwing up my hands. "Don't you have someone else you'd rather annoy?"

"Right, because I clearly planned a whole car accident just to piss you off. Makes *perfect* sense," he shot back.

Heat rose in my face. "Don't even *joke* about a thing like that. You have no idea what you've done to people. *To me.*"

He let out a sharp laugh. "Last I checked, that was a side effect of *amnesia*. And for someone who clearly hates me, you're being awfully cagey about it."

"Maybe because I don't buy the whole amnesia story. Convenient, isn't it?"

His brows furrowed. "What? You think I'm lying or something?"

I crossed my arms. "You said it, not me."

His jaw tightened, and he leaned back in his chair, staring at me like I was the world's most frustrating puzzle. "Why the hell would I lie?"

"Why wouldn't you?" I snapped.

He exhaled sharply, running a hand through his hair. "You know what your problem is? You don't even want to hear the truth. I think you just like being mad. Ever thought about that?"

"Y'know what?" I stood so fast my chair scraped against the floor again. "I refuse to work in these conditions. Beside you, near you... on the same *planet* as you. I'm done."

Cole blinked at me, unaffected, and casually held out a pencil—the pencil I'd "borrowed" from him earlier. "Here's a parting gift before you go."

My vision went red. "*Unbelievable.*"

"What?" he said feigning innocence. "Clearly me being nice to you isn't working. You can't blame me for trying a different tactic."

I snatched the pencil from his hand and snapped it clean in half before slamming it back onto his desk. "Well, I don't want *anything* from you, and I'm not wasting another second of my time here."

I spun on my heel, fully intending to walk away, but his voice stopped me in my tracks.

"One can only be so lucky." he called after me, his voice dripping with mock relief.

That did it.

I whirled back around and stormed toward his desk. "Excuse me if I don't take anything you have to say seriously when a *child* has a better grasp of crossing a street than you do. Haven't you ever heard of *looking both ways?*"

He grinned, like he was suddenly enjoying this. "Haven't *you* ever heard about not being so pretentious? Did you miss that day of school or something?"

I let out an exasperated huff and dropped back into my seat because honestly, storming off wasn't an option anymore—not when he'd just spin it into a victory. "Wow, Cole. Why don't we just give you a gold star for that one, then?"

For a split second, his smirk faded, and his eyes narrowed as he gave me a once-over. "Well..." he started.

I folded my arms and raised an eyebrow. "Go on. Don't hurt yourself trying to remember my name, hun."

"I... I *can't* remember it, though."

"*Right...*" I paused, just in case adding. "It's Gracie. Not that it matters, though."

"Gracie..." he repeated slowly, leaning back in his chair again. And then he smiled—which, quite frankly, was a bold move for someone in the middle of an argument. "Okay, Gracie. We could go round and round about this all day, but *I'm* more curious as to why you seem to dislike me so much."

I scoffed. "We're really doing this?"

"Yeah, we're doing this." His tone was annoyingly calm. "Because if you're holding a grudge, I'd love to know why. Or is this just how you treat everyone?"

"Don't flatter yourself," I shot back. "You're not special. I could care less about you."

"Could you, though?" he asked, tilting his head with a maddeningly smug look. "Because it feels like you're putting in a lot of effort to argue with someone you don't care about."

I glared at him, trying to ignore the heat creeping up my neck.

He wasn't wrong—even with his alleged memory loss, we were always arguing. Fighting. Getting under each other's skin. Whatever you wanted

111

to call it. It was like we just couldn't help ourselves, no matter how many second chances the universe or whatever tried to give us.

"Well, why are *you* arguing with *me*?" I asked, folding my arms tighter across my chest. "Shouldn't you be off, I don't know, rediscovering your personality or something?"

"Maybe this is part of it," he shot back without missing a beat. "For all I know, I've always been like this."

"Oh, trust me. You have."

"Good to know, then."

"I don't believe you have amnesia." I blurted out suddenly.

"Excuse me?"

"Think about it," I said, fanning my hands flat out on the desk as if to present the obvious. "Your life's a mess, you basically have no friends, and no one really likes you. I'd pretend to forget my shitty life if I were you too."

His jaw tightened, the smugness draining from his face. "I don't have to prove anything to you."

"Oh, I think you do," I said, a wicked smile tugging at my lips. "In fact, let's test that spotty memory of yours, shall we? See what's actually *real* or not."

"I'm not playing twenty questions with you."

I laughed dryly. "Oh, this one's not a game."

His eyes narrowed, but he didn't say anything.

"Let's start simple. Do you remember the time in ninth grade when you 'accidentally' poured chocolate milk all over my pants and told everyone I'd pissed myself?"

His expression darkened. "No."

"Hmm, interesting," I said with mock sweetness. "How about when you and your friends thought it'd be funny to lock me in the janitor's closet

112

after gym one time? I was stuck in there for an hour and a half before someone found me."

His lips parted, but no words came out.

"Still nothing?" I clicked my tongue, growing more irritated. "Okay, how about the time you spread that rumor about me? The one in middle school? You remember that one, don't you, Cole?"

Gotcha.

He couldn't resist holding that over my head even if he tried. And even though I hated falling on the sword of my past like that, I hated Cole even more. It was for the greater good.

I leaned closer, lowering my voice. "Go on. If you're really faking this whole thing, now's your chance to say so. I know you want to."

Suddenly, his face went pale, like all the blood had drained from it. His expression blanked, and his eyes... they weren't even looking at me anymore.

"Cole?" I prompted, waving a hand in front of his face. "What are you doing?"

Nothing. His eyes remained distant and unfocused, as if he was seeing something that wasn't there.

Oh, great. *Another act.* "Seriously? You're just gonna sit there like that? You can just say you remember, and we can move on."

Still nothing.

"I'll even keep *your* weird little secret. For a price, obviously. I'm thinking..." I stopped myself then, an uneasy feeling hitting me.

He would've said something by now, wouldn't he? Not just about the rumor, but anything?

"Cole," I said again, sharper this time. "Are you okay?"

No response.

I shot a frantic glance at Miss Holland, who was leaning over some girl's paper, blissfully unaware that one of her students was either messing with me or actively dying.

"Cole!" I hissed, shaking his shoulder. His skin was unnaturally cold. "Snap out of it! Seriously. This isn't funny anymore."

No movement. No reaction.

My heart pounded against my ribs.

What's happening? A stroke? A seizure? A side effect of amnesia? My brain scrambled for answers, but all I could really think was, *Please don't let this idiot die in front of me. That'd be impossible to explain.*

Finally, after what felt like an eternity, he sucked in a shaky breath, his whole body shivering like ice water had been dumped on him.

I yanked my hand away from his shoulder like he'd burned me, crossing my arms tightly to cover the fact that they were trembling. "What the hell was that?" I demanded, and then (slightly) softer: "Are you... are you okay?"

He blinked, his eyes refocusing on me like he'd just realized I was there. "Whoa," he muttered under his breath, running a hand through his hair.

"*Whoa*? That's all you have to say?" I snapped, more out of discomfort than anger. "You just scared the shit out of me, and all you can say is *whoa*?"

He didn't answer, his gaze darting around the room like he was searching for something.

A flash of frustration crossed his face. "Where are the bathrooms?"

"Uh... down the hall and to the right?" I said hesitantly, my eyes narrowing. "But are you—"

"Thank you," he interrupted, pausing briefly to give me a once-over. "*Gracie.*"

And then he was gone.

Chapter Ten:

C ole

    I'd been standing in the bathroom for what felt like forever, my knuckles locked around the edges of the sink so tightly they'd turned white.

The fluorescent lights buzzed faintly overhead, bouncing off the cracked floor tiles and somehow making the dark, purple bags under my eyes look even worse.

The guy staring back at me looked familiar, but that was the problem—he only *looked* familiar. I didn't actually *know* him.

Dr. Andrews had said my memories weren't gone forever, just... misplaced. Like I'd shoved my whole life into a mental junk drawer and lost the key.

Yeah. Real helpful. Thanks, Doc.

I leaned in closer to the mirror, like staring hard enough would make something click.

It didn't.

And then there was the memory I had just gotten.

There I was, sitting on a boat with a man who looked like an older version of me. My dad, maybe? We were laughing about something until the line I was holding jerked.

I could feel the excitement of younger me as I reeled in the biggest rainbow trout I'd ever seen in my life. Then, the man scooped me up in celebration—just as the boat rocked, sending us flying into the water.

It was simple. It was perfect.

But it was also completely useless.

I squeezed my eyes shut, trying to block out the stabbing pain behind my temples as the memory played again. And again. And again.

What the hell was I supposed to do with it? It didn't explain why my sister wouldn't even look at me. Or why everyone at this school acted like I had the damn plague.

It didn't explain *anything*.

When I opened my eyes, the guy in the mirror was still there, still a stranger.

My breath fogged the glass as I leaned closer, searching for... what? Clues like some kind of kiddy detective? A spark of recognition? Anything?

Nothing.

Without thinking, I slammed my palms against the sink, the sharp clang echoing through the empty bathroom. My head dropped forward as I forced myself to breathe, but it came out heavy and uneven.

What the hell was wrong with me? Why couldn't I just *remember*?

I had nothing to go on. Only a single memory that didn't fit anywhere. A face that didn't feel like mine. And a past that everyone knew except for me.

But the biggest question—the one that wouldn't leave me alone—was why I'd been in the middle of the road in the first place.

According to the driver that night (and what he ended up telling the cops), I'd stepped onto the road on purpose. Like I'd *wanted* to get hit.

And the worst part? I didn't know if he was lying. I didn't even know if *I* was lying to myself.

I mean, I was supposed to be this amazing quarterback, right? That's what everyone had been telling me since I'd woken up in the hospital, at least. There's no way I wouldn't have seen a car coming.

I could've dodged it. I *should've* dodged it.

But here I was, waking up with no memories and no explanation for it. For *any* of it. I mean... I'd been hit by a fucking *car*. Those things didn't just happen, did they?

Had I been suicidal?

The bathroom door creaked open, and I halfheartedly looked up and met the eyes of some guy with earbuds dangling around his neck.

I gave him a small, courtesy smile because what else was I supposed to do in that situation?

Nothing to see here. I'm not having a fucking existential crisis in the bathroom right now at all.

But that's when his face went sheet-white, his hand freezing on the doorhandle, like he'd caught me murdering a litter of newborn puppies.

"Oh. Uh..." he mumbled. "I'll just... come back later. Sorry, Cole."

The door clicked shut behind him before I could say anything.

Not that I *had* anything to say.

I stared at the empty doorway, then back at my reflection.

Great. Add "scaring people out of bathrooms" to my growing list of talents—another stellar moment in the life of Cole Whatever-My-Last-Name-Is.

A slow breath hissed out through my teeth.

Maybe that guy had the right idea. Maybe avoiding me was easier—for him... for everyone.

Anger surged through me, and my foot shot out before I could stop it.

The trash can behind me slammed against the wall with a metallic crash, spilling paper towels, empty wrappers, and a crushed soda can across the floor.

The noise echoed louder in the room than I'd expected, and I flinched, my chest heaving as my pulse roared in my ears. "Damn it," I muttered.

For a second, I just stood there, staring at the mess I'd made.

I almost wanted to leave it there. As if to say *see? My problems should be your problems too.* But the frustration twisting inside me quickly cooled to something heavier—something closer to shame.

I sighed, crouching as I started grabbing the crumpled paper towels and shoving them back into the can. The soda can had rolled to the farthest corner of the bathroom, and I stretched to reach it before throwing it back in too.

When everything was cleaned up, I stood and wiped my palms against my jeans, my gaze landing back to the mirror.

I didn't like what I saw.

I reached out and turned on the faucet, letting cold water pour over my hands, before splashing it onto my face. *I just need to calm down. And then I can figure everything else out.*

Eventually, I forced myself to take a deep breath as ice water dripped from my chin and slid down my neck, soaking into the collar of my shirt.

My pulse even returned to normal, the pounding in my skull easing up enough for my thoughts to at least stop spinning in every direction.

When I opened my eyes again, I turned off the water and straightened, gripping the edges of the sink for a second before stepping back.

I just had to make it through lunch and two more classes, and then I'd be home free. I could do this.

I wasn't suicidal. Accidents just happen.

Four Years Earlier
Gracie

The last car pulled out of the parking lot, and I exhaled slowly, watching the taillights dissolve into tiny red dots before vanishing into the night.

It's just me now.

The wind picked up, slipping underneath my sweater, and I had to clench my arms around my guitar to keep from shivering.

The only real light left was the glowing white cross at the front of the building. Everything else had faded into shadows that seemed to press closer together the longer I sat there.

It wasn't like this was the first time Mom had forgotten to pick me up after practice. *She isn't even that late yet*, I told myself. But that didn't stop my imagination from running wild as the minutes dragged on.

Bear was probably still at the ice rink with her. I bet they hadn't even realized what time it was.

I tried not to let it bother me. But it did.

My sheet music sat in my lap, crinkled from where I'd accidentally bent it, and I squinted in the dim light, trying to work through the chords I'd struggled with earlier.

If I kept my mind busy, maybe I'd forget I was in a church parking lot all alone.

The creak of a door swinging open behind me made me jump to my feet, and I turned sharply, clutching my guitar like a shield, as someone stepped out of the shadows and into the faint glow of the cross.

Guess I wasn't as alone as I thought I was.

"Hey, Gracie," the bass player said cheerfully. He moved closer, hands in his jacket pockets as his shadow stretched long across the pavement.

"Hi." I hated my voice for how small it suddenly was.

I forced a polite smile anyways, hoping he'd just say 'have a good night' or something, and leave.

But instead, he nodded toward my guitar, tilting his head. "Still working on that song?"

"Uh, yeah." My fingers fidgeted with the sheet music, folding and un-folding the corner. "I didn't think anyone else was still here."

"Just locking up," he shrugged, not moving away. "You sounded good tonight, though. Got a ride coming?"

"Yeah," I said quickly, nodding like I could will my words into reality. "My mom's on her way."

He smiled, but it didn't feel quite right. "I could take you home. Save you the wait."

"*No*," I said forcefully. "I mean... no, that's okay. She'll be here soon."

His eyes dragged over me, lingering on my breasts for an eternity longer than I was comfortable with before meeting my eyes again. "You sure? You shouldn't be out here alone. It's a dangerous world for a pretty girl like you."

My throat tightened, but I managed to croak out, "I'm fine. Really."

He leaned in just a fraction, and his voice dipped low. "I could have you home before your mom even realizes you're gone."

A cold, sick feeling crept into my stomach, rooting me in place. Every muscle in my body screamed at me to move, but my feet had stopped listening.

He reached out, his fingers brushing against my cheek as he tucked a strand of hair behind my ear. My breath hitched, and I almost wanted to vomit.

"Too pretty to be out here alone," he murmured again.

Suddenly, headlights swept over the parking lot, slicing through the darkness.

Mom's car rolled up to the curb, and I stumbled back a step, still clutching my guitar. "Well, that's her," I blurted, my voice shaking as I hurried toward the car.

I yanked open the passenger door and slid inside, fumbling with the seatbelt as my hands shook uncontrollably. The buckle clicked into place, but I didn't let go—I held onto that strap for dear life as I tried but failed to calm myself down.

"Sorry I'm late!" Mom said brightly. She was smiling, oblivious to what had just happened, already launching into a story about Bear's game and how great he'd done in net.

I nodded along, forcing a smile that barely lifted the corners of my lips.

My gaze stayed fixed straight ahead, unwilling to meet her eyes, feeling guilty for something that hadn't even been my fault.

Or had it? I didn't even know.

Against my better judgement, I stole one last look at the rearview mirror.

He was still there, standing in the glow of the cross. He waved once, slowly, before turning and disappearing back into the shadows.

I bit my lip, my fingers drifting to the strand of hair he'd touched. An unfamiliar wave of disgust rolled through me.

I wanted it gone. I wanted to grab a pair of scissors and hack it all off. Every last piece of hair he'd touched. As if that could erase the memory, erase *him*.

Was that insane? Was *I* insane?

"Everything okay?" Mom asked, her cheerful tone dipping slightly as she glanced at me.

"Yeah," I said quickly. My voice sounded strained, but I forced it to stay even. "I was just thinking about getting a haircut."

Mom perked up, her smile returning. "We can set something up for tomorrow. I think I have a coupon for one lying around the house somewhere."

The conversation shifted back to Bear's game, but I couldn't focus.

I couldn't stop replaying his words in my head. *I could have you home before your mom even realizes you're gone.*

It sounded like a threat.

And I couldn't shake the feeling that he had no problem making good on it.

Chapter Eleven:

PRESENT DAY: SEPTEMBER 25TH

Today was the day. The most important day of my life—the day of the FFA presidential vote.

It was a big deal, not just for our chapter, but for the way things ran all year. Not only did the president organize events and lead meetings, but they also basically set the tone for everything we did.

Thankfully, at that point, I had already decided that was the perfect job for Emma.

She was at the back of the room, crouched by the supply cabinet, rummaging through a pile of papers when I walked in.

Her blonde ponytail swayed back and forth, keeping time with Taylor Swift's "Cruel Summer" playing faintly from her phone.

I twirled a strand of my own hair between my fingers, watching her.

Between that and tapping on my glasses, it was one of my many nervous habits of mine. This was one I'd picked up in eighth grade when I'd chopped it all off in a moment of rebellion (or maybe desperation).

Let's just say: getting that bob had been one of the worst decisions of my life. It basically gave *Dora the Explorer*—if Dora had gotten it cut by a toddler in the dark. But at the time, it'd felt like a way to reclaim "myself" in a way.

Fast forward to today, it'd finally grown back to a decent length, grazing just above my mid-back.

I liked having long hair better. It felt more like me.

Well, as much of me as I *could* be given the circumstances.

"Gracie, can you grab the ballot box?" Emma asked suddenly, slightly muffled as she stretched deeper into the cabinet.

I sighed dramatically, pushing myself off the counter I'd been leaning on. "You mean this highly advanced, state-of-the-art wooden box that one of the seniors carved during shop class last year?" I held it up, squinting at the slightly crooked edges. "Yeah, sure. Real fancy."

Emma didn't even look up as she laughed. "You know our budget isn't what it used to be. It was nice of Colin to make that for us before he left."

I snorted, setting the box down on the table in front of her. "It was only *nice* because you had a crush on him. If you ask me, we could've done a whole hell of a lot better by getting a box from a haunted garage sale."

Emma popped up from behind the cabinet, grinning with arms full of papers and a clipboard. "Well, good thing I *didn't* ask you, then."

I stuck my tongue out at her, but my attention drifted toward the door before I could come up with a better response.

My fingers brushed the edge of the ballot box as I asked, "On a different note, have you seen Bear? He promised he'd be here today for the vote."

Emma paused, her grin softening. "No, but I was wondering where he was. I thought he was coming with you."

"Yeah, he was supposed to..." I said, biting my lip, trying to sound like I wasn't worried at all. Like my first thought wasn't that he had fallen down somewhere and couldn't get up, or was choking to death on his own vomit... All the *fun*, big sisterly things. "I think he went to the bathroom or something, but he's been in there awhile if that's true."

Emma tilted her head slightly, studying me. "Should we go look for him? Just... in case?"

I waved her off with a tight smile knowing she was just trying to help. But honestly, it was only making me even more nervous.

My brother is supposed to stay an inside problem, not an outside. I didn't want anyone else to be involved in my shitty life—even if it *was* my best friend. "No, he's fine. He'll be here any second. I'm sure of it."

She didn't look convinced, but thankfully, didn't push it.

"Here," she said, grabbing the clipboard from the pile she'd gathered, handing it to me with a little smile. "Something to take your mind off of everything while we wait. Just make sure we have all the right forms for the election."

I took it gratefully, knowing Emma had probably checked these papers one-thousand times over already. But leave it to her to let her pride take a backseat if it meant giving me a distraction.

I clicked the pen attached to the clipboard twice and began to skim through the files.

She was leaning against the table now, arms crossed as she watched me. "Speaking of," she started casually, "what's it been like having Cole back in your science class?"

I groaned. "Nice segue, Em. Tell me how you really feel, huh?"

"*What?*" she giggled. "You can't blame me for being curious! It's Cole Brown, for Pete's sake. Quarterback of the football team? The guy every girl in school has drooled over since the fifth grade? How is that not the juiciest thing *ever*?"

"Because it's *Cole.*"

She raised her eyebrows. "You can't seriously still be mad about middle school, can you? Besides, he has amnesia now. He doesn't even remember what he did to you."

I narrowed my eyes. "Correction: he *allegedly* has amnesia. And *I* remember. That's all that matters."

Emma bit her lip, too polite to beg me outright for more details. But after a minute of puppy dog eyes, I sighed and gave in. "He's been trying this whole... fake nice guy thing lately. Like yesterday, he asked me how my day was going. *Twice.*"

"And you...?"

"I ignored him. *Duh,*" I said with a shrug, flipping a page on the clipboard.

Emma gasped, clutching her chest in mock horror. "You're *kidding*. You ignored the guy who literally has no idea who he is right now?"

"How is that my problem?" I shot back. "I didn't tell him to go play Frogger in real life."

"Gracie..."

"What?" I asked, raising an eyebrow. "I'm just saying, natural selection works in mysterious ways."

Emma frowned. "And *I'm* just saying you could cut him a little slack. He almost died in that car accident."

"Yeah, well, I almost died as Utah's very own Scarlet Letter because of him," I snapped, finally giving up on doublechecking the papers and tossing the clipboard onto the table. "Pretty sure we're even."

"People change, Gracie," she said softly.

I rolled my eyes. "Please, spare me the after-school special."

Before she could respond, her phone buzzed on the table.

She glanced at the screen, and for a split second, her face fell. But just as quickly, she smoothed it over, slipping the phone into her pocket.

"Everything okay, Em?"

"Yeah," she said a little too brightly. "I just realized I have to leave earlier than planned. Totally slipped my mind." She gestured vaguely toward the discarded clipboard. "Let's get this vote over with, shall we?"

I pursed my lips skeptically at her tone but let it slide. "What about Bear? We can't start without him. He said he'd be here."

Emma hesitated, shifting her weight from one foot to the other. "I know, but... maybe we should just do it now? We've been putting it off for weeks, and we should really have a president by the next meeting."

I stared at her, frustration bubbling up in my chest. "Emma, he's my brother. He promised he'd be here. Can't we just wait five more minutes?"

Her face twisted in the guilty expression she always made when she thought she was about to let someone down. "I really have to go, Gracie. We can't keep stalling."

I sighed, glancing at the door one last time, hoping he'd walk in at the last second. But the hallway beyond it remained empty.

"Fine," I muttered, grabbing a scrap of paper from the desk. "Let's vote, then. But you know the drill—it has to be unanimous."

"Wait, Gracie,"

I ignored her.

"*Gracie*," she repeated, firmer this time.

I sighed and looked up. "What?"

She hesitated, her cheeks flushing pink. "My vote is for you."

That stopped me.

I froze, my pen hovering above the paper. "Excuse me?"

"You should be president," she said simply.

I dropped the pen onto the table and scoffed. "You can't just say that. Especially not without writing it down. That's not how this works."

She crossed her arms. "Does it matter? You know I'm serious."

"No, you're not," I shot back, my voice rising before I could stop it. "You're the president. End of story."

Emma shook her head. "Gracie, come on. You've been the one holding this chapter together since day one. You're passionate, you care about every detail, and you're not afraid to speak your mind. You're *exactly* what this team needs."

I laughed bitterly. "Yeah, because a president who loses her temper every five seconds is *so* great for morale. Be so for real right now."

She sighed, her voice softening. "Gracie, whether you like it or not, this job was made for you."

"Well, good luck, because I'm not voting for myself," I said, grabbing the paper and crumpling it into a ball. "So, I guess the jury's hung."

"Gracie—"

"You know what?" I interrupted, snatching my bag off the table. "Forget it. I'm gonna go find Bear."

"Gracie, please—"

But I was already at the door, yanking it open.

I glanced back over my shoulder one last time. "Good luck finding someone else to do the job, *Madam President*."

And with that, I slammed the door behind me.

Cole

I stood outside the weight room, staring at the metal door, as if I could separate the present me from who I was supposedly before.

The quarterback. The hero of the story. The guy who always got the girl, who walked through these halls like he owned the place. I deserved that life again, didn't I? Deserved to feel... invincible?

Coach Williams stood next to me, his potbelly brushing against the clipboard he was carrying. He was talking, but his voice sounded distant, muffled under the bass-heavy rap music pounding through the door.

The sound should have stirred up some memory, but instead, it just made me feel smaller.

"Your dad," Coach Williams said.

That did it. My thoughts snapped back into focus like a rubber band at just the mention of him.

"Back when I coached him, he had that same drive. That same fire to win," he chuckled to himself, as if replaying a memory in his head. *Huh. Must be nice.* "He was a quarterback too, you know. The apple didn't fall far from the tree."

I forced a polite smile.

It wasn't the first time someone had mentioned my dad, and knowing this town, it wouldn't be the last.

But every time they did, I just felt like a piece of myself was missing and everyone else knew it too. I didn't even have the memories to fill it in either.

Just a collection of things people had told me for almost a month since I'd woken up from my coma.

He sounded like the kind of guy who was worth remembering, and that only made it worse.

"You're lucky," he added, tapping the clipboard against his leg. "Some guys don't get that kind of legacy to live up to."

Lucky. Yeah...

I swallowed hard, shifting my gaze back to the door.

Lucky isn't exactly what I'd call it. It felt more like a bar set impossibly high, with everyone watching and waiting for me to trip on the way up.

"This weight room was practically your second home, Cole," Coach Williams went on. "Thought it might help to see it again, maybe jog something loose."

"I hope so," I muttered, more to myself than to him.

His eyes suddenly lit up. "You wouldn't happen to be cleared to start playing again, would you? Maybe taking the weights for a spin would do you some good."

"No, sir." I said. I caught the flicker of disappointment on his face and quickly added, "But I'll let you know when I am."

The corner of his mouth twitched into a soft smile as he reached for the doorknob. "Just... take it all in, alright? No pressure."

Right. *No pressure*. Just my dead dad's reputation hanging over my head. Totally no big deal.

The second the door cracked open, the thumping bass of the music hit me like a physical wave. The smell of sweat and metal (a mix of gym socks and old rubber mats) rushed out into the hallway, and I braced myself as Coach Williams pushed the door open wider.

I expected the place to be empty since school had ended an hour ago, maybe a couple of stragglers lifting weights or screwing around.

But no, it was packed.

Almost the entire team was in there, spread out across the room. A couple of guys were spotting each other at the bench press, one was loading plates onto the squat rack, and a group in the corner was half-lifting, half-laughing over something I couldn't hear over the music.

Then somebody noticed me.

"Yo, Cole's here!"

"QB's back, baby!"

"Look who finally decided to show up!"

It was like flipping a switch. A ripple of excitement went through the room, and before I knew it, I was surrounded.

Slaps on the back, handshakes, someone tossing me a water bottle like I was going to start lifting with them right then and there...

"You gonna suit up, man?"

"Team's not the same without you!"

"Dude, you remember me, right? I'm Eric!"

Not really, Eric. But I nodded anyway.

Coach Williams clapped his hands together. "Alright, alright! Give him some breathing room! Let's get back to work!"

The crowd reluctantly started to scatter, but not before a few more slaps on the shoulder and a couple of "good to see you, man" comments.

As the noise settled, I let out a breath I hadn't realized I was holding.

Every day since my accident had been like that—little bursts of attention that never felt as comfortable as they should've been.

I sat with the team at lunch, waved back when they called my name in the halls, and laughed when I thought I was supposed to. But it all felt hollow.

Like I was playing the part of the legendary quarterback and didn't really fit the role.

Because I didn't really understand what *that* guy was supposed to act like.

The team respected me. So, maybe pre-amnesia had the right idea personality-wise. But respect wasn't the same as belonging, and belonging was a lot harder to fake when I couldn't remember the guy they were all rooting for.

On the bright side, names were slowly starting to stick—Michael, Hayden, Alex...

But when you're trying to relearn a group of people who assume that you just *should* know who they are, it's like being handed a thousand-piece puzzle with no box to show you what it's supposed to look like.

Coach Williams came up behind me, patting me on the shoulder and breaking me from my thoughts. "I've got to take a quick call, but I'll be back in a minute."

He gave me a nod before heading toward the door, leaving the faint sound of his ringtone trailing behind him.

Shit. Don't leave me here by myself.

But being alone didn't last too long because almost immediately, I spotted Max.

He was near the back of the room, stacking more weight onto the barbell like he hadn't noticed me walk in.

I watched him for a second, hoping he might glance up and give me a nod or something. But, no—he just kept doing his thing, completely ignoring me.

Unlike the rest of the team who'd made sure to go out of their way to welcome me back, Max had kept his distance since day one.

That might not seem like a big deal, (he didn't exactly seem like the loud, rah-rah type of guy) but after almost a month of being back at school, I'd picked up on something:

He wasn't just any guy on the team—he was *the* guy. The captain.

And if you were on his team, you were supposed to be his priority. At least, that's how the other guys talked about him.

He was the kind of captain who'd hype up a freshman just for showing up early. The kind of guy who would stay late just to help someone work on their form. A "team-first" guy, through and through.

Except, apparently, when it came to me.

Sure, I'd seen him around—in the hallways or whatever. But he never sat with the rest of the team at lunch and didn't hang out with anyone after school if I was there.

It wasn't like he was a total loner, but when it came to me, there was this... gap.

And it didn't make any sense.

Everyone else treated me like I could do no wrong. Which, yeah, made sense. Apparently, I was a god when it came to football—or so I'd been told, over and over again. Coaches, teammates, even the random kids in the hallway who *weren't* afraid of me—they all acted like my name was some kind of magic word.

But not Max.

It bugged me more than it should have. Not because I wanted him to kiss my ass like everyone else, but because... well, I didn't know why.

Maybe it was because, from what I'd heard about him, I would've thought he would've been the one to ask me how I was doing after being hit by a *fucking car*.

But he hadn't. Not once.

So, then, I had to ask myself: Did Max, like basically everyone else at this stupid school, have a reason to hate me?

Because that would explain a lot, wouldn't it?

I stood there for another second, glaring at the barbell in front of me. Then, before I could talk myself out of it, I headed for him.

If Max had some kind of problem with me, I might as well figure it out right here and now. I already had enough to deal with without adding "why does Max hate me?" to the list.

I weaved through the machines and groups of guys swapping sets, stopping just short of where Max was standing.

He was focused on adding another plate to the barbell, barely glancing up when I stepped into his space.

"Hey," I said, crossing my arms and forcing an easy tone. "*Max*, is it?"

This time, he straightened, meeting my gaze. "Yeah. Max," he said, reaching out his hand. "Nice to meet you... again."

That last word hung in the air, and I couldn't tell if he meant it as a jab or if I was just reading into it.

"So, captain, huh?" I said, leaning against the nearest machine. "That's... awesome, man. Guess Coach Williams thought you were the right guy for it?"

I forced my smile to stay put, even though irritation was starting to burn a hole through my chest.

Max paused, studying me, like he was sizing me up just as much as I was him. A faint redness crept up his dark complexion as he rubbed the back of his neck. "Yeah, he, uh... said he wanted someone who worked hard and led by example."

My jaw tightened. *Worked hard? Led by example?* Right. I guess to him, barely even acknowledging me was "leadership."

"Interesting..." I replied, giving him a once-over. "Because you don't really strike me as the type to care about, you know, *everyone* on the team. Not exactly captain material, if you ask me."

He sighed, tipping his head toward the door, calm as ever. "Hey, it's kinda loud in here. Wanna step out into the hallway for a second?"

Still steaming, (probably even more so now that he'd just totally ignored my comment) I let him grab a towel off a nearby bench and sling it around his shoulders as I followed him out.

But as we stepped out into the quieter hallway, the shift in the air was noticeable.

Max leaned against the wall with his shoulder, weirdly relaxed in a way that made me feel like I was already losing whatever argument we were about to have.

Finally, he let out a soft chuckle, shaking his head. "Captain... *ha*. You've always had a one-track mind, buddy. I was waiting to have this conversation again."

My chest tightened as I crossed my arms. "Excuse me?"

Max's smile faded, and he straightened slightly, his eyes meeting mine. "You don't remember, do you?"

"*Obviously*."

"The night before the accident," Max said quietly. "You called me."

A flicker of something stirred in the back of my mind, but I couldn't quite catch it. "I did?"

"Yeah..." he hesitated for a second, as if he were wondering how much he should actually tell me. "You told me to step down. Said you should be captain instead."

I opened my mouth to respond, but nothing came out.

Max pushed off the wall slightly, his shoulders tense now.

"Any other time, I think... I think I would've. I would've gone to Coach and asked him to give you back the position. I would've stepped down. But I just... couldn't. I couldn't do that this time."

I swallowed hard, forcing the words out. "And why's that?"

"Because they need someone who treats them like they matter," Max said simply. "Like they're worth fighting for."

He let the words hang for a second before he went on, his tone still steady but more vulnerable now. "Boston. Sophomore year, his parents were going through a divorce, and he started skipping practices because he didn't have a ride there anymore. I drove to his house every morning to take him to school, then to football.

Sean? His grades tanked two years ago. I helped him study for finals so he could stay on the team. And Eric? He blew out his knee last season. I sat in the hospital with him while they figured out his surgery."

Max shifted uncomfortably, rubbing the back of his neck again. "To you, this was always just about football, but... it's not. It's about giving them someone they can trust. Someone who's there, no matter what. Like... I was for you."

"*Me?*"

"Yeah," Max said, his voice quieter now. "Eighth grade. The summer your dad died. You were at my house every day. We'd play catch in my front yard until it got dark, especially after your stepdad moved in. My mom used to joke that we should've made up a room for you with how much you were there."

I blinked as I tried to picture it: me and Max, younger versions of ourselves, tossing a football back and forth like the world outside didn't exist. Like we were just two normal kids.

But it was never normal, was it?

Waking up from my accident... having to lose my dad all over again... it was like ripping open a wound that hadn't even started to heal yet.

I barely knew my *name*, but I knew that.

But also in that moment, I finally understood what kind of person it took to step up for someone like me.

The kind of person who could see past all the anger and hurt and still stick around. The kind of person who could lead by example.

A captain, if you will.

If anything, Max *should* have hated me. But he didn't. I'd gotten him all wrong.

"A captain should be a lot of things. Respected. Firm. Hardworking. But never feared." His eyes locked onto mine. "Fear might get people to follow you, but it'll never make them trust you."

I didn't say anything right away, letting it sink in, feeling it shift something fundamental inside me.

Finally, I nodded. "You're a good captain, Max. I mean it. You deserve the title."

Max blinked, surprised by the sincerity in my voice, but before he could say anything, I cleared my throat and added, "Hey, maybe we could catch up sometime? Outside of scho..."

That's when a loud crash echoed from down the hallway.

Max whipped his head toward the sound, his brows snapping together in an instant.

We locked eyes, the same thought sparking between us without a word.

He took off first, but I was right behind him.

The scene in the foyer came into view fast. Three linebackers, Dylan, Aiden, and Josh, were towering over a smaller kid I didn't recognize.

His bag was gutted, notebooks and papers spilling out across the floor.

I skidded to a stop, Max just behind me. And for a second, I froze.

What am I supposed to do?

Was *this* it? The moment when I finally reembraced my old self—the guy everyone *said* I used to be? The guy who didn't take nothing from nobody? The guy who scared people like this shrimpy-looking kid shitless?

With the football team, I wasn't an outcast. I was *one* of them.

But the rest of the school? They'd never see it that way. To them, I was still the kid who fell from grace, the reminder of what *not* to be.

Which made me wonder: did it even matter how good I tried to be if no one else cared enough to notice?

Falling back into what was supposedly old patterns was an easy way out. It was a chance to reclaim my old life—whatever that was.

So, why don't you just join them?

Because if I stepped in, if I did the "right" thing and saved this kid, there was no way in hell the football team would take me back.

Losing my memory was already difficult enough without adding "wuss" to the list.

It was either him or me. Was I really ready to risk it all for someone I didn't even know? Was it worth it?

Him or me?

Him or me?

Him or me?

But then, I heard it. The right thing to do.

"Fear might get people to follow you, but it'll never make them trust you."

Trust.

That's when it hit me—*that* was exactly the person I wanted to be. Someone who was trusted. *Not* feared.

Not anymore.

The second that Dylan, the biggest of the three, hauled the kid up like he was nothing, tossing him between his friends like some sadistic game of hot potato, my feet started moving forward, closing the gap before I could even process how big of a decision I'd just made.

"Leave him alone."

Max stayed back, watching me cautiously, like he wasn't sure if I'd just stepped up or stepped off a cliff, but the words felt solid. Like I'd been meant to say them all along.

Dylan turned to me, his smirk dropping as our eyes locked. "Cole, what's wrong? We're just having some fun."

"Put. Him. Down."

The kid hung over Dylan's shoulder like a rag doll, his eyes squeezed shut, like if he wished hard enough, he could make all of us disappear.

"I won't ask again."

Dylan blinked at me, looking more confused than threatened. "What are you smoking, Brown? You usually get a kick out of this stuff."

I tried to swallow down the guilt that clawed at my throat. Yet another reminder of who I was before my accident.

And maybe I *still* was that person. A failed attempt at a "rescue mission" wasn't exactly a change in character.

Before I could roll over and wash my hands clean of this whole thing (maybe I'd get lucky and Dylan would believe I was just messing with him), I turned my focus back to the kid one last time.

But as I did, something tugged at the corner of my mind.

His eyes... there was something familiar about them. Something I couldn't really place but also couldn't ignore.

Had I known him before the accident?

That's when it clicked for me. The reason he looked familiar. His eyes looked almost exactly like...

"BEAR!"

I turned just in time to see Gracie barreling down the steps, practically flying as she skipped them three at a time.

She shoved past me without hesitation, throwing herself in front of Dylan like she was some kind of human shield.

"Cole, I don't know what you're doing to my brother, but I swear if you try anything else..." *How is this **my** fault?*

"You'll what?" Josh piped up, "You'll punch him aga—"

"Not if I punch you first, you little jerk..."

That's when she lunged for the group with more rage than sense.

I barely had time to react before I caught her, scooping her up like she weighed nothing and spinning her out of the way.

"Alright, alright, that's enough of that," I said, setting her firmly down beside me. "I was *handling* it."

"Clearly," she snapped. "You're doing a *fantastic* job so far."

Sarcasm, funny.

Honestly, at this point, though, I expected nothing less from her.

But I still couldn't help the smirk tugging at my lips. "You know, if you keep sweet-talking me like that, people might think we're actually friends."

She shot me a glare that could've melted glaciers. "In your dreams, Brown."

Meanwhile, the guys were staring at the two of us like we'd just dropped in from another planet.

Dylan's smirk was now gone, replaced with something closer to irritation.

"Fine," Dylan said, finally setting Bear down and shoving him back to us. "You wanna play hero? Go ahead. This isn't even fun anymore."

I couldn't help but raise my eyebrow at that. "Fun? Yeah, because nothing screams 'fun' like beating up on a kid who's half your size."

His face flushed instantly. "Whatever," he muttered, his eyes darting to the ground. "Let's go, guys."

Aiden, ever the genius, glanced back at me and vowed, "This isn't over, Brown."

"Wow," I said, tilting my head in mock awe. "Really branching out from clichés, aren't we? What's next? 'You'll pay for this?' 'Curse you, Perry the Platypus?'"

Gracie snorted (actually *snorted*) before clamping her hand over her mouth like she couldn't believe the sound had just come out of her.

But the guys didn't seem like they had anything else to say about it because Dylan and the rest of his lollipop guild cleared out before anything else could happen.

Glancing back, I realized even *Max* had left at some point. Now, it was just me, Gracie, and her brother.

I let out a deep, shaky breath, running a hand through my hair. It hadn't even been a month since I'd been back to school, and I was already making more enemies than I had to start with.

Hopefully, that didn't come back to bite me in the ass.

Gracie, meanwhile, had already spun toward Bear. "Are you okay? *Did they hurt you?*"

Bear shook his head but kept his eyes fixed on the floor. "I'm fine," he mumbled.

"*Fine?*" she snapped, gripping him by the shoulders. "Bear, I've been looking *everywhere* for you. You scared the shit out of me! You were supposed to wait for me after school."

"I know," he said, scuffing the toe of his sneaker against the floor. "I was heading to the FFA meeting, but then they..."

"Forget the meeting," she interrupted, losing steam. She bit her lip and took a deep breath. "It got canceled—long story. Just... wait in the car for me, okay? I'll be there in a minute."

"But—"

"*Now*," she said firmly, pointing toward the door. "And text Emma to let her know you're fine. She's probably freaking out too."

Bear muttered something under his breath but followed directions anyways, turning and heading for the exit.

"And don't forget," she called after him. "I'm helping you with your English paper tonight, so don't even think about procrastinating again."

"I know," Bear replied without turning around.

"And you better remember to take your meds tonight. I swear if—"

He spun around. "Gracie, I *know*."

She raised an eyebrow, clearly taken aback by his reaction, but quickly crossed her arms over her chest as if to pretend like it hadn't affected her. "Good. Get moving. *Now*."

He let out a frustrated sigh and turned back around, pushing the door open with more force than necessary.

I tried my best to look uninterested as I leaned against the closest lockers to me, watching this all go down, but it wasn't easy.

Seeing Gracie boss her brother around was like watching a general command an army—intense, kind of terrifying, but also fun to witness if it wasn't directed at you.

She didn't coddle him, didn't treat him like he was fragile, but she still managed to get her point across.

She hid the fact she cared, but that didn't make her love any less. And realizing that hit me in a way that didn't really make sense.

Maybe I'd been wrong about her too.

Not that I was about to tell *her* that, though.

Gracie turned to me suddenly, letting out a long, dramatic sigh. "I guess I should thank you for risking your precious popularity for some random kid."

I let out a laugh before I could stop myself. "Well, that's a start. I'd say you're about fifty percent of the way to a proper thank-you."

She scoffed. "Oh, don't flatter yourself. If anything, I'm regretting not letting Dylan drop kick you across the school."

"Believe it or not, Gracie, I'm not a total jerk."

Her eyes narrowed again, like she was trying to figure me out. But after a beat, she must have decided on *something* because she shook her head and started to turn away. "Whatever," she muttered.

"You know," I called after her, "you're welcome, by the way."

She spun back around. "I didn't *ask* for your help. I've been handling this kind of thing for sixteen years, Cole. And it's mostly been from people like you!"

"People like me?" I asked, arching a brow. "What's *that* supposed to mean?"

"Oh, *I'm sorry*. Let me clarify." She replied, holding up her hand and ticking off fingers like she had a list ready to go. "Bullies, people on the football team, people with fake country accents..."

"My accent's not fake," I cut in, a little too defensively. My voice cracked at the end though, which only made it worse.

Her brown eyes sparkled with amusement. "*Right*. Sure it's not."

"Will we ever have a conversation longer than five seconds without you going all psychotic on me?" I shot back, trying to recover whatever shred of dignity I had left with her.

She rolled her eyes. "I'm not *psychotic*, you asshat."

"Could've fooled me," I said, smirking now. "You know, if you weren't always calling me names, I'd think you were kinda cute."

Her face twisted like she wasn't sure whether to laugh or gag. "Did you just call me *cute*?"

"In a roundabout way... maybe." I grinned. "Why? Worried you'll accidentally fall for someone as devilishly handsome as myself?"

"*HA*! I'm worried that you suffered more brain damage than just the amnesia," she shot back, spinning on her heel as she turned for the door. "By the way, your fly is down."

I glanced down automatically, then caught myself. "Wow. Real mature, Gracie," I called after her.

She didn't even slow down—just threw her middle finger over her shoulder.

I couldn't help laughing at that, shaking my head as she pushed through the exit and disappeared out of view.

She was exhausting, irritating, and impossible to keep up with. But for some reason, I didn't want to stop trying.

Maybe "enemy" was too strong of a word for what we were. Maybe we were something else entirely.

Chapter Twelve

SEPTEMBER 26TH

G racie

By the time I'd made it halfway down the hall to fourth period, I could already feel the beginnings of a headache starting.

The morning had been an absolute disaster.

Bear's IVIG infusion had gone way longer than expected, even though I'd gone out of my way to reschedule it for during lunch. *Why?* Because Dad flaked on me. He had an "emergency" or whatever at the restaurant, which suddenly made Bear my problem. *Again.*

So now, not only was I late to class, but I also hadn't even had time to eat yet, and my stomach was making noises that could have passed for a dying whale.

Lovely.

I adjusted my bag on my shoulder and picked up the pace, weaving between clumps of kids who apparently had nothing better to do than stand in the middle of the hallway.

If I didn't make it to class soon, Ms. Newman would lose her *shit* and give me another lecture about "timeliness and responsibility" or something.

Right. As if *I* needed any advice on being "responsible," like I wasn't actively taking care of a literal kid on *top* of all my stupid homework in that class.

Don't get me wrong. I cared about Bear more than anything in the world. But sometimes, it felt like I wasn't allowed to exist outside of being *just* his sister.

No one ever asked me how *I* was doing. Not my parents, not my teachers, and certainly not anyone in this godforsaken hallway. Instead, they were all just brainwashed into feeling sorry for Bear.

Even Cole... okay, scratch that: *especially* Cole.

Ever since the accident, he couldn't seem to resist jumping on the "let's feel sorry for the kid who's about to die" bandwagon. Which made absolutely no sense because this was the *same* Cole who'd started all the bullying in the first place.

Old Cole would've made fun of me for being Bear's babysitter. He would've called me an entitled princess. He would've made my life miserable on *top* of having a sick brother. But the new Cole held doors open. Asked about my day. Asked about *Bear*.

He'd never been the "hero" type, so, what had changed?

Even though I kept waiting for it, he hadn't slipped up with his little 'amnesia act' at all. And honestly, I was starting to wonder if *I* was the crazy one for doubting him—because there was no universe that *I* lived in where Cole would have been the "good guy" under normal circumstances.

But if he *did* have amnesia, that meant that he didn't care about my pathetic life because he *wanted* to; he cared because he thought he *had* to.

Be nice to the girl with the sick brother and divorced parents... that's the right thing to do.

Well, maybe I was sick of people doing the "right" thing because they had to. Maybe I just wanted someone who actually wanted to be my friend.

Suddenly, something slammed into me.

My bag slipped off my shoulder, sending my books scattering across the floor, and my glasses flying off to who-knows-where.

I stumbled backward and hit the ground with a less-than-dignified "oof."

Today just keeps getting better, huh?

"Whoa, sorry about that!"

I blinked, squinting at the blur of shapes and colors around me, fumbling along the floor for my glasses.

I'd barely brushed my fingers over the frame when another hand beat me to it.

"Here. Sorry about that, again."

I slipped the glasses back on my face, glancing up at the asshole who barreled into me, and there he was.

Cole. Freaking. Brown.

Holding out a hand to help me up like some kind of knight in shining armor.

I stared at it, pursing my lips in frustration. "What, no white horse?"

He smirked. "Left it in the shop. Budget cuts."

I sighed, mostly because refusing his help would inevitably mean spending even *more* time on the disgusting tile floor, and reluctantly took his hand.

He pulled me to my feet with zero effort, like I weighed nothing at all, which was just *insulting* to my Italian foodie ancestors. *Damn him.*

"You okay?"

And that's when I was slapped across the face with reality.

We're really close right now.

His chest was flush against mine as he searched my face for an answer I was suddenly blanking. But for some reason, not knowing what to say in that moment wasn't the most *terrible* thing in the world.

I kind of liked it...

I needed to move. I *should* move.

Somehow, my brain finally kicked in, and I quickly shoved him back. "I'm *peachy*. I love it when my stuff ends up on the floor." I gestured to the mess of books and papers scattered around us.

Cole chuckled softly, crouching down to grab my books before I could stop him.

"*I've got it*," I said sharply, already scooping up some papers, but he ignored me. Because of course he did.

"You know, we really need to start working on your *thank you's*," he grinned, holding out the notebook for me to take.

I snatched it out of his hand. "I'm not *thanking* you for running into me."

He picked up another paper, standing and holding it just out of my reach, inspecting it like it was the most fascinating thing he'd ever seen. "What's this? A list of the people you hate? Poetry? A secret love letter?"

"It's calculus homework," I snapped, shooting up from the ground to swipe it from him. "But I wouldn't expect you to understand basic derivatives even if they hit you in the face."

"Relax, Einstein," he sighed, handing me back the paper. "I'm just asking for a simple *thank you*. An actual one, please?"

I put on my sweetest, most sarcastic smile. "Okay... *thank you* for being a douche. Happy?"

I brushed past him, my bag now welded to my shoulder. I was going to be really late to class, *thanks* to him.

"Delighted," he called after me, his voice dripping with amusement.

I rolled my eyes without looking back. "You should stop talking."

Unfortunately for me, that only baited him even more.

His footsteps sounded behind me as he caught up to me with ease. "But then how would I get to know you?"

I shot him a frustrated glare. "You wouldn't," I said flatly, before quickening my pace again.

"Come on, Gracie, don't be like that," he said, his voice still annoyingly light. "You haven't even told me your favorite color yet."

"Black. The color of my soul. Now you know everything there is to know about me. *Congratulations.*"

"What is it really?" he pressed, letting out a low chuckle.

I stopped abruptly, spinning on my heel to face him. "If I tell you, will you leave me alone?"

"You have my word," he said, grinning as he held his hands up in mock surrender.

I sighed, crossing my arms over my chest. "*Fine.* I usually tell people it's blue because that's easier for them to remember. But it's not just *one* color. It's... it's the sunset. My favorite color is the sunset."

He tilted his head slightly as his grin softened into something more curious. "Go on."

"*Y'know*," I said, avoiding his eyes, "that perfect moment when the sun dips down and the whole world is on fire? I like how the sky blends together to create something really beautiful."

I shrugged, keeping my tone as indifferent as I could possibly manage. "I could never decide on just *one* color as a kid, so I picked something with all of them. It felt... alive. Like it had so much potential. Like it could burn the bad to start fresh the next day."

When I met his eyes again, his expression had softened in a thoughtful kind of way I wasn't prepared for, which quickly made me regret saying anything at all.

"That's..." He paused, searching for the right words to say. "That's not what I expected you to say."

"Well, sorry to disappoint then," I mumbled, suddenly hyper-aware of my honesty. My cheeks burned, and I took a step back, uncomfortably adjusting my bag on my shoulder again. "I have to get to class."

Cole stepped in front of me, his grin returning, though it was mellower now. "What's another couple of minutes? You're already late."

I scoffed. "Late-er isn't exactly the goal here."

"Come on," he said, sidestepping when I tried to walk around him. "You can't just drop something like that and run off."

"Watch me," I shot back, making another move to pass him, but he blocked me again, his hands raised like I was some kind of wild animal he didn't want to spook.

"Gracie, please," he said, his tone dipping just enough to make me pause.

When's the last time I had a conversation with Cole freaking Brown where I didn't want to gouge both his eyes out with a rusty spoon afterwards?

Never. The answer was never.

Even still, I pulled my arms tight across my chest to make up for the fact that I was still there, giving him any time of day at all. "I think you're reading too much into my answer. I'm still the girl with the 'black soul'. That didn't change just because I have a favorite color."

"I don't think anyone whose favorite color is the sunset could have a black soul."

I groaned. "You seriously can't just take things at face value? Why do you have to overanalyze everything I say?"

"Why do *you* have to be so closed off all the time?"

"Why do *you* have to be so damn annoying?"

"Ouch." He pressed a hand to his chest like I'd physically wounded him. "You really know how to flatter a guy."

"I try," I said dryly, stepping to the side again.

This time, he let me pass, but only because he followed. "You know, pushing me away only makes me want to get to know you more."

I ignored him, my heart beating faster for entirely too many reasons. We were walking side by side now, and I could feel his eyes on me, studying me.

Then, he reached out, gently catching my arm.

I froze.

Not because I was scared—because, surprisingly, that was the first time a guy had touched me in a while and I *hadn't* been scared—but because his touch felt entirely too... nice. It threw me off-kilter.

"Gracie," he said softly, "What is this really? Why are you so against having a conversation with me?"

"Because talking leads to a friendship, and we can't be friends," I said simply as if I were a trained parrot.

"And why not?"

"You'll understand when you get your memories back," I mumbled, pushing past him again.

"What?"

I spun around, my chest tightening as I repeated myself, louder this time. "I said, you'll understand when you get your memories back!"

He blinked, stunned. "What's *that* supposed to mean?"

"It means," I snapped, "just because *you* forgot everything doesn't mean *I* did. You and me? We weren't friends before your accident, and we aren't friends now. I'm not going to play along with this... this whim-of-the-day thing you've got going on, and you can't just expect me to be all buddy-buddy with you after doing something nice for my brother *one time*."

Cole's jaw clenched, and he raked his hand through his hair.

"Just so you know," he said tightly, his voice rising with frustration. "I risked a lot standing up for your brother to those guys. They were my friends before. At least, I think they were... *Look*, it doesn't even matter because now they won't even *talk* at me. But I did it because it was the right thing to do."

I gave a dry laugh. "*Oh*! I didn't realize that doing the right thing was *such* a hard decision for you. That must've been tough hurting your precious man-ego over trying to right a wrong that was *your fault in the first place*!"

"Gracie, no. Come on, I didn't mean it like—"

I cut him off. "No! Let's be real for a second since you're so into honesty right now. I didn't ask you to do that. I didn't *need* you to. Because again, I don't need or want your help. Not now, not ever."

"So, what was I supposed to do? Just let them pick on him?"

"I was *handling* it!" I exclaimed, throwing my hands into the air.

"Oh, along with the five-thousand other things that you're doing for your brother? *I bet*. Sounds like you've got it covered."

My eyes narrowed. "You have no idea what it's like to be me, so don't you dare act like you do."

Cole's mouth twisted into a humorless smirk. "Yeah? Well, you don't exactly make it easy to figure you out, do you? Heaven forbid anyone tries to get close. Or worse, *know your real favorite color*?"

He let out a mocking gasp, hand to his chest like he'd just uncovered the world's biggest scandal. "Will the townsfolk riot if they figure out your favorite color isn't actually blue?"

I glared at him. "Ever think I just don't like people? Maybe I don't want a bunch of them up in my business."

"And *yet*," he paused for a second, giving me a once-over as a sly grin slowly grew on his face, "you argue with me every chance you get. You enjoy this as much as I do."

"Oh, I'm sorry. I should just roll over and agree with everything you say, shouldn't I? That *is* what you're used to, isn't it? *Oh, Cole! I'm so helpless! Oh, Cole! You're my hero!*" I said with sarcastic reverence, batting my eyelids. "Everyone at this damn school eats out of the palm of your stupid hand!"

Cole raised a brow, a slow smirk tugging at the corner of his lips. "Oh, forgive me, Your Highness. Didn't realize I was making everything so much harder for you by simply existing."

My breath hitched at that. *Your Highness.*

It wasn't exactly *Princess*, but it was close enough.

Did he even know what he was saying? The tone was the same, the context was the same, *he* was the same... It was like pre-accident and post-accident Cole were *this* close to their paths crossing, blurring into something eerily familiar.

But was that just an accident? His stupid personality bleeding through? *Wouldn't he have called me 'princess' if he still had his memories, though?*

153

I huffed, trying to take things for face value for once in my life, rather than worrying about him lying to me or something. *I had enough to deal with already*. "What's your problem, anyways? Why can't you just leave me alone?"

"Maybe because I'm trying to figure out why the hell you hate me so much. Ever thought of that?"

I stepped past him. "Because you're an asshole."

"And you're a runner," he called after me. "You don't like me? Fine. You want me to leave you alone? Great. But at least admit it to my face instead of walking away every chance you can."

I spun back around. "You want me to say that? You want me to tell you to leave me alone?"

"Go ahead!" he snapped, his voice rising. "We both know you're going to say it anyway!"

"*Fine*! I—"

The words lodged in my throat as something in his expression shifted. His face paled, the color draining so fast it was almost unnatural. That's when something pulled at my memory: *this isn't the first time he's been like that*.

It was in class. His first day back after the accident... he'd frozen just like that before running out on me.

"Cole...?"

"I'm fine," he muttered, though his voice was strained, and he refused to meet my eyes.

"No, you're not," I said, taking a step closer even though I shouldn't have. "You look like you're about to pass out. What's wrong? *Not* that I care, by the way. I just..."

154

The thought trailed off as his shoulder continued to slump. He bent forward, his hands braced on his knees as his breathing shallowed. His head hung low for a second before he slowly craned his neck up to look at me, his face damp with sweat.

He let out a bitter, strained laugh. "What? You gonna play nurse now? Fix me up like you do your brother? I said I'm—"

His knees buckled, cutting him off as he crumpled to the floor before he could finish.

Chapter Thirteen:

C ole

A blinding white light hit my eyes as tiny steel drums pounded in my ears, each beat syncing up with the throb in my skull. I grimaced, pressing a hand to my forehead.

Calling it a headache would've been a gross understatement—it was like my brain was waging war against itself.

I forced my eyes open completely, squinting against the fluorescent lights overhead. I blinked once, twice... just before panic shot through me.

The hospital.

Before I could think it all the way through, I sat up. *Too* quickly. My head immediately protested, dizziness crashing over me like a wave.

I gripped the edge of... something, trying to steady myself. *I can't go back. I can't lose everything... again.*

My name is Cole Brown.

I am (or was) the quarterback for Hillview High.

People don't really like me here.

But as the room came into focus—faded blue walls instead of the artificial white I remembered from the hospital, not to mention the couch I was lying on was covered in that cheap crinkly paper, I realized that I was still at school.

In the nurse's office, to be exact.

And I still remembered everything.

Well, at least everything I did when I woke up this morning.

I rubbed my temples, trying to piece everything together, as bits and pieces of the last hour or so slowly came back to me.

Gracie. I'd run into her, and we'd argued... again. *About what?* The details were fuzzy, but I remembered her eyes—full of anger, maybe even a little hurt. And then... *nothing*.

The pounding in my head exploded like it was punishing me for trying to remember too much at once. But there was something else, buried in the fog—an image that had been burned into my mind so clearly I could almost feel it.

A memory.

My family didn't know that I was remembering things off and on yet. I mean, what was I supposed to say? *Hey, I'm starting to realize why everyone hates me now...?*

No, I couldn't do that to them.

I had amnesia, not stupidity. I *saw* the fear in people's eyes when they looked at me. I *knew* how much people resented me for whatever I had done.

Not remembering made it easier to avoid the guilt, sure, but it also left me terrified of my past.

I was more scared of myself than a whole *room* of people could ever be.

Knowing I couldn't stay in this room forever, even if I wanted to, I slowly peeled myself off the couch and glanced around.

How did I even get here anyways?

That's when I saw Gracie to my left. She was sitting on a chair in the corner of the room reading a book... *The 48 Laws of Power*. I almost snorted.

I'd heard a rumor from one of the cheerleaders that Gracie was trying to master the "dark, psychology arts." I guess reading that book was the perfect, natural descent.

She hadn't noticed me yet, and there was something different about her in her element—no yelling or anything. Just Gracie, completely lost in her own little world.

Her glasses slipped down her nose, and she absentmindedly pushed them back up with her finger, scrunching her nose almost like it annoyed her.

She then tucked a strand of hair behind her ear, her eyes narrowing as she leaned closer to the book. Her lips moved a little, mothing the words without realizing it.

It was... weirdly cute seeing her like that. She looked... softer somehow, *content*.

Without thinking, I shifted, knocking a tray off the couch with a loud *bang*.

Her head jerked up, and I braced myself for her signature glare whenever I bothered her (which apparently, was all the time). But instead, for a split second, I saw something else in her expression—*concern*.

Or, I must've imagined it because the next second, it was gone and replaced with annoyance, like she'd remembered *I* was the one she was getting worried about. *And Heaven forbid.*

I pretended it hurt a lot less than it did and cleared my throat. "Hey," I murmured.

"Hey, yourself," Gracie replied dryly, eyes shooting back down to her book. "You're in the nurse's office, BTW."

The abbreviation rolled off her tongue like she couldn't be bothered to say the full word. Not that she had to. Although, it would have been nice if she threw me a fucking bone every once in a while.

I glanced around again, trying to get my bearings. The pounding in my head was making it hard to think straight, but one thing was clear: I hadn't dragged myself here.

That left only one option.

"Did you—"

"Nope." She cut me off before I could even finish the question.

I raised an eyebrow. "So, I just magically teleported here, then?"

Her lips twitched, almost like she was fighting a smile. *Almost.* "You're heavier than you look, just so you know," she muttered, flipping a page in her book with exaggerated force.

That settled it.

She'd hauled me here herself, no matter how much she wanted to pretend otherwise. She acted like she didn't care, but the proof was right there in front of me: the way her fingers tapped impatiently against the book's spine, the way she kept stealing quick glances at me like she was making sure I hadn't keeled over and died.

Gracie Lewis *cared* about me. Wow.

"Do you need some aspirin?" Gracie asked after a beat, flipping another page of her book. "The nurse is outside right now, but I'm sure I could find it if I tried hard enough."

I breathed a sigh of relief, thankful that I didn't have to ask. She just understood. "Sure, thanks."

Gracie let out a loud groan and threw her book down as she got up from her seat, as if she wasn't the one who had just offered to help in the first place.

She headed over to the cabinets, muttering something under her breath that I didn't quite catch but was sure wasn't very ladylike.

Bottles clinked as she rummaged through the drawers, and I closed my eyes again, grateful for the second of quiet(ish).

After a while, she returned, holding out a tiny pill and a paper cup of water. "Don't choke," she deadpanned as she handed them over.

I rolled my eyes but couldn't stop a smirk from growing on my face as I swallowed the pill and downed the water in one gulp. "I'll try not to just for you."

She didn't answer, just moved to a fan in the corner of the room, plugging it in and angling it toward me.

Then, she walked to the sink, wet a washcloth, and placed it gently on my forehead.

I blinked up at her, stunned. "Gracie—"

"Don't." She cut me off, flopping back into her chair and picking up her book again. "I was hot, and I wanted to cover up your stupid face. That's all."

And just like that, we were back to square one.

But I couldn't help it—I let out as much of a laugh as my headache would allow before grimacing.

Despite me legit passing out in front of her less than an hour ago, she couldn't stop herself from giving me hell.

And for some reason, that was reassuring to me. Unlike the rest of this school, she didn't act like she was scared of me. I could actually have a conversation with someone without them shitting themself.

Yeah, because I'm the one doing it instead.

Like I said before, Gracie was not for the weak.

"What's so funny?" she snapped, glaring at me over the top of her book.

"Nothing, nothing," I said, grinning. "You just make a surprisingly good nurse, that's all."

Her eyes narrowed as she sputtered. "You take that back right now."

"Never."

She huffed. "Fine. Whatever. I've reached my quota for arguing with the iron-deficient amnesiac for today anyway."

"Oh! I didn't know there was a limit. You should have said that sooner. Maybe we could've actually, I don't know... *gotten along* for more than five minutes or something?" I mumbled.

I heard her snort faintly but she didn't say another word.

The fan's hum filled the silence between us, and for a minute, I let myself relax, the cool air and the wet cloth doing wonders for my headache. But Gracie, apparently, couldn't handle quiet for too long.

"So," she said finally, setting her book down on her lap, "do you have some weird underlying health condition that I should know about? Or did you just feel like collapsing dramatically in the hallway?"

I hesitated, sitting up slowly as I rubbed the back of my neck.

Her question deserved an answer—or at least something close to one. After all, she'd brought me in here when she didn't have to.

"Sometimes it just happens," I admitted, avoiding her gaze. "Headaches, blackouts... stuff like that."

Memories... I wanted to add. But I didn't want her to give me a hard time for it, and there was a good chance that she would: her being Gracie and given our history—whatever *that* was.

Her dark eyes studied me. "That's vague."

"Yeah, well, it's all I've got right now."

Gracie leaned back in her chair, crossing her arms. "You should see a doctor."

"I've seen plenty."

Her eyes narrowed like she was about to argue, but she didn't push it.

For a second, I thought that might be the end of the conversation, but then I found *myself* speaking again.

"I had a memory." I blurted out.

Gracie raised an eyebrow.

"It wasn't anything good," I continued. "Just... me being a jerk. Freshman year. There was this kid, Garrett. He was quiet, always reading sci-fi books. I made fun of him in front of everyone, gave him some dumb nickname, and it stuck."

"Okay. And?"

"And... I don't know. I'm seeing pieces of who I was before the accident, and they kind of suck. I feel bad."

She shrugged. "So, go apologize to him."

I blinked, caught off guard. "What?"

"You heard me. Go apologize to him," she said again. "Own it."

"That's—"

She cut me off. "What? Hard? Awkward? Yeah, it is. But you don't get to sit here and feel sorry for yourself because you finally figured out you're an ass. You want to change? Do better. Fix what you did."

Her words were brutal, blunt, but honestly, exactly what I needed to hear, even if I hated it.

I swallowed hard. "Yeah... maybe I should."

"*Maybe*?" she scoffed, picking her book back up. "You're unbelievable."

The room went quiet again, except for the sound of the fan humming in the background and the occasional flip of her pages.

I glanced at her again out of the corner of my eye.

She'd probably... no, *definitely* dragged me all the way to the nurse's office, sat here even though she didn't have to, and then insulted me.

She was a walking contradiction, and I couldn't decide if I liked or hated that about her.

But before I could say anything else, the door swung open, and the nurse walked in, clipboard in hand. "Feeling any better, Cole?"

I quickly cleared my throat. "Yeah, a little."

"Good. Principal Hawkins wants to see both of you in his office."

Gracie's head snapped up, her eyes wide. "Wait—what? Why me?"

The nurse didn't answer, already halfway out the door.

Gracie shot me a look that was equal parts confusion and irritation. "What did you do now?"

I smiled weakly. "Guess we'll find out."

She groaned, grabbed her stuff, and muttered under her breath. "I swear, if you got me in trouble for dragging your unconscious body to the nurse's office, I'm leaving you in the hallway when you pass out next time."

I chuckled softly, wincing as I stood. "Noted."

"Come in," a voice called from behind the door.

Gracie and I filed into Principal Hawkins' small, square office.

Two leather armchairs sat across from his desk, which was neatly positioned in front of a nearly panoramic view of the courtyard outside.

I glanced around the room, feeling a strange sense of familiarity—though not in a comforting way. It reminded me of a fever dream: hazy, warped, and a little twilight zone-y.

"How many times have I even been in here?" I muttered under my breath, half-joking as I fought the urge to check for the impression of my ass in the chair across from him.

Gracie didn't respond, but I caught the sharp, nervous exhale she let out beside me as her eyes darted around the room.

"Cole, it's nice to see you again," Principal Hawkins greeted, standing as we entered.

"You, too, sir," I replied, shaking his outstretched hand.

His grip was firm but not overbearing—the kind of handshake people train for. I wondered for a second, as I let go, if someone had ever taught me how to do this.

Maybe my dad—or stepdad? Or some grandfather I couldn't remember had drilled it into me that a good handshake was important.

It would probably be one of the endless little mysteries about my past that I'd never solve.

Principal Hawkins turned to Gracie next, sticking out his hand.

She froze instantly—like she physically stopped breathing for a second. Her eyes flicked to his hand, then to me, and then back again.

She squeezed her eyes shut and sucked in a breath before extending her hand out to meet his, but at that point, her hand was shaking so badly that it was impossible to miss.

Her hand dropped just before making contact, wiping it on her jeans as she let out an awkward little laugh. "Uh, hang on," she muttered.

The principal waited, smiling as if he didn't notice anything, but *I* did. How the hell could you not?

She tried again, but her hand was trembling even worse now. And before she could go through with it, she panicked and pulled back again, giving him a small wave instead.

"Hi," she mumbled, her face bright red. "Good to see you."

Principal Hawkins didn't even blink as he dropped his hand. "Good to see you too, Gracie."

We sat down, and I shot her one hard look.

She looked like she was about ready to cry, her shoulders stiff as a board in her seat.

I could tell she was trying to act like nothing was bothering her, but something *was*. And weirdly enough, I wanted to fix it for her. Even if I didn't know *what* was wrong or *how* to even make it better.

"So," Principal Hawkins started, snapping me back to the present, "I wanted to talk to you both about something important."

Gracie stayed silent, and for some reason, an even bigger weight landed on my chest. *Please don't cry.*

Without thinking, I jumped in. "If this is about me skipping lunch detention last week, I swear it was because—"

"It's not about that," he interrupted, smiling like he was ignoring the fact that I'd just thrown myself under the bus.

Gracie broke out of her own thoughts just enough to shoot me a *what are you doing?* look. But I just shrugged.

If anyone was going to take the fall for anything, it was going to be me, not her. She didn't need to get upset over something I (probably) did. I didn't like the idea of that at all.

Principal Hawkins cleared his throat. "Cole, as I'm sure you are aware by now, you aren't medically cleared to play football until further notice. However, you need an extracurricular to graduate." He paused, looking at Gracie. "And as it happens, I've heard your FFA Vet Science team is in need of an extra member to compete at State this year."

Gracie's head snapped up. "Wait. Where is this going?"

"I'd like for Cole to join your team," Principal Hawkins answered, as if it were the most reasonable suggestion in the world.

Gracie blinked, then turned to me with wide eyes. "Cole? On the Vet Science team? *No.* Absolutely not."

"Wow," I said, leaning back in my chair and crossing my arms. *At least she's talking again.* "Thanks for the support, *captain.*"

"*President,*" she corrected, her face already flushing. She whipped her head back toward Principal Hawkins. "You're joking, right? He's not actually joining the team?"

"I'm serious, Gracie," he said patiently. "Your team needs another member, and Cole needs an activity. It's a win-win."

She turned back to me, narrowing her eyes. "Do you even *know* how to suture an animal?"

"Sure." I paused, then added, "And just to make sure, why don't *you* describe it for me...?"

She groaned, throwing her hands in the air. "This is already hopeless."

I raised an eyebrow. "Well, maybe you could tutor me, then. I promise not to bite."

"*Actually*, it'd be more realistic if you did."

Principal Hawkins cleared his throat between us. "Gracie, I understand your concern, but I think this could be a good opportunity for both of you. And if the team brings home a win, it could even attract new members."

She opened her mouth, as if she wanted to argue, but slowly, her shoulders sagged as she realized there was no way out of this.

She let out a long, dramatic sigh before finally mumbling, "Fine. I'll give it a shot."

Chapter Fourteen:

OCTOBER 2ND

The bell rang.

English was over. *Finally.*

I'd just survived an hour and a half of Mr. Hayworth droning on about *The Great Gatsby* while I sat there, staring at the back of Gandork's... I mean, *Garrett's* head, trying to figure out how the hell I was supposed to apologize to him.

I mean, it should've been easy, right? The guy sat directly in front of me. We'd been breathing the same air for nearly two hours. But there was a big difference between *wanting* to apologize and actually doing it.

I'd spent the weekend wallowing in self-pity, replaying every awful thing I'd ever said or done to him on a constant loop in my head—and those were just the things that I could *remember.*

But Gracie was right. I had no right to sit around and feel sorry for myself. I'd messed up, and it was time to own it. Time to fix it.

I slung my bag over my shoulder, watching Garrett shuffle out of the row with his head down as if he were trying to escape the classroom before anyone noticed him.

Unfortunately, he wasn't quick enough.

"Hey, Gandork!" Josh shouted, followed by a burst of laughter from Dylan and Aiden. "How goes it?"

I grimaced. That nickname should've died in middle school. Guess that meant it had stuck—thanks to me.

Thankfully, though, Garrett kept his head down and somehow managed to slip past them without further damage.

I didn't get off so easy.

"Yo, Brown!" Dylan called. "Me and the guys are heading to the gas station. You in?"

I hesitated for just a second longer than I should've.

Honestly, there was a part of me that wanted to go—wanted to pretend like I was a normal guy for once, a guy that didn't have to go on an apology tour just to be able to live with himself.

But then my eyes flicked back down the hallway, where Garrett had disappeared into the crowd, and the memory I'd had of him a couple days ago slapped me across the face all over again.

I need to do this.

"I'm not in the mood," I said finally, stepping around Dylan.

He shifted in front of me, blocking my path with an obnoxious grin. "You're getting slow, Brown," he said, tossing a football from one hand to the other. "Careful, or I might just steal your QB spot next season."

"You wouldn't be quarterback even if the position came with someone to throw for you," I shot back without thinking.

Whoa. Calm down, Cole.

But Dylan being Dylan, just laughed. "Relax, man. I'm just saying, you could lighten up. You've been acting, I dunno... weird lately."

"I'm fine," I muttered, brushing past him and scanning the hallway.

Where'd he go?

"C'mon, Brown! It'll be fun," Dylan said, falling into step beside me. "We're just gonna mess around for a bit. Convince the old lady working there to give us beer or something. Nothing crazy."

It would've been easy... *too* easy to shrug this whole apology off and follow them. And I might've. Until I heard Max's voice in my ear: *"Fear might get people to follow you, but it'll never make them trust you."*

I wanted to be trusted. I wanted to be known as a better person.

I had to be.

"I said no, Dylan," I doubled-down firmly.

"Lame," Dylan muttered, finally backing off. "Catch you later, loser."

I didn't even look at him as I pushed further into the hallway, zigzagging between people as lockers slammed left. But as time went on, I starting feeling more and more frustrated.

Where in the world is he?

Maybe this was the universe's way of telling me to bail on the whole thing. Apologizing was gonna be awkward as hell anyway. Would he even care? Or would he just tell me to screw off and keep walking?

No. Find him. Apologize. Be a man about it.

And as it turned out, after really committing to it, finding him wasn't as hard as I thought it'd be.

He was by a row of lockers, fumbling with the straps on his giant backpack as he pulled out *The Lord of the Rings* trilogy before stuffing it back in like he couldn't decide if he needed it or not.

Maybe the name *Gandork* wasn't entirely off...

Okay, what the hell? Shut up, Cole.

He must have noticed that someone was watching him because he looked up, his eyes darting around the hallway before landing on me.

And then he froze.

Not exactly a confidence booster.

I cleared my throat, stepping closer but keeping enough distance to not freak him out any more than he already was. "Hey, uh... Garrett."

He flinched, (like, *actually* flinched), his whole body stiffening like I'd just walked up to him with the intention of punching him.

Then, his eyes dropped to the ground and he started fiddling with his backpack as if he was prepared to chuck it at me if this whole thing went south.

This is already going great.

"I, uh... I wanted to talk to you," I said, shoving my hands into my pockets to keep *myself* from being nervous.

Still no eye contact. He just kept fumbling with the zipper on his bag.

The tension in the air was so thick I could cut it with a knife—a metaphor I *probably* shouldn't use around Garrett, who looked like he half-expected me to be packing one.

I felt like I was towering over him, even though I was still standing a few feet away. The dude was small, like *really* small, and it was painfully obvious that this was the last place he wanted to be right now.

Honestly, same, man.

My palms were sweating in my pockets, and I was starting to feel like an even bigger jerk.

I'd come over to apologize to him, but all I was doing was freaking him out.

171

I could almost hear Gracie's voice in my head telling me to spit it out before he went into cardiac arrest in front of me.

"I just wanted to say I'm sorry," I blurted out suddenly. "For, you know... being a jerk to you and giving you that nickname. It was wrong, and I—"

"I—It's fine," he stammered, cutting me off. He glanced up for a split second before his eyes darted away again. "No big deal."

But he was lying. I could tell. Anyone with *half a brain* could tell. And knowing that I could make someone feel like they couldn't tell me the truth—messed me up more than I wanted to admit.

This was my fault. I'd done this to him.

If Gracie were here, she would've told me off by now. Chewed me out for being this much of an asshole long before it ever came to this.

I almost smiled at the thought of five-foot-something her going toe-to-toe with me—someone almost twice her size. And that's when the thought hit me out of nowhere.

What if she's scared of you, just like everyone else?

"You touched me..."

Gracie's voice. Clear as day.

And the crazy thing? Deep down, I *knew* she'd said it before. Or at least, I thought she had.

But that couldn't be right. Gracie wasn't like that. She wasn't afraid of me.

Was she?

"You touched me..."

What had I *done* to her?

"Cole?"

172

Garett. *Right.* I had forgotten all about him, which, considering everything going on in my head, seemed pretty fucking ironic.

I blinked, forcing myself to refocus on him. He was still standing there, waiting for me to say something else instead of just staring off into space like an idiot.

"You touched me..."

"It *was* a big deal, though," I said, my mouth dry, fighting to keep it together as Gracie's voice continued to echo in my skull like a damn siren.

"You touched me..."

The apology caught on the lump lodged in my throat, but somehow, I managed to force them out. "To *you*. It was a big deal. I get that now."

He still wouldn't look at me, but his shoulders eased a little, like maybe he wasn't bracing for me to lose it with him anymore. Then, he swallowed hard. "Yeah... yeah, I guess it was."

"You touched me..."

"I'm really sorry, man," I said, still trying to block out Gracie's voice. "For everything. For how I treated you back then. It wasn't cool. I'm not expecting you to just... forgive me, but I wanted to tell you I've been thinking about it. A lot."

"You touched me..."

Her voice came back even stronger that time, more insistent. And that's when her face flashed in my mind.

She was wide-eyed and pale. She looked *scared*.

I felt sick to my stomach.

Garett hesitated, glancing around the hallway like he was still hoping for a way out.

The hall was starting to clear out now, but he didn't move.

"I can... learn to forgive you," he said slowly, like he was picking his words carefully. "Not because I have to. But because I *want* to. Freshman year sucked for everyone. Even you... probably. I just know I wouldn't want to be defined by every mistake I made back then, so I'm not gonna do that to you. That's only fair."

"You touched me..."

The floor tilted underneath me.

I need to get out of here...

"Thank you, Garett. I appreciate it," I muttered, forcing the words out as I fought to stay tethered to reality. "I, uh, gotta go. But we'll talk later?"

"Sure," he replied, his voice distant now, like he knew something wasn't right with me but didn't want to ask.

Or maybe... he didn't feel like he could.

Because you're a fucking monster.

I turned and bolted down the hallway, the walls closing in around me as her voice slammed into my brain over and over again.

"You touched me. You touched me. You touched me."

I stumbled past classroom doors, my feet barely aware of where they were taking me.

Suddenly, I was in front of a janitor's closet. The door was cracked open, and without thinking, I slipped inside, throwing the door shut behind me.

Darkness.

Silence.

Only my ragged breathing filled the space.

But her voice wouldn't stop.

"You touched me..."

My fists clenched at my sides, the memory of *her*... in pain, tearing me apart from the inside.

Then I punched the wall. Hard. Once. Twice.

The pain shot through my knuckles, but it was better than hearing Gracie's voice like that.

I hit it again. And again. And again.

Anything to make it stop.

But it wouldn't. It just wouldn't stop.

Gracie

"First rule of Vet Science," I called out as soon as I spotted Cole jogging toward me in the school parking lot. "Don't be a dick and make your saint of a teacher wait outside the school for you for an hour. FFA is *all* about punctuality, Brown."

I kicked my car in a half-hearted attempt to silence the radiator, and my engine ticked in protest like it might explode if I even *thought* about starting it back up again.

I prayed Cole wouldn't notice—or worse, *say* something about it.

The last thing I needed was him thinking we were even in anything.

Bear's infusion had run long again, and I'd barely managed to get back here in time for practice. If Cole hadn't been late, I probably wouldn't have made it back before he noticed at all.

Not that I was about to tell *him* that.

He slowed to a stop in front of me, looking annoyingly composed for someone who had just full-on sprinted across the parking lot. His gray eyes locked on me, and something about the way he looked at me made my stomach dip.

It was different somehow… *softer*.

Nobody had ever looked at me like that before. Ever.

"Hey," he said quietly.

I blinked at him. *Why the hell is he acting so weird?*

But instead of asking that, I cleared my throat, pushing off my car as I shoved the thought down as quickly as I could. "Don't 'hey' me. You're late."

"I know," he said, voice still low, *apologetic* even. He glanced at the ground for a second, then back at me. "I'm sorry."

I stared at him like he'd grown a second head. "For being late?"

"For that…" He shifted on his feet, scratching the back of his neck. "And for other stuff too."

"*Other stuff?*"

He gave me a small shrug, looking at me like I might shatter into a million pieces if he said the wrong thing. "You know. For being a jerk to you. For spilling chocolate milk on your pants and saying you wet yourself… or locking you in that janitor closet… or—"

"Wait, hold up." I held up a hand, trying to wrap my head around what he was saying. "You *remember* doing that?"

"I—" He hesitated, his gaze flicking to the side. "I remember you telling me about that, but—"

"*Oh.*"

The apology hung in the air between us.

He shifted again, stuffing his hands into his pockets and staring at the ground like it might somehow save him from this conversation.

"What else do you remember?" I asked carefully. His jaw tightened.

"I remember enough, okay?" he said sharply. But then, he took a deep breath as he glanced back at me, his tone soft again. "Look, I was an ass to you, and I'm sorry, Gracie. For everything."

For a second, I didn't know what to say.

It wasn't his apology—because Lord knows, it could've used some work. He at least could have springboarded it off someone before trying it out in real life... But it was the way he'd said it. How he looked.

Vulnerable.

Cole Brown was many things in my life (mostly a pain), but I'd never planned on *that* version of him existing. And I definitely hadn't planned on him apologizing to me.

For *anything*.

It didn't make any sense.

But if I was being honest with myself, nothing about him had made sense since his accident.

The apology wasn't perfect. It wasn't an end-all-be-all fix for the years of history between us, but it was something. Something I'd never thought I'd get from him in a million years.

And, for reasons I didn't fully understand, that *something* hit harder than I wanted to admit.

"*Damn*," I said, clicking my tongue, brushing past the uncomfortable knot in my chest. "You really suck at apologies, y'know that?"

His lips twitched like he might smile, but it didn't stick. "Sorry," he mumbled again.

We started up the hill past the school, but Cole walked just a step behind me, hands shoved into his pockets, like he was trying to disappear.

It wasn't like I wanted him right beside me or something, but the space he kept between us felt... weird. Not *weird* weird—just off, like he was physically trying to keep his distance from me, and I didn't know why.

This whole thing already felt like a waste of time anyway.

I knew how this was going to go: we'd sit down, crack open my vet science binder, and within twenty minutes (maybe less if I was *really* trying) he'd throw in the towel.

Cole didn't exactly have a reputation for sticking things out (memory loss or not), and if I'd dragged him straight to a group meeting with Emma and Bear, I'd have to explain why he wasn't coming back for a second one.

This was better. He'd be sick of me (and FFA) before we even made it to his house. Which, by the way, he had insisted on practicing at for some reason.

"You even know where you're going?" he asked finally after a couple minutes of dead silence.

"Of course I do," I said, waving him off like it was the dumbest question I'd ever heard. I pointed vaguely in the direction of the bowling alley. "You live over there. Everyone knows that."

Out of the corner of my eye, I saw him bite back a smirk. "Not even close. Other side of town, Gracie."

My face burned as the heat crept up my neck. "*Oh.*"

He tilted his head slightly, studying me. "Oh, what?"

I let out a sigh, realizing there was no point trying to hide it. "*Fine.* I guess I was just hoping your house was over by the bowling alley because... I might've egged a house over there once?"

"Excuse me?"

"The first night I had my license," I said quickly, the words spilling out. "I took Emma out, and we were supposed to go grab milkshakes or

178

something. But I talked her into buying eggs instead—she was *very* against it, by the way—and then we drove to what I *thought* was your house and... well..."

I trailed off, giving him a sheepish look.

For a second, Cole just stared at me, wide-eyed. Then, all at once, he threw his head back and laughed.

"*No way*," he said. "You egged some random person's house thinking it was mine?"

"Shut up, Cole," I groaned, blushing as I looked away. "You deserved it."

"I guess I did," he smirked. "Well, if you feel like giving me a second chance, my *actual* house is this way."

I snorted. "Don't worry, I think I've outgrown my egging phase."

"Shame. Sounds like you had potential."

We started walking again, but as much as I hated to admit it, I was beginning to see a different side of him—the kind that wasn't totally unbearable.

And for the first time, I wasn't dreading having this practice.

I didn't have to guess which house was his.

If it wasn't his literal truck in the driveway that gave it away, it was the fact that this was *exactly* the house I would've pictured a stuck-up, asshole jock having: a basketball hoop in the driveway, a lawn that looked like it belonged in *Better Homes and Gardens*... oh yeah, and the biggest two-story home I had ever seen?

It wasn't a mansion, but compared to my cramped, borderline-trailer of a house, it might as well have been.

Everything about it was bigger, neater, and more polished than anything I was used to.

It was the kind of place that looked like you never had to worry about leaky faucets or overdue bills. Or better yet, sick brothers or your parents randomly divorcing and leaving you.

Cole must've caught me staring because he glanced at the ground, shoving his hands back into his pockets. "It's just a house," he muttered.

"Yeah, *right*..."

He cleared his throat uncomfortably as he guided me the rest of the way to the front door, fumbling with his keys as he went.

As he reached the porch, he paused to glance back at me with a crooked smile. "You ready?"

Apparently, not at all.

The inside was even more impressive than the outside, if that were possible.

To my right was a sunken living room, plush with cream-colored carpets and furniture that looked too expensive to touch, let alone sit on. Above it hung a chandelier so sparkly it made the whole room glow.

Straight ahead, through a wide archway, was the kitchen.

Even from the entryway, I could see stainless steel appliances glinting under pendant lights, and a huge dining table off to the side (y'know, not a foldable one shoved back in the corner next to your fridge like mine was?).

I couldn't even believe people actually got to *live* like this. No wonder he'd thought he walked on water before the accident. I would've felt that way too if this were my life.

Cole scratched the back of his neck as he stepped further inside, noticing my silence. "You okay?"

I cleared my throat, snapping back to reality as I looked at him. "Yeah, just... taking it all in, I guess."

He nodded, glancing toward the living room. "You'll have to ignore the mess," he said sheepishly.

I followed his gaze and saw... nothing.

Well, nothing except a toolbox sitting by the fireplace.

If he thought *that* was a mess, he'd go into cardiac arrest just by setting foot into *my* house.

"We're redoing the fireplace for my mom's birthday," he continued, his face turning red. "My stepdad and I started it last month, but, uh... it hasn't been going well."

I stepped around the one *singular* object on the floor: the toolbox, trying to hold back my amusement. "You guys must be terrible at surprises. Or do you blindfold her every time she walks into the living room?"

That made him laugh, and for some reason, the sound made my cheeks warm. "Yeah, she definitely knows by now."

We wandered into the kitchen, as I was still trying to process the sheer size of everything.

"Does Gordon Ramsey cook here or something?" I quipped, gesturing toward the double ovens that probably cost more than my future college tuition.

He shot me a wry look as he opened a cabinet, pulling out two fancy glass jars and filling them with water from the sink. "I'm starting to realize that my mom just... likes things a certain way," he said, sliding one of the jars over to me. "It's fine, though. Whatever makes her happy."

There was something about the way he looked at me—almost like he was testing the waters, trying to gauge my reaction.

181

"What about you?" I asked finally, leaning against the island counter. "How do you feel about it?"

He hesitated, then smiled faintly, his gray eyes flicking toward the chandelier above us. "Honestly? Sometimes it feels like I live in a museum."

Unexpectedly, a laugh escaped me. "Yeah, I can see that. No touching the exhibits, right?"

"Exactly," he said, his grin widening. "But hey, at least this museum has snacks."

He sat down next to me, close enough that our knees brushed under the counter. I couldn't help myself and stiffened instinctively, my back going ramrod straight.

The contact was light, (*definitely* unintentional) but it was like an alarm had gone off in my chest. And suddenly, every nerve in my body because hyperaware of the fact that we were *touching*.

Cole didn't seem to notice, though. I think if he did, he would've moved away like he *had* been doing all day.

Instead, he leaned forward, resting his elbows on the counter, his fingers drumming lightly against the surface.

He shifted slightly, like he was trying to give me space without calling too much attention to it, but he didn't move far enough. His knee was still brushing mine.

The longer it stayed, though, the less *I* wanted to pull away. He wasn't crowding me or crossing any lines. He was just... there. And weirdly enough, that was okay.

Maybe this is how normal people feel—that touch isn't a big deal. Maybe they can just... exist and enjoy in the moment.

"You don't agree, though," he said, misreading my silence as an answer.

I blinked, realizing I hadn't been paying attention, and that instead, my finger was nervously tracing the rim of my water glass. "It's not that I *don't* agree," I answered, slowly. "It's just... I don't know what it's like to live like this. It's different."

The words came out softer than I had intended, and I was thankful that Cole didn't push for more. He just stayed quiet, his gaze steady on mine, like he was giving me the space to say more if I wanted to.

And I *did* want to, for some reason.

"In my house," I started hesitantly, "there's not a single picture on any of the walls. Everything feels like it could be packed up and gone in a day. Like we're always one bad thing from falling apart. And when my brother got sick..."

I cleared my throat, trying to push myself to keep going. "My mom left. My dad checked out emotionally. And I had to grow up fast because... someone had to."

Son of a bitch, I actually said it.

And I hated myself for that because the biggest thing I'd learned over the years was that people didn't like being reminded of the ugly parts of life.

In friendships, relationships... it was easier to smile, to pretend everything was fine. That way, people stuck around. They didn't make excuses to leave just because you made them uncomfortable by being yourself.

And let's be real. I was a walking, talking reminder that life...

Sucked.

Cole and I had (surprisingly) been doing so well, and I had to go and do what I always did: ruin it by being too honest, too much like myself. *Way to go, Gracie.*

"Anyway, it's not a big deal. Just your classic tragic backstory. Y'know me... I'm super fun at parties."

Cole didn't laugh, didn't even crack a smile.

His eyes stayed locked on mine, like he could see straight through me, and suddenly, I felt even *more* vulnerable.

But not as embarrassed like I thought I would be by sharing...?

"You're the strongest person I know, Gracie," he said after a minute.

I wrinkled my nose instinctively, trying to deflect. "Eww, don't say that to me."

"I *mean* it," he said simply.

I quickly cleared my throat and picked up my FFA binder, using it as an excuse to give my hands something to do.

"Can we actually start studying now?" A beat between us passed without a word, "Please?" I threw in for good measure.

"Okay, Gracie... If that's what you want."

That's when his gaze flickered downward as he reached for one of his notebooks. I followed it, only to notice what he did—our knees. Still brushing under the counter.

Before I could even protest (although why *would* I? This was Cole Brown we were talking about), he shifted, scooting back just enough to break the contact.

Losing that feeling hit me harder than I expected, like something small but kind of important had been ripped away from me.

It was almost like he had stumbled across a nice little secret that I was keeping all to myself, and now it was ruined.

I forced myself to look up, unable to stop from opening my mouth. "What? Afraid you're gonna catch the plague from me or something?"

His cheeks flushed as he ran a hand through his hair, looking everywhere but at me. "No, I just... I didn't want to make you feel uncomfortable."

My face burned.

Even the kid with amnesia knows you're a freak. People can see you're different than everyone else. Did you really think this would be easy for you?

I rolled my eyes, trying to shove the thought away. "What? Was I screaming or something?"

His brow furrowed slightly at that. "You have before... haven't you?"

Great. Of all the things this guy could remember, he had to latch onto that. His first day back after the accident, when I'd lost it in class and become the "weird kid" poster child.

I broke eye contact, embarrassment hitting me like a truck (pun intended), and my eyes drifted to his hand resting on the counter.

There has to be a way out of this. Maybe I can use Bear as an excuse or something. Perks of having a sick brother, I guess.

"I, um, actually have to..."

That's when I noticed the black and purple bruises covering his knuckles.

"What happened to your hand?" I asked, reaching out without thinking. I turned his hand over, inspecting the bruises before he pulled back, tucking it into his lap.

"It's nothing," he said quickly. "Messed around with some equipment during practice. Dumb of me."

I thought he wasn't medically cleared to play yet...?

Wasn't that the whole reason he had to be on the Vet Science team in the first place?

I pursed my lips, letting skepticism color my face, but didn't push.

His business was his business, but I wasn't just going to sit around and do nothing about it. "Yeah, well, that's a great way to end up with an infection. You're supposed to clean your wounds, stupid."

With exaggerated exasperation, I stood, grabbing soap and a washcloth as I waved him over to the sink. "Come on, let me fix it."

He hesitated, his shoulders suddenly stiff, as if he were trying to maintain an invisible boundary between us. "You don't have to—"

"*Hand.* Now."

He bit back a smile, finally giving in and stepping closer. "You're bossy, you know that?" he muttered under his breath.

"Only because *you're* helpless," I shot back, a grin growing on my face too.

A comfortable silence settled over us as I worked on tending to *the* Cole Brown's wounds, and for once, I didn't feel the need to fill it in.

After a minute, though, he nudged my shoulder lightly, his voice quieter this time. "By the way... thanks, Gracie."

I glanced up and must've got caught in the moment because the words that came next tumbled out of my mouth before I could stop them. "What are friends for?"

His smile widened slightly, and honestly? Mine did too.

Cole

What are friends for?

Gracie had gone home a while ago, but I couldn't stop thinking about the afternoon I'd spent with her (that part specifically) as I flipped burger patties on the stovetop.

I hadn't expected her to say that.

In fact, up until today, I was pretty sure she hated me. But no. *What are friends for?* We were *friends*. I was actually friends with *Gracie Lewis*.

Take that, old me.

A stupid smile tugged at my lips, and I pressed down harder on the spatula to try to shake it off. The burgers sizzled louder under the pressure, and some grease even splattered on me, but I didn't care.

Because *I* had a friend.

Besides that, though, practice with Gracie had gone as I had expected it would.

She was about as encouraging as a drill sergeant.

"What's the name of the organism that causes coccidiosis in cattle?"

I'd bull shitted my way through some half-formed answer, and she'd cut me off in the middle of it, raising an eyebrow. *"Eimeria. It's literally in the study guide, Cole. Maybe try reading it?"*

She wasn't afraid to let me know she was better at this than I was—and honestly, she probably was. Gracie had this sharp, competitive streak that showed up in everything she did. She wanted to be the best, period.

I'd told myself it was annoying. That's what I was *supposed* to feel, the old me being "mortal enemies" with her, after all.

But the way her nose scrunched up when she got something right, or how she tapped her pen against her glasses when she was trying to remember a term for something... yeah, that stuck with me more than I wanted to admit.

Honestly, though, I'd thought I'd be better at the whole vet science thing.

I worked on a ranch, for crying out loud. I should've had that in the bag. But all the textbook answers felt like some kind of foreign language.

I knew how to physically do things—haul hay around, treat wounds, mend fences (thanks to the ranch owner's son... or nephew or something, Steve). But regurgitating textbook definitions?

You might as well have been asking me to remember my entire life before the accident: blurry, frustrating, and basically impossible.

The burgers hissed again as I flipped them one last time.

And then there was that other thing...

"You touched me..."

The memory (or what I *thought* was a memory) had clawed its way back into my mind more than once today.

I was *sure* she'd said it to me at some point. And even though I didn't know what it meant or why she'd said it, the idea that I could've done something to scare her like that made me want to vomit.

It didn't matter that I didn't remember. The possibility of what I could've done was enough.

Which was why I was keeping my distance.

It wasn't about what I wanted—because yeah, I *wanted* to get closer to her. But if staying away meant never making her feel that way again, then that's what I'd do.

The front door opened suddenly, and three pairs of feet shuffled into the living room.

Chloe kicked off her shoes (straight into the wall, like always) and her dance bag hit the floor with a heavy thud.

My stepdad was in the middle of one of his rambling jokes, the kind that took seven detours before finding a punchline, while Mom laughed as she pulled off her scarf and hung it by the door.

It felt weird, listening to them settle into the house while I stood in the kitchen like an outsider to it all.

I wanted to do something for them—to prove that I wasn't just a screw-up taking up space in their lives. And actually, Chloe's complaints about wanting hamburgers earlier in the week had sparked the idea for the meal.

But now that they were actually here, doubt was starting to creep in. *Maybe I shouldn't have...*

But I didn't have time to finish that thought, because my stepdad's voice boomed from the doorway. "Something smells good!"

Mom followed, stepping around him to get a closer look at the set table. "Cole, is this all for us?"

I nodded, shifting awkwardly as I turned the stove burner off. "I just... wanted to say thank you. For everything you guys have done for me, especially since the accident."

Her eyes softened, and for a second, I thought she might start crying right then and there. "Cole..." she started, but I cut her off, stumbling over the next words.

"Sorry... *Mom*," I said, the word still feeling strange in my mouth. It was like saying somebody's name too soon after meeting them—like I wasn't sure I'd gotten it right, even though I knew I had. "I just wanted to..."

"Cole," she said, stepping forward as she rested her hand on my arm. "This is beautiful. Thank you."

I exhaled, feeling a wave of relief as I gestured toward the table. "You guys sit down. I'll handle the rest tonight."

As they moved toward their seats, I turned back to grab something for my stepdad to drink out of.

We were out of regular cups, so I reached into one of the upper cabinets and pulled out a mug that had been shoved way in the back. It was dusty, but after a quick wash, I figured it'd work.

I set it down in front of him. But just as he was about to drink from it, he paused, quickly setting it back down. "Oh, Cole," he said, his voice thick with surprise. "I don't have to use your mug."

I frowned at him. "*My* mug? What do you mean?"

Mom's eyes widened as she leaned in, her hand covering her mouth. "I can't believe we still have that."

"What are you guys talking about?" I asked, glancing between them.

"That's your dad's old mug," Mom said quietly. "He used to use it every morning before he went to work."

The room seemed to shrink around me as I looked down at the mug.

My *dad's* mug.

I picked it up slowly, turning it over in my hands. The faded logo on the side (some local mechanic shop) blurred as I tried to focus.

It wasn't just a mug, though—it was a breadcrumb, a piece of the map leading back to him. But the lines didn't connect, even though I tried like hell to at least remember *something*.

"You wouldn't let anyone touch that mug after he passed," my stepdad said, his voice softening. "Where did you even find it?"

I shrugged, still staring at it. "It was in the back of one of the cabinets..."

Silence fell on the room again, and not being able to take it anymore, I cleared my throat, attempting to use the excuse to find a different cup as a mercy kill.

I turned, digging through the cabinet one more time and pulling out one of Chloe's old plastic mugs.

"There you go," I said, trying to sound normal as I set it down, though my voice felt tight in my throat.

My mom gave me a small, uncertain smile. "Thank you, Cole,"

That was it. I needed to change the subject, to move *past* this.

I turned toward Chloe. "I, uh—remembered you saying you liked burgers a few days ago. I wanted to make something special for you."

She looked down at the burger, then at me, and then over at Mom. A little pout settled on her lips, making me worry I'd misheard her a few days ago.

Maybe it hadn't been burgers. Maybe she hated them. Maybe she was allergic. Hell if I knew.

My shirt collar felt tight as I waited for her to say something. *Could tonight get any worse?*

Mom glanced at my stepdad, and then back at Chloe. "That was really sweet of Cole, wasn't it, Chloe? Now, what do we say?"

"Thank you." she mumbled, barely meeting my eyes.

"Honey," Mom pressed gently. "Say it louder so Cole can hear."

Chloe hesitated, her pout deepening. "*Thank you,*" she repeated, just a little louder, before quickly adding, "Can I go to my room now?"

Mom gave me a sympathetic look before nodding at her.

Chloe was gone before I could say anything else.

"She's just tired," Mom said to me softly.

I nodded, forcing a small smile as I sat down across from them.

But as I poked at my food, I couldn't help but wonder if she really *was* just tired—or if she wanted nothing to do with me.

Chapter Fifteen

FOUR YEARS EARLIER

G racie

"She's such a slut."

It was said just loud enough for me to hear as I walked past a group of seventh grade girls in the hallway, and because I'd always been someone who loved a good dose of gossip in the morning, I glanced over my shoulder.

The finger pointed directly at me made me take it all back.

I only loved gossip if it *wasn't* about me.

"I heard she slept with some college guy!"

Suddenly, this game wasn't so fun anymore.

The air drained from my lungs before I could stop it. *No, no, no...*

"She's fat and ugly anyways," another girl chimed in. "Who would even want *that*?"

This couldn't be real. Like it physically *couldn't* be.

I need to get some air... But my feet wouldn't move, no matter how much I begged them to.

So instead, I kept listening to them.

Middle school was funny that way. Everyone lived in this... fishbowl of sorts. Tiny scandals were massive, and rumors always had an ugly reputation of rearing their head and revealing darker truths.

Like the fact that my brother wasn't expected to make it past that year.

Or that my parents were getting a divorce.

Or that...

No.

He promised he wouldn't say anything. He *promised*.

"Good girls don't cry, Gracie,"

But here I was... drowning in what felt like the end of my life. And maybe it should've been. Maybe that would have been better.

That's when footsteps rounded the corner... *Cole.*

The blood rushed to my head.

I watched, feet still glued to the floor, as he gave me a once-over and smirked. He *smirked* at me. Like he didn't realize how big the can of worms he'd opened was.

Then, acting as the nail in the coffin, and just loud enough for everyone in the hallway to hear, he said, "She probably couldn't keep up with him. What a freak."

Okay, maybe he *did* realize how big the can was.

"Good girls don't cry, Gracie,"

"Good girls don't cry,"

"Good girls..."

"Don't... Cry..."

Before I could really process what was happening, I turned and bolted, my shoes slamming against the tile as I raced into the cafeteria.

It didn't matter where I went. Just anywhere but there.

By the time I stopped, I was alone. Alone in a room full of people who didn't care enough to notice that I was falling apart—losing my dignity, my reputation, the one *safe* place I had away from everything else going on in my life...

That's when the tears finally started to stream down my face.

I pressed my hands to my chest, willing my heart to stop racing, but it wouldn't. My mind kept screaming the same words over and over again: *He promised. He promised.*

Sobbing turned to hiccupping as I fought to pull myself together before Cole and his friends found me. But I couldn't stop. I just couldn't stop.

Why would Cole say something?

How did he even know what happened?

Why does he hate me?

Because that was the only explanation there was for him spilling my secret. He hated me. Always had. Always would. No matter how "nice" I was to him.

And it was right then and there, in the middle of the cafeteria, that I made a promise to myself—a promise born out of the lowest, loneliest moment of my life: I would never let Cole treat me like that again.

I would never let *anyone* treat me like that again.

They'd never get close enough to me to have that chance.

Present Day: October 24th
Gracie

Holy shit.

I was fully awake in a second, shooting upright so fast that the room spun.

It took me way longer than I would've liked to even remember where I was... my room. My heart was pounding so hard in my chest that it was difficult to concentrate on much of anything.

One thing stuck, though: I was disgusted.

Disgusted with myself. Disgusted with *him*...

I wanted the memory gone.

I wanted to physically scrub it all away, so hard until my skin bled.

It'd be worth it, though, if I could reverse the past so that it would *only* be a bad dream.

But I couldn't. It didn't work like that.

I shoved the tangled mess of bedsheets around my legs onto the floor, forcing myself to take a breath as I glanced around the room again.

Everything was still here: the blinds, the carpet, my dumb comforter that was now lying on the ground.

Safe. I'm safe, I'm safe, I'm safe...

But was I really?

I hated how easy it was for my brain to drag me back there. Middle school was a lifetime ago, but it might as well have been yesterday for how well I remembered it.

Condoms buried in my mash potatoes. People telling me I was gaining weight and *had* to be pregnant, no matter what I did. Even when I stopped eating altogether at one point and accidentally lost twenty pounds...

It'd been... awful.

195

I couldn't escape my past back then, and sometimes I *still* couldn't. Words stuck and rotted, and they didn't go away. No matter how old you got.

To this day, I still didn't know how Cole had found out about my secret, and now that he couldn't even remember, it wasn't like I could ask. But it didn't matter. Because of him, what happened to me became its own legacy, one I was forced to live with.

The truth didn't matter when the story was better.

And yeah, maybe everyone eventually moved on from middle school for the most part, but *I* hadn't.

I was still stuck there.

Still wearing my favorite leopard print yoga pants that I had to throw away after the first time it'd happened, still wondering if I had fucked up my whole life, still wondering how I could come back from it...

Sometimes, I envied Cole for not having anything to haunt him like that.

So, that was why by the time third period had rolled around, even though I still sat next to him in class, I didn't say a word to him.

Because Emma was right. How could I hate someone who didn't even remember what he had done?

No, seriously. I was asking. *How the hell can I keep hating this guy?*

It was easier than trying to be his friend, at least.

"What's going on in that pretty little head of yours?" Cole asked, leaning over just enough for his (surprisingly) nice cologne to hit me.

I didn't look at him. Mostly because I was too busy shading in a stick figure version of him getting launched into a volcano on my homework packet.

He glanced down at my paper. "Nice drawing. Has my eyes," he dead-panned.

I slammed my packet shut, ears turning red before I could stop it. "Isn't there someone else you can go bother right now?"

Truthfully, it was probably easier (and for the best) if he agreed with me on that. If he told me to just fuck off and go have an attitude somewhere else. If he told me he didn't have time to continuously deal with my shit (even if it was well deserved).

Like I said before—it'd be easier to hate him.

But now everything was just too complicated, and I didn't know what or how I was supposed to feel.

I mean, it wasn't like there was a pamphlet out there on what to do if your mortal enemy gets into a car accident, loses their memory, and then, tries to become your friend not remembering that they actually hate you or something.

"I'm just tired," I muttered, opening up my packet again—this time with the actual purpose of *doing* it.

"Were you up all night with your brother again? Is he doing alright?"

My grip tightened on my pencil so hard I thought it might just snap in two.

There it was. Even in my *own* damn conversations, Bear was still the main topic of the whole thing.

I couldn't ever just be "tired," (not that I even was, I just didn't know what to say around Cole right now) it had to be for a reason. And I guess to most people, Bear was the *only* reason I had. Because I was his sister.

And that was all I ever would be.

"I'm not tired because of him," I shot back. "Shocking, I know. Some-times I just don't sleep."

For a shining moment, I hoped that'd be enough for him.

I should've known it wouldn't be for the new and improved version of himself. *Ugh.*

"Well... something's off," he concluded finally. "You've had at least *three* perfect chances to make fun of me for tragically having amnesia in the last half hour, and I've gotten nothing. Not even a pity smirk at my suffering."

A tiny smile tugged at my mouth before I could stop it, and I had to keep shading in the volcano so he wouldn't see.

Dammit, why did he have to make this all so much harder than it had to be?

Before his accident, we couldn't even be in a room together without something exploding, and now he was asking about how my brother was doing? How did that make sense?

He shifted in his chair, like he was waiting me out. "You know I'm not going to drop this, right?" His tone was light, but the way he said it told me he meant it. "I'll just sit here until you crack and tell me what's up."

I rolled my eyes, but he didn't fill the silence after.

He just sat there, being all quiet and patient with me, and it did something weird to my chest... it *settled* it. Like somehow even it knew I didn't have to pretend like everything was fine around him.

So why try?

But telling him about the nightmare I'd had last night? Absolutely not.

If he remembered what happened in middle school, we'd be right back to where we started. No more asking about how well I had slept, or about my brother... he'd stop talking to me forever.

He'd think I was a freak all over again.

And *sue* me for starting to enjoy these dumb little conversations with him.

So, I was determined to do the selfish thing and keep the truth for a little while longer. Because why the hell not? It wasn't like *he'd* know the difference.

"You're the reason I lost my job at Mary Anne's," I blurted out. "And I'm... mad at you for that. Still."

His head tilted as he processed my words, his brow furrowing. "Wait, what? How?"

I sighed, quickly realizing that maybe talking about the ranch was a horrible idea because the answer would lead to more questions, (especially about our history together) and then we'd be back in the same place we were if he found out about the rumor. It was a lose-lose situation.

Great.

"It doesn't matter," I said quickly. "Forget I said anything."

But Cole shook his head. "No, it *does* matter. If it was my fault, I want to make it right."

I couldn't help but laugh at that. "And how exactly do you plan on doing that? You gonna march up to Mary Anne and demand she rehire me?"

Cole's lips turned upwards into a grin. "I could call in a favor from Steve."

In all my many (*many*) years of working there, I had never seen nor heard of a guy named Steve. I gave him a look as if I were the one with amnesia.

"Excuse me? Who?"

"You know, Steve—Mary Anne's aunt's cousin's nephew or whatever? Look, I've only seen him like... once. He showed me how stuff worked on my first day back after the accident. But he's cool. He'd help."

I stared at him for a beat, my brain working overtime to try and figure out who the hell he was talking about. Finally, "I'm sorry... do you mean *Shawn*?"

Cole snapped his fingers like he'd just solved the world's greatest mystery. "Shawn! That's right. Knew it started with an 'S.'"

I shook my head, rolling my eyes as another involuntary smile tugged at my lips. "You're such a dork."

He grinned wider, clearly pleased with himself for making me laugh. "Is that a compliment? Because I'm taking it as one."

But before I could respond, a loud, mocking gasp sounded from across the room. "Hey, it's Slutty and Co.!"

Heat rose to my face as recognition of the voice hit me... *Dylan.*

Cole had been horrible to me in middle school, there was no doubt about it, but the Bonnie to his Clyde, Dylan, had been *just* as bad.

Sometimes, I wondered if there had ever been a board meeting between two of the biggest asses at this school just to come up with nicknames for me. ("Slutty" was Dylan's pick after Cole had settled on "Princess"—still up for debate on which one was arguably better).

I cleared my throat, trying to act unbothered by him (fear was what bullies like him fed on, after all—even if it sucked to admit that). "*Dylan!* Don't you have a rock to crawl under?"

He just snorted as he handed Miss Holland a slip of paper from the office. "Chill, Gracie. Just saying hi."

Cole's eyes drifted to mine for a second, and then fell on Dylan's like a heat-seeking missile.

Before he could give this any kind of *rational* thought (because of course not), he pushed his chair back, the sound making a horrendous screeching sound as it slid across the linoleum as he stood, his jaw tight.

"Is there a problem here, Dylan?"

My eyes widened as the color drained from my cheeks.

I yanked his arm, trying to force him back down. "*What are you doing? Sit down.*"

Dylan's smirk widened at that. "Yeah, listen to Slutty. Relax, man. We're just having fun."

Cole laughed, humorlessly. "Oh, really? Because it doesn't look like *she's* having fun."

I gave his arm a firmer tug. "Cole, I'm serious. Sit."

I must have been louder than I had meant to be because Miss Holland's head suddenly snapped up, giving the three of us a sharp look (I was just destined to never be on her good side in this class, was I?).

"Mr. Brown. Mr. Casey. Miss Lewis. Is there something you'd like to share with the class?"

Dylan raised his hands in mock surrender. "I'm just checking in with my *friends.*"

If I were being completely honest with myself, I'd barely gotten around to the idea of *Cole* being "my friend," let alone imagining Dylan as being one, and the thought of it made me physically ill.

But it was a moot point because before I could tell him that very same thing, Miss Holland shot him a glare that could have melted ice, and Dylan surrendered, slinking out of the room as he muttered something incoherent (and probably not very PG friendly) under his breath.

I sighed to myself, my gaze landing back on my drawing of Cole flying towards an active volcano.

The makings of guilt pulled at my stomach right then. After all, what had he done to me recently (except defend me... not that I NEEDED it) to deserve dying on my homework?

"What was that about?" Cole asked finally, sinking back into his seat beside me.

"Don't worry about it," I said automatically.

"Gracie..." His tone softened even more, like he was trying to handle me like I was five and my parents were getting a divorce.

Oh, *wait*—they already had! My bad.

I was starting to feel less guilty about the whole volcano thing.

"It's fine," I cut in, sharper this time. "Just... drop it, okay?"

Cole's jaw tightened, and for a second, I could see him considering pushing further (he was like me in that). But instead, he studied me for a beat, his eyes full of questions he wasn't sure he should ask, and then he turned back to his packet.

I kept my eyes glued to my desk, pretending the packet's blurry words and drawings provided by *moi* weren't swimming in front of me.

My chest burned, but it wasn't just from Dylan's stupid comment. It was because of Cole, too. The way he had looked at me—like there was something broken inside of me, something that wasn't normal.

He probably didn't even realize he was doing it. But the way he went out of his way to avoid physical contact with me, treating me with kiddy gloves based on the things he *thought* he knew about me. Or how he offered to get my job back at Mary Anne's, like it was that simple...

And now this—jumping up to defend me against Dylan, like I couldn't handle it myself or something?

He didn't *see* me. He saw a problem to solve, a girl to save.

Because that's who I was, wasn't it? Gracie, the girl with the sick brother. Gracie, the girl with divorced parents. Gracie, the mess, the charity case, the freak, the slut. That's what people saw when they looked at me—a list of things that happened *to* me.

Not someone who was whole.

And the worst part was, I didn't even know if they were wrong to see me that way.

I didn't want their pity. I didn't want their judgement, either. I didn't want them looking at me and seeing the cracks first. The things I couldn't control. The things I couldn't change.

I didn't want to be a headline. Or a punchline. Or a cautionary tale.

I just wanted to be *Gracie*.

Whoever Gracie was.

Chapter Sixteen:

OCTOBER 26TH

C ole

The sound of the level clattering to the floor yanked me out of my brain. I hadn't even noticed it slipping from my hand.

"You good?" my stepdad asked, bending down to pick it back up.

"Yeah," I mumbled, steadying the mantel. "Just tired, I guess."

Which wasn't entirely a lie. After weeks of sanding, painting, and piecing together the fireplace for Mom's birthday, I was exhausted—but mostly, I was nervous.

I wanted this to be perfect in a way that wasn't just about the mantel; it was about proving I could actually do something worthwhile for someone for once.

"You've got that look on your face again," my stepdad said as he fished a pencil from behind his ear and marked spots for the screws.

"What look?"

"The one that says, 'I've got ten questions I'm too scared to ask.'"

A humorless laugh escaped me before I could stop it. "Alright, fine, you caught me. Can I ask you something real quick?"

He stepped back, examining the mantel before nodding. "Shoot."

"You know that ranch I work at?"

"Mhmm."

"Well, Gracie, she's a friend of mine—said she got fired there. Because of me, apparently." I paused, shifting my grip on the wood. "I was hoping to get her job back for her. But Shawn said to talk to Mary Anne, and I never know where she is. I don't even know *who* she is."

My stepdad chuckled softly as he held the level up to the mantel. "Mary Anne's not exactly the easiest person to track down when she doesn't want to be found."

"Yeah, I'm starting to pick up on that," I muttered, adjusting my weight as I helped him set the mantel down. "Do you, uh... happen to know where I could find her? Or maybe—"

I rubbed the back of my neck, suddenly feeling a little awkward for asking about things I *should* have known the answer to, even though it wasn't entirely my fault I couldn't remember. "Do you still have my resume from when I applied lying around somewhere? Like, maybe there's a number I can call or something?"

His hand suddenly stilled on the level. Then he turned to me with an expression that was something between amusement and hesitation.

"Kid, you didn't apply for that job,"

I blinked. "What?"

"You didn't apply," he said again. "You're doing community service there."

My stomach gave out from under me. "Wait, what are you talking about?"

He sighed and gestured for me to sit on the couch. "Let's take a break for a minute. This might take some explaining."

Reluctantly, I followed him to the couch, my mind already racing.

Community service? What the hell?

Sure, I'd been the school bully—I'd found *that* one out the hard way. But whatever I'd done before the accident, it was supposed to stay in school, right?

But I guess I'd never really stopped to think about why I was still working at the ranch to begin with.

Yeah, I'd thought it was a little weird that I was putting in full days of manual labor even after skidding across an entire *highway*... you'd think being the concussed guy who couldn't even get medically cleared to play football would've been enough of a pass to take it easy. But I had never questioned it.

I never thought I *had* to.

I should've known nothing about my life would ever be that simple.

He sat down next to me, resting his elbows on his knees. "Cole, about a year ago, things were... complicated. You got yourself into a little trouble."

I frowned. "What *kind* of trouble?"

"Serious enough that the judge wanted to send you to juvie," he said gently. "But Mary Anne stepped in. She fought like hell for you to work at the ranch instead. Said it would be better for you than being locked up somewhere."

I stared at him, my mind reeling. "Mary Anne? The Mary Anne who owns the ranch? Why would she do that?"

He hesitated again, like he was searching for the right way to drop the next bombshell. Finally, he said, "Because she's your grandmother."

I felt like the floor had been yanked out from under me. "My... what?"

"Your grandmother," he repeated. "On your dad's side."

For a second, I thought he must've been messing with me. But the look on his face said otherwise.

All this time, I'd been working for her—*my grandmother*—without even realizing it. That was insane.

I let out a hollow laugh, the kind you make when there's nothing else to do. "So lemme get this straight: I've been shoveling horse shit and scrubbing troughs for her for months, I haven't seen her once since I got *hit by a car*, and she's my *grandma*?"

"She's... not exactly hands-on these days," he admitted. "She leaves most of the day-to-day stuff to Shawn."

"Well, I haven't even seen *Shawn* in a while. It's starting to feel like I'm the only one ever there."

"Mary Anne has her reasons for keeping her distance, but it doesn't mean she doesn't care."

I leaned back into the couch, trying to wrap my head around it all. "No one thought to mention that I've been working for my *grandmother* this whole time?"

"Your mom wanted to keep it under wraps," he said. "She didn't want to make things any harder for you. Thought it'd be better if you remembered on your own."

I scoffed, running a hand through my hair. "Yeah, because that would've been so much better..."

He shot me a look.

"Look, I get it. It's a lot to take in. But you need to understand something. The people in your life—your mom, Mary Anne, *me*—we try to make the best decision with the information we have at hand. We've made mistakes, sure, but we love you and want you to succeed. That's not nothing."

I opened my mouth to argue, but the realization slowly dawned on me that...he was right. They *did* love me. By showing up, by being here, even though I was a lot to deal with sometimes.

Since waking up from the accident, I'd been running on the idea that I had to figure everything out on my own, like I was the *only* one going through this.

But taking care of a kid with amnesia was a new thing for *everyone* in my family. It wasn't just something I was dealing with.

"Thank you," I said after a long pause, my voice quieter this time.

His brow furrowed slightly. "For what?"

"For being here," I said, my throat tightening. "For... sticking around."

"You're family, Cole," he replied simply, his expression softening. "That's what family does."

"I'm gonna make you proud," I said, the words spilling out before I could stop them. "You, Mom... my dad, Mary Anne. All of you."

He met my eyes, a small smile crossing his face. "You already do, kiddo."

I sat with his words for a minute, letting them settle in my chest.

I'd spent so much of my time feeling like I needed to prove something to everyone—prove that I wasn't still the "bad kid", prove that I could be more than a past that I couldn't really remember. And yet here my stepdad was, telling me that it didn't matter what that past looked like.

I could still turn around and come back home, no matter where I ended up, or what I'd done.

He was giving me the chance to move forward.

"Okay," I said, standing up from the couch and brushing my hand on my jeans. "Where's that number? I think it's time I met my grandma."

Finding Mary Anne's number wasn't as hard as I thought it'd be. My mom had it on a 3x5 card buried in the back of one of her drawers in the office.

Actually calling her, though? *That* was the tricky part.

It took me three tries before I finally hit the call button. Even then, I almost hung up the second she answered with a sharp, "Who's this?"

After stumbling over my name and managing to explain that I was told... well, that I was her *grandson*, she got quiet for a minute.

When she finally spoke again, her tone had softened—sort of. "Took you long enough. I'll be in the barn all afternoon. Come by if you want."

Now, sitting in the driver's seat of my truck with the entrance to the ranch looming in front of me, I felt like everything I'd planned to say to her had vanished.

She was my *grandmother*. But she was also a stranger.

How was I supposed to talk to her? What was I even supposed to say?

I gripped the steering wheel, taking a deep breath as I scanned the property.

The barn was set back a little, surrounded by paddocks and fields that stretched out for acres. It was peaceful out here, even with the occasional distant whinny of a horse.

Too bad I was about to wreck all of it.

Just then, I caught a glimpse of movement in the barn.

There she was, Mary Anne... sorry, *my grandmother*, moving slowly from stall to stall. She was smaller than I'd imagined she would be, with silver hair pulled into a loose braid.

As I reluctantly stepped out of the truck and got closer, I noticed something else—her eyes. Steely gray, just like mine.

Just like dad's.

The pit of my stomach settled a little at the realization.

She wasn't just a stranger, even if the memories were gone. She was a *part* of me. And suddenly, talking to her didn't seem so bad anymore.

She was struggling to open a stall gate when I reached the barn, muttering under her breath as she yanked at the latch. "Damn thing won't budge," she grumbled.

"Here. Let me help you." I offered automatically, closing the gap between us.

She turned, raising an eyebrow as I grabbed the latch and gave it a firm yank. The gate creaked open, and I stepped aside to let her through.

"Thanks, kid," she said, brushing past me, heading straight to the horse inside—a black-and-white spotted mare lying down in the corner.

At the sound of her voice, the horse groaned and got to her feet, trotting over to nuzzle Mary Anne like she'd been waiting all day for her.

"Oh, stop it," Mary Anne muttered, scratching the mare's neck. "You're fine, you big drama queen. I thought you were dead, but no—you were just lying down, being lazy. You tired, big girl?"

The horse whinnied, nudging her pocket for a treat. Mary Anne sighed and pulled out a peppermint, which the mare took eagerly.

I watched, amazed at how natural she was with the animals. It wasn't just that they trusted her—it was like they understood her.

"You gonna stand there gawking all day or are you gonna tell me what this is about?" she asked, not looking up from the horse.

Her honesty threw me for a second, and suddenly, I was nervous all over again. "I, uh... I found out you're my grandma."

She snorted. "You said that on the phone already. Or did you forget about that too?" She paused, shaking her head. "I bet your mother didn't even tell you about me."

"No," I admitted, shifting awkwardly. "My stepdad did."

"Figures," she said clicking her tongue. "Your mom was always a steam-roller—either you're paving the way for her, or you're getting flattened. Poor Luke didn't stand a chance."

"That's not true," I said instinctively, rushing to defend my mom, though I wasn't sure why.

I hated to admit it, but I'd thought the same thing at one point. Sometimes, I *still* did. It felt like she had moved on from my dad way too quickly.

My grandmother arched an eyebrow at me then. "What would you know about it? You can't even remember your own name!"

The horses snorted as heat crept up my neck. I opened my mouth to respond, but she waved me off with a roll of her eyes.

"Relax. I'm just messing with you. Come on—let's walk and talk. Shut the gate behind you, dear."

As we started down the breezeway, I noticed the small limp in her step and how her hands brushed against each stall like she was trying to steady herself.

Before I could give it a second thought, and that to me, she was *still* a stranger, I offered her my arm.

"Here, why don't you hold onto me?" I asked gently.

Her eyes flickered with a flash of hurt pride, but after a second of hesitation, she slipped her hand through my elbow.

"I hate getting old." she murmured, letting out a long sigh through her nostrils.

"You? Old? No way. Can't be a day over twenty," I teased, flashing her a grin.

She snorted, a faint smile reaching her lips.

We fell into silence as we walked—a silence that I quickly rushed to fill with something. "How come I never saw you after the accident? Not at the ranch, not anywhere,"

She stopped mid-step, giving me a look like she thought I was stupid. "I was always here, you dummy. Where do you think these horses came from, the tooth fairy?"

I frowned. "I don't remember seeing you."

Her face softened then, and she sighed. "That's because I stayed out of sight. Figured it was better that way."

"Better?" I echoed, my brow furrowing.

She hesitated. "You're a walking, talking reminder of what I lost? And me?" She gestured to herself. "I'm the same damn thing for you. You didn't need me hanging around, making it harder."

My throat tightened a little at that. "But staying away... that couldn't have been easier."

She looked at me then, her gray eyes clouding over in the dim barn light. "No," she said softly. "It wasn't."

We stopped in front of the hay barn, and my grandmother bent down slowly to pick up a fallen pitchfork.

Then, she made her way to the cart tucked in the back of the barn and yanked it from a pile of hay. The wheels squeaked in protest, and that's when I realized one of them was actually flat.

"I didn't expect you to come today," she huffed, pausing to catch her breath as she dragged the cart further out.

I stepped forward immediately, taking the cart's handle from her. "Let me help, Grammie."

Whoa, where did that name come from?

Her head snapped toward me, just as surprised as I was by it. "Wow," she murmured. "You remembered... You used to call me Grammie when you were little. Haven't heard that in years."

Her hand came up to brush back a stray wisp of hair, leaving a faint smudge of dirt on her forehead. "I missed it," she admitted quietly.

I laughed thoughtfully to myself. "Grammie..." I repeated, trying it again and liking the way it felt. "Please don't tell me you do this every day when I'm not here."

"My nephew, Shawn, was supposed to come up and help," she muttered, leaning against the pitchfork. "But he's been too busy with his new, fancy city job. Damn him."

It clicked for me then what ranch life actually looked like for her, one where Shawn *wasn't* around. One where I wasn't around much either, only when I had to be.

And honestly? There was no way I was going to let her keep hauling broken carts around the barn by herself after today. Not when I was perfectly capable of lightening her load.

"I'm gonna start coming by every day to help you then," I concluded firmly.

"What? No." She shook her head quickly. "I couldn't do that to you. You've got school, y'know."

"I'll make time, Grammie. You and your safety are important to me." I insisted, meeting her eyes with a determined gaze.

Her expression softened, and for the first time, she laughed—a warm, hearty sound that filled the barn. "If you're up for it... but it's a lot of work, kid. More than you *have* been doing."

I grinned. "And I know the perfect person who would love to help."

October 28th

Gracie

I slammed the car door shut behind me and stepped out onto the familiar dirt road, shivering as my breath clouded the October air.

My car's heater had decided to give out on me this morning, and now my fingers were numb, tucked as far into my jacket pockets as they'd go.

Typically, something as horrible as losing the only thing keeping my body from freezing to death meant that we were in for a hell of a ride, but maybe not today...

We'd see, I guess.

I spotted Cole almost immediately.

He was across the field, tossing hay bales into the back of his truck like it was nothing. *Showoff.*

His white T-shirt stretched over his shoulders, his backwards hat barely keeping his messy brown hair under control. And for a second, I just... stood there, watching.

He looks good up there, don't you think?

Whoa. Okay. No. Where did *that* come from?

I blinked hard, shaking the thought out of my head. But before I could pretend like it'd never even happened, Cole looked up, his face breaking into an easy, sunlit grin.

"Gracie!" he called, hopping down from the truck bed. He jogged over, wiping sweat off his brow with the back of his hand. "You came."

I rolled my eyes, but a smile still crept in anyway. "You *called*, doofus."

He laughed, brushing dust off his jeans. "Come on—I've got something to show you."

I hesitated for a split second before following, keeping enough distance to remind myself of who we were to each other: Cole and Gracie: oil and water. Enemies turned... friends. *Just* friends.

But Heaven help me because it was getting harder to ignore the way my pulse jumped as he glanced back at me with that grin again.

The barn quickly came into view, the smell of hay and leather drifting through the air in waves. But as soon as we reached the doorway, wide open and dark beyond, old memories tugged at me, stirring up an uneasy feeling deep in my chest.

I slowed my pace, letting Cole step ahead of me.

It wasn't the dark itself. It was what could *happen* in the dark. Things I couldn't stop. Things people wouldn't believe me for. Even though I knew logically I was probably getting worked up over nothing, it wasn't something I could let go.

I knew Cole wasn't like that. Even before the accident he wasn't like *that*. But my body didn't seem to care what I knew—it only cared about what it remembered.

Normal girls don't get this way, Gracie. They actually appreciate surprises.

I know, I know...

"Gracie?"

I blinked up at Cole, realizing I'd just zoned out probably for a lot longer than socially acceptable. He was standing a few feet ahead, his face softening when he looked back at me.

Embarrassment flooded my cheeks. *He probably thinks I'm crazy right now.*

He tilted his head at me. "You okay?"

"Yeah," I replied quickly, plastering on a tiny smile that didn't quite reach my eyes. "It's just darker in here than I remembered."

I braced myself for him to start laughing at me. I mean, that's what usually happened when I let on more about myself than I should've.

But instead, he smiled gently. "Hang tight. I'll fix that."

He walked toward the wall, and a second later, the barn lights flickered on with a hum. The shadows melted away instantly, and (thankfully) so did the tightness in my chest.

"Better?" he asked, glancing back at me.

I nodded, a more genuine smile growing on my face this time, and came closer to the entryway, taking in the scene before me.

A huge banner stretched across the top of one of the stalls, reading *Welcome Back, Gracie!* in big, bold letters.

Painted Lady, my favorite horse, stood in the stall beneath it, chewing on a tuft of hay with a bored expression. A pink party hat dangled lopsidedly from one of her ears, and I had to bite back a laugh.

"Oh. My. Gosh."

Cole grinned at me as he walked over to her and gently pulled the hat off. "Figured she'd tolerate it for at least five minutes. Guess I gave her too much credit." He turned back to me, tucking the hat into his back pocket. "So... what do you think? I mean, I can't take all the credit. Grammie helped a little..."

Wait. *Grammie?*

I blinked. "I'm sorry. *Who?*"

He chuckled, rubbing the back of his neck. "Turns out Mary Anne's my grandma. Found that out a couple of days ago."

That realization was probably more out there than a horse with a party hat on.

But I guess it finally made sense as to why she'd chosen him to stay over me in the first place. Family was family... even though she was family to *me*.

For once, though, I didn't let the hurt settle into my gut. Not when there was literally a guy who'd gone through all the trouble of throwing me a freaking *welcome back party* when he hadn't had to standing right in front of me.

"I can't believe you did this."

"Well, yeah," he said, his cheeks flushing. "And, uh, I got your job back too." His voice trailed off, and he looked down at the barn floor like he wasn't sure if he'd done enough—or if he'd done *too* much.

I honestly didn't know what to say. Nobody had ever done anything like this for me in my entire life.

Most people only remembered my brother, or treated me like the school harlot. But this didn't feel like one of those weird instances where Cole pitied me.

It felt like one where he'd gone out of his way to be nice to me. Actually nice to *me*—not nice because he was worried about Bear or knew what had happened to me.

Before I could overthink it, I crossed the space between us and threw my arms around his neck.

He stiffened for a second, surprised by the contact, but then his arms slowly wrapped around my waist, pulling me in closer.

I let myself sink into the warmth and surprising dizziness of it all for just a second longer than I probably should have.

And *that's* when it hit me. This fluttering, weightless feeling coursing through my veins was terrifyingly wonderful, and I hated that I loved it.

Maybe this is what it feels like to be normal.

"Thank you," I murmured.

"Yeah," he said softly. "Anytime, Gracie."

Chapter Seventeen:

NOVEMBER 10TH

Cole

"Good morning!" I turned to see Gracie, glowing in the soft morning light, all dark messy waves and rosy cheeks.

Over the past month, we'd gotten into the groove of things—showing up early to help Grammie before school and then coming back again in the afternoons.

I'd told myself it was just to make sure she didn't overdo it, but the truth? I didn't mind the work.

Actually, I *more* than didn't mind it.

And it was all because of Gracie.

She made everything feel like it mattered a whole lot more than it actually did (not that Grammie's ranch *didn't* matter).

There was this fire about her—like the way she'd rant about some book she stayed up all night reading, or how she'd argue with me over little things, just because she could.

It was the kind of thing that felt off-putting at first. I mean, let's be real, Gracie was *intimidating*. But once you saw it, like *really* saw it, it was like you couldn't imagine having her any other way.

"I brought you coffee," she said simply, holding out a Styrofoam cup. Then she pursed her lips, hesitating before quickly adding, "But don't get used to it. I just had an extra."

I grinned. "Right. An extra coffee exactly how I like it? What are the odds?"

Her face turned pink as she rolled her eyes, thrusting the cup at me. "Just take it, Cole."

I took a sip, chuckling. "Thank you," I said, softer this time. "I mean it."

She rolled her eyes again, muttering something about how I shouldn't make it a thing. But it *was* a thing.

It was her remembering the little stuff and playing it off like it wasn't a big deal. It showed she cared, showed that she got it, even when she pretended not to.

Just like she does with her brother. She cares in her own, special Gracie way.

As we continued to nurse our drinks, a weird, slightly awkward silence fell over us.

Normally, Gracie would've filled the space with some sarcastic comment or another hot take about a book she was reading, (those were always my favorite).

These past couple of weeks, I'd even found myself reading some of the books she'd mentioned—books like *Animal Farm* and *The Giver*—just so we'd have things to talk about. And listen, I was *not* a book kind of guy. But for her, I was.

Today, though, she was quiet.

Unusually quiet.

I glanced over, ready to ask what was wrong, when I noticed the tips of her ears turning pink under her hair.

She's cold. Obviously.

Without a second thought, I shrugged off my jacket—the one I'd really only started wearing because she was always telling me that I was *one gust of wind away from freezing to death.*

What could I say, though? I didn't really get cold.

But she clearly did.

"Put this on," I said, holding it out to her.

Gracie looked up at me, laughing as she tried to hide the fact that her lips were literally turning purple. "You're not even gonna put it on me? What kind of gentleman is your mother raising?"

I hesitated, not sure what to do with that.

I knew she was joking. But I also knew what *not* to do: don't screw things up by crossing a line and making her uncomfortable.

The memory of my first day back—how I'd accidentally brushed against her in class and she'd freaked out—was practically burned into my damn mind at this point. Same with her saying *"You touched me..."*

And then in the principal's office, when she wouldn't even shake his hand.

There was something she wasn't telling me, and I didn't want to accidentally stumble across a landmine and do something to ruin the trust she'd put in me.

Not after everything we'd done to build a... friendship.

221

Yeah, we're just friends... that's it.

But this felt different.

She wasn't pulling away now. If anything, she was waiting for me to get over myself.

"Fine," I gave in softly, stepping closer.

Carefully, I slipped the jacket over her shoulders. It was huge on her, the sleeves hanging well past her hands, and a small, amused laugh escaped her lips.

"I bet I look so stupid in this," she muttered, grinning.

"Hold on. I can fix it."

My fingers took her hair as I gently lifted it out from under the jacket, letting it fall free.

It was softer than I expected, but honestly, I wasn't shocked. Gracie had always been full of surprises.

I didn't step back. I *should have*, but I didn't.

Her back was pressed lightly against my chest, and the smell of her shampoo (something faintly vanilla and floral) drifted between us.

She tilted her head slightly to look up at me, and that's when I realized she was waiting for me to say something else.

I quickly cleared my throat, forcing myself to speak before I accidentally blew up our *just* friendship. "There," I murmured, "Much better."

My hands hovered just above her shoulders, unsure of what to do with themselves, unsure what would happen if I moved *just* an inch.

Would she mind? Would she hate me for it?

Her eyes flicked up to mine, hesitantly, then to my lips—just for a second, before snapping back to meet my gaze, and stomach did a weird flip, the kind you get before something major happens.

Suddenly, I couldn't move even if I tried.

She angled her head up, just a little more, and before I could stop myself, I was leaning in too.

It wasn't like I'd planned it—hell, I wasn't even sure I was breathing at this point. All I knew was that her eyes were closing, and mine probably were too, and everything felt like it was leading up to this one moment...

Then she froze, her breath hitching as she pulled back just enough to break the spell.

"For the love of God," she muttered, a breathy laugh slipping out. She shook her head slightly, her expression torn between frustration and something softer. "I don't know why this is so hard for me."

Before I could say anything, she broke free from me, spinning around to give me a playful shove on the chest.

"Well, let's get back to work, then," she sighed, her eyes sparkling with that familiar, guarded look as she stepped even further away, tugging at her sleeves like it wasn't *my* damn jacket practically swallowing her whole.

She gave me a small smile like nothing had just happened. Meanwhile, I was pretty sure I'd aged at least six years in the last thirty seconds.

"Coming?" she asked, her voice unnaturally light.

I let out a shaky laugh, raking a hand through my hair in an attempt to pull myself together. "Yeah... I'll catch up in a second."

She nodded, her gaze staying on me for another half a second before she turned and jogged toward the barn.

I watched her go, my heart still pounding like I'd just run a marathon.

She was the most confusing person I'd ever met.

But damn it all if she didn't make me want to figure her out.

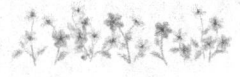

I leaned against the pasture fence, watching as the horses devour the feed I'd just put out for them.

Gracie had gone to take a call from her dad, which was fine. I didn't mind the time to myself. In fact, I kind of needed it.

Between our almost kiss earlier and her pulling away like I'd fucking burned her, I wasn't exactly in the greatest headspace.

She'd be the death of me one of these days, that was for sure.

Because how do you get that close to someone just for it all to slip through your fingers? She'd been *right* there, and for a second, I thought maybe she felt the same way I did.

Then she pushed me away and left me standing there like a complete idiot, replaying the entire interaction in my head and trying to figure out where I'd gone wrong.

I sighed, realizing it wasn't just Gracie, though. I was frustrated with *everything*.

I felt like I'd been dropped into someone else's life and told, "Here, kid. Figure it out."

Like I'd been handed the keys to a car that was already in motion, not knowing where it was going or how much gas was left in the tank.

Clearly, I had done something wrong with my life the *last* time I'd lived it. That much was obvious.

But now that I'd re-entered a video game with all the cheat codes unlocked, given the perfect restart, I had no memory of what didn't work.

Did a relationship with my family work?

Did being a quarterback work?

Did *Gracie* work?

I tossed the empty bucket into the bed of my truck and climbed into the driver's seat, leaning back for a second and letting the world as I knew it split in two: my past and present.

I could almost see him (*past me*) sitting here in the same seat, same body, same silence, staring out at nothing, feeling...

Well, probably the same damn thing I was feeling right now: *lost*.

I let the engine grumble as I started up the truck and rolled up the dirt path toward the barn.

The fences blurred by as my mind wandered back to Gracie before I could stop it. She was probably up there already, leaning against her car with that little smirk she always wore when she beat me back.

I liked seeing her like that.

Maybe a little too much.

You're just friends, Cole. Right, right.

Besides, her reaction to almost kissing me this morning was proof enough: she wanted nothing to do with me.

I pulled up to the barn (before her, surprisingly) and let out a low chuckle despite the knot still in my gut.

She'd be pissed when she found out I'd made it back before she had, and I almost turned around with the intention of stalling for a second so she could "win" right then and there.

But then again, maybe some healthy competition was exactly what we needed to get things back to normal between us.

"Gracie?" I called out. "Guess I beat you back today!"

Nothing. *That's weird.*

It usually didn't matter where she was. At first mention of any kind of thing she *could* win, she'd just materialize out of thin air and join in.

But after a minute or two of waiting for a response, I gave up and headed to the hay barn to check for her. Empty.

Then the chicken coop. Still nothing.

The barn door creaked as I pushed it open, the dim light spilling over the breezeway.

"Gracie?" I said again, softer this time, hoping that maybe a change in tone would convince her I wasn't trying to jump her or anything.

I mean I could take the hint if she was avoiding me from earlier. But at the same time, I wondered...

Was she?

The horses shifted in their stalls, hooves scuffing against the floor, but other than that, there was no other sound.

I ran a hand through my hair as I stepped further inside.

She was probably fine. *Definitely* fine. She was Gracie, for crying out loud.

She'd show up any second with some excuse about losing track of time or maybe just to tell me off for worrying about her at all.

Still, I couldn't help it. Protecting her—it wasn't just instinct. It was something I *wanted* to do. I'd felt that way since I met her. Well, met her *again*, at least, since I couldn't really remember... before.

"Gracie," I tried one last time, glancing around the barn. "Where are you?"

That's when I heard it. Just as I was about to leave, a faint sniffle came from Painted Lady's stall. I recognized the sound instantly.

Shit.

Had she gotten kicked or something? Was she okay?

"Gracie?" I rushed to the stall, yanking the door open and stepping inside.

There she was, huddled in the corner, knees tucked to her chest and her face streaked with tears.

I dropped down a few feet away, not wanting to crowd her, though every instinct screamed at me to do *something* more. "What's wrong?"

"Nothing," she mumbled, her voice cracking. "Just leave me alone."

I scoffed, leaning back on my hands like I wasn't going anywhere. "You're a terrible liar, you know that?"

Her eyes narrowed. "And you're a terrible comforter," she snapped, swiping at her face with the back of her hand.

If she hadn't been crying, I probably would've laughed.

Leave it to Gracie to argue with me, even when something was obviously the matter.

"You know, it'd be easier if you talked to someone about it. It's better than sitting out here all alone."

"Shut up, Cole."

"Fine, I can wait." I shrugged, settling into the silence, though my gaze stayed on her.

I couldn't help but think back to all the therapy sessions Mom had forced on me after the accident. At first, I'd hated it—hated someone digging into my head. But, over time, it actually helped me feel better about some things.

Maybe Gracie didn't need a therapist, but she needed *someone*.

And I wanted to be that someone for her.

If she'd let me, that was.

Her shoulders shook with another sob, and I couldn't just sit there and watch her like that anymore. *Fuck letting her come to me first.*

"Gracie, come here," I murmured.

To my surprise, she moved, sliding across the dirt floor until her head rested against my chest.

My pulse kicked up, but I refused to let it show. Instead, I wrapped an arm around her, letting my fingers hover near her shoulder—not quite touching, but close enough for her to feel the space she could fill if she wanted.

She let out a shaky breath, her tears soaking into my shirt. "Tomorrow's my birthday," she admitted quietly. "Seventeen. I don't even think my dad remembers. He just called to make sure I was still watching Bear."

"Gracie..."

"And I get it. I'm used to it. Bear's more important. He always is," she continued, her tone bitter. "It was just another stupid day anyways. One year closer to the sweet release of death. *Yay...*"

I clenched my jaw at that.

How the hell could her parents treat her like she didn't matter? Like she wasn't important enough to have one special day?

"That's not fair. You deserve better."

She shrugged against me. "What's the point of caring, though? They don't."

"Well, I care," I said firmly. "And I'm not letting you spend your birthday like this."

"It's not up to you, dummy. You can't force them to be there."

"You're right, I can't," I responded thoughtfully. She let out a humorless laugh as if to say, *see? I told you so.* "That's why you're coming to my house tomorrow: dinner, cake, the whole thing. Bring Bear too. My family will love you."

That's when Gracie suddenly lifted her head, glancing at me in shock, like she thought I were crazy for even *suggesting* the idea.

But slowly, her lips twitched up into a smile. "I don't know if I like your tone, Brown."

"Fine. *Please*, Gracie?"

She hesitated, scrunching her nose in that way she always did when she was thinking too hard about something and trying to find a way out of it. Damn, she was stubborn.

"Don't you think it'd be weird?"

"Absolutely not. Especially if you bitch about me to my sister," I joked, nudging her in the shoulder. "She'd eat that up."

She clicked her tongue, that smile of hers spreading wider. "Ah, yes. Winning over the approval of an eight-year-old. That's exactly what I'm aiming for in life."

"Don't underestimate her," I teased. "Being on her good side can get you places."

I let a beat pass between us but didn't give her a chance to argue. "So it's settled. Dinner tomorrow. I'm bribing you with cake and free food, and there's no getting out of it."

"But—"

"It's just dinner. You'll survive one night with me. I promise."

She shot me a sharp look, before sighing dramatically.

"Fine," she said, drawing out the word like she was saying it against her own free will (though her eyes had noticeably cleared up). "But don't expect me to be all cheerful or anything."

"Deal." My grin widened as I leaned back slightly, trying to mask the weird dip in my stomach at the thought of her coming to my place for dinner—*and* meeting my family. "I'll be cheerful for the both of us."

Gracie rolled her eyes but stood, brushing the dirt off her jeans.

She held out her hand to me, and I let out a small chuckle as I took it.

Just can't stand being a damsel in distress for more than a minute, can we now, Gracie?

Her palm was smaller than mine, warmer too, and I didn't let go right away. "By the way, Gracie," I said softly, giving her hand a gentle squeeze, "happy early birthday."

She smirked, tugging her hand back as her cheeks flushed just enough to give her away. "Early birthday wishes don't count, y'know."

I tilted my head, matching her smirk. "Well, then I guess you'll have to stick around for the real thing."

That time, she didn't argue.

November 11th

Gracie

"Is your *boyfriend* coming to pick us up?" Bear asked, as I stood in front of the bathroom mirror, attempting to curl the loose, flyaway hair around my face.

"He is *not* my boyfriend..." I shot back, my face already warming. "But yes, he's picking us up. So, get ready."

"I *am* ready," Bear grumbled, crossing his arms. "And for someone who's 'not your boyfriend', you sure are putting a lot of effort into how you look."

"My hair was messy," I said defensively, setting the curling iron down. "I don't want his parents thinking I'm some hobbit in the woods."

Bear rolled his eyes. "I think you're starting to care too much about what people think—especially him."

I turned to the mirror, catching my reflection.

My hair looked fine. More than fine now, actually. But the girl staring back at me didn't feel like me at all.

I adjusted the bandana tied in my hair—red, white, and blue (perks of having a Veteran's Day birthday)—and tried to push the nerves down.

Maybe Bear was right about me caring what they thought of me... of *us*, but he was also conveniently leaving out the full picture.

"I just don't want them thinking we're... y'know..."

Bear frowned. "Charity cases?"

I sighed, tearing my eyes from the mirror. "I just want to make a good first impression, okay? I already feel bad enough for crashing their dinner."

He didn't say anything, but I could tell by the way his shoulders were sagging that just being awake was draining on him. His IVIG infusions were tomorrow, and he always felt his worst the day before.

Maybe I was being selfish by dragging him along to this. Maybe I should've called Cole and canceled...

The truth was, though, I didn't *want* to cancel.

I mean, let's be real: I *never* wanted to. I just usually did. Because Bear came first.

But then my mind rebelled against me and replayed Cole and I's almost-kiss at Mary Anne's.

Something between us had changed that day, and I couldn't figure out if it was good or bad.

I didn't know if I liked him. I didn't know *what* I felt. All I knew was that the waters had gotten murkier the more time we spent with each other.

But if Cole ever remembered our history, I was almost positive he'd stop talking to me all over again.

Maybe that's why this whole thing felt so intoxicating for me. I knew it wasn't going to last, but I could at least let myself enjoy the journey a little. Even if it was wrong to build a friendship with him based on a lie.

Well, not a *lie*—just not the truth of who I was to him.

I wasn't ready to lose what we... were.

"Also, I thought *Emma* was the only one allowed in our house." Bear said, interrupting my thoughts.

Normally, *no one* was allowed over. It wasn't like I was dying to host some open house for people to judge the Lewis Zoo: featuring my divorced parents, sick brother, and the pathetic screw-up I was.

I'd learned pretty early on that most people only wanted to come over for a chance to gawk at the exhibit. But Emma was different.

It was nice. She never looked at my family with pity. Never pried or asked really personal questions. She just wanted to hang out with *me*. The real me—not the one with the messed-up family life.

But Cole and I? We didn't have that kind of history. As far as I knew, the second he pulled up to my house (if you could even call it that), he'd freak out and leave.

And I couldn't blame him if he did.

His family was clearly loaded. Meanwhile, my house looked like it was one gust of wind away from collapsing.

Who was I kidding?

If I were Cole, I wouldn't stick around either.

The thought left a sour taste in my mouth. Cole had been so insistent about today—something about it *being my birthday* and I *deserved a good day*. But maybe I was only kidding myself thinking this whole thing wouldn't end in disaster.

The doorbell rang suddenly, and my stomach did a nervous flip—not a full one, but just enough to make me pause in front of the mirror one last time.

"Just know," Bear called from behind me, his tone as dry as ever, "if he brings you flowers, I'm officially calling him your boyfriend."

I rolled my eyes, though the laugh that escaped was more nervous than amused. "Don't even *joke* about a thing like that. Grab your coat."

I took a deep breath, wiping my suddenly sweaty palms on my pants as I made my way to the door.

My fingers hovered over the doorknob for just a second too long, like I could buy myself a little more time. But no amount of stalling could prepare me for what came next.

I swung the door open, and there he was.

The porch light caught on the messy tumble of his dark curls, and he had on a flannel, the sleeves rolled up just enough to show the tan line on his forearms. His boots scuffed lightly on the wooden step as he shifted.

For a second, I was completely at a loss for words. There was something about the way the light wrapped around him, outlining the faint stubble on his jaw, that made it feel like the universe had slowed down just for this moment.

I hated that feeling, and it made my palms sweat even more than they already were.

Cole cleared his throat, the corner of his mouth twitching into a grin. "Hey, Gracie,"

My brain finally caught up to the moment, and I realized I was staring. *Great.*

I crossed my arms, trying to sound indifferent even as my heart was pounding against my ribs. "Before you say anything about our house," I blurted, "just know I warned you it'd be trashy. So, that's not my fault."

Bear groaned from behind me, his voice dripping with mock irritation. "What she means to say is, *Oh my gosh, hi. Thanks for the flowers.*"

Cole chuckled, completely unbothered by my comment. "I was going to say," he said, holding out the bouquet in question. Sunflowers... my favorite. *How the hell does he know that?* "That it's great to see you both. And these are for you, Gracie. Happy birthday."

My throat tightened.

"Thank you." I managed, reaching out for the bouquet. My fingers accidentally brushed his, and an unfamiliar warmth shot straight to my cheeks. "These are... nice. Really nice."

Bear let out a low whistle, finally pushing his way into the middle of me and Cole. "She's speechless. Wow. I guess it really *is* possible."

Cole laughed again, scratching the back of his neck as if the idea amused him more than it should have. "I wasn't sure if you were into the whole 'getting flowers' thing, and Heaven forbid you actually tell me. But they reminded me of you, and I... had an extra."

Ahh, yes. Back to the whole coffee thing.

Sure, I'd made a point to remember how he takes it (black with *exactly* two creamers) less than twenty-four hours earlier. But could you blame me? It was an easy order to remember.

And now here he was, extending an olive branch of his own with *flowers that apparently reminded him of me.*

Somehow, we'd stumbled from being mortal enemies to acquaintances... and now, we were in this weird gray area of...

I don't know *what* we were, or what bizarro world I was living in where I thought spending any time with Cole outside of work and school was a good idea, but here I was, genuinely *excited* for tonight.

"You guys ready to go?" Cole asked, his eyes drifting from me to my brother.

Bear grinned. "Oh, yeah. I can't wait for this disaster to unfold."

Chapter Eighteen:

I couldn't believe I was sitting in *the* Cole Brown's truck, on my way to a birthday party that he was throwing for *me*.

The whole thing felt surreal, like stepping into a movie where the plot twist hadn't hit yet.

The inside of the cab was nothing like I'd expected and somehow everything I should've known it would be.

The cracked vinyl bench seat had clearly seen better days, but was broken in just the right places—like a pair of worn-out boots. And an old tape deck with a still-intact radio sat above a dog-eared fishing magazine tucked into the pocket below.

I ran my hand over the edge of the door panel. "You know," I started, "I think I might actually be obsessed with this truck."

Cole glanced over, his hand resting casually on the gear shift. A small, lopsided smile tugged at his lips. "Yeah? She's old, but she's got personality."

"How'd you get her?" I couldn't resist quickly adding, still joking, "If you can even *remember*, that is."

His grin faded for just a second (a blink-and-you-miss-it kind of thing) before settling into something more neutral.

"Funny," he said flatly.

Regret hit me immediately. I hadn't expected him to react like that. Although, I guess I understood how he felt. I'd be mad if I couldn't remember anything about myself either.

"Sorry. I didn't mean to... It was a stupid joke. I'm sorry."

"Nah, it's fine." He waved it off, glancing back at the road. "You're right. My memory sucks right now."

I fidgeted with the hem of my denim top, unsure if I should let it drop, but Cole must've caught onto the hesitation in my silence because his voice softened and he said,

"But I do remember that story. It's not much of a one, though. My dad bought her when I was a kid. We were supposed to fix her up together, but..."

He trailed off, before finding the words again. "But he died before we could finish. He was a cop. Died in a DV dispute. The husband was on drugs, threatening to kill his wife. My dad jumped in front of the bullet before it could hit her."

He paused, his jaw tight. "Died instantly... a *hero*. That's what everyone says, anyways."

Even *more* guilt overtook me. "Cole, I—"

"I don't remember him, Gracie," he cut me off. "Not his laugh, not his voice, not even the little things. Just one memory of us fishing. And the only reason I know about fixing up this truck is because my mom told me.

237

That's it. The truck's the closest thing I have to him, besides a damn mug I have at home. I can't even picture his face without a photo."

The cab of the truck suddenly felt smaller. I swallowed hard, trying to find the right words, though I wasn't sure they even existed.

"I am so, so sorry, Cole. I didn't know. I mean, I know he died, but... I'm sorry. I can't imagine how hard that must be."

He shrugged, but the motion was stiff. "It's fine. It was a long time ago, and like I said, I can't even remember it. But this truck... it helps, I guess. Makes me feel like I've got a piece of him, even if the memories are gone."

I looked at him then—like, *really* looked at him.

I'd always thought of Cole as this untouchable guy. The perfect life, perfect family, perfect, shiny future playing football... But in that moment, he wasn't *untouchable*.

He was human. And he was hurting.

And I *wanted* to fix it for him. Even though I didn't really know how to.

"I kind of get it," I said after a while.

He glanced over. "What do you mean?"

"I mean, I don't really see my dad much. He's not... gone, not like your dad, but in a way, he kind of is. He's always working. Always too busy to notice what's going on at home."

Cole stayed silent.

"Growing up, I had to be the 'man of the house'. It was lonely. It still is. And it's hard not having someone who understands that, who's gone through that."

His expression softened. "I understand," he said quietly.

I gave him a small smile. "I know you do."

The truck slowed as Cole pulled into his driveway. The house looked cozier at night, with warm porch light spilling onto the steps, glowing against the November air.

He killed the engine and unbuckled his seatbelt, flashing me a grin, like he'd just pushed all the heavy stuff about his dad into a box, locked it, and thrown away the key. *Holy hell, he's just as bad as I am.*

"Ready to finally meet the circus?"

I laughed softly, wondering how I hadn't noticed the similarities between us before. "Ready as I'll ever be."

Bear hopped out first, but Cole stayed behind, his hand brushing against my lower back as he guided me toward the door.

The touch was borderline not even there, if I were being honest, but it sent my stomach dipping in an oddly intoxicating kind of way.

He opened the front door, and even though I'd been in his house about a million times over for FFA practice, the scent of home still hit me unexpectedly—a mix of cinnamon, pine, and something vaguely buttery.

It was the kind of smell that made you want to curl up on the couch with a blanket and never leave.

Inside, a petite woman stood at the kitchen counter, her platinum blonde hair swept into a loose ponytail.

A man was behind her, his arms wrapped loosely around her waist while he whispered something in her ear that made her laugh softly.

At the sound of us shuffling further into the room, the man glanced over his shoulder, his expression lighting up the second his eyes landed on us.

"Gracie!" he said, his smile wide as he disentangled himself from who I assume was Cole's mom and rounded the kitchen island.

I knew Cole and his stepdad weren't biologically related, but in my opinion, you never would have guessed it. They shared the same easy grin, muscular build, and dark hair.

But as I was noting even *more* similarities between them, movement towards me flicked across my peripheral vision.

I barely had time to register what was happening before Cole, catching on immediately, stepped in closer to me. "Uh, Peter—" He reached out as if to intercept.

But Peter was already there, his arms opening wide. "It's so great to finally meet you!" he said, wrapping me in a hug.

My muscles tensed instinctively, a familiar wave of discomfort prickling at my skin.

I expected the worst. After all, that was all I'd ever known.

And yet...

His hug wasn't like what I'd expected. It wasn't overbearing or suffocating or unwanted. In fact, I knew if I wanted to, I could break away at any time. But I didn't. Because it was warm... and nice.

When the hug ended, I felt a slight shift in Cole beside me—his hand brushing my back, hovering for a second as if checking if I was okay.

To my surprise, I realized I *was*.

"And you must be Bear!" He turned to my brother, wrapping him in an equally enthusiastic hug.

Bear, who wasn't exactly a fan of physical affection either, but for entirely different reasons, looked caught off guard but didn't pull away.

"Nice to meet you, sir," he mumbled, a hint of a smile tugging at his lips.

Cole's mom wiped her hands on a dish towel and came over next. She hugged Bear first before turning to me. *That hug wasn't bad either.*

"It's so nice to finally meet you both!" she said, holding me a second longer than Bear. "And Gracie, happy birthday, sweetheart."

"Thank you, Mrs. Brow—" I froze mid-word. *Crap, crap, crap.* Cole didn't go by his stepdad's last name, but his mom and sister did.

Heat rushed to my face as I realized my major mistake.

Way to go, Gracie. Bring up her dead husband in the first five seconds of meeting her. Great start.

"Sharon's just fine, dear," she said kindly, her smile never falling. "You're family now."

I let out a shaky breath; grateful it wasn't as big a deal as I thought it'd be. "Thank you... Sharon."

Bear shot me a look that screamed *close call* as we followed everyone to the table, and I was suddenly glad he was there right alongside me, jumping into the deep end.

Meeting the parents, even just as... friends, was its own kind of personal hell.

As I slid into a chair, Cole's hand brushed against my thigh before settling on the back of my chair.

The movement was casual, (and kind of cocky, if you asked me) like he was hoping it'd make my heart do a somersault.

Good news: it did.

And suddenly, all I could think about was how close his fingertips were to my shoulder.

If I leaned back *just* enough...

"And this," Cole said. My gaze shot back to his, a blush creeping up my face as if he could hear my thoughts or something, "is my little sister, Chloe."

241

At the end of the table sat a small girl with blonde curls, her attention focused on her silverware as if it were the most interesting thing she'd ever seen in her entire life.

I smiled, hoping that she wouldn't notice I was going slightly hormonal on her literal older brother. "It's nice to meet you, Chloe."

She barely looked up.

Wonderful, I thought wryly. *Now I'm offending the kid too.*

"You'll have to excuse her," Sharon said, her tone apologetic as she settled into her seat. "She hasn't been much of a talker lately..."

I glanced at Cole, catching the slight tension in his jaw. His arm twitched behind me for a second before he relaxed again.

"No worries, Mrs. B... *Sharon,*" I said quickly, my cheeks flaming again as I stumbled over the correction. "I understand."

Luckily, the conversation quickly shifted to lighter topics—school, sports, and everything under the sun. Sharon passed me a basket of rolls, and I tried to focus on the weather and whatever else they were saying.

But every time Cole moved, I felt it.

The slight brush of his fingers against my hair. The warmth radiating from him. The way he leaned in to whisper something about how Peter always ate too many of his mom's homemade rolls.

I laughed softly at it all, but my voice felt distant in my ears. My thoughts were a jumbled mess, and every time I glanced at him, I got lost in the curve of his smile or the way his eyes crinkled at the corners.

What is happening to me?

"Gracie?"

"Huh?" I blinked, realizing Sharon had just said something to me.

"I was just asking how old you are now," she said with an amused smile as she handed me a dish of mashed potatoes.

"Oh! Seventeen," I replied, my face burning.

"Ahh, same age as Cole, then," Peter observed, leaning back in his chair as he took a sip of his drink.

"That reminds me..." I turned to Cole, trying to regain my composure. "We never talked about when *your* birthday is."

His cheeks flushed slightly, and he gave an awkward laugh. "Oh, well..."

"August 20th," Sharon interjected, a knowing glint in her eyes.

I blinked as my stomach twisted with a weird mix of surprise and regret.

I'd *missed* his birthday.

And I actually *cared* that I had.

"Yeah, that's it," Cole muttered, his free hand raking through his hair.

Across the table, Bear's brow furrowed as he adjusted himself to see over the coloring book that Chloe had snuck to the table with her. "Amnesia really makes you forget all that?"

Cole's eyes suddenly lit up realizing this was the "in" he'd been waiting for to connect with my brother. "Yeah, it's crazy, seriously," he started, a dopey grin spreading on his face.

"I've got this thing called acute retrograde amnesia, which means everything before my accident is gone. It's like my brain just hit the reset button. I still remember how to do the basics, like reading or, you know, using the bathroom," he added with a slight chuckle, "but all the personal memories aren't there anymore."

Bear pursed his lips in thought. "Do you know if you'll ever get your memories back?"

Cole hesitated, his gaze flickering briefly to me before settling on his plate.

There was something in his eyes, like he was searching for something, and I was the only one with the answer (for some reason).

"I'm... not sure just yet," he said finally, his voice softer, "I hope so, though."

Then, out of nowhere, Chloe piped up. "I hope you don't get them back," she said, not even looking away from her coloring book. "You're a lot nicer to me now."

She didn't say another word for the rest of the night.

After dinner and Chloe had gone to bed, I stayed behind with Cole in the kitchen.

From the other room, I could hear Sharon and Peter with Bear on the couch, lost in conversation.

You were really a hockey goalie? That's so cool!

I wish I were that flexible.

What's your favorite class in school?

I glanced back at Cole, who was already stacking plates by the sink.

"I'll help with the dishes," I said, stepping closer.

"You don't have to," he replied automatically, glancing at me with a flicker of surprise at the offer.

"I *want* to, dummy." I grabbed a sponge and flicked on the tap, letting the warm water run over my hands. "You don't just get to throw me an entire birthday party and expect me not to help with cleanup. That's not how this works."

Cole smirked as he handed me a plate. "You're stubborn, you know that?"

244

"And *you're* annoying." I shot back, grinning. "Must be part of your stupid charm."

"Did *the* Gracie Lewis just give me a half-assed compliment?"

I let out a breathy laugh. "Don't get used to it."

I stole another look at him, wondering why he'd stopped laughing beside me, only to find that he wasn't looking at me anymore. His jaw was tight as he rinsed a dish, and I could only imagine that the Chloe thing from earlier was still bothering him.

I got where she was coming from, though. I used to hate Cole before too.

Even still, I didn't have to live with him. Chloe *did*. And that made the healing process a whole of a lot harder.

"She'll get there," I said softly.

He shook his head, the corners of his mouth pulling into a faint frown. "You heard her. She's *scared* of me."

"What I *heard*," I countered, "was that she can see how hard you're trying now and loves you for it. Even if she doesn't know how to say it yet."

He didn't respond right away, his hands moving absently as he scrubbed another plate.

"I just... I want to be better for her. She's my little sister, you know? And she deserves an older brother she feels safe around, not..." His voice trailed off, and he swallowed hard.

"You're not that guy anymore, Cole."

For a minute, the kitchen was quiet except for the sound of water running over the dishes. Then, in a quieter voice, he said, "You don't have to stay and help. You could be out there, enjoying your birthday."

I looked over at him, his face half-lit by the warm glow of the kitchen light overhead, how perfect this night had been, how perfect *he'd* been... and then it hit me. "I *am* enjoying it."

Really truly, I was.

A small, almost relieved laugh escaped him. "Me, too."

When the last plate was dried and put away, I finally turned to face him, leaning back against the counter.

To my surprise, he was already standing back just a little, his eyes fixed on me.

"Tonight was really wonderful," I said softly, "Thank you."

He shrugged casually, his expression turning playful again. "*Ahh*, and that's where you're wrong. The night's not over yet."

I laughed. "What else could there possibly be?"

A mischievous smile formed on his face, and he grabbed a towel, drying his hands before tossing it over his shoulder and holding out another one for me.

Then, he reached into the fridge and pulled out a small box wrapped in pastel paper that shimmered under the kitchen light.

He turned back to me with a grin. "Come with me,"

I snorted but followed to the back porch anyways.

The crisp air wrapped around us as Cole lowered himself onto one of the steps, patting the spot beside him.

I hesitated for a second before easing onto the step, our legs brushing as I settled.

The contact was quick, almost nonexistent, but it sent the best kind of shockwave through me. Like the space between us (whether physical or mental) was shrinking as the universe nudged us closer together.

Warmth radiated from him, and I decided I liked it even *more*.

More than I should've, probably.

He sat the box down in his lap, his fingers tracing the bow, like he was trying to gather his thoughts.

"So, what's the deal with that?" I prompted, trying to push any rebellious thoughts of him (and me and him *together*) away.

His smile was small, almost shy. "Close your eyes and find out."

I rolled my eyes, but obliged, trying to steady my breath as the sputter and hissing of a matchstick being struck sounded, followed by the faint crackle as it caught fire.

Warm, soft light danced through my closed eyelids, and the faint, earthy scent of smoke filled my nose.

"Okay, on the count of three you can open your eyes, okay? One... two... three!"

My eyes flew open, revealing the open box with a tiny birthday cake inside. The candles flickered, the flames casting soft shadows on his face, giving him an almost ethereal glow.

That's when he began to sing, "Happy birthday to you..."

And it was in that moment when I realized that I could sit here with him forever—just listening to him sing, or talk about everything and nothing at all.

It was more than I ever imagined my birthday would or *could* be.

When he finished, he leaned closer, his breath brushing against my ear. "Make a wish, Gracie."

I closed my eyes, but this time, I didn't wish for anything.

Because everything I could've ever wanted was right beside me.

Chapter Nineteen:

NOVEMBER 13TH

Well... as of today, Cole was coming to one of our actual Vet Science practices. Asking him had felt like a fever dream—probably because it happened at two in the morning.

I'd woken up to a text from him that said, *"Absolutely! I'll see u there"* and immediately panicked, scrolling up to confirm what I already knew. Sure enough, there it was: my late-night message practically begging him to come. *Fan-freaking-tastic.*

As much as I hated my sleep drunken screw-up, shamefully practicing with Cole for State in secret wasn't exactly ideal either. At least this way, everything was out in the open.

Well... sort of.

After today, Emma and Bear would be in the loop. There was no going back after this.

It was easy when it was just me and Cole. But now? I was bringing more people into it, and the thought was terrifying.

I hovered outside the ag. science room, as my stomach churned with guilt and nerves.

If I can just get this over with, then everything will be fine. Well, hopefully, anyways.

The sound of footsteps echoing down the hall made my chest tighten even more. I didn't need to turn around to know it was him. "Gracie! Hey!"

I glanced over my shoulder just in time to see Cole jogging over, his brown hair a little messy, like he'd been in a hurry to catch me. I couldn't help the corners of my mouth twitch upward into an almost smile.

He's such a dork.

But before I could savor the moment, or even think about the consequences of my actions, I blurted out, "I need to tell you something."

His expression shifted, his smile fading slightly as he instinctively stuffed his hands into his pockets. "Sure," he said carefully, like he wasn't sure where this was going. "What's up?"

I opened my mouth to explain myself, but suddenly, the words caught in my throat.

There had to be a way to justify hiding him away from my *best friend and brother* for the past couple of months—something that wouldn't sound awful, or make me look even more selfish than I was already by talking to him while he couldn't remember our history.

But no bright ideas came to mind, so instead I said, "Nobody knows you're on the team yet. I've kind of... been keeping it a secret."

His eyebrows rose, but he didn't say anything.

"It's not—" I stammered, trying to find the right words. "It's not be-cause I'm embarrassed by you or anything. I just... I wasn't sure it was the right time to say something before. That's all."

Cole studied me, and for a second, I thought he was going to press me for a better reason.

Instead, he just let out a soft exhale. "Okay," he said finally, though his voice was quieter than usual. "I mean, I kind of figured... it's not like people were lining up to be my friend before the accident. I know it's going to take time for people—" he hesitated, "—for *you* to trust me. And that's okay. I get it."

He didn't sound angry, thankfully. But that didn't mean it probably didn't hurt.

I bit the inside of my cheek, guilt twisting inside my gut.

I guess that's just what happens when you try to be friends with me. I ended up disappointing the hell out of people.

He must have seen my face drop, because Cole, ever the saint he so clearly was, quickly added, "Gracie, trust me. I get it. We have a weird history together."

There it was again.

Our history.

I'd been using that line on him since the accident, and at first, I thought it was well-deserved. But now, I didn't know what was up or down anymore.

I mean, how much more was the guy supposed to do before I fully trusted him? Throw me *another* birthday party?

To be fair, though, I couldn't just get rid of the memories *I* had of him.

He was still the guy who'd spilled my secret to the world in eighth grade or locked me in a barn or made fun of my brother for just existing...

Everyone else was willing to move on. They cared about who he was now—the one who stood up to bullies, who threw birthday parties and was genuinely "better."

But better wasn't enough for me. Better didn't erase what happened.

I blew out a frustrated sigh suddenly. "Look, it's not about you, okay? It's about... *I don't know*, timing?"

He tilted his head, his eyes searching mine. "*Timing*," he echoed, like he was testing out the word. "That's what this is?"

I nodded quickly. "Yeah."

But even as I said it, I knew that wasn't it.

It was about keeping control—about not letting anyone get too close. Cole wasn't just a person I could plug into my world without consequences. He was a risk.

And I was too scared to make that jump.

"You think you're protecting yourself," Cole said quietly, after a minute. "But you're just shutting everyone out. Me, them... *yourself*. And I don't know how to prove to you that I'm not the same guy I was before. I don't know how to make you believe in me."

The worst part was that he wasn't wrong. The truth was, I didn't know how to let him in and not expect the worst.

I wanted to believe I could trust people, that I could trust *him*. But it was hard.

Keeping my guard up... *expecting* to be screwed over... it meant I couldn't get hurt. Because nobody could let me down.

"I—" I started, but no good words came to me.

I wanted to explain to him the type of girl I really was, *why* this was so hard for me. I wanted to tell him, *I'm trying. I want to trust you, I really do.*

But no matter how much I pushed, I couldn't bring myself to do it.

251

Cole stepped closer to me, his voice softening. "It's okay," he said. "You don't have to explain. If you're not ready, you're not ready. I'll wait."

He was so calm about it, so *patient*, and it made me want to scream—not at him, but at myself.

Why couldn't I just meet him halfway? Why couldn't I stop being so *stuck*?

The whole school knew me as "Slutty" or as a "freak"—I just wanted to seem normal in somebody else's eyes for once.

But of course, I was ruining that too.

He turned to leave without another word, and that's when regret swelled inside of me. Before I could even think about what I was doing, my hand shot out, my fingers wrapping around his wrist.

"Wait."

He froze.

Slowly, he turned to face me, his eyes meeting mine.

The heat rushed to my face so fast I thought I might puke as my brain scrambled to catch up to my mouth. "I... I want you to stay,"

I couldn't explain to him why I was the way I was, or why I couldn't let him in—at least not without him thinking I was a freak. But at least I could do *this*. And this had to be something, right?

His lips twitched, the hint of a smile softening his face. "Then I will," he said simply.

I nodded, looking away as I yanked my hand back like his skin had burned me.

Without another word, I pushed the door open to the ag. science room, praying that Cole couldn't notice how badly my hands were shaking.

Inside, Bear and Emma were talking in the corner, but the second we walked in, the conversation stopped cold.

Their eyes locked on us, and I bit my bottom lip, the last shred of calm I had jumping ship. *Off to a great start already, aren't we?*

I cleared my throat, hoping the heat creeping up my neck wasn't as obvious as it felt. "Okay, you guys, listen up," I said, forcing artificial confidence into my voice. "I have an announcement to make."

I glanced at Cole, and he gave me the smallest nod, like he was telling me it'd be okay. *At least he's on my side before this all goes to hell.*

"Cole's officially joining the team. It was Principal Hawkins' idea to start with, but I... think he'll make a great addition to the team too."

I paused, waiting for some sort of response. But none came.

No Emma fangirling about "finally getting to be a part of the Cole drama". No Bear shooting me an *I told you this would happen* look.

Nothing.

"And that's... it," I finished awkwardly, shifting on my feet. "So, yeah. Welcome him. Or don't. Whatever."

That's when the silence in the room popped like a bubble.

Bear snorted, not bothering to hide his laughter, and Emma just rolled her eyes, a smirk tugging at her lips.

"What?" I asked defensively, crossing my arms.

Emma covered her mouth as she giggled. "Gracie-girl, you do realize we've known this for *weeks*, right?"

"Yeah," Bear added. "Principal Hawkins asked us first before asking you. You know... just to make sure you didn't try to kill him during a competition or something."

I blinked. *Wait, what?*

All the stressing, all the guilt of going behind everyone's backs, the whole big deal I'd made about this... it had all been for *nothing*?

I shot Cole a look, half-expecting him to be as shocked as I was, but instead, he just grinned. "Sorry, President Gracie. Looks like your big surprise is a bust."

"As I have said *many* times," I started, quickly shaking off the surprise and tossing Cole a well-deserved glare as I moved to sit down. "I'm not the president. Emma is."

Everyone else followed my lead, Cole grabbing a chair next to me.

I tried to ignore the way my heartrate picked up at that.

"In this democracy, I think we get to vote," Bear said, smugly.

"*Fine*," I shot back. "Let's take a vote, then."

Right on cue, Emma pulled out her FFA binder, flipping to the first page and reading dramatically, "The rules state that the president must be unanimously voted in, yada yada, so on and so forth..."

"Should I get the ballot box?" I interrupted, arching an eyebrow.

Emma smirked. "No need. Cole, would you like to do the honors?"

He laughed as he adjusted in his seat. "What I think she means to say, Gracie, is that, we all collectively agree that our vote is for you."

My cheeks burned as I looked at him.

"You have such a hunger for world domination and power. This job is perfect for you!" he added, giving me a soft nudge.

"I—"

Bear cut me off, his tone uncharacteristically serious now. "Gracie, you're the glue that holds this team together. You've got the drive; you've got the determination... You're the best choice."

Cole nodded, growing just as thoughtful now. "You care about this team more than anyone else. Hell, you've been studying with me every week for *months* because you're so committed to this. You've already been leading us, whether you've realized it or not."

I met Emma's eyes about to protest some more, but she just smiled softly at me. "You've got a vision, Gracie-girl," she said. "And you've always been the one pushing us to be better. Learn to finally take the credit for once in your life."

As I scanned the room, my eyes flicking from face to face, my chest tightened.

I hated admitting it (even to myself), but I was terrified.

Terrified of screwing everything up, of failing so spectacularly that I'd let the entire team down.

My *friends* down.

What if I couldn't live up to everything they expected me to be? What if I made the wrong call and everything fell apart?

What if I was the reason we lost everything we'd worked so hard for?

"When have we ever steered you wrong?" Emma asked softly, breaking through my thoughts.

I opened my mouth to reply, but the *truth* was, they never had. None of them.

They all believed in me.

And maybe I could start believing in myself too.

"Alright. I'll do it."

Chapter Twenty:

NOVEMBER 16TH

C ole

I didn't fit in with these guys the same way anymore, and admitting it to myself felt like swallowing broken glass.

Football was my thing. It still *was* my thing. I'd been counting down the days until I got cleared to practice again, holding onto this idea that everything would snap back into place once I was back on the field.

But now, standing here in the weight room, I couldn't shake the feeling that something was off.

It wasn't like I didn't love football anymore. I *did*. But ever since I'd woken up from my coma, being *just* "the quarterback" like everyone said I was felt like trying to wear a shirt you'd outgrown but couldn't bring yourself to throw away.

And to make things worse, Coach Williams kept giving me these looks—the kind that screamed, *step up and be the guy we need, Cole.*

He wanted me to rally the team together, to be the leader I used to be. But I wasn't that guy anymore—not entirely, anyway.

I stayed there, leaning against the weight room wall, watching the scene unfold around me.

Dylan and his friends were gathered around a barbell stacked with way too many plates, hyping each other up like they were trying out for a WWE audition, and a couple of the other guys were chucking groin protectors at each other.

You should be with them. I thought.

But instead, I hung back, feeling even more like an outsider than I already was.

"Crazy, huh?"

The voice made me jump, and I turned to see Max standing beside me.

I hadn't even noticed him walk over.

"Sorry, man," he said quickly, holding up his hands in surrender. "Didn't mean to sneak up on you. I was just saying—it's crazy that people can lift that much."

He nodded toward Dylan, who was now mid-lift, veins popping out of his neck like he was trying to deadlift the entire planet.

"Yeah," I said, managing a polite shrug. "Pretty crazy."

Max studied me for a second, then smirked.

I raised an eyebrow at him. "What?"

"Nothing. It's just... you're different now," he said, almost like he was amused. "You don't seem like you even want to be here anymore."

"*Not true,*" I said automatically, though it wasn't entirely a lie. "I do."

He gave me a look like he wasn't buying it, so I sighed, leaning my head back against the wall to let him know that he'd caught me.

"I still love football," I admitted. "But it's not everything for me any-more. Does that make sense?"

He slowly nodded.

We'd been hanging out more lately—small stuff, like catching up be-tween classes sometimes and now, we even ate lunch together with the rest of the team when I wasn't hanging with Gracie.

It wasn't like we were best friends again (not that I was much of a good friend to start with), but I wanted to try, I wanted to be *honest*.

I owed him that much.

"Look, I know you've got a lot going on," Max started. "But if you're not feeling it, you don't have to force it, you know? Coach can survive without you running the whole show all the time."

When I broke eye contact to steal a look at the ground, he cleared his throat and added, "But for real, man, I wanna see you at our last game. And not as a benchwarmer. In the stands. Have fun, live a little. Bring Gracie. Whatever it takes to get you there."

Gracie.

Just by hearing her name, my brain veered off the road like it didn't care that I was in the middle of a conversation with someone.

I could picture her clear as day—her nose scrunched in the way it did when she got annoyed at something, the way she smelled... like vanilla and flowers even though we worked in literal horse feces all day, every day.

And suddenly, focusing back on Max became impossible.

The thought of her was addicting. It was enough to make a man go insane.

And apparently, I wasn't hiding it well, because Max let out a low laugh like he already knew exactly where my head went.

"What?" I asked, raising an eyebrow.

"Nothing," he said, smirking. "I just never would've expected you and Gracie... *never mind*. I'm serious, though. Invite her. And maybe afterward, we can catch up. Like, really catch up."

I smiled then. "You got yourself a deal, Captain. I'll see you there."

November 17th

Gracie

I wasn't into football as much as I was to hockey, but that wasn't going to stop me from going and dragging my buzzkill of a brother along with me.

Originally, though, it had just been Cole and me planning to go. Not that he'd explicitly *asked* me or that I'd officially invited myself...

It all started with one of those ironic twists of fate that seemed to be happening a lot more lately.

I'd stayed late at school, trying to retake a test that I hoped would bump my grade up by two percent (from an A- to an A) because, yes. I was one of *those* girls who needed to maintain her 4.0 GPA.

As I was walking back to my car in the parking lot, I smelled the team long before I had even heard them—which meant that the odds of running into Cole were way higher if I slowed down *just* a bit...

So, I did.

Yeah, shame. Shame on me.

But sure enough, right on cue, Cole came jogging down the stadium steps, his messy hair plastered to his forehead in a sweaty, teenage guy way that *should* have grossed me out. But it didn't.

He caught me staring almost immediately, and to my surprise, instead of acting like he didn't know me in front of his "cool" teammates (not that he *would've*, although the old Cole might've), he grinned, changed directions, and headed straight for me.

"Gracie! Hey!"

I laughed, my pulse picking up as he got closer. "Hey, Cole."

He closed the gap between us faster than I'd expected. So much so that when he reached me, he skidded slightly against the pavement, stumbling right into me.

I braced for the inevitable—death by football player, *how fitting*.

My hands flew up instinctively, connecting with his chest.

But before I could fall straight on my ass, his hands shot to my waist, steadying me with a firm, warm grip that made my breath hitch defiantly.

Oh crap, oh crap, oh crap. What do I do?

Neither of us dared to move first.

My palms stayed pressed against him, mostly because I'd suddenly forgotten how to breathe at that point, while his hand lingered at my waist.

But I could have sworn that his fingers curled around me ever so slightly as if to hold me closer.

"Whoa, sorry about that," Cole exhaled.

"It's okay," I managed to croak out.

His gaze trailed down to where his hand rested on my waist, his smile shifting to something gentler.

Slowly, he tilted my chin up with his thumb as his eyes scanned my face. "You sure you're alright, Gracie?"

"Totally fine," I said finally getting a grip over myself and stepping back a half step, though my legs felt unsteady, "You just... caught me by surprise, that's all."

He let his hand drop, but for some reason, I still felt him... and maybe even *missed* being that close?

So why in the world did I just push him away, then?

"My apologies, m'lady," he teased, tipping an imaginary cowboy hat with a playful smirk, "I don't know what got into me there."

An uncomfortable silence fell over us suddenly—the kind that makes you hyperaware of every little sound. Cole shifted his weight, his gaze drifting to the ground as if he were searching for something else to say.

Which was *weird* because we never ran out of things to talk about. Ever.

I cleared my throat, desperate to fill the space with something. "So, umm, how was practice?"

The words tumbled out faster than I'd meant for them to, making me squeeze my eyes shut in hopes that the universe would have mercy on me and just erase this moment from both of our memories.

Thankfully, though, Cole's face relaxed at the question. "It was... fine," he said, though his tone sold him out.

I raised an eyebrow. "Just fine?"

"Well," he hesitated again, running a hand through his hair, which only made it look messier—and unfairly better, "Max wants me to go to their last game."

"And?"

"And I want to go to support him," he admitted, shrugging.

I clicked my tongue awkwardly. "Well, sports are fun. I love sports."

Cole snorted. "Oh, for sure. You're still a Vegas Golden Knights fan, right?"

I crossed my arms, a smirk tugging at my lips before I could stop it, "Good to know the amnesia didn't *fully* destroy your brain. At least you remember all the important stuff."

"Hey, I might have a few gaps, but I've got a knack for remembering the essentials. Always have been."

A flutter rippled through my stomach. *Am I one of those essentials?*

I pursed my lips, trying (but probably failing) to act like I didn't care about knowing the answer. *What does it matter to me, anyways?* "Good to know I haven't been completely forgotten about."

Cole grin deepened. "Oh, you're definitely not forgotten. You're practically tattooed on my brain, Gracie Lewis."

"Well then," I said quickly, trying to sound unbothered as I stepped back even further to put some much-needed distance between us before my body went all hormonal on him, "maybe I'll see you at the game, then."

His gaze lingered on me for a second longer than it needed to. "Maybe you will."

And then: *bam*. We were going together.

Our little group doubled by the time the game actually started.

Obviously, my brother was either coming with me, or I wasn't going at all. Leaving him home alone for an entire football game wasn't an option, which was the only other choice I had, thanks to my dad, who'd "picked up an extra shift at the restaurant" on his day to watch him.

Emma had somehow gotten roped into joining us too (probably the most excited of us all), even going as far as to bring pom-poms and foam fingers for all of us.

The stadium was packed when we finally managed to wrangle four tickets.

We couldn't have even imagined how crowded it would be there, even Cole, who, according to him, in the bits of his life that he actually remembered, had never been watching the audience—only the cheerleaders (which oddly made my blood boil to temperatures unnecessary for "just a friend").

And as for the rest of us, we'd never been "cool" enough to go to a game.

Eventually, we managed to squeeze into the last row of bleachers, crammed against a metal fence. And because God had a twisted sense of humor, Cole ended up sitting right next to me.

We hadn't talked since finding our seats, but I was painfully aware of every move he made—the way his laughter vibrated through the stands, the small adjustments in his spot, and how his shoulder would occasionally brush mine.

It was sending my already frazzled nerves into overdrive, and I could barely focus on the game—especially since Cole was so much more entertaining anyway.

Every so often, I'd catch him muttering under his breath, coaching the players as if they could hear him. His brow furrowed with intensity, and I could see the way his lips formed instructions: *Fake left. Watch the pass.*

It was oddly... adorable, in a way.

And it made me realize that this wasn't just about football for him; it was a piece of himself—something he *hadn't* lost from the accident. Which made it even harder *not* to like him for it.

NOT that I liked him! Obviously. That would be stupid of me. I mean to fall for my lifelong sworn enemy? Crazy...

"Gracie?" The warmth of his breath against my ear snapped me out of my thoughts.

"Hmm?" I tried to sound disinterested, even though it suddenly felt like someone was taking a hammer to my chest—one word, one word from him was all it took for me to lose my cool.

Damn me.

In one fluid motion, he draped an arm over the back of the bench, his gray eyes swirling with mischief, as if he knew exactly what he was doing to me.

My gaze betrayed me then, dropping to his lips before I could stop myself.

Do NOT stare at his lips! My brain screeched, and I pushed myself from him like he had burned me, sliding back until the metal fence dug into my side.

His lips quirked into a partly amused/partly questioning grin. "I'm going to the concession stand. Want anything?"

I blinked, the air finally returning to my lungs. *Just a normal, friendly request. Nothing to worry about...* "Oh... um, yeah. I could go for a soda, I guess."

"Come with me," he said, standing and offering out his hand. "You can pick what you want."

I hesitated, but it didn't last long.

Like I said. I was too busy being a hormonal teenager to even care about my pride anymore.

It was also in that moment, as we took the other's requests for snacks and made our way down the steps still hand in hand, that I knew if I didn't figure out what the hell was going on with me soon, I'd be completely screwed.

"So," Cole started as we neared the concession stand, "you were really in the zone up there. What were you thinking about?"

I felt my face turn bright pink.

Logistically, actually telling him what I *was* thinking would be "bad for the friendship" or whatever, so instead, I just blurted out the next best thing I could come up with in hopes it sounded semi-normal.

"I was just thinking about how into the game you are. I heard you back there, Mr. 'Fake Left, Fake Left'!"

He laughed, loosing up a little at the admission (was he worried that I was thinking something bad about him up there or something?) as he ran his free hand through his hair.

"Old habits die hard, I guess. But you know, I'm pretty sure we'd be winning right now if they listened to me."

"Obviously." I teased, quickly regaining my footing in the conversation. "The game's outcome rests entirely on your shoulders."

He grinned. "See? You get it."

As we reached the front of the line, I scanned the menu one last time. "What are you getting?"

"Probably just a hot dog." he replied, "Keeping it simple."

I snorted. "Bold of you to trust a group of teenagers working minimum wage with your culinary choices."

Cole laughed as he handed the cashier a bill to cover both of our orders. It wasn't a big deal. Or maybe it *shouldn't* have been a big deal.

Honestly, I never thought I'd see the day when I would *willingly* let a guy pay for me, let alone Cole freaking Brown. But today was just full of surprises, wasn't it?

Or maybe it was an entirely friendly thing to pay for my $1.50 drink, and I was just going insane.

I took the soda from him anyway. "Thank you," I murmured, wrapping my hands around it as normally as I could like my heart wasn't suddenly doing Olympic gold medalist gymnastics in my chest.

He smiled, and Lord help me...

As we made our way back to our seats, Bear was in the middle of telling what had to be his favorite story—the one he always swore was the funniest hockey game of his life.

"Okay, so there's a minute to go in the third period, right? Well, my team was down by one, so Coach pulled me. But to make matters *worse*, as I was skating to the bench, I wiped out in front of everyone, and the other team ended up scoring anyway. We never *did* get that extra attacker on the ice..."

When Bear finally finished the story, Cole was laughing so hard that he had to take a second to respond. But when he did, he clapped him on the back. "If I'd been there, I'd have gone down too. Solidarity, you know?"

Emma's smile grew as she ruffled Bear's hair. "As would I, Bear-Bear."

I stayed quiet beside them.

Emma's response to Bear didn't surprise me. She was my best friend, and at this point in our friendship, I knew everything about her. Of course she'd support my brother like that.

But Cole... Cole was good at this too. Not just being polite but actually caring.

It didn't feel like some rehearsed act he had to get through. He wasn't faking it. He just... *was*.

And that scared me.

Because this new version of him wasn't at all what I'd expected out of him.

He wasn't the boy I'd sworn I hated. He was kind. And thoughtful. And funny. And maybe a little too good at making me forget all the reasons I'd told myself this couldn't work out between us.

But was *this* real? Was *he* real? Or was it just some awful joke the universe had decided to play on me—dangling someone in front of me that I couldn't have, only to snatch them away when I started to believe in it?

This wasn't ever supposed to have happened—me falling for Cole, that was.

If that's what this even was.

People like me didn't get the guy, people like me got used and left behind.

That's how it'd always been.

I'd spent so long keeping myself locked up, pushing people away before they could get a chance to hurt me, and now, here I was.

Sitting next to the one person I knew could ruin me if I let him in.

And for some reason, I *wanted* to let him in.

But what if I did and he realized I had nothing to offer him? That I wasn't some shiny, perfect girl with everything figured out?

I was messy. Insecure. Full of failures I was trying so hard to hide, failures that he used to make fun of me for.

Failures that were disgusting.

Would he still want to be here if he saw all of that? If he remembered?

I just... couldn't do this again. I couldn't let him in, knowing that the possibility of getting hurt again was looming over my head. It was too much. I couldn't...

"Gracie?"

My brain shut up then, making me realize that my head was buried behind my hands and I had physically shrunken myself as small as I could go against the chain link fence.

But when I looked up at him, with his gray eyes locked on mine, I wondered why I'd fought it for so long. Because the noise from my thoughts, the stadium... it was all gone. Everything but him had just disappeared.

"You see those guys down there?" he asked, nodding toward the field.

I nodded, slowly, trying to find some kind of snarky comeback to say like *"Obviously. I have eyes."* or *"What about them, stupid?"*

But the problem was, we'd spent enough time together these past few months for him to know my fronts. And always being "on" was getting pretty damn exhausting.

So instead, I just nodded, waiting for him to speak again.

"I used to be one of them," he said, his tone quieter now, almost wistful.

I bit my lip, raising an eyebrow at him as if to say, *"Okay. And?"*

His lips twitched in a small smile, but his eyes stayed serious.

Then, slowly, his hand brushed mine, almost like he was asking for my permission to have it turn into something more.

*I want it to be more. I want **us** to be more.*

I swallowed hard, my eyes dropping to where his hand now rested against mine like he was reading my mind.

His fingers waited a second before curling around mine, threading together like it was the most natural thing in the world.

"Sometimes," he said, "you just have to take the risk. Even if it's scary. Even if it doesn't make any sense. Because sometimes, it's worth it. And sometimes, you find out exactly where you're supposed to be."

The crowd around us erupted into cheers then, the bleachers shaking beneath us. Somebody had scored.

Probably us, since y'know... we were the home team. But suddenly, I didn't care enough to look at the scoreboard. I just let myself keep my hand intertwined with his.

I wanted to believe him. I wanted to believe that taking a risk could lead to something good, something real.

But deep down, there was this quiet, stubborn voice in the back of my mind still whispering that girls like me didn't get happy moments like this.

I wondered, though, what it would feel like to try. To stop running, stop hiding, stop fighting, and let myself fall. To let him catch me.

But I knew what that leap of faith would mean.

And that terrified me more than anything.

Chapter Twenty-One:

DECEMBER 25TH

C hristmas was a complete bust.

Bear and I had been promised about a thousand times over that we'd all be together as a family this year. But as the day dragged on, waiting for the door to open to reveal one (or both) of our parents turned out to be a complete joke.

There were no presents under the tree (that I'd set up by myself, by the way). Not that I was expecting any.

Between Bear's medical bills, Dad working every shift he could to stay blissfully ignorant about what was happening at home, and Mom doing... her thing, there wasn't much room for extra stuff.

I was okay with that, though.

What I *wasn't* okay with was the fact that this very well could've been Bear's last Christmas at the rate things were going, and no one was here for it.

I'd tried my best to salvage the day. I'd pulled up a recipe online for gingerbread houses and dragged our fold-up table out from behind the fridge, hoping that Bear and I could at least do something productive with our boredom.

But I was starting to think that even *that* had crashed and burned.

"Gracie," Bear started after putting the final touches on his third gingerbread house of the night: a two-story mansion complete with a gingerbread army lined up in perfect formation.

I glanced over at my own (arguably kind of sad in comparison) attempt of a home. The walls were layered with icing so thick that it was almost impossible to see the cookie beneath it.

But the universe must've had a sense of humor because no amount of frosting was going to save the leaning monstrosity... *or this day*.

"Yeah?" I replied, setting down the piping bag.

"This is kind of pathetic," he said bluntly, a small smirk tugging at the corner of his mouth.

I sighed. "I know."

He quieted, but I could see the gears in his mind turning as he fidgeted with one of the gingerbread men. "So, I was wondering..."

I had to curb my immediate impulse to laugh first and ask questions later.

With the seventeen years of experience I had in life (fourteen with my brother), any time someone started a sentence off with that phrase (*especially* Bear), we were all in for a wild ride.

Well, at least *I* was, being that we were still home alone... on Christmas day.

"Can I hang out at a friend's tonight?" he blurted out.

I blinked.

Of all the crazy requests he *could* have asked for, that was the last one I was expecting.

Not to say that he *didn't* have friends, because Heaven knows being known as the "sick" kid came with its perks in that regard... (thanks guilt and pity!). But he hadn't actually hung out with a friend in... what? A year? Two, maybe?

Had it really been that long?

"Please, Gracie? It's not like anyone will notice. Nobody else is here."

My gaze fell right back on the front door again.

To what? Prove him wrong? I knew I couldn't.

Mom wasn't flying in from God-knows-where, and Dad wasn't going to magically appear after swearing (yet again) that he wouldn't miss Christmas for anything.

And then back to Bear... He was trying to look hopeful, but I could see in his eyes that he was preparing for the inevitable: for me to say no.

It wasn't fair.

Nothing about his life had been fair.

His childhood had been chipped away piece by piece by doctor's visits, treatments, and a stupid disease he never asked for. He just wanted one day to be normal. To be a kid.

And I could understand that feeling better than anyone.

Being the "responsible one" in the family wasn't something I chose; it was something that had been forced on me.

I'd spent so much of my life trying to hold everything together, trying to make up for the love in this house that we didn't have.

But Bear didn't have to grow up like that, did he?

Why not give him the chance to do something fun? To "sneak" out of the house and hang out with his friend like a normal fucking teenager for once?

"Gracie?"

Do it. Just say yes. One time. He deserves that.

I bit my lip, all the things that could possibly go wrong swarming my mind.

He could forget to take his medication and get really sick again, he could choke on his food if it wasn't made properly, he could pass out somewhere...

But he would also never get today back.

And who's to say none of that stuff wouldn't just happen here anyways? At least at a friend's, he'd be socializing with someone his own actual age.

"Fine," I said finally, "But you have to text me. Every hour. And don't stay too late, okay?"

The doorbell rang, and I glanced toward it, pursing my lips as if to ask *seriously?* "You went behind my back and made plans anyway, didn't you?"

Bear shrugged, completely unapologetic. "Well, if you said no, I was thinking about jumping through the window."

I rolled my eyes, a grin spreading across my face. "I'd like to see you try."

He laughed. "I'll see you later. And thank you for this." he paused, a sly expression hitting his face as he opened the door, "I'd say I owe you one, but I already went to dinner with you and your boyfriend."

"He's *not* my boyfriend!" I shouted, laughing too as I grabbed a piece of cookie from the table and chucked it at him. It hit the door with a soft thud as it closed behind him.

It wasn't much of a Christmas, but maybe it was just enough for him.

And as for me? Well, I could handle being the adult. It's what I'd always done, after all.

When I'd let Bear go to his friend's, I hadn't realized just how lonely the house would feel without him.

I'd thought about watching a Christmas movie, but Netflix only wanted to shove cheery holiday specials in my face. Y'know... families around dinner tables, singing carols, unwrapping presents by roaring fireplaces, all while living happily ever after?

Yeah, no thanks. Not today.

Instead, I flopped onto the couch and opted for scrolling through Instagram. At least then, I knew I was safe with hockey game highlights and the occasional funny meme.

But then there was this one reel—a college football ref accidentally getting run over by a player (it looked a lot funnier than it probably was for the guy).

My mind went to Cole before I could stop it.

He'd probably find it hilarious, especially after how much he'd enjoyed that football game we went to a couple of weeks ago...

Bad idea, Gracie. Don't do it.

I scrolled past it quickly, already feeling the heat start to creep up my neck.

He'd sent me a few reels here and there before, I guess, but I'd never started the conversation. *Not once.* And I wasn't *that* pathetic to try and get one going myself, was I?

But the more I scrolled, the harder it was to stop thinking about it.

He'll like it.

He'll probably make that stupid laugh he always does—y'know, the one that starts off as just a little snort, like he isn't sure if he's even allowed to let himself enjoy the moment, before giving in and leaning into a full belly laugh... the kind that you feel no matter how bad of a day you're having...

I froze, my thumb hovering over the screen.

*Whoa. Okay, where did **that** come from?*

I sighed to myself, but before I could just delete the Instagram app altogether, I scrolled back up, found the reel, and hit send.

No big deal, right? Just a funny video. For Cole. Totally normal. Totally fine. Totally...

My phone buzzed almost immediately.

He'd "liked" the message.

***That's** it? That's all you're going to say? Jerk.*

I groaned and tossed my phone onto the cushion beside me, suddenly regretting every choice I'd made ever up until this point.

I would've been completely fine with an "LOL, that's hilarious" or "You know me so well, Gracie." Not just... a "like" and move on.

See, *that's* what I got for sending the first message. I seemed like a desperate loser who...

My phone buzzed again.

> **Cole: Haha, that's what I wish would've happened at the game a couple weeks ago.**

I stared at the screen, my heart doing a dumb little flip, as the corner of my mouth defiantly twitched up into a smile.

One text. That's all it took. Good God, I was a mess.

Then, another buzz.

> **Cole: Btw, Merry Christmas, Gracie. Did u have a good day today?**

Well, *that* smile didn't last long.

Maybe I should've just come out with the honest truth: that I was home alone, and my life was currently in shambles all around me.

The old Cole would've made fun of me for admitting *any* of that. But then again, the old Cole and I wouldn't have been talking.

Okay, let's be real. We wouldn't have even been *friends* if it hadn't been for the accident.

There was no telling when his memories would come back, and when that happened? I'd lose this... thing we had going for us. So, what was the harm of using him while I had him here?

Emma was in the Dominican Republic with her dad over the break, Bear was with his friend, I was *home alone on Christmas day* for crying out loud...

Oh, screw it. I quickly thumbed out a new text and hit send before I could overthink it.

> **Gracie: Honestly, today sucked. I'm Kevin Mc-Callister-ing up in this MOFO.**

> **Gracie: That was a *Home Alone* reference in case you didn't get it.**

> **Gracie: Sorry, I'm being a dork right now.**

My face reddened, and I set the phone down again.

Way to go, Gracie. Scare the guy, why don't you?

But before I could spiral too hard, my phone started buzzing. Not a text this time—a *call*.

I fumbled with the screen, already bracing myself for the absolute worse: Bear was stranded in a ditch somewhere, calling me to come rescue him... my parents were getting *another* divorce...

But it wasn't Bear.

Or my parents.

It was *Cole*.

For a second, my brain just short-circuited. I'd almost forgotten about how he'd insisted on getting my number "just in case of an emergency."

Apparently, to Cole, this was it: the grand moment he'd been waiting for.

Swiping to answer, I pressed the phone to my ear, trying to sound normal despite the fact that my heart was now jackhammering inside my chest. "Hello?"

"Hey."

And just like that, all my nerves started to untangle in the pit of my stomach.

I'd never been one for phone calls to *begin* with. In fact, there were probably still a few aunts and uncles waiting for a response back from voicemails they'd left me in *middle school*, but it was different with Cole.

I'd almost... *missed* his voice since school had let out for winter break? Crazy, I know.

"You're seriously home alone—by the way, yes, I understood the reference—on Christmas?"

He sounded shocked, honestly.

Oh, to have present parents...

I forced a small laugh. "Yep, that's me. Little Miss Kevin McCallister."

"Gracie..."

The way he said my name made my chest flutter in this weird, unfamiliar way, like I simultaneously wanted to hear it a hundred more times and tell him to shut up because I knew he was just feeling sorry for me.

"No, eww. Don't do that," I said, wrinkling my nose even though he couldn't see it. "I don't need your pity."

"It's not pity," Cole said, a laugh softening his voice. "I'm just thinking about how I'd feel if I were in your place. My parents... well, let's just say Christmas is kind of a big deal in my house."

That caught my attention.

I tucked my blanket tighter around my legs, surprising myself with the fact that I was genuinely curious to hear more about his homelife. "Yeah? Like how so?"

"We've been going at it since six this morning. At first, I thought it was to keep the magic alive for Chloe and stuff. But honestly? I think my mom and stepdad love it just as much. My mom's side of the family's been here since noon. That's why I couldn't call earlier."

He wanted to call me today?

My face heated, and I thanked every star in the sky that he couldn't see me right now.

"No worries," I said, trying to sound nonchalant. "Bear and I were *pretty* busy decorating gingerbread houses all morning anyway. I probably wouldn't have even noticed if you tried to call."

The second I said it, I wished I hadn't.

Great, now it sounds like I don't care.

It'd honestly be a miracle if by the end of this conversation, he didn't think I hated him.

But Cole, bless him—that car must've hit him into certifiable sainthood because he just laughed.

"Well, if you're not too wiped out from your very intense ginger-bread-making session, you should come over. We're about to start decorating sugar cookies *ourselves*. You can meet everyone. I'll pick you up."

I almost dropped the phone right then and there.

Cole was inviting me to his house (not unusual). But to meet his *entire* family? On Christmas? Was this normal? Was this what normal people did?

And was it bad that I *wanted* to spend Christmas with Cole freaking Brown?

Now there's a sentence I never thought I'd say.

"Okay," I said finally, the word wobbling on its way out. I cleared my throat, trying to sound more indifferent than I actually felt. "I mean, I'm not doing anything else, I guess. But *only* if the rest of your family is good with that."

In the background, I heard a high-pitched voice shriek, "Cole, catch me!" followed by a loud *oomph* as if they'd just launched themself at him.

"Addie," he said, chuckling. "I'm talking to Gracie right now, but I'll play with you in *just* a second."

A laugh escaped my lips too. Of course he was already the favorite.

Cole had this way of charming people—kids, adults, probably even goldfish—until they adored him. Versus me who literally had the energy of Wednesday Addams a good ninety-eight percent of the time.

"Sorry about that," he said, coming back on the line. "It's a little crazy here. Crazy in a *good* way. Don't freak out. I still want you to come."

Like I needed much convincing these days.

He could've openly admitted he was going to put poison in the icing, and I *still* probably would've come.

"Fine, you convinced me," I said, sighing dramatically for effect. "I'll come. *If* you pick me up."

I thought that was the end of it until he added, softer this time, "Oh, and Gracie?"

"Yeah?"

"My family loves you. You'll be just fine."

I stared at the screen long after the call ended, my heart doing this dumb, fluttery thing in my chest.

His family loves me.

How was I ever supposed to survive this?

Cole

Snow fell in soft waves, swirling under the amber glow of the streetlights as I drove through the almost vacant roads.

The rhythmic swish of the windshield wipers filled the silence, and for once, I didn't mind it. It gave me time to think.

Thank God Gracie had agreed to come over.

The idea of her spending Christmas alone didn't sit right with me—not because I had some moral obligation to make sure she wasn't lonely, but because it genuinely bothered me.

She deserved something good in her life.

She deserved... well, *everything*, really.

280

The funny thing was, I could tell myself all day about why I wanted her there. But deep down, I knew it wasn't just because we were friends. I *needed* being around her in a way that was kind of hard to explain.

She had this way of making me feel less... broken, like I wasn't as messed up as everyone else (including myself) thought I was.

Speaking of mess...

Christmas dinner with my family (in as polite of terms as possible) had sucked. No one knew what to say to me anymore, and that made everything awkward as hell.

Sure, I knew my reputation wasn't exactly stellar, but you'd think having *amnesia* would at least make them ease up a little.

Nope.

To them, I was still the same screw-up I'd always been—now, *I* just couldn't remember.

I'd spent most of the night pretending not to notice how everyone was avoiding me.

The adults didn't even bother hiding it, and my cousins (except for Addie, who'd decided I was alright, I guess) would've rather taken the monsters underneath their beds over me.

Getting banished to the kiddy table was just the universe's way of driving the point home: I didn't belong there.

It didn't matter how much I'd tried to change. In their eyes, I was still the kid who couldn't do anything right and only ever made bad decisions.

Yeah, that was me.

By the time dinner was over, I'd wanted to slink back into my room and hide away from the world forever.

But I knew how much Mom had worked on making sure the night was perfect for everyone, so I disappeared into the kitchen with a bunch of dirty plates and cups instead.

Cleaning up seemed like the perfect excuse to escape everyone. Anything to avoid the conversations I knew they didn't want to have with me (the feeling was mutual, by the way).

"So... are you back to playing football yet?"

"The weather's been nice lately..."

"Do you really have amnesia? Or is that a joke?"

Yeah, being stuck in the kitchen alone was better.

For *everyone*, probably.

I gave myself permission to let my mind wander as I stacked the plates into the sink, pretending just for a second, that Gracie was there. That she'd rolled up her sleeves, playfully shoving me to the side and telling me I was doing it all wrong.

It was stupid, maybe. But it made me feel less alone.

Just as I was elbow-deep in soapy water, debating with "Gracie" about whether or not *Die Hard* was a Christmas movie (I was obviously losing the argument), Grandma Ruth shuffled over.

She stuck around just long enough to hand me her dishes, her expression softer than the rest of the family's but still uneasy, like she wasn't sure what to say around me.

"Thank you, Cole," she murmured, "It's nice of you to help."

I nodded, not looking at her.

By now, I was used to the half-hearted politeness, and it was easier to just keep busy doing something no one could hate me for.

She hesitated, her fingers tightening around the edge of the counter for a second, and then she said it.

"You remind me so much of your dad."

But before I could even process that, she turned and left the kitchen, her footsteps fading into the other room like she thought she'd just handed me a compliment wrapped in a bow, something to make me feel better for spending Christmas basically alone.

It didn't.

The faucet was still running, the suds still clinging to my hands, but suddenly, I couldn't move... or even think.

How was I supposed to feel about that? Grateful? *Honored*?

I couldn't remember his laugh or how he smelled after work, whether he wore a tie to dinner or if he'd ruffled my hair on the way out the door.

I didn't know what his favorite Christmas tradition had been—or if he'd even liked Christmas at all.

And that's when the thought hit me aggressively out of nowhere, like I was homesick over it: *I want my life back.*

Not the life everyone said I'd ruined, but the one I couldn't remember.

The one where my dad was alive, and I was just a kid. A kid who didn't have to carry around the guilt of being the fucking family disappointment.

And maybe, selfishly, I wanted it back for Gracie too.

She deserved better than the guy who spent every waking moment trying to piece themselves back together.

If I could just remember, if I could just figure out who I was, I could be better for her.

I could be better for my dad.

I could be better for *myself*.

That's when my truck's headlights lit up her driveway, the snow crunching softly under the tires.

To my surprise, though, she was already outside, waiting for me in jeans and an oversized red sweater, with little reindeer and Christmas trees on it. Her dark hair was even pulled back with a matching bow.

Leave it to her to make me feel better. I thought, a smile already starting to overtake me.

I put the truck into park and reached over to pop the passenger door open for her. She climbed in quickly, her cheeks already pink from the cold.

"You didn't have to wait outside for me," I said, concern lacing my voice as I stretched my arm towards her, vigorously rubbing her thigh. She shivered.

"It's not *that* cold," she shot back through chattering teeth. Then more honestly, "I guess I just didn't want to be in an empty house for that long."

The way she said it so casually twisted something inside of my chest, but I tried to keep my voice light. "Next time, wait for me inside," I said, flipping on the heater. "You'll die from hypothermia out here."

She rolled her eyes, but a smile formed on her face. "Okay, *Mom*."

We drove in a comfortable silence, the streets quiet except for the steady hum of the heater. That is until we turned the corner, and suddenly, the night lit up.

At the end of the street, a house stood glowing, decked out in an insane amount of Christmas lights.

A giant inflatable snowman swayed in the yard, surrounded by plastic reindeer, glowing candy canes, a Santa waving from the porch, and "Jingle Bell Rock" blasting from a couple of hidden speakers on a loop.

Just as I was mumbling that their neighbors must love them, Gracie gasped, her eyes brightening. "Oh my gosh, I *love* Christmas lights."

I almost did a double-take.

Gracie, of all people, was not the kind of person I would've pegged to enjoy a holiday like Christmas.

Halloween, maybe. But *not* something that came attached to a man in a fat suit delivering "joy to the world."

When I glanced back over at her, though, I realized she wasn't kidding.

Her face had gone soft with wonder, her chocolate brown eyes reflecting the glow from the decorations as she rolled down the window and stuck her head out like a little kid.

The icy wind turned her cheeks even pinker, and...

I looked away, hard. Because the thoughts crowding in my brain weren't exactly *friendly* anymore.

"Look at that one!" she giggled as she pointed to the next house with an elf popping out of a present.

Fine. Fuck it. I thought suddenly as I turned back to face her fully.

If I was going to fall for her, I was at least going to enjoy myself as I did it.

I split my time between looking at her and the road as we drove. And if I wasn't worried about crashing us into a mailbox (and you know, getting into my second car accident in less than a year), I wouldn't have given a damn about traffic laws at all.

I'd never seen Gracie smile that big before.

And I... yeah, I kinda loved it on her, really.

"You should see your face." I teased, glancing at her, "You're like a little kid right now."

She pulled her head back in. "Christmas lights are just so magical. It's like... a little piece of the North Pole, right here in Cedar City."

"If I'd known this would make you so happy, I would've taken you on a tour of them forever ago." I joked.

She nudged me playfully. "Well, now you know. Congratulations. You've unlocked the secret to my happiness."

"Good to know," I chuckled. "Maybe I'll have to step up my decorating game next year. I've got to keep up with the competition."

A mischievous look glinted in her eyes. "Just don't fall off the roof and lose your memory again. You're not exactly known for your good luck with that, y'know."

I laughed, shaking my head. "I promise to stay firmly on the ground. I think one memory reset is more than enough for a lifetime."

"Good," she replied, covering her mouth as she giggled again. "I don't want to have to reintroduce myself all over again. I might just have to start making up stories about 'who you actually are' or something."

"Oh yeah?" I said, smirking. "What would you say?"

"That... your name is actually Frank, and you used to be an FBI agent who gave it all up to live a humble life in the middle of nowhere Utah."

I burst out laughing. "Where were you when I was in the hospital? *That* would've been fun to wake up to."

She grinned, leaning back in her seat. "Next time you decide to walk out into traffic, call me first, and I'll be there."

I snorted. "Yes, ma'am."

For a second, everything (especially our conversation) felt... easy. Like *this* was supposed to have been my life all along.

I'd felt like I had to force a lot of things into place since the accident: football, school, my family... but never this.

Never Gracie.

And I wanted that feeling to last as long as it could.

Suddenly, an idea popped into my mind. "Oh, hey! There's this street around here... Christmas Lane. It's supposed to have the best light display in town. You've heard of it, right? We could..."

She stiffened so fast it was like I'd flipped a switch.

Her face dropped as she turned toward the window, the light from a passing streetlamp catching the red creeping up her neck. "Umm, no. It's okay. I got a little carried away anyway."

I instinctively opened my mouth to apologize. *For what?* I couldn't tell you. I just knew that she looked like she was three seconds away from bursting into tears.

But before I could say anything, she let out a shaky breath.

"It's just..." she paused, like she was deciding whether or not to say more. Then, it all came spilling out. "Before my brother got sick, my family would go to Christmas Lane every year. It was our thing. Now we don't even spend Christmas *together*."

Her voice cracked in a way that made it feel like someone had taken a bat to my chest. *Please don't cry...*

I don't want you to be upset.

"I wish I could go back," she whispered, her eyes on her lap now. "It was way easier being a kid. Everything was so perfectly simple. Christmas used to be magical, and now, it's... not."

I didn't know what to say. Words felt useless, and I wanted to physically take her pain away and promise that she'd never be alone again. Not when I was around.

But I also knew Gracie and knew that she didn't want someone to fix it. She just wanted someone to listen.

I reached over and gave her hand a quick squeeze. "Gracie, I'm sorry. I didn't know."

She swiped at her eyes with the back of her hand. "It's fine. It's stupid to cry over it. I don't want to talk about it anymore, okay?"

I nodded, understanding how she felt more than she realized.

I was the same way about my dad. It was hard to talk about—knowing that the memories (ones I didn't even have to *begin* with) were better than the reality we lived in.

She didn't say anything else for the rest of the drive, and I didn't push.

Instead, I took the long way back to my house, driving her past neighborhoods I knew had decent Christmas lights. Not Christmas Lane, (obviously), but enough to fill the quiet with something warm.

Every so often, I'd glance over at her.

The lights outside flickered across her face, catching the tiny curve of her lips when she found a display she liked. And for someone who'd just poured her heart out to me, she looked... peaceful.

The kind of peaceful that made me want to *keep* driving, even if it was all the way to fucking *Arizona* just so she wouldn't lose it.

By the time I pulled into my driveway, parallel parking between my aunt's minivan and one of my cousin's cars, I couldn't even imagine going inside.

I wished I could just freeze this moment. Just hit pause and stay right there, with her next to me.

I let the truck idle for a second longer than I should've, hoping she'd start talking again. I didn't care what it was about: something random, something she thought was dumb... I just liked hearing her voice.

"You don't look too excited to get in there," she finally teased softly.

Thank God she said something.

I gave an apologetic smile (although how sorry could a guy *really* be for talking to a girl as complex and interesting as her?), before turning my body towards her.

"My bad. I was just... thinking."

She smirked, clicking her tongue. "Ah, a dangerous pastime."

I laughed, the tightness in my chest easing up just a little.

Might as well just go in there and rip the band-aid off then.

But as I reached for the door handle, she stopped me, her hand brushing against my arm. "Hey."

Her voice was different now... softer, almost shy, which was weird for her. But then again, this whole *night* had been weird for the *both* of us.

You better not let yourself fall for the only friend you have right now. You know how she feels about you. Move on.

For a second, her eyes held mine before darting away. "You'll be great in there," she said quietly. "And if there are any stragglers who can't accept that you're different now, they're complete morons. So, who cares what they think anyways?"

I nodded, trying to swallow down the lump forming in my throat.

"Thank you, Gracie," I murmured.

But when I said her name, it hit different. Like I wasn't just thanking the part of her I was "just friends with." I was thanking *her*. All of her.

She looked up at me again, and the space between us caught on fire.

Her hand was still resting against my arm.

I should've pulled away. Instead, I leaned in.

Barely an inch.

Her breath caught.

And then...

"Well, then," I said quickly, jerking back before I did something I couldn't take back. "You ready?"

If she noticed my almost slip-up in trying to kiss her *again*, she didn't say anything.

Instead, that beautiful grin of hers returned, brightening her face in a way that made everything else fade into the background.

"I was born ready."

And just like that, everything felt lighter again. No weird history between us, no relatives who were scared of me... just Gracie and me.

Even if we were "just friends."

By the time we'd finished decorating cookies, Gracie's sweater was splattered with every color of the frosting rainbow.

The rest of my family had gone to bed hours ago, but neither of us were ready to call it a night. So, I led her back downstairs to the living room and queued up *Home Alone*.

It was a win-win: partly because I liked the movie (thanks to my mom, who made me watch it with her a few weeks ago since I couldn't remember it) and partly an excuse to spend more time with her.

She'd been a natural with my family, by the way. I should've been annoyed at how little time I'd gotten with her, but I couldn't be. She was perfect. This *night* was perfect. And I didn't want it to end.

We sat with just enough space between us to keep things friendly, even though I had to practically glue myself to the cushion to keep from closing the gap.

But every once in a while, (and what made me like the movie even more) she'd lean in closer to whisper a joke or comment between fits of giggles.

I didn't always catch every word she said, but her laughter was enough to make up for it.

"It's amazing to me that Harry and Marv aren't dead yet," she laughed, scooting in close enough so that her breath was warm against my ear.

I fought the urge to kiss her right then and there.

But instead, I leaned slightly toward her, lowering my voice to match hers. "Oh, yeah? You're telling me you couldn't survive getting hit in the face with a paint can?"

"*That*, and stepping on nails barefoot, getting my head blowtorched, and the spider thing? I would simply pass away."

Before I could stop myself, I reached out and poked her side. "I wonder... could you survive something like this?"

Gracie squealed, swatting at my hand as she squirmed away. "*Cole*!"

I grinned, poking her again. *Is that a weakness, I see?*

"Is *the* Gracie Lewis ticklish? Never thought I'd live to see the day."

Her laughter bubbled up as she tried to fend me off. "Cole, stopppp!"

"Make me."

In an instant, she launched herself at me, turning the moment into a full-on tickle fight.

We tumbled back on the couch, laughing as we went down, and she started trying to wrestle her way back to the top.

My heart raced from how close she was. Her warmth, her energy... she was everywhere, and it felt as natural as breathing. *I'm screwed, aren't I?*

"Just so you know, tickling," she managed between giggles, "is *not* the same thing as a paint can to the face. Stopppp! You win, you win!"

"Good. Glad we agree on that," I grinned, finally letting up as we both collapsed back onto the couch, breathless and laughing.

I couldn't talk myself out of stealing another look at her just as the credits started rolling.

Her eyes were still on me, her lips pursing as she gave me a once-over.

Slowly, she leaned in, her hand resting lightly on my chest, and I silently prayed that she couldn't feel my heart slamming against my ribcage.

Just friends. I reminded myself again.

But damn it all if I didn't selfishly want something more.

Instincts took over, and I closed the rest of the gap between us, one arm snaking possessively around her waist, pulling her into my lap.

She fit against me like she belonged there. I liked that.

Her gaze fell on my lips.

Just say the word, Gracie. Say you want this too.

But then, just as quickly, her eyes fell on the staircase, and she pulled back slightly without warning. "I... I should probably go, shouldn't I?"

"Wait. *What*? What do you mean? I..."

"*Cole*..." she murmured, her gaze still fixed on the staircase.

I forced my eyes to follow her line of sight.

Addie... standing at the top of the steps in the new Christmas pajamas all the cousins had gotten tonight, holding a copy of *How the Grinch Stole Christmas* in her hands.

"What are you doing out of bed, Adds?" I asked, my voice cracking slightly as Gracie took the opportunity to inch even further away from me.

"I think someone wants you to read her a bedtime story," Gracie replied, standing up and smoothing out her clothes before giving Addie a warm smile.

My younger cousin grinned. "Yes, please!"

I looked back at Gracie.

Please don't make me choose between the two of you. I don't want to be a jerk to the only family member I have who's willing to me right now.

But before I could say anything, Gracie stood up, heading for the hall to grab her shoes. "Let's get a move on, Cole."

Guess the decision had been made for me.

I sighed, standing reluctantly. "I'm just going to take Gracie home, and then I'll be right back. Okay, Addie?"

She nodded eagerly.

Knowing Gracie, I shouldn't have been surprised she was letting herself out as I trailed behind her like a lovesick puppy—or even, that she was already at my door with my Carhartt jacket, holding it out to me like she owned the damn thing.

But here I was, completely and utterly fascinated by her for all of it.

What the hell is happening to me?

"Tonight was a lot of fun, Cole. Thanks for inviting me."

"Thanks for coming." I managed to choke out.

Tonight was a lot of things for me.

Confusing was the word for half of them.

Chapter Twenty-Two:

The house was empty without Gracie.

I shut the front door softly behind me, the quiet pressing in all at once.

Ghosts of her, my cousins, and even my sister from when Gracie had somehow managed to rope everyone into a game of hide-and-seek that she insisted had to be played "to the death" still danced around me in the dimly lit room.

Any normal food fight would have been chaotic, but with Gracie, it was complete mayhem that left everyone howling on the floor with laughter.

My eyes drifted to a streak of frosting on the wall from the fight in question, making a mental note to clean that up later.

A small smile tugged at my lips from the drive back with her.

"Well, here we are," Gracie said, lightly slapping her thighs as I pulled into her driveway.

"Here we are." I echoed, putting the truck in park to get a better look at her. "You have..."

"Frosting all over me? Yeah, I figured," she covered her face with her hand as she giggled. "Can't take me anywhere, I guess."

I wetted my thumb with my tongue, gently wiping off the pink frosting smeared across her cheek. "I'm glad I did, though."

The thud of footsteps on the stairs broke me from my thoughts, and Addie appeared again, still holding onto her book.

Her face lit up when she saw me.

"Ready for that story, Addie?" I asked, catching her as she launched herself into my arms.

"Yes!" she said, wrapping her arms around my neck.

Her book banged against my back as I carried her up to her room, and when we finally made it upstairs, I blindly attempted to maneuver around a few of my other younger cousins in various sleeping positions on the floor to her very own pull-out bed.

"Story time!" she begged, holding out the book as I set her down.

I grinned. "Gotta tuck you in first, Adds. I don't make the rules."

She huffed dramatically, yanking the closest blanket onto herself, while knocking the rest onto the floor.

A laugh escaped me as I rolled my eyes and bent down to scoop them back up, "Alright, tornado, let me help you out. This is a trick my mom taught me when I was about your age."

Wait, what was I talking about?

Addie settled back into the bed, looking up at me with her big, green eyes—waiting for the promised trick in question. But I...

That's when my hands started moving instinctively as I tucked the blankets around her, like they'd done it a hundred times before—even though my brain couldn't remember.

"A stuff-stuff here and a stuff-stuff there..." I started, smoothing the covers into place.

What the hell is happening to me right now?

But as I was in autopilot, the words, the motions...it was all bringing back this hazy, bittersweet familiarity.

My mom's hands flashed in my mind.

It wasn't exactly a memory I could fully grasp, but the feeling was imprinted somewhere deep, like it'd always been a part of me.

I thought back to what Gracie had said earlier: *I kind of wish I could go back to before... It was way easier being a kid.*

She was right.

Kids lived life with a... spark. They were imaginative, curious... they could start up a conversation with any stranger, never pausing to take a breath. They believed in magic and Santa Claus and the good in humanity.

But somewhere along the line, life wore you down, and that spark faded.

So, when had mine burned out?

I didn't need all my memories to know that I hadn't always been the "school bully".

Like that memory of the time that I'd gone on a fishing trip with my dad. The world had just been... perfect.

What had happened to *that* kid?

Was it too late to find my way back to him?

"Then we roll your little toesies in," I said, coming back to reality as I finished the last corner of the blanket, "and wham-bam, you're a burrito."

Addie burst into giggles from under the covers, her eyes widening. "Aunt Sharon really taught you all that?"

I blinked at my hands in awe, then at the finished product, a beat passing between us.

"Yeah, I guess she did."

"I love Aunt Sharon. She's the best." Addie beamed.

I smiled, the warmth in her voice catching me off guard. "She is. I got really lucky with her," I said, realizing for the first time just how much I meant it.

Clearing my throat quickly, I picked up her book, running my fingers over the cover before flipping to the first page. "Let's get started on that book, shall we?"

Addie nestled closer to my side as I began, her hands grasping the blanket in excitement.

I was midway through describing the Grinch's scowl when I noticed movement out of the corner of my eye.

Chloe.

She stood in the doorway, half-hidden by the frame.

Her fingers gripped the edge of her pajama shirt, as if she were caught between wanting to join us and being too scared to ask.

I didn't waste another second in throwing out the offer. "You wanna join us, Chlo?"

Her eyes shot towards me then, like she was surprised (and a little scared) that I'd even asked.

But then her gaze fell back to the book in my hands, and the tiniest hint of a smile tugged at her lips.

"Can I?" she asked, shyly.

"Of course," I said, patting the space next to Addie.

Relief washed over me as she crossed the room.

It wasn't like she was jumping for joy at the thought of spending time with me, but it was a step. And I was okay with any kind of movement as long as it was in the right direction.

I tucked the blanket around her and Addie before picking up the book again.

This time, I leaned into the voices a little more. Addie let out a wild cackle every time I got dramatic, and her laughter was so contagious that Chloe couldn't help but giggle too.

As the story went on, I felt Chloe letting go of something. The distance between us didn't feel so heavy anymore.

She leaned closer, her eyes wide as the Grinch crept into Whoville, and for the first time, it felt like we were just... siblings. We weren't broken or distant. I was just an older brother reading his little sister a bedtime story.

By the time the Grinch's heart grew three sizes, both girls were starting to crash.

Addie was the first to give in, her head dropping until it landed on my arm. Chloe wasn't far behind.

I finished the last page in a whisper, closing the book softly, and for a minute, I just sat there, not wanting to risk waking them.

Here's what I knew about past me: he was captain of the football team, the most popular kid at school, he supposedly had it all...

But he didn't have *this*.

And honestly? I'd take what I had now over what he'd lost any day.

Chapter Twenty-Three:

THREE YEARS EARLIER

G racie

What nobody ever tells you about growing up is just how lonely it can get.

Instead, they throw the blanket term around of "everything happens for a reason" in hopes that one day, you'll just give up the fight and stop asking those *hard-hitting* questions.

I hadn't meant to join the worship team at my old church. It kind of just fell into my lap. And the funny thing was, I remembered my parents saying that it'd been such a "God thing", such a blessing for our family to be a part of something *great*.

I was finally making them proud.

In hindsight, fourteen *was* a young age to be on an all-adult worship team. But back then, I'd thought I was so mature and grown up for being the only kid there.

I thought I knew everything.

I was wrong.

The first time it happened, I convinced myself that I'd made the whole thing up.

Little kids are notorious for their overactive imaginations, and no one at that age looks at an adult and thinks that *they're* the ones in the wrong.

If anything, we blame ourselves.

And the second time it happened, that's exactly what I did.

Flash forward a couple of months: I hadn't meant to, but I'd woken up from a nightmare.

My parents were still together, and all I needed in that moment was my mommy and daddy.

I knew it was late, but I could hear them watching some TV special about a girl from Utah from behind their bedroom door. Elizabeth Smart, I think?

Anyway, as I raised my hand to knock, I heard my dad make this joke to my mom: *She deserved it, you know. You can tell she had daddy issues.*

And in the middle of me preparing to confess every secret I'd been keeping from them in the past year—every place he had touched me, everything he had said, everything I had *felt*... I stopped.

Because maybe, they were right.

Maybe this was *my* fault somehow.

But in the back of my mind, I wondered... how could something that made me feel so terrible happen to me inside of a church that was supposed to make me feel safe?

How could God watch this happen to me time and time again and choose to do nothing about it?

Did He not care about me?

Was I really just *that* unlovable?

After Bear got sick, I chose to keep my dirty, little secret hidden from everyone.

I knew that my parents were too busy dealing with Bear, and I didn't want to be a burden. I didn't want them to be mad at me or think I was disgusting. After all, one more thing would've caused the family to implode.

But I guess that would've happened either way.

Slowly, us going to church as a family every week stopped.

My parents blamed God for what was happening to Bear, and I blamed Him for... what had happened to *me*.

It happened three times.

Three.

God's perfect number.

Like my life was some kind of sick and twisted joke to Him... and him.

Years later, I still couldn't be around men without being forced back into a memory with him.

Even *good* men.

People would never understand why the one and only time I'd ever been asked to a school dance, I'd purposely overdosed on ibuprofen just so I'd be too sick to go. Because I was scared.

Scared of being alone with a guy.

They'd never understand why I'd started taking a knife out of my family's kitchen every night, half for protection if he ever came for me again, and half to cut out the beast that was clearly inside of me.

After all, good girls didn't have this happen to them.

No matter what angle I tried to look at it from, I knew that God must have made a mistake in making me... making my life.

I'd spent my entire life dreaming up a Prince Charming to save me from myself yet failed to realize one very important thing: for people like me, Prince Charming never comes.

Because why would he? I wasn't a princess.

She deserved it.

Me, too.

Present Day: January 11th

January mornings consisted of the kind of cold that no matter how many layers you piled on, you could still feel.

The sun hadn't fully climbed over the horizon yet, leaving Mary Anne's ranch draped in a faint, silver-blue light, and snow blanketed everything around us—its crisp surface only broken by the faint tracks Cole and I left behind.

It didn't take us long to fall into a rhythm of mucking the stalls together in the barn. But even still, every so often, I'd pause for a second to blow on fingers, desperately trying to will some life back into them through my gloves.

"You good over there?" Cole grinned on what felt like my sixteen hundredth time of doing so.

His cheeks were a firetruck red, so I could only imagine that he was probably just as cold as I was. *Even if he was too much of a wimp to admit it.*

"Totally fine," I lied. "Who doesn't love getting hypothermia bright and early in the morning?"

He laughed, and the sound oddly enough warmed the pit of my stomach.

Just think, if he keeps doing that, maybe skinny dipping wouldn't be out of the question this month.

Oooh, skinny dipping with *him*?

STOP IT, GRACIE.

"It's growing on me," he admitted. "There's just something about the frosty air that makes everything feel more alive, don't you think?"

"Oh!" I exclaimed sarcastically. "I didn't know you were the head of the PR team for the Jingle Bell Rock song. My apologies."

"Hey! I'm just saying." he gestured toward the open barn door. Outside, the snow-covered mountains stretched out in every direction, the light catching on the ice crystals like the ground itself was glowing. "You have to admit it's kind of magical out here."

"Save it for next Christmas, Buddy the Elf." I grinned, rolling my eyes.

"Okay, *Scrooge*."

We continued to move in sync, the way you do when you've done something together a hundred times before.

Toss, scrape, haul. Joke. Toss, scrape, haul. Joke.

"I'll give it to you," I said after a while, leaning against the handle of my pitchfork. "This wasn't the worst way to spend a morning."

Cole glanced over, a smirk tugging at the corner of his mouth. "Careful, Gracie. You're starting to sound like you're enjoying this."

"Oh, *whatever*, Cole."

He grinned. "Just you, me, and a bunch of horse shit. What could be better than that?"

"When you put it that way, it sounds less romantic." I snorted, shaking my head.

"Who said anything about romance?" Cole winked, tossing another shovel full into the wheelbarrow.

I rolled my eyes again but couldn't stop the smile spreading across my face.

"Speaking of romance, though... Did you hear that Emma's in charge of the planning committee for prom? I keep trying to convince her to do a *Fifty Shades of Gracie* theme."

"Would you actually like something like that? I thought you had an image to maintain."

"What? The image of my dark and brooding-ness?" I shot back, grinning at him, "And maybe you don't know me as well as you think you do."

He chuckled, holding his hand to his heart in mock pain. "Whoa, there, Gracie. Hit me where it hurts, why don't you?"

As we finished mucking out the last stall, the sky had lightened to a pale blue, signaling the approach of sunrise.

The horses nickered softly in their stalls, and Cole and I both stepped back to admire our work, leaning on our pitchforks, breathing heavily (at least *I* was) from the effort.

"Not bad for a couple of amateurs," Cole said, grinning at me.

"Speak for *yourself*. I'm a seasoned pro."

I picked up my pitchfork and headed for the storage closet at the front of the barn, feeling the ache of manual labor vibrate through my bones. *I'm definitely going to be sore tomorrow.*

Cole jogged to follow, catching up with me easily, even though he'd put in as much effort this morning as I had. *Yeah, I know. He was used to it because of the football thing...*

"You know," he started, "You never struck me as someone who'd be into going to prom."

I stuck my tongue out at him. "Contrary to popular belief, I *am* a girl who wants to feel like a princess sometimes too."

Even though the *last* dance I'd tried to go to had been an absolute disaster. I hadn't even made it out the door before I'd started vomiting all over the place and had to call and cancel on the guy.

But Cole didn't know that (at least... he didn't *remember* that).

"I get it," he said quietly. "You deserve to have that moment."

Even though he hadn't been the "old Cole" in awhile, I was still surprised when he said stuff like that.

Surprised in a good way, though. It was nice to talk to someone like that sometimes.

I shrugged, a wistful smile pulling at my lips. "I just hope it lives up to the hype."

After all, it was kind of a rite of passage for high schoolers to go to prom. And even though my life had made enjoying something like that harder, I still wanted to go.

I wanted a chance to be "normal" for a night.

Just one.

We reached the storage closet, and I placed my pitchfork alongside the others, turning to face him.

"Well," he started, a mischievous smile spreading across his face as he leaned against the doorframe, "if the night doesn't live up to all your hopes and dreams, you'll at least have someone to keep you entertained."

I raised an eyebrow as I laughed. "And who might *that* be?"

"Me, of course. Who else?"

I rolled my eyes, trying hard not to grin. "You're a dork, y'know that?"

"And you love it," he replied, winking.

I didn't think so. But maybe I was starting to.

Chapter Twenty-Four:

FEBRUARY 5TH

I settled into my usual spot in the ag. science room, surrounded by textbooks, flashcards, and an assortment of color-coded notes that screamed I couldn't be *more* stressed for the upcoming state competition.

Across the table, Cole sat with his sleeves pushed up, flipping through his notes like he wasn't worried about this at all.

He glanced up, catching my eye with a grin. "Did you know that a cow has four stomach compartments?"

I twirled my pen between my fingers as I smirked back at him. "Obviously. And you should know that too. Get it wrong on the written test, and I will literally hunt you down and hurt you."

Cole raised his hands in mock surrender. "Relax, Dictator Gracie. I've got the cow guts part down. It's the pharmacology section that's going to kill me... if you don't first, that is."

I playfully slapped his elbow, my heart doing a dumb, little flip at how solid and warm his arm felt. *Ugh.* "Funny. Just remember: Amoxicillin is for bacterial infections, Ivermectin is for parasites, and everything else... you can just guess."

"Solid plan... maybe I'll just copy off your paper."

"In your *dreams*, Brown. Guess you'll just have to figure out which end of the cow is which all on your own."

His laugh made my face heat up, but I didn't dare let it show.

Instead, I grinned back, matching his energy, like this was just another normal day and conversation. Like my stomach wasn't tying itself in a hundred knots for no reason.

I hadn't meant to ignore everyone else in the room, it was just... Cole being Cole, I guess.

He had this way about him that was slightly addicting. Like I knew he was bad for me for so many reasons (reasons I was honestly starting to forget), but I just couldn't help myself.

I wanted to live in this moment as much as I could before he remembered who I was and started hating me again.

But unfortunately, the bubble around us popped when I looked up.

Bear sat at the end of the table, head propped on one hand as his pen dragged across the page with the other, as if it weighed a hundred pounds.

We were late on his IVIG infusions, so obviously it made sense that he was going to feel like crap until he was able to see someone for it.

He was actually supposed to go in and get it a couple of weeks ago, but his doctor decided to jet off on a vacation without telling anyone.

And apparently, since he was the only person in *all* of Southern Utah who could do the procedure, we had to wait until he came back.

Yeah, I was still pissed about that.

Next to him, though, Emma was weirdly quiet, too.

Normally, she'd be the one rattling off some random fact about anatomy or steering the discussion back to studying when Cole and I managed to get off track (which seemed to be happening a lot lately).

But today, she was hunched over her notes, refusing to make eye contact with anyone.

I shifted in my seat, guilt slowly creeping in. *She probably thinks that I'm leaving her out.*

Cole and I had been doing *so* well together lately (not on purpose or anything, it just kind of happened) that I hadn't spent as much time with her as I would've liked to. She hadn't even been over to my house for a sleepover in *months*.

This was my first time having a... Cole, and clearly I didn't know how to navigate it well if my best friend thought I was replacing her or something.

"Hey, Emma," I blurted out, saying the first thing that came to mind. "Where'd you get your top? It's super cute."

She blinked, her head snapping up like she'd forgotten I was there, before glancing down at the lavender sweater and tugging the fabric lower over her wrists. "Umm, my dad got it for me."

The way she said it felt flat, like there was a whole story there that she didn't feel was worth telling.

She must really hate me right now, then.

Normally, we could've talked forever about what she affectionately called her "healthy" addiction to shopping.

I cleared my throat, attempting to try again. "Oh! I talked to Principal Hawkins about transportation..."

That got her attention.

Her head shot back up, and for the first time all day, there was a spark of interest in her eyes. "What'd he say?"

Getting to and from the competition had always been a problem before, even when we had more members. Now, with just the four of us, it was basically impossible.

But it was the president's job to make everything work, so that's what I'd done. That was the *Gracie Lewis way*.

"It took a lot of badgering—" I started.

Cole chuckled, leaning back in his chair with a grin. "I would expect nothing less from you by now, Gracie."

I rolled my eyes but couldn't stop my mouth from twitching into a smirk. "But," I continued, "I managed to convince Principal Hawkins to let us use the school van."

"The school has a van?" Bear snorted, lifting his head. "Like one of those sketchy, free-candy-on-the-side kind of deals?"

Emma giggled softly, her eyes flickering to Bear with a tiny smile. "Maybe we can get the windows tinted, add some flames for dramatic effect."

He laughed. "Make it the coolest creepy van ever? Heck yeah, I'm in."

"*That's* a hard pass," I countered, shaking my head as I grinned. "Emma's just too nice to tell you how bad that idea actually is."

She shrugged. "I mean, I wouldn't say *bad* exactly. Just... an excuse to end up on a police scanner or two."

My brother tapped his pen against the desk, nodding solemnly. "Alright, alright. No flames. But if we break down in the middle of nowhere, I'm calling dibs on painting *Free Puppies* on the side."

Cole clapped his hands together, rolling his eyes. "Okay, so we've got a questionably legal school van, a guaranteed lack of parental supervision... should I *ask* about the road trip playlist?"

Emma smiled the most she had all day. "Strictly Taylor Swift, buddy."

He groaned, slumping dramatically in his seat. "This is going to be torture."

"Oh, shut up, Cole." I teased, giving him a playful shove.

For a minute, everything felt like it was back to normal.

Like we weren't four stressed-out teenagers cramming for the most important competition of our entire lives. Like Emma didn't feel left out because of the Cole thing and Bear wasn't so pale and lethargic that it hurt to look at him.

It was just us, sitting in a classroom, teasing each other about the stupid stuff and pretending the world wasn't as heavy as it felt.

But little did I know that this was the calm before the storm.

February 14th

Bear had been up all night.

At first, I hadn't thought much of it. He'd had bad nights before, and sure, this one *felt* different, but he'd bounce back. He always did.

Didn't he?

He'd gotten more and more sluggish over the past few days while we waited for his doctor to get back from the Bahamas or wherever the hell he was.

He'd stopped eating, stopped moving—just *stopped*. The last day I could even call "normal" was our latest FFA practice... *had it really been that long?*

I stayed up with him, watching from the couch as he shuffled back and forth, barely being able to hold himself upright.

His face was pale. His breathing was weird. He was *being* weird.

But I told myself it'd all be okay. He just needed rest. Or food. Or something.

Sometime around 2 AM, I got him to lie down in his room. "Just try to get some sleep, okay? For me?" My voice wobbled slightly as I pulled a blanket over him.

I moved to brush the damp curls off his forehead, trying to ignore my stupid shaky hands.

Bear nodded (if you could even *call* it that) before his eyes fluttered closed.

I sat next to him, resting a hand on his shoulder, as if being there could somehow make everything better. But the truth was—I had no idea how to help him. I had no idea what was *happening* to him. And the thought of not even knowing what to do made me want to vomit.

I stayed there for a minute, watching his breaths shallow out until he finally started snoring softly.

If we were a normal family, I probably would've made fun of him for making noise while he slept.

But we weren't, and I was just glad he was *able* to sleep.

Eventually, I slipped out of his room, setting up camp back on the couch—because there was no way I was going to sleep now. Not when he wasn't doing well.

I kept the door to his room in my line of sight and told myself I'd hear if he needed me at all.

If anything went wrong (*which it wouldn't*), I'd hear it. I'd see it. I *had* to.

I just needed to keep myself awake.

I shifted on the couch, pulling my knees up to my chest as I tried to focus on anything I could to help me stay up—the faint creak of the house settling, the dim glow of the streetlight filtering through the curtains, the ticking clock on the wall, the hum of the refrigerator...

But my thoughts started to spiral, suddenly descending into fragmented lines that looped and tangled as I fought to keep my eyes open.

Did I remember to charge my phone? What if I need it to call Mom or Dad about Bear? What if I need to call 911? No. It'll be fine. He'll be fine. Besides, I plugged my phone in... I think.

Bear looked worse tonight than he did yesterday. Was that my fault? No. He just needs sleep. Or food. When was the last time he ate? Shit. When was the last time I ate?

If I close my eyes for just a second—no! Stay awake. Stay awake.

I lifted my glasses off my nose and rubbed my face as I fell back against the cushions, staring at the ceiling.

Dad used to say Bear looked like me when we were little. I don't see it anymore. His hair's lighter, and he's thinner now, way too thin.

What if I should've called someone earlier? What if... No. He'll be okay. He has to be. He'll call if he needs me. He'll...

The ticking clock blurred into the background as my eyelids grew heavier. I had one job, but sleep crept in anyway.

When I woke up, it was like getting yanked out of a nightmare.

The house was silent.

Too silent.

I swung my legs off the couch, the cold floor sending shockwaves to my brain beneath my bare feet.

Something wasn't right. I could feel it.

That's when it clicked.

"Bear?"

I skidded across the floor to his room, the door creaking as I pushed it open.

His bed was empty, and the blanket I'd put on him earlier was folded at the foot of the bed like he'd never been there at all.

Panic started to claw at my chest.

"Bear!" This time, my voice came out sharper. Had he fallen down somewhere? Had he tried to give up? Was he...?

Then I heard it—a weak, strangled wheeze.

My legs felt like lead as I stumbled toward the noise.

No, no, no.

I shoved the bathroom door open.

And there he was.

Bear, crumpled on the floor looking unnaturally pale.

His forehead was bruised, and there was blood—just a little, but enough to make me feel physically sick to my stomach.

I hit my knees beside him, hands shaking so hard I couldn't even think straight. "Bear!"

"Come on, come on," I whispered, hands hovering uselessly.

I needed to get him up. Get him *somewhere*. But my arms wouldn't stop shaking. Normally, I could carry him easily. Hell, I just *had* earlier that night, but my stupid body betrayed me.

I can't do it. I can't lift my brother.

"Bear, please wake up."

Either it was adrenaline or sheer desperation that took over, but by some miracle, I managed to pull myself together enough to get him to the car.

The next thing I knew, I was flying down the road, hands locked so tight around the steering wheel that it hurt.

I didn't care, though.

I didn't care about speed limits or cops or *anything* except getting him to the hospital.

Something that I should've done in the first place...

"Stay with me, Bear," I begged, over and over again. "Please, stay with me."

I was screaming for help before I'd even reached the emergency entrance.

Nurses and doctors swarmed around us, yanking Bear from my arms, and I just *stood* there.

Frozen. Shaking. Watching as they disappeared through the heavy double doors, taking my baby brother with them.

And then I was alone, leaving myself to replay every moment, every bad decision, every missed sign. *I thought he'd be okay.* I thought letting him sleep was the right thing to do.

I was wrong.

This was my fault.

A memory slammed into me, one I didn't want. The dream. The man in the tiki mask.

He's your brother, don't you love him?

I hadn't saved him in my dream.

And now, I hadn't saved him in real life.

Where it mattered.

Chapter Twenty-Five:

C ole

    I tapped my pen against the desk, glancing at the empty seat next to me. It wasn't just empty, though; it was *wrong*.

Gracie Lewis—queen of perfect attendance, color-coded notes, and military-precision organization—was *missing*.

She didn't skip class. She didn't even *sneeze* in class without permission. If she wasn't here, something had to be seriously wrong.

By the time class had ended and there was *still* no sign of her, my worry had officially outpaced my amusement.

I shoved my books into my bag and pulled out my phone, thumbing through my contacts until her name popped up.

The hallway was loud with lockers slamming around me with people on their way to lunch, but all I could hear was the ringing in my ear as I waited for her to pick up.

One ring. Two rings. *Come on, Gracie.* Three—

Finally, the call connected, and I couldn't help but breathe a sigh of relief.

At least she was alive.

"Cole..."

"Hey, Gracie," I said, trying to sound casual and not like I was ready to bolt out of the school to go find her. "You okay? You weren't in class today."

There was a pause, and for a minute, all I could hear was the faint hum of background noise—beeping, clanging doors, a voice paging Dr. *Someone* over a loudspeaker.

Shit. That wasn't good.

"I'm... at the hospital right now," she admitted finally, "Bear had a really bad night, and I had to bring him in."

I leaned against the nearest wall, the conversations around me suddenly fading into white noise. "Is he okay?"

"He is now," she said, her voice still strained, "But they're keeping him overnight for observation. I just... I couldn't leave him. I *won't* leave him."

I nodded, even though she couldn't see me.

That was Gracie for you: strong, loyal, determined to carry everything on her shoulders, even if it crushed her in the process.

She was a force to be reckoned with, but even *she* needed a break sometimes.

"How are *you* holding up?" I asked gently.

She let out a laugh that broke apart halfway through.

"That's a loaded question," she said, her voice crumbling into something rawer and more fragile. "I just... I dunno. He's so sick right now. He can't eat half the time without choking, and he barely has the energy to walk from his room to the bathroom. Which is why we're in this fucking mess to begin with, and..."

316

She took a shaky breath, attempting to right herself, "And I'm supposed to... I don't know, fix it all? Be there for him? But I don't even know what the hell I'm doing. I'm just..." her voice cracked, and when she spoke again, it was barely a whisper. "I'm the worst big sister in the world, aren't I?"

My chest tightened like a vice.

How could you ever think that?

The silence stretched between us for a minute as I tried to come up with the right words (if there were any) to say.

"I asked how *you* were doing," I said finally. "Not what you're doing for Bear. Not whether you've got it all figured out. I just want to know how *you* are."

She inhaled sharply. "I..."

I knew her well enough to know she was shutting down, trying to handle it all on her own. But before I could call her out on that, she caved.

"I'm *scared*, Cole. I'm so scared I can barely think straight. I keep telling myself that if I'm strong enough, he'll be okay. But it's not enough. *I'm* not enough. I'm not my parents. I can't fix this... I can't be the big sister he needs."

"But you *are* enough, Gracie," I said softly, "You're doing everything you can, and then some. You're holding his world together, and that's not something everyone could do. You're incredible."

Her breath caught, and she cleared her throat quickly as if she were trying to force her feelings back down.

That's when a pit formed in my stomach. I could hear it all: the exhaustion, the fear... *everything*. And all I wanted was to take that pain from her.

"It doesn't feel like it," she whispered. "It feels like I'm just... failing. Over and over again."

"Gracie." Her name left my lips slowly, like I was trying to pour every ounce of certainty I had into it. "You are *not* failing. I know you think you have to be strong all the time, but it's okay not to be. It's okay to lean on someone else for once. You don't have to carry all of this alone."

There was another pause before she blurted out. "And I really wanted to go to prom." Her voice cracked like she hadn't meant to say it.

"Gracie..."

"No, I know it sounds stupid," she said quickly. "It's just a dumb dance, right? And it's probably for the best. But I'd been planning it for *months*: the dress, the shoes, the whole thing. And now I'm here, and *Bear's* here, and I feel awful for thinking about *prom* when he could literally die. But I can't help it. I wanted one night where everything felt... normal. Just one night."

"It's not stupid," I said firmly. "Not even close. You deserve that. You deserve *all* of it. And wanting something for yourself doesn't make you a bad sister or a bad person. It makes you human."

Suddenly, an idea came to me. "You know what? If you can't go to prom, then prom's coming to you."

"What are you even talking about?"

"You said you wanted one night to feel normal, right?," I asked, already running through the possibilities in my mind, "Then that's exactly what you're going to get."

She sighed. "Cole..."

"I'm serious," I interrupted. "You deserve this more than anyone."

She was quiet for a bit, but when she finally said something, her voice was softer. "You're crazy," she murmured.

"Maybe," I said, staring up at the school's tiled ceiling, still thinking. "But crazy works sometimes."

"Cole..." she started again, but I cut her off.

"I want to give you this, and I'm going to, alright? Just sit tight."

And I meant it. Whatever it took, whatever I had to do, she was getting her night. Because if anyone deserved to feel special (even just for a minute), it was her.

Now all I had to do was figure out how to pull it off.

February 15th

Nervous didn't even *begin* to cover it.

I felt sick. Like I'd eaten too much candy and was about to regret it.

Or maybe it was more like the exact second before knocking on the door of the girl you liked. Hoping the makeshift prom you'd put together in less than twenty-four hours wasn't about to crash and burn.

Wait, no, scratch that. It was *exactly* like that.

My fingers drummed against the steering wheel as I tried to give myself a half-hearted pep talk, but my mind kept drifting back to the damn bouquet of sunflowers and roses sitting in my passenger seat—the ones that I'd spent way too long picking out just because I wanted them to be perfect.

I didn't know why I was freaking out about this.

Emma had helped me pull this off, keeping Gracie distracted all afternoon and even convincing her to dress up how she would've for prom under the idea that they'd have a *stick-it-to-the-man* snack run and movie night.

It was the perfect setup.

Especially since Gracie wouldn't let herself get too excited about the dance to begin with, not after everything that'd happened with Bear.

Even though he was back home now. Even though he was doing better. I *knew* her.

But I also knew that the second I knocked on that door, this wouldn't just be an idea anymore. It would be real. My *feelings* for her would be real.

And I wasn't sure if she wanted that.

Somehow, I was able to push my nerves down enough to grab the bouquet from the front seat and force myself out of the truck.

But before I could even raise my hand to knock, the door swung open—and there she was.

Fastening an earring with one hand, she looked up at me with those beautiful brown eyes of hers, and just like that, every word I'd planned on saying completely disappeared from my mind.

The silver dress she was wearing caught the porch light in a way that made her shimmer, and the thin straps left her shoulders bare.

Her dark hair tumbled in soft waves, and I had the sudden urge to run my fingers through it.

"Wow," I breathed. "You look like a princess."

Her eyes widened, and for a second, I was worried that I might've said something that upset her.

But then, her cheeks turned the softest shade of pink, and a small smile tugged at her lips.

"Thank you, Cole," she murmured, her fingers fidgeting with her earring still. "I didn't know you were coming. Otherwise..."

She trailed off, but she didn't have to finish. I knew what she meant.

Otherwise, she would've canceled her plans (even though, technically they weren't *real* plans) *for me.*

That was a good sign, at least.

I swallowed, still nervous for some reason.

We'd basically hung out every day for months, but now when it mattered most, I was a complete wreck? How did *that* make any sense?

I quickly held out the bouquet, praying she couldn't see my shaky hands. "I hope you don't mind, but we've got other plans for tonight."

Her brow furrowed as she took the flowers, bringing them to her nose and inhaling softly. "Other plans? What did you do?"

I grinned, holding out my arm. "You'll see."

She hesitated, but only for a second before slipping her hand into the crook of my elbow.

Her touch was light, more delicate than I was expecting, but it still sent a jolt of electricity through my chest, like she had a direct line to my pulse.

We made it halfway to the truck before she suddenly stopped, her face falling. "Wait, shoot. I can't do anything tonight. I have plans with Emma..."

I let myself breathe a little easier. If *that* was tonight's biggest hump, it'd be smooth sailing from here on out.

"She's in on it, too," I said, shooting her a wink. "On her way right now to watch Bear, actually. So that means we have a night to ourselves. Don't worry."

Gracie blinked at me, stunned for all of two seconds before her surprise melted into laughter. "Well, you've just thought of everything, haven't you?"

Damn, I hoped so.

I helped her into the truck, my fingers brushing against hers. I let the touch stay a beat longer than necessary, memorizing the warmth of her skin.

I hope tonight is as perfect as you are.

321

"So," she said, her voice teasing as I slid into the driver's seat and started the engine, "are you going to tell me where we're going, or are you just going to keep being all weird and mysterious?"

I turned toward her, just as a strand of hair was falling across her face. Without thinking, I reached out, gently tucking it behind her ear.

"Mysterious suits me, don't you think?" I murmured.

Her eyes locked onto mine in soft surprise, and the world seemed to narrow to just the two of us.

But then she rolled her eyes, breaking the moment with a laugh.

It was alright, though. I knew what I was getting myself into with her, and honestly? Her smile was something I wanted to spend the rest of my life chasing. No matter how complicated she thought she made it sometimes.

"Just trust me, Gracie," I said, quieter this time. "Please?"

She looked at me then. *Really* looked at me.

And I swore right then she could see everything I wasn't saying.

That she was incredible.

That she was beautiful.

That she was *everything* to me.

Her fingers brushed absentmindedly over the petals of the bouquet in her lap, and she smiled again.

Damn, I love her smile.

"Okay, Cole," she whispered. "I trust you."

Gracie

As much as I tried to guess where we were going—the only parking garage in all of Southern Utah, the Little Caesars down the street... *heck*, maybe even McDonald's—nothing could have prepared me for Cole pulling into West Canyon Park.

But it wasn't just *any* park. It was *the* park.

The place where people my age went on first dates and stuff.

Oh my gosh. Is this a date?

And why didn't I really mind if it was...?

I didn't want to let my mind wander into all the what-if's, but as the truck engine silenced and Cole turned to flash me that lopsided grin, I didn't fight them either.

It wasn't the worst thing in the world just to... hope a little.

The park stretched out before us like a painting come to life.

A weather-worn bridge arched over the river, the water catching the fading sunlight and scattering it like tiny diamonds. Just past it, the river cascaded over smooth rocks, pooling beneath a massive oak tree.

And under that tree, there were fairy lights strung through the branches casting a shimmer over a perfect little picnic spread with finger sandwiches, fresh fruit, and enough cheese to clog every artery in my body.

I stared, speechless. It wasn't just *romantic*—it was intentional.

It wasn't one of those Netflix-and-chill things where the guy forgot your name halfway through. It showed he'd been listening to me. Like he actually *cared* to make this memorable in the best way.

"Holy crap..."

He glanced over, a little sheepish. "Is it too much?"

I shook my head. It wasn't too much. It was *everything*.

Before I could stop myself, I threw my arms around him, pressing my face to his chest.

He froze for half a second before his hands slid around my waist, holding me tight.

Please don't let me go.

As settled onto the blanket with the smell of wildflowers and oak wrapping around us, I realized that it wasn't just gratitude I felt. It was something bigger, warmer... *scarier*.

And it was also *him*: the way his eyes crinkled when he laughed. Or the way he spun a story. Or the way he leaned in like every word I said was worth hearing.

It was the kind of night that'd stay between Cole and me, locked away just for us to know because it's too perfect, too *ours*. A memory so private that even if I tried to put it into words, it wouldn't come out right.

But to my surprise, the night wasn't even over yet, because after we'd finished eating, Cole stood up and held his hand out to me. "Gracie, may I have this dance?"

I grinned up at him, rolling my eyes as I slipped my hand into his.

He pulled me to my feet, leading me onto the makeshift dance floor as *Beautiful Crazy* began to play softly through his phone.

"Is this a Luke Combs song?" I asked, biting back a laugh.

Cole scratched the back of his neck, and suddenly, he was the most self-conscious I'd ever seen him.

"Yeah. Is that okay?"

I didn't answer right away. Instead, I grabbed a fistful of his shirt and pulled him down so that we were eye-level. Our lips hovered close enough that I could feel his breath against my skin.

"It's more than okay," I whispered, my teasing grin widening. "It's perfect."

His eyes darkened slightly, emotions flickering behind them. And then, without another word, he spun me around and pulled me closer, hands firm on my waist as we swayed to the music.

The space between us grew smaller, *quieter*, as my forehead brushed against his lowered one.

I closed my eyes for just a second, letting myself sink into it. Into *him*.

But then, breaking the spell with a voice that wavered just slightly, he spoke.

"You know," he started hesitantly, "I was really worried you'd hate all this. I didn't want to cross a line or... mess things up between us. I just..." He exhaled, his grip on my waist tightening slightly. "I just wanted to tell you... to *show* you... how much I..."

His words hung in the air, heavy and unfinished.

I tilted my head back, meeting his gaze, and my chest tightened.

Because here's the thing: I'd spent so much of my life insisting that I hated this boy. He was cocky and infuriating. He'd been my absolute worst nightmare for years. And yet... he *wasn't* the same Cole anymore.

This was the Cole who'd gone ridiculously out of his way to give me the best night of my life. The guy who I enjoyed being around, who I *actually* trusted. The guy who was the living, breathing definition of *if he wanted to, he would*.

And now, he was standing here, looking at me like I was something worth wanting.

Me.

I could barely hear the music anymore over the sound of my own beating heart.

325

Was this what love felt...?

I didn't know. I'd never known.

Whatever this was, though, it was terrifying. It was exhilarating. It was too much and not enough, all at once.

But Cole must've taken my silence as rejection because he plowed on.

"I just..." He took a breath, his voice lower and uncertain. "I didn't want to ruin this, you know? I wanted tonight to mean something. For you to see that you *mean* something. And maybe I'm reading too much into things, or maybe I'm completely off base, but I just needed to try. To show you that I—"

Oh, for the love of all things good and holy.

"Cole?" I cut in.

He blinked down at me, his ramble stalling. "Yeah?"

"Shut up."

His brows lifted in surprise, but before he could say another word, I tightened my grip on his shirt, stood on my tiptoes, and kissed him.

No hesitation. No second-guessing. Just everything I didn't know how to say, poured into a single moment.

His lips softened against mine as his hands stayed firm on my waist, steadying me as my hands slid up to his shoulders. The way he held me made it impossible to remember why I'd even been so scared in the first place.

When we finally pulled apart, the world felt different—quieter, softer, more beautiful, like it had reshaped itself around us. I kept my forehead resting against his, and watched as his lips curled into a small, breathless smile.

"Interesting way to get me to shut up," he said, his voice teasing but still a little uneven.

I huffed out a laugh, my heart racing. "It worked, didn't it?"

His eyes opened, and the way he looked at me (like he couldn't even believe I was real) sent my stomach flipping straight off a cliff.

"Yeah," he murmured, his thumb brushing lightly against my cheek. "It worked."

And in that moment, I didn't care if I didn't have the words to describe what this was.

The kiss was enough.

This night was enough.

We were enough.

Chapter Twenty-Six:

The world felt... brighter.

Was it brighter?

I wasn't sure, but everything around me—my house, the porch light, the freaking *sky*—was now in full-blown technicolor.

Or maybe I just had too much adrenaline coursing through my veins to process anything normally anymore.

My hands were still shaking as I dug into my dress pocket (that's right, my dress had *pockets*), looking for my house key.

Meanwhile, Cole stopped a few steps behind me, hands in his pockets too, watching me with a quiet, amused look on his face.

Eventually, I found the key and jammed it into the lock, but just as my fingers brushed against the metal, I hesitated.

I wasn't ready to go inside. I wasn't ready for the night to end... for *this* to end. And if I went through that door, I was worried this would all disappear.

Because that's how these things usually went for me.

I used to believe in happy endings. A long time ago, before Bear got sick, before my parents divorced, before I learned that nothing good ever lasted.

But the universe had a way of yanking things out from under me, as if it were just waiting for the chance to prove I didn't deserve them.

And now, I wondered if this... if Cole, if tonight, if *everything* was just another thing I was destined to lose.

But then, another voice... something softer, quieter, something *Cole* would probably say, pushed its way in.

This is different.

This was *mine*. I had chosen it. I had chosen *him*.

Cole had been my first kiss.

That was something *I* got to decide, and I'd chosen to share it with the boy who had spent the entire night proving to me that I was worth it for some reason.

That I wasn't broken beyond repair.

That I wasn't disgusting or a disappointment to anyone.

To him, I was just Gracie.

And as Gracie, the girl who'd had so many firsts taken from her, this felt like... everything to me.

It wasn't just about the kiss. It was about the fact that for the first time, I'd given a piece of myself away willingly. And I'd given it to someone who deserved it.

It was the fact that Cole was thoughtful and sweet and amazing and somehow completely unaffected by the walls I had built around myself.

He didn't try to tear them down or sneak past them. He just... *waited*.

And tonight, I'd let him in.

I let my fingers slip from the key, turning to face him. He tilted his head at me just slightly.

"You okay, Gracie?" he asked softly.

I let out a breath, a tiny smile tugging at my lips. "Yeah," I breathed, and somehow, that one word felt bigger than I thought it'd be. "More than okay, actually."

The corner of his mouth lifted. "Good." He took a small step closer. "Tonight's been the best night I've had in a long time."

"And it's not just because of the kiss, right?" I teased.

His grin widened. "It's because of *you*, Gracie. All of it."

Something lodged in my throat, something warm and... kind of wonderful, and I had to force out a breath to keep my heart from doing something ridiculously dumb.

"You're pretty amazing, Cole. You know that?" I murmured.

He smirked. "I've been told." Then, with a shrug. "But hearing it from you makes it mean a whole lot more."

A beat passed between us as we stood there. Caught in this stupid, perfect moment that I didn't want to break.

The air smelled like rain-soaked pavement and pine, and somewhere in the distance, a cricket chirped. Above us, the sky was a deep blue, scattered with stars, and just as I looked up, a streak of light cut across the darkness.

A shooting star.

I made a wish before I could stop myself.

Let this last. Just a little longer. Please.

Cole shifted, rocking on his heels. "So," he said, playfulness creeping into his tone, "you think maybe we could do this again sometime?"

"You mean go on a date, kiss, and then awkwardly stand outside my house for ten minutes?" I teased, my cheeks going warm.

330

"Something like that." His eyes danced. "Minus the awkward part."

I giggled, shaking my head. "Joke's on you. I actually happen to *like* the awkward part."

"Good to know." Then, quieter, "So... that's a yes?"

"It's a yes, definitely, absolutely."

His expression softened, something unspoken passing between us. "Good." His gaze fell on my lips for a split second before meeting my eyes again. "So, I'll see you tomorrow?"

"Tomorrow," I echoed.

He took a step back, slowly, like he didn't actually want to leave. "Goodnight, Gracie."

"Goodnight, Cole."

As I closed the door behind me, I leaned against the wood, my hands gripping the fabric of my dress as I tried (and failed) to stop the giddy smile spreading across my face.

If someone had told me a few months ago that my first kiss would be with *the* Cole Brown, I would have called them crazy. But now?

Now, I couldn't imagine it being with anyone else.

I climbed into bed, hugging my pillow close, still feeling the ghost of his kiss on my lips, the warmth of his laugh still surrounding me.

And as I fell asleep, I dreamed of him.

February 19th

Cole

The bell above the door jingled as Max and I stepped inside.

Brad's, the old burger joint, was *the* spot for our team—at least, so I'd been *told*. We'd all pile into a booth in the back after games and stick around until the staff gave up and let us close the place down.

But today, it was just me and Max.

The checkered floors stretched out beneath cherry-red booths, and the walls advertised photos of past Hillview High sports teams.

My eyes snagged on one—me, hoisted on one of my teammates' shoulders, grinning ear to ear with the state championship trophy clutched tightly in my fist.

I stared at it, waiting for pride to bloom in my chest, or at least some flicker of recognition.

Instead, that life felt distant, like it hadn't ever even been mine to begin with.

"That was last year," Max said, following my gaze as we slid into a booth. "First time Hillview won state... well, since your dad."

My stomach dipped.

My dad... the *football legend*. How could I forget?

I let out a dry laugh to myself. *Maybe don't answer that.*

"Must've been a good season," I said instead.

Max's grin widened. "A *great* season. Dude, we were unstoppable. *You* were unstoppable. You made everything look so damn easy. It was like you were born to do it."

"Thanks," I muttered, fiddling with the edge of a napkin.

He meant well, I knew he did. It was just hard to picture being good at something you couldn't even remember *doing*.

He leaned back, a little too wistful. "Man, your dad would've been so proud. Everyone always said you got his arm—his instincts."

I nodded stiffly, the knot in my chest tightening.

The napkin in my hands was starting to fray.

"He was something else," Max kept going, not even realizing that I wasn't meeting his eyes anymore. "He wasn't just, like, *your* dad. He was *everybody's*. He used to come to our practices back in middle school and just hang out on the sidelines. We all played harder when he was there. Like, we didn't want to let him down, even if we were just running drills."

My jaw clenched.

Why. Can't. I. Just. Remember?

My eyes flicked to my picture again, suddenly feeling a seed of jealousy start to grow in my chest.

The guy I used to be—he got to remember my dad.

Hell, the whole team had probably been best friends with my dad, and I couldn't even remember what he *looked* like without a picture.

Max laughed under his breath like he was reliving it. *Must be nice.* "He even taught me how to throw a good spiral. Must've taken a hundred tries at least, but that didn't stop him. Back when my dad—"

He hesitated for a second. "Back when my dad bailed, your dad didn't have to step in. But he did. He was there for me in ways mine never was. He was... like a second dad, you know?"

Second dad.

My hands froze on the shredded napkin.

Second-fucking-dad. That's what he said.

Why did Max get to have that? To have *him*? Why did *anyone* get to have him?

"That's nice," I said flatly.

333

Max kept going, like we were strolling down memory lane *together*. "You don't find guys like him anymore, you know? He was the kind of guy who made everyone feel like they mattered, even when you felt like you didn't. He was a *saint*."

I nodded again, slower this time. It should've been comforting.

It wasn't.

"And when he died..." Max's voice softened. "The whole town felt it. The service was packed. It was like the world just stopped. Because we all loved him. We all missed him."

Something cracked inside me then.

Something sharp and ugly.

"*We?*" The word slipped out before I could catch it.

Max blinked. "What?"

"You said *we* missed him," I repeated, my voice tight. "Like you lost him too."

"Well, yeah..." Max said carefully, as if he was trying to read where this was coming from. "I mean, not like you did. Of course not. But he was—"

"Like a second dad." I finished dryly.

Max frowned, shifting in his seat. "I didn't mean—"

"You didn't mean *what*?" I snapped, cutting him off. "You didn't mean to make it sound like you knew him better than I did? Like you have more memories of my dad than *I* do?"

"Cole, that's not what I—"

"Then what *did* you mean?" I shoved the napkin aside.

Heads turned to our booth, while Max ducked his in embarrassment. But I didn't care. Max's feelings meant absolutely fucking nothing to me right then.

"Because from where I'm sitting, it sounds a hell of a lot like you're the one who got to keep him. Like *you* get to remember every damn thing about him while I'm stuck with nothing."

"That's not fair—"

"Not fair?" I let out a sharp laugh. "You're right, Max. It's *not* fair. It's not fair that you have all these stories and memories and moments with him, and I can't even picture his face without looking at some shitty photo on a diner wall."

Max opened his mouth to respond, but I didn't let him.

"Do you have any idea what that's like? To know that someone you're supposed to love, someone who's supposed to be the most important person in your life, someone you're supposed to *remember*, is just... gone? No, not just gone. *Erased*? Like he was never even there to begin with?"

"Cole—"

"*No*." My voice steeled. "Don't act like you understand. You *don't*. You can't. So just—stop."

The silence that followed was deafening.

Maybe this blow up had been a long time coming. Maybe it'd always been there. I didn't know anymore. It was too much.

It was all *too much*.

Max swallowed, finally speaking. "I'm sorry, man. I didn't mean to..."

But I wasn't listening anymore.

Max had memories of my dad. *My dad*.

And I had nothing.

I shoved out of the booth. "Just leave me alone."

I didn't wait for a response. Didn't look back.

My footsteps pounded against the checkered floor as I stormed to the door, throwing it open hard enough to send it slamming behind me.

335

Fine. He could keep his stupid memories of my dad.
See if I care.

Chapter Twenty-Seven:

FEBRUARY 23RD

I lied about wanting pizza for dinner.

Mom didn't question it, though.

I guess she was so thrilled I was *acting normal* again since my conversation with Max that she'd buy pizza every night if it meant getting back the version of me she recognized...

The version of me that *I* recognized.

Too bad he didn't exist right now.

If he *ever* did.

I watched from my bedroom window as her car backed out of the driveway, and the second she disappeared down the street, I double-checked the quiet.

My stepdad was at work, my sister was at dance practice, and *now*, I had the place all to myself.

Minutes. That was all I had.

But it was all I needed.

My pulse hammered as I made my way across the hall to her office door. This was a stupid idea. The kind that could only end badly.

Not that it mattered to me.

He was *my dad*. And yet I remembered nothing about him. There was just a black hole where he should've been.

Why did *Max* get to have memories of him? Why did *he* get to have something that should've been mine?

"He was... like a second dad."

It wasn't fair.

I paused for a second, my hand hovering over the knob.

Mom never specifically said I wasn't allowed in here, she never had to.

But she also never talked about Dad. Never offered pictures. Never told stories... It was like me losing my memory was the perfect opportunity she needed to erase him from our lives entirely.

But not anymore. That ended today.

I twisted the knob, flinching at the faint creak as the door swung open.

Even though I *knew* the house was empty, my heart jumped like I was in some shitty horror movie.

I peeked over my shoulder one more time just to be sure I really was alone.

Nothing. The coast was clear.

I slipped inside, easing the door shut behind me as quietly as I could.

"Better make this quick, Cole," I muttered under my breath.

The office was like the rest of the house—immaculate and soulless.

Everything was exactly where it was supposed to be, like a photo in a catalog, and it made me feel out of place—like I didn't belong there. But that was nothing new.

I went straight for the desk.

The drawers opened smoothly, and inside, everything was neatly organized: pens lined up in their compartments, a stack of sticky notes, and a box of paper clips.

I sifted through them quickly, finding nothing remotely useful or relevant to me.

My fingers brushed a small bundle of envelopes tied with twine before shutting the drawer, and my breath caught.

Letters, maybe? Pictures?

I yanked them out, but the return addresses were all boring—bills, receipts, some legal firm.

No dad.

Frustration started to claw at my insides, but I shoved it down.

I wasn't done yet.

I moved to the bookshelves, scanning titles—tax manuals, law references, self-help books... I ran my hands along the spines, looking for anything that didn't belong. Photo albums, records, *something*—but there was nothing.

That's when I spotted the closet.

Don't do it. Don't do it. Don't do it.

I yanked the door open anyway.

The inside was crammed with boxes, file folders, and a few jackets hanging on the bar.

My throat tightened as I stared at it, taking it all in. Somewhere in this mess, there *had* to be something about him. Something that wasn't locked away in a memory.

I pulled down the first box I came to: **"Family-Misc."**, bringing it over to the desk and prying the lid off.

The first few things I grabbed weren't helpful—a Christmas card from five years ago, a pair of baby shoes I didn't recognize, some old hospital bracelet.

I rifled through them faster, a growing sense of urgency hitting me. *Come on. Come on.*

Then—

A floorboard creaked downstairs.

I froze. *Shit.*

They weren't supposed to be home yet.

I still had at least... my eyes shot to the clock on the desk—at least *ten* more minutes.

I tried to calm my breathing, but suddenly, I felt sick.

How the fuck am I going to explain me being in here?

Thankfully, though, after a few excruciating seconds, the silence returned.

Must've just been the house settling.

Maybe. Probably.

I let out a shaky breath and turned back to the box. But my hands felt clumsy as I continued to dig through it.

That's when I knocked the edge of the box, tipping it over just enough to send a folder and a few loose papers sliding to the floor.

The sound wasn't loud, but in the quiet, it may as well have been a gunshot.

My back went ramrod straight as I stayed there, waiting. Listening.

Still nothing. *Thank God.*

I winced, crouching to gather the mess as quickly as I could.

But as I did, one paper that was thicker than the others caught my eye. It was folded neatly with my name scrawled across the front in big, block letters.

Cole Henry Brown.

My fingers hovered over it, a weird, sinking feeling hitting my stomach as I unfolded the paper and skimmed the first few lines.

"It is the finding of this court that Cole Henry Brown acted recklessly while driving under the influence."

Fuck. No, no, no, no.

*"...destruction of property to Mary Anne Brown's back pasture fence. The **ACCUSED** acted irresponsibly and illegally, being not only a danger to himself, but the general public as well..."*

My breathing quickened as the words blurred together.

I didn't remember this at all.

Obviously not, you moron.

"...since this is not an isolated incident and rather a string of reckless acts and misbehaviors, it is in the best interest of the court that remediation be served..."

The paper fell from my hands as I stumbled back, my head spinning.

This was it. This was why I was doing community service.

Because I was a *habitual* screw-up.

I stared at the paper now on the ground as the corners of my lips twitched into a dry, humorless smile.

Maybe I should just put it back, pretend I'd never see it. That'd be fitting, wouldn't it? Just to "forget" this all ever happened.

That'd be real poetic.

But the sound of the front door opening (for *real* this time) slapped me with the reality.

I needed to get out of there. *Now*.

I lunged for the paper, shoving it into my pocket without thinking. Hands shaking, I slammed the lid onto the box, shoved it back onto the shelf, and yanked the closet door shut.

But just as I was turning to leave, something on the floor stopped me cold.

A photo.

I bent down, my gut twisting as I picked it up.

What now?

It was a little weathered around the edges, but the faces were unmistakable, (and *I* was the one with amnesia)—me, Mom, Dad... and a tiny baby swaddled in a pink blanket.

My sister.

I stuffed the photo into my pocket too.

The floorboards creaked again, and I bolted out of the office, pulling the door shut behind me as quietly as I could.

My heart was still slamming against my ribs, but I forced my expression blank. Forced my heartbeat to slow as I took the stairs, one at a time.

Calm. Normal. Nothing to see here, folks.

"Cole? Where are you?"

I froze mid-step, my hand gripping the banister.

Gracie. Shit. I guess she'd let herself in.

My pulse jumped for an entirely different reason now, which was stupid because I *was* happy to see her.

But not like this.

Not when I couldn't tell her anything about the court case, or the DUI, or the photo burning a hole in my pocket.

Not when she'd only *just* started to accept me as someone different now. Someone who was getting better.

I wasn't about to wreck that with all the shit I had going on.

She must've sensed me on the steps, zoned out on her, lost in my own thoughts, because she turned, her eyes locking onto mine like a heat-seeking missile. "You weren't at practice today."

I opened my mouth. Nothing came out.

"You *missed* practice. Y'know, for the competition that's in a couple of weeks?"

Shit.

"I..." I trailed off, my mind scrambling for an excuse.

I mean, I couldn't tell her the truth, could I?

She didn't need to know that I'd just spent the last hour tearing through my mom's office like a criminal.

Well, *more* of a criminal than I guess I already was.

"I lost track of time."

Gracie sighed, shaking her head. "You can't just blow off practice. This is something that's *very* important to me, and if you're not going to take it seriously—"

"I *am* taking it seriously," I snapped before I could stop myself.

She flinched, her face dropping for a split second before she masked it.

Guilt instantly hit me seeing her like that. Knowing I'd made her *feel* like that.

"Sorry," I muttered, raking a hand through my hair. "It's just... been a long day."

She didn't answer right away, just watched me with that look—the one that always made me feel like she could see straight through me.

And maybe she could.

Maybe she knew I wasn't telling her the full truth.

Then, after a long minute, she took a step back. Creating space.

"Well then..." she said slowly, "Think of me as your FFA fairy godmother or something. Here to save your ass like always."

The corner of her mouth lifted at her comment, as if she were proud of herself for it. But there was something about that smile that didn't quite reach her eyes, and I hated it.

I hated the space between us, the look she gave me, and most of all, the fact that I deserved every bit of it.

"Fairy godmother, huh?" I muttered finally, trying to lighten the mood. "Does that mean you're here to turn my shitty mood into a pumpkin?"

Gracie's hand brushed against my arm as she passed by me on her way to the kitchen. "No," she called over her shoulder, "it means I'm here to *fix* your mood before you scare all the woodland creatures away."

I followed, dragging my feet. "I'm not really in the mood to practice today, Gracie."

"Too bad," she opened the fridge, the faint hum filling the room as she rummaged through it. "You can mope later. Right now, you've got a fairy godmother on a deadline."

"Gracie..." The protest was weak even to my ears.

She turned. "*Cole*," she mimicked, wrinkling her nose. "Don't make me pull out the magic wand, okay? It's glittery, and I *will* use it."

That did it, and suddenly, I couldn't help but smile a little.

Even though every part of me wanted to sulk alone for the rest of my life, I found myself letting her push... let myself feel a bit better just because she was here.

I settled onto one of the stools at the kitchen island, and Gracie slid into the spot next to me, close enough that her knee brushed me.

344

She let out a dramatic sigh. "You do realize there are other foods in the world besides vegetables, right? Where are your Oreos?"

I laughed, the sound surprising even me right then. "You were looking for Oreos in the fridge?"

Her eyes widened, feigning scandalized shock. "You don't keep Oreos in the fridge?"

"You *do*?" I asked, a real grin finally starting to break through. "Don't they get soggy?"

"Absolutely not," she declared, leaning in closer. Her voice dropped to a playful whisper. "Fridge Oreos are life-changing, Cole."

"*No way*. Oreos belong in the pantry, like a normal person's snack."

Gracie leaned in even more, her face so close that I could see the mischievous glint in her eyes. "Okay, first of all, if vegetables are a 'normal person's snack' to you, your opinion's already invalid. *Secondly*, cold Oreos taste like happiness."

I let a sharp exhale escape my lips, trying to focus on what she was saying, and not the fact that I had just caught a whiff of her: vanilla and flowers.

That scent had been stuck in my head for days.

Hell, it was probably carved into my skull by now, right alongside the memory of her kiss.

But it wasn't just the way she smelled, or the way her laugh made the world suck less. It was *her*.

The way she filled every space she walked into with an undeniable energy, like gravity worked differently around her. Like maybe... everything could just be okay if I stayed close enough.

Warmth prickled across my skin, spreading up my neck.

I swallowed hard, as she closed the small space between us until we were just inches apart.

"Fine," I murmured. My eyes flicked down to her lips before I could stop myself. "Next time, I'll put the Oreos in the fridge. Just for you."

Because I'd do *anything* for her.

I loved the sight of her sitting beside me to the point of obsession.

I loved how at certain angles, the sunlight made her berry-colored lip gloss shimmer. I loved the the way she lived her life so unapologetically her. I loved the way she kept me honest. I loved... *her.*

I loved her.

The realization hit me like a sucker punch. *I loved Gracie.*

But I also didn't deserve her.

Not like this, anyway. Not when I was a walking disaster who couldn't even keep his own head on straight.

She deserved someone normal, someone who could make her laugh without dragging her into their messes. Someone who could actually remember their life. Someone who didn't make her upset like I was doing right now.

She deserved someone who... wasn't me.

I must've tensed up, because her smile dropped. "Hey," she said, tilting her head. "Are you okay?"

I tried to respond, but my throat felt like it was full of broken glass.

"This is about... *before*, isn't it?"

"What?" I blinked, dragging myself out of my own spiraling thoughts.

"The kiss," she clarified. "I don't know, maybe you regret it or... or maybe I—" She bit her lip, cutting herself off. "I've just been thinking, and I feel like maybe I've been... unfair to you."

"Unfair?"

"*Yes*, unfair. I mean..." she laughed softly, but it didn't reach her eyes. "Look at us. Our history's... complicated. I don't want you to think that

346

the second you lost your memory, I just *swooped* in and forced you to do something you weren't comfortable with because I know... I know what that's like, and I would hate myself if I ever made you feel..."

"Gracie, no. That's not it at all." I croaked, but she barreled forward.

"No, no. Let me finish. I should've explained this to you better instead of making you have to guess about your past with me... because the old Cole wouldn't even have wanted to be in the same room with me, let alone *kiss* me. And I just... I don't want you to think I'm taking advantage of that, of *you*."

"You're not."

"Obviously that's not how you really feel," she challenged, her tone slightly frustrated. "That's why you've been so weird lately, and I just..." Her shoulders slumped as her face softened. "I just wanted to say I'm sorry. I shouldn't have let us become friends, or... or kiss you..."

Fuck it.

I needed to say it now. To tell her that's not how I actually felt, not by a long shot.

Say it, Cole. Say you love her.

But suddenly, my chest tightened, and the edges of the room began to blur.

Dammit. *Not now. Not now.*

I clenched my fists so hard my knuckles ached, trying to focus on her face and the way her beautiful brown eyes were locked on mine, waiting for me to say something.

My heart screamed to hold onto this moment, to *her*, because if I lost it, I knew I'd lose her too.

I couldn't let that happen. Not when I needed to tell her. Needed to make her understand.

She wasn't using me. She was my *everything*.

I loved her.

A shudder tore through me, and I gasped for air, clawing desperately at the present as the past dragged me under.

I fought it with everything I had, my whole body shaking violently.

Her voice sounded in my ears, but it was underwater.

"Cole...?"

"Gracie—" I choked out, barely able to form the word. I reached for her, my hand brushing hers as my vision blurred.

I couldn't let her go—couldn't lose this.

But the memory slammed into me, swallowing me whole.

And just like that, she was gone.

The low hum of an engine whistled in my ears. Darkness clouded my vision, but through the haze, LED lights flickered intermittently, casting a harsh, eerie glow on my dark blue jeans.

I finally realized where I was (my truck)—driving, to be exact. But something was off.

The memory and the sense of where I was and what I was doing, kept slipping through my fingers. No matter how hard I tried to focus, everything seemed to blur and fade in and out.

An urgent feeling gnawed at the edges of my consciousness, but at the same time, I felt... giddy. And warm?

The sound of the engine grew louder, distorted, as if the world around me was warping and twisting together.

The dashboard lights flickered faster.

The road ahead blurred.

Then, out of nowhere, a muffled sound pierced the silence—a scream. MY scream.

And then everything went dark.

"Cole, I'm seriously getting worried about you."

I must've been losing it because the voice sounded a hell of a lot like Gracie.

The words rattled in my skull, and it took a minute before I looked down and realized how tightly I was gripping the edge of the countertop.

I forced myself to release my hold, peeling my hands off the counter like they were glued there.

My chest heaved as I fought for air, my head spinning as memories and reality blurred together.

I shook my head, trying to snap out of it, but I couldn't.

"Cole," the voice—I looked up just to make sure: it *was* Gracie, said again, softer this time as she stepped closer.

Her hand hovered near mine like she wanted to reach for it but wasn't sure if she should. "You need to sit down, okay? Just take a second and breathe."

But I am sitting down.

Except... I wasn't.

My feet were firmly planted on the kitchen floor, steps away from the island where I *just* was.

How the hell did I not notice myself getting up?

The pounding in my head grew louder, like someone was slamming a sledgehammer against my skull.

I tried to piece together how I'd ended up like this, how Gracie had ended up here, why there were papers scattered all over the floor...

"When..." my voice came out hoarse, raspy. I swallowed and tried again, but the words tangled in my throat. "When did you get here?"

"Cole, you're *scaring* me. Sit down. You're shaking."

But I couldn't focus on her.

The pounding in my head only got worse, the memory clawing at the edges of my consciousness like a feral animal.

The hum of the engine, the blinding lights, the scream... that *scream*. It echoed in my mind, louder and louder until it was drowning out everything else.

My legs wobbled, and I staggered back, fumbling for something, *anything* solid to hold onto.

I reached for the countertop, but it wasn't there anymore.

I forced my gaze to Gracie again. Her lips were trembling as if she were seconds from crying.

You're scaring her. Stop.

The thought gutted me, making my heart twist in painful, unnatural ways.

I didn't want to scare her, didn't want to make her feel unsafe. And here I was... *hurting* her, the one person I wanted to protect more than anything.

"Gracie, I..." my voice cracked.

But I didn't know what to say. Didn't know how to fix it.

The memory roared louder, overlapping with the sickening realization that I couldn't stop this. I couldn't stop myself.

That's when a new wave of anger surged, swallowing the guilt and leaving something hot and uncontrollable in its place.

The more I tried to calm down, the worse it got.

The harder it became to breathe.

"I need you to leave." My voice came out rough, barely scraping past the lump in my throat.

I squeezed my eyes shut.

My chest burned, my head continued to pound, and my thoughts were jumping everywhere.

Stop it, calm down, don't scare her. But I didn't know how.

"I'm not leaving you. Especially not like this. I'm getting you a glass of water, and I'm *making* you sit down."

She didn't understand what was happening to me. *How could she?* She was treating me like I was suffering some psychotic break, and maybe I was. But she couldn't fix this.

She couldn't fix *me*.

"Gracie," I forced out. "I need you to stop for a minute."

She ignored me.

Because *of course*, she did.

When she came back, she was holding a mug with both hands. "Here. Take a sip, okay? Just—"

"Gracie, I said *stop!*"

I slapped the mug out of her hands before I even realized what I was doing.

The crash was deafening.

Ceramic exploded across the hardwood, and water splashed everywhere—her shoes, my jeans, the cabinets...

I looked down.

Dad's mug.

I froze, staring at the shattered pieces.

The chipped handle spun to a stop in the puddle of water.

What the hell did I just do?

"Cole..." Her voice was smaller than I'd ever heard it before.

"That was my dad's mug."

"I'm sorry—"

"That was *my dad's* mug," I repeated, sharply.

"I didn't know. I'm sorry."

I took a step closer, and her hands twitched at her sides.

"Of *course*, you didn't Gracie," I scoffed, my voice rising, shaking with the effort to hold it together. "Because you never *know*. Not if it has something to do with someone who's not you."

"Cole—"

"It was one of the last things I had left of him. And now it's *gone*. You don't *listen*, Gracie. You *never* listen! I told you to stop. I told you to leave, but you just keep *pushing*!" The words came faster and louder as I took another step toward her. "You try so hard to 'fix' everything, but all you do is make it worse. Every. Single. Time."

Her eyes were glassy, her mouth trembling like she wanted to argue. But she didn't. She just stood there, taking it.

"My life isn't something that needs fixing, okay? I'm not some passion project for you to work on when you're feeling bad about yourself!"

Still nothing from her. Just that same, damn quiet look.

"You're not my savior, Gracie!" I spat. "So, stop acting like you are! You can't fix *this*. You can't fix *me*. You're just—" My voice caught, but I forced the words out. "You're just making everything harder."

I took a shaky breath, but I couldn't stop myself. The words kept spilling out.

"We are *not* the same. You have a life outside of this, outside of *me*, and you need to start living it."

"Is this just about the kiss? Because I—"

I pointed at the door, my chest heaving. "GO HOME, GRACIE!"

Suddenly, something snapped inside of her. And she moved. *Towards* me.

"The only reason I haven't walked out of here is because you're important to me," she said quietly. "But don't think that I'll keep letting you talk to me like this. Now... I think we should sit down and—"

"GO FUCKING HOME, GRACIE."

The force of my voice cracked through the air like a whip, echoing off the walls.

She flinched.

Like I'd hit her.

My stomach twisted, but not enough to apologize. At least not right then.

Instead, I stumbled forward, my shoulder brushing past nothing. She must have moved. Or maybe she wasn't as close as I thought.

I didn't look back to check.

"Place one hand on your stomach. One on your chest," I muttered, my voice shaky. I wasn't even sure if I was doing it right anymore. "In through your nose. Out through your mouth."

Dr. Andrews had told me this would help. It *had* to help.

But it wasn't working. The air felt like I was breathing through a straw.

I gritted my teeth, trying to stay focused on the steps that weren't helping. "Deeeeep breath. In. Out. Repeat."

The room spun around me, and I stumbled back, hitting the counter.

I pressed my palms to my face, digging my fingers into my hair as I mentally counted the seconds.

One. Two. Three. Four...

Each breath came slower. The pounding in my ears dulled. The room steadied. My lungs burned as I forced in air, the ache in my chest shifting into something deeper—*more hollow.*

My hands dropped to my sides as I blinked back into focus.

The silence that followed wasn't peaceful. It was *suffocating.*

And Gracie's face was stuck in my head.

She'd been *afraid* of me. Actually afraid.

Like everyone else was.

"Gracie, I'm—" But she was already gone.

"Sorry," I whispered to the empty room.

My legs buckled then, and I sank to the floor, the cold hardwood pressing against my skin.

It felt like the fight had ripped out everything I had left. The anger, the adrenaline was all gone now, leaving behind this raw, nasty, gnawing ache.

Hot tears welled up before I could stop them, spilling over and running down my face.

I tried to pull it together, to hold on to something—*anything*—but the harder I tried, the more it all slipped through my fingers.

She was gone. My *dad* was gone. Everything was... gone.

I curled up on the floor, my knees to my chest, my whole body shaking. I didn't care how pathetic it looked. I didn't care about anything anymore.

I'd fucked up. Big time. And I didn't know if I'd be able to fix it. Or if I even deserved to.

Chapter Twenty-Eight:

FEBRUARY 24TH

I felt... numb.

My fingers curled weakly around the stiff hospital sheets, my eyes searching for something that made sense. But it felt like I was trying to grab smoke with my bare hands.

People would come in every so often, poking their heads into my room, asking the same useless questions over and over again.

"How are you feeling?"

"Do you know why you're here?"

"What do you remember?"

I wanted to scream at them. I wanted to demand to be left the hell alone. But I didn't. What did it matter, anyways? They didn't care.

They left. And then they'd come back. And then they'd leave again. An hour would pass, and it would start all over, the cycle repeating like some twisted, never-ending loop.

Time stretched and folded in on itself until I couldn't tell if I'd been here for hours or days.

The door creaked open again, but I didn't bother looking. Instead, I stubbornly closed my eyes so that I wouldn't have to talk to anyone.

I was exhausted. I was embarrassed. I was frustrated. I didn't know what was going on...

I never knew what was going on.

"I don't think you understand, Dr. Andrews."

My mom's voice.

The first one I'd actually recognized since I got here.

"The day started off completely normal," she continued, her words tight. "We left him alone for a few hours, and when we came back... we found him curled up on the kitchen floor sobbing."

Was that what I'd really been doing?

No, that didn't sound right.

I racked my brain for some kind of confirmation either way, but my thoughts were a tangled half-formed mess of images and static.

Then, out of nowhere, a face surfaced in my mind.

Gracie.

She was crying. *Why was she crying?*

My pulse spiked. *Had I done something to her?* We were at my house earlier—we'd fought...

No, wait. That wasn't right either. Because she wasn't in my house in the memory.

She looked... younger. And we were at school...

But that didn't make any sense. How could she be younger?

What the hell was going on with me?

But there she was—clear as day. Gracie hunched over, her shoulders shaking violently as she sobbed on the floor.

A sharp, sour taste crept into my mouth. That didn't happen. It *couldn't* have.

But it felt so real.

And I'd done *nothing* about it.

I did nothing as the most beautiful soul in the world fell apart *right in front of me*.

After what felt like a lifetime's worth of my own personal hell, I forced myself to take a step forward. *Towards* her.

And that's when a hand clamped down on my shoulder.

"Dude, come on."

I turned. Dylan... laughing, completely oblivious of what was happening right there in front of us. Or maybe he *wasn't* oblivious. Maybe he just didn't care.

I hesitated. Just a second. Just long enough for him to pull me away. I didn't say anything. I didn't do anything.

Why didn't I do anything?

And then—

The hospital room slammed back into focus.

My pulse spiked as panic clawed its way up my throat.

Was she okay? Did she need me to come get her? What even was that?

I couldn't breathe. I needed to talk to her. To make sure she was okay. *Now.*

I fumbled for my phone, my hands shaking as I reached toward my bedside table—

It wasn't there.

Right. Because I'm in the fucking hospital right now.

"Cole," Mom started, coming quickly to my side, "lay back down."

"I just need to—"

"Cole. *Lay back down*." Firmer this time. Her hand hovered over my arm, ready to push me down if I didn't listen.

I sank back into the bed, heart hammering, reality sloshing around in my brain like water.

She then turned back to the doctor. "You mean to tell me that my son experienced a clear psychotic episode and 'there's nothing you can do'?"

"I didn't say *nothing*."

She exhaled sharply through her nose, not buying it. "And how *are* you feeling, Cole?"

I hesitated as my mind flashed back to Gracie. *Like absolute shit.*

But I couldn't say that.

Instead, I forced a smile that didn't feel even remotely real. "Good. Better."

She studied me for a second longer than I was comfortable with, then nodded, relief softening her face. "Good. That's good to hear." But just as quickly, she turned back to Dr. Andrews. "I still want a second opinion. You have no idea how scary it is to walk in on your child like... *that*."

"I understand your concern," Dr. Andrews replied evenly. "But medication is a last resort. We need to understand the underlying causes of Cole's episodes before considering that step."

Mom's jaw clenched. "So, what do we do then?"

Dr. Andrews turned to me, his expression serious. "Cole, how long have you been getting these memory flashes?"

I swallowed hard, my throat dry. "On and off... for a few months."

He nodded thoughtfully.

Mom's sharp inhale cut through the room.

I turned just in time to see the look on her face—wide eyes, parted lips, the question forming before she caught herself.

Why didn't you tell me?

But she didn't ask out loud.

Instead, she pressed her lips into a thin line, her gaze darting between me and Dr. Andrews. "If this happens again..."

"We'll cross that bridge if we come to it." Dr. Andrews assured her. "For now, let's focus on getting Cole the help that he needs. The first step is to track these episodes. Keeping a record of when and where they happen might help us identify a pattern."

Mom's fingers curled tighter around her arms. "And what if there *isn't* a pattern? What if this... this *just happens*?"

"It's too soon to make assumptions. But I can promise you this: we'll keep digging until we know more. These things don't happen without a reason."

She was quiet for a long second before finally nodding. "Fine. But I'm holding you to that."

Dr. Andrews turned back to me. "Cole, this isn't something you have to figure out on your own anymore. Whatever's going on, we'll face it together. You've got people in your corner."

I nodded, even though it felt like I'd pushed the one person I *wanted* in my corner down a path of fucking self-destruction.

If I could just call her, hear her voice, make sure she's okay...

Dr. Andrews stood. "Get some rest. We'll set up a follow-up appointment to talk more about next steps."

Mom waited until he left before stepping closer, her hand hovering over the edge of the bed like she wanted to reach for me but wasn't sure if she should.

"You should've told me," she muttered.

If my mind hadn't been somewhere else (on Gracie), the thought of freaking my mom out would've gutted me. But it *was* somewhere else. On someone I hated hurting even more.

She has to be okay. Just give me a chance to fix this.

Please.

Mom let out a tired sigh, one that carried more than just frustration. It carried *fear*—real, bone-deep fear.

"Get some sleep, Cole. We'll talk later."

And then I was alone again.

You've Goat Mail FFA Group Chat:

MARCH 3RD

> **Gracie:** Just got an email from Principal Hawkins... our practice room is being used by *shiver* the Ag Mechanics team.

> **Emma:** what??? they cant just do that. we've had mondays booked for like... forever

> **Gracie:** I know. It's stupid. Anyway... does anyone know where we can study instead? We could really use the practice before State.

Cole: I mean, I'd offer up my place, but my mom's redoing the countertops in the kitchen. I don't think there'd be room for all of us

Gracie: Ahh, yes. No room in that mansion of yours. Makes sense...

Cole: ??

Gracie: Well, we can't use my house. Mom's back in town, and it's really awkward when my parents are together in the same room right now.

Cole: I didn't know ur mom was back in town?? Why didn't u say smth?

Gracie: Clearly you were busy.

Emma: as much as i love being in the middle of these little lover spats, we really need to figure out a plan

Bear: I second that, for the record. BTW Emma, it's even worse seeing it in person. Gracie looks pissed RN.

Bear: Attachment: 1 Image

Gracie: I'm not above blocking you from this chat, Bear. Don't test me.

Cole: I think u and I should talk, Gracie. Outside of the group chat... if that wasn't clear

Gracie: What for? You've got an audience right here. Might as well make it a show.

Cole: Because I was a jerk. And u deserve an actual apology

Gracie: Well, I don't wanna hear it.

Gracie: Now, the plan, please?

Bear: What about Emma's place?

Gracie: THAT'S BRILLIANT! And exactly why I keep you around. What do you say, Em?

Emma: i dont know, you guys... isnt there someplace else we can go?

Gracie: C'monnnnnn! I've never even been to your house before. Please?? It'll be fun!

Emma: gracie, i dont think it's a good idea

Gracie: Please, please, pleaseeeeee? I'll be your best friend!

Emma: you already are??

Gracie: Even MORE of your best friend?

Cole: I'm not sure whether I should take offense to this or not

Gracie: Shut up, Cole.

Emma: uggh. ok, fine. but only for a few hrs. nothing more.

Gracie: YOU'RE THE BEST!

Cole: Gracie, I'm serious. Please. Just five minutes. U don't even have to talk. Just let me explain

Gracie Lewis Has Left the Chat

Chapter Twenty-Nine:

MARCH 5TH

G racie
The second I walked into Emma's house, I wanted to walk right
back out.

The air reeked of cigarette smoke, though someone had clearly gone
to war with a can of Febreze to try and cover it up. But the smell of fake
lavender only made it worse, like the whole house was trying to convince
us it wasn't as miserable as it felt.

The walls were bare—no photos, no art, nothing that made it feel like
someone actually lived here—kind of like *my* house. Just with decaying
wallpaper instead of boring beige paint.

"So," I said, setting my bag down on a couch cushion that looked like it
came complete with an array of STDs. "This is... cozy."

"I tried to warn you," Emma sighed, biting her lip.

"No, no, no... it's just... unique." I scanned the depressing interior. The combination of stale cigarette smoke and Febreze was starting to make my eyes water. "What'd you say your dad does for a living again?

"Let's not talk about my dad, okay?" Emma replied quickly, her voice tight. "Where's Bear?"

I gave her a look. She was being cagey, but I didn't push.

If she didn't want to talk about it, fine. I wasn't exactly an open book either.

"Probably passed out in the driveway," I muttered, flipping open my notes.

Right on cue, Bear stumbled in, looking like death warmed over. "If anyone needs me," he said dropping onto the couch, which literally *caved* under his weight, "I'll be over here, slowly dying."

Bear's infusions were late again, thanks to his doctor deciding to prioritize his family or whatever. His wife just had a baby, so naturally, that meant Bear had to suffer.

The timing was *truly* unbelievable. And let's just say, the infusion center received a *very* lengthy voicemail from me about it... complete with a few of my favorite choice words.

The door opened again.

Cole.

He stayed by the entrance like he wasn't sure if he was allowed inside (he *shouldn't* have been, if he was).

But just as I was thinking that, his eyes flicked to mine, and my heart betrayed me.

You want him here, you liar.

After much deliberation, (or maybe *no* deliberation, and I was just trying to convince myself that he cared) he came all the way in, sighing as he set his bag down next to Bear's.

We accidentally made eye contact again, and he gave me a half-wave.

Instead of waving back, I whipped my head back around to my FFA binder and buried myself in the text just so he couldn't see my reddening face.

"You okay, Gracie?" he asked softly in a way that made my stomach dip. But I still refused to look at him.

"Peachy."

He exhaled sharply at that. "Can we just talk for a second, please?"

"We're talking right now." I shrugged, flipping to the next page I was pretending to read.

"*Gracie.* Please?"

I snapped quickly, slamming my binder shut to glare at him. "*What*, Cole? What do you want?"

His jaw tightened, and for a minute, he didn't say anything. Just stared at me with those stupid gray eyes that looked like they were full of lies and fake apologies that I didn't want to hear.

"I just..." he raked a hand through his hair, seemingly struggling to find the right words. "Have I ever made you... cry?"

That threw me off.

Maybe I'd rather have a fake apology.

"*Excuse me?*"

His eyes searched mine for a beat. "Have I ever done something to make you cry?"

I quickly looked away, afraid of what he might see.

"*That's* what this is about? Seriously?" I stood from the couch, crossing my arms. "No, Cole. I could care less about you."

It was a lie, of course. A big, fat, obvious lie. But it was the best defense I had.

The truth was, I'd cried about Cole more than I wanted to admit.

I'd cried on the drive home after our argument, cried at school the next day when he wasn't there (probably avoiding me instead) and cried every night since like some pathetic idiot.

And I hated myself for it.

Because no matter how much I tried to convince myself otherwise, Cole Brown was all I could think about.

The way his hair always fell into his eyes. The way he leaned in when he laughed, like he wanted to share the joke only with me. The way he'd kissed me that day in the park...

My stomach did a nosedive.

It was true, wasn't it?

Our problems had started after we kissed. He regretted it. He *had* to. He thought I was using him. Taking advantage of the fact that he couldn't remember anything.

I'd my suspicions when I went over to his house the other day, *a house I basically broke into, by the way.*

But he was too freaking nice to tell me he was uncomfortable, so instead, he chose to scare the living crap out of me in the comfort of his own home.

See what having a crush did to me? I didn't know how to handle my feelings, and now, he probably thought I was psychotic.

"I don't believe you," he said finally.

I rolled my eyes, deflecting. "Believe what you want, Cole. I don't care."

But I *did* care. Too much.

Heaven help me.

I folded my arms tighter against my chest, trying to create a barrier between me and Cole—*or maybe just me and my feelings.*

Why couldn't he just stay away from me like in the good, ol' days before his accident?

But **were** those good ol' days?

I didn't want to know the answer, so instead, I quickly doubled-down. "I've never cried because of you. That's all in your head."

"Classic gas lighter move," Bear mumbled under his breath.

Cole's brow drew together, that stupid furrow that made him look both confused and determined, ignoring Bear completely. "I don't believe that."

"Well, you should. Because it's true." I stepped around the couch, turning my back to him. "Let it go. I'm fine."

Cole took a step closer. "Gracie, I know you. You're not fine."

I laughed bitterly. "Oh, you *know* me, do you?" I whirled around to face him, my eyes narrowing. "Because last I checked, you couldn't even *remember* you."

His jaw tightened again, but he didn't look away. "I don't have to remember everything to know when you're upset. And I know I hurt you. Just tell me how, Gracie. Please."

"*Why?* So, you can do it again?"

Emma cleared her throat behind us uncomfortably. "So... anatomy... who wants to start?"

"Gracie," Cole pleaded. "What did I do?"

I clenched my fists, my nails digging into my palms so I couldn't just give in right then and there. I just had to keep reminding myself: *we don't work, we don't work, we don't work.*

369

"You didn't *do* anything, okay? You just... exist. And that's the problem."

"I know you don't mean that."

"Don't tell me what I mean." I fired back.

"Then don't tell *me* that I don't know you."

Emma cleared her throat again, tucking a strand of blonde hair behind her ear. "Um, sorry to interrupt whatever... *this* is, but can we please focus? The competition is in four days."

She held up a stack of flashcards like a peace offering. "I made flashcards?"

"Ooh, flashcards. Riveting." Bear grinned, inspecting the stack.

"*I'm* ready for this competition," I said pointedly, my eyes flicking toward Cole. "Can't say the same for everyone else, though."

He sighed, sitting back down in his chair as he crossed his arms. "Oh, *I'm sorry*. Was that aimed at me?"

I didn't look at him as I slid into the open spot next to Emma. "If the boot fits, Brown." I grabbed Emma's flashcards. "Let's just focus on the reproductive systems of cattle or something."

Emma's eyes widened as I rifled through her stack. "Uh, those are actually in alphabetical order—"

"Don't care," I muttered, flipping one over and reading aloud. "Question: What is the gestation period of a cow?"

"Two hundred eighty-five days," Cole answered automatically, not even looking at the card.

His eyes never left mine.

"Great. You can go home now," I said flatly, tossing the card onto the table.

He scoffed. "Why do you always do this?"

"Do *what*?"

"Push people away the second they get close to you."

I froze, the rest of the flashcards slipping through my fingers and scattering across the table. "I don't push people away," I said simply.

"You do too."

A bitter laugh slipped out. *He has some nerve saying that to me...* "Oh, and *you* don't?"

"Guys," Emma cut in. "Seriously, we need to—"

"You're scared, Gracie," Cole observed. *Wrongly*, I might add.

"I am *not*."

"You are," he pressed. "But I'm not going anywhere, Gracie. No matter how hard you try to push me away."

"Oh, do you say that to *all* the girls you yell at?" I shot back, shifting further away from him on the couch.

But *not* because I was scared. Because I was... I don't know. Confused by him? Angry? Ugh. I didn't even know anymore.

"I was an asshole, and I'm sorry. I want to—"

"Cole," I warned. "Don't."

"Don't what?" His voice rose slightly, frustration bleeding through. "Don't care about you? Don't try to understand you?" He leaned closer, stubborn determination in his gray eyes. "I made a mistake, and I want to own up to it."

Bear groaned dramatically. "If you two are gonna fight all night, can we at least make it entertaining? Throw something. Ooh! Maybe a flashcard."

Emma buried her face in her hands. "Oh my gosh."

"You don't know everything, okay?" I said quietly, my voice losing its edge as I looked directly at him. "I'm doing you a favor."

"No, Gracie." He shook his head, his voice softer. "You're trying to do *yourself* a favor. But we both know this isn't what you want either."

Before I could respond (or deny it), the low rumble of the garage door opening shattered the moment.

Emma's eyes went wide, panic shooting across her face as she shot to her feet.

"You all need to leave. *Now.*"

My eyebrows furrowed. "What do you mean? Emma, are you okay?"

"I SAID LEAVE."

None of us moved for a second (mostly from shock). In all the years I'd known her, she'd never been *this* upset before.

But the spell quickly broke, and Bear and Cole started scrambling to pack up their stuff, sensing the urgency in her voice.

I grabbed my backpack, finally, too, hurt but compliant.

Fine. Whatever. Kick me out of your life, why don't you?

We filed out of the house in silence, but halfway down the driveway, I realized...

"Shoot. My binder," I muttered, stopping short.

"What?" Cole asked, glancing at me over his shoulder.

"My binder's still inside," I said, already turning back.

"Gracie, just leave it," Bear called, already tugging on the passenger side door of my car.

When it didn't budge (because I hadn't unlocked it yet), he shot me an impatient look, lifting the handle again as if that would magically open it.

I sighed and pressed the button on my key fob, the lock clicking open. "There. Happy now?"

Bear rolled his eyes but climbed in without another word.

I turned back toward the house, muttering under my breath, "I'll be right back."

"Gracie—" Cole's voice followed me.

I held up a hand, flipping him the bird without breaking stride.

He scoffed, "Seriously?"

"Seriously!"

When I reached the door, it was already ajar (I guess we'd accidentally forgotten to shut it on our way out the first time), swinging open just enough to make me think twice about going straight inside.

Something felt... wrong.

I stepped across the threshold anyway, my sneakers scuffing against the linoleum as the door creaked closed behind me.

The whole house felt eerily empty.

*Where's Emma? She was **just** here.*

My heart thudded faster, and I swallowed hard, trying to shake off the unease creeping up my spine.

This was stupid. I was being stupid. I just needed my binder, and then I'd be out.

That's when I saw it.

"Why the hell are there people in my driveway?" an older man, who I assumed was Emma's dad (I'd never met him before), barked as he stormed into the living room from the garage.

His face was red as Emma trailed behind him, looking like she wanted to disappear into the walls. "What did I *tell* you about having people over?"

"I'm sorry." Emma's voice quivered, tears already streaming down her face. "I'm so sorry. I didn't mean—"

"*Sorry?*" he cut her off, spinning around and shaking the case of beer in his hands like it was some damning piece of evidence. "Oh, I get it. Sending me to the store was all a ruse so you could have your little friends over, huh? You little weasel!"

"No, no, it wasn't like that!" Emma stammered, "We were just studying..."

"*Sure,*" he scoffed, narrowing his bloodshot eyes at her. "And how much beer did you take from me, huh? *Answer me!*"

"None," Emma shook her head frantically. "None. I promise."

"Don't lie to me, girl," he growled, stepping closer and grabbing her arm with a grip that made her wince.

"I'm not lying!" Emma sobbed, trying to pull away. "We didn't drink anything, I swear!"

But apparently, she wasn't convincing enough because he yanked her harder, and in one swift, enraged motion, he threw her to the floor.

She cried out as she fell into the coffee table, her hands flying up to protect her face.

But he wasn't done. He stalked around the (now broken) table with the beer in hand. "You want some alcohol, *sweetheart*? Well, here—"

Before I could even react, he slammed the entire case down on her.

I must've screamed then, because both their heads whipped toward me.

Emma's face crumpled with mortification, "Gracie! It's not what it looks like!"

But it was.

It *absolutely* was.

I didn't bother shutting the front door behind me as I bolted toward my car.

Cole was leaning against my driver side door when I reached it, concern flooding his eyes the second he saw my face.

"Gracie?" he said softly, stepping closer. "What's wrong? Did something happen?"

"Not now, Cole!" I snapped as I fumbled with my keys.

"Wait—" He reached for me, his hand brushing my shoulder as if he wanted to try to calm me down. But I pulled away, shoving past him to yank the car door open.

"What's going on?" Bear asked as I threw myself in the driver's seat.

I was causing a scene, but I couldn't think… couldn't *breathe*. All I could picture was Emma and…

"Just *wait* for a second. Please…" Cole tried again.

But I slammed the door shut, cutting him off.

At that point, my hands were shaking so badly that I could barely get the key into the ignition. But somehow, I managed, flooring it on the gas, leaving him—and the house behind me.

The drive was a blur of taillights and streetlamps, my mind racing with images of Emma's dad *hurting* her.

How had I not seen this before? Was I really so obsessed with myself that I didn't notice that she was in trouble?

And yet, even now that I knew, I'd run. *Left* her there. Like a coward.

I bit back a sob, gripping the steering wheel tighter as the realization dawned on me…

I wasn't just a terrible friend. I was a terrible *person*.

Only a few minutes later did I remember that I'd left my binder back in that house of horrors.

Chapter Thirty:

MARCH 9TH

It was the day before the biggest competition of my entire life—y'know, the one I'd been studying for all year? And I couldn't even enjoy it.

Why? Oh, just the small detail of being sandwiched in a van on the way *to* it between my best friend, who was silently begging me not to expose her dad as the raging monster it turned out he was, and my sworn enemy turned... crush? (the details on that one were still a little murky.)

Thankfully, though, just a few, short hours later, we lurched to a stop in front of our hotel.

And I still hadn't said a word to anyone.

I pushed my way out first, immediately being slapped in the face with thick, humid air.

But I didn't care. I just needed to breathe for a second.

"Gracie."

Emma stood a few feet away, arms wrapped tightly around herself. She glanced between Cole and Bear, who were busy grabbing their bags (well, Bear was *trying* to—I'd have to help him in a second), then back at me.

"Can we talk?"

My first thought was *absolutely not*, only imagining what this "fun" little talk was going to be about. But I nodded anyways.

She led me around the side of the van, where it was quieter. Her face was pale, eyes darting around like she was afraid someone might overhear us.

"Gracie," she whispered. "You can't say anything. Not to anyone."

"Emma—"

"I mean it," she cut me off, eyes wide and pleading. "It's not what you think. He... he's just stressed right now. It's not always like that."

My chest tightened. "I don't think it should *ever* be like that."

"Please." Her voice cracked as she grabbed my hand, gripping it tightly. "If you tell someone, it'll just make everything worse. You don't understand. I just need to make it to graduation. That's it. Then I'm gone, and none of this will even matter."

"But—"

"Gracie, I'm asking you as my *friend*, please don't say anything."

It wasn't like I had the greatest example of a dad to go off of, but saying *nothing* really couldn't have been better... could it have?

But then again, maybe she was right. Maybe it *was* just a one time thing.

I mean, the guy literally took Emma on freaking vacations to places I could only *dream* of going every other weekend. Not to mention, he was always buying her the prettiest, most expensive things ever...

It couldn't have been *all* bad. Right?

But before I could say anything else, she squeezed my hand one last time, her fingers trembling. "Please," she whispered, then pulled away, walking toward the hotel like nothing had happened.

Pretending. She's pretending. I can do that too. I can...

Suddenly, another shadow fell over me.

"Are you okay, Gracie? What's up?" Cole asked softly.

I spun around, hardening my face as quickly as I could. And even though I knew that I shouldn't have, I just muttered, "I'm *fine.*"

Because I knew if he really tried, he could get me to talk. And I'd *let* him because I was a wuss. And then, I'd screw-up Emma's stupid secret.

So instead, I marched straight for the reception desk, ready to check us in and ignore everything else.

But of course, he followed.

Out of the corner of my eye, though, I noticed that there were two bags slung over his shoulder—his (obviously) and *Bear's.*

Sweet mother of Abraham Lincoln.

My brother wasn't the type of person to ask for help, (he was too proud for that) and *I* definitely hadn't asked. But there was Cole, acting like the knight in shining armor he thought he was.

And he *was.*

Even with the argument we'd had a couple days ago.

He shouldn't have still been nice to me. Especially not now, with me treating him like the scum of the earth all over again.

The *old* him wouldn't have put up with that, at least.

I pushed, he gave up. That way, I didn't have to feel guilty.

I didn't have to feel anything at all.

But now, he was this genuinely good guy. Just one who made mistakes every once in a while (y'know, like a normal freaking person?).

It wasn't that I couldn't forgive him for getting mad at me. I mean, I would've been pissed at me too. I accidentally broke his dead dad's mug for crying out loud.

I just couldn't ignore the little voice screaming in my head that people like me don't deserve people like him.

Maybe before the accident, we'd actually had something in common with each other. But now, we were in two completely different places in our lives. One where he *could* get better, and one where I only got worse.

For right now, though, I had to pretend like everything was fine and like I *wasn't* a complete disaster.

And that's exactly what I did as I squared my shoulders and stepped up to the reception desk, shoving the mess of my thoughts into a corner of my mind where I could ignore them.

Mostly.

The receptionist, a woman in her late thirties, glanced up at me as I approached her. "Hi! How can I help you?"

I matched her smile... or at least *tried* to. "We have a reservation for the Hillview High Vet Science team. We just need to check in and get our room keys."

She nodded and started typing away on her computer.

After a minute, she handed me four keycards. "Here you are. Rooms 412 and 414. Just to let you know, our elevators are currently out of order, so you'll need to use the stairs."

Wait. **_Four_** *flights of stairs?*

There was no way Bear could handle stairs on a *good* day, let alone going on week three without his IVIG infusions.

I blinked as my mind scrambled to find a solution. "Umm,"

Then suddenly, out of nowhere, it hit me...*Cole could carry him.*

And just like that, my brain took off like a racehorse.

I pictured it—Cole, scooping Bear up in his arms, climbing those four flights of stairs like some kind of gorgeous fireman from one of those overly dramatic romance novels Emma was always talking about.

The image shifted in my mind, uninvited but incredibly vivid and shirt-less: Cole's arms flexing, his jaw set with determination, Bear resting securely in his grip while he muttered something wildly hot under his breath, like, *"It's no big deal, Gracie, I've got this."*

Damn me.

"I, uh, actually..." I stammered, focusing back on the receptionist so fast it gave me whiplash. "Is there any way we can get a room on a lower floor? My brother has a disability, and stairs aren't really an option for him."

Her expression softened like it usually did whenever people found out about Bear's condition (hooray for pity!), and she nodded. "Let me check what's available."

She typed some more, her brow furrowing as she scrolled through the reservations. Finally, though, she looked up. "We *do* have one disability-accessible room available, but it's not part of your block. It's usually reserved for emergencies or last-minute needs."

Relief washed over me. "We'll take it."

She nodded, printing out the key. "Room 102, first floor."

"Thank you."

I headed back to my group, handing the first key to Bear. "You guys are in Room 102, first floor. No stairs."

In the few steps it'd taken to walk from the receptionist's desk back to my group, I'd turned over every possible room combination in my head a thousand times.

It was already bad enough starting this trip knowing that Bear wouldn't realistically end up in the same room as me, so I could watch him (because putting Emma with Cole was *not* happening, and I couldn't exactly shove Cole and Bear in with me either).

But now, not to even have him be on the same *floor* as me?

I almost wanted to turn around and go home right then and there.

But I couldn't.

So, it meant that I really had to trust this decision to trust *him*. Even if that went against everything I'd ever learned growing up.

I turned the second keycard over in my hands once. Twice. Still thinking it over.

I'm really choosing to put my faith in Cole over myself, aren't I?

With that, I took a breath, slowly giving up control.

His hands closed over the card, but he didn't move. He just stood there, looking at me.

I cleared my throat, willing the words out of me. "You'll be... with Bear."

"I'll make sure he does alright. Okay, Gracie?" he said softly.

I nodded quickly, ripping myself from his contact and looking anywhere but at him. Because I knew if I let myself meet his eyes, it'd be *game over* for me. "Okay," I whispered.

"Alright, kid," Cole said, slipping the key into his pocket and turning to Bear with a grin. "Let's go see what kind of view this first-floor has to offer."

Bear smirked. "Yeah, sure. I bet it's got a great view of the parking lot."

I watched as they walked away, surprising myself when I didn't feel worried like I thought I would. Instead, I felt something quieter... more deeply intimate by trusting him.

Yeah, yeah. I knew this whole *Cole and me* thing couldn't work. He'd get his memories back and realize it too. But that didn't mean I couldn't hold onto this Cole 2.0 a little longer, right?

"Wow," Emma breathed next to me. "That was big of you, Gracie-girl. I'm proud."

I smiled at her. Because even though we were in a tough spot right then, leave it to Emma to still be my biggest cheerleader.

And for once, I didn't feel the need to stress about the worst-case scenario. This Cole had it covered.

March 10th

The morning came way too quickly, with gray light creeping around the edges of the blackout curtains.

I hadn't slept much.

Between Emma getting a call from her dad as soon as we got to our room and being holed up crying in the bathroom for most of the night, to the upcoming competition, to still worrying about Bear (even *with* Cole watching him), it was bound to happen.

I gave up on sleep around 3 a.m. and lay staring at the ceiling, thinking about everything and nothing at the same time. And when my alarm buzzed, I was already almost out the door... making my way to Room 102 with a tray balanced in one hand before I could even process what I was doing.

Bear opened the door almost immediately. "What's up?' he asked, his voice scratchy with sleep.

"I brought you breakfast," I said, handing him a yogurt. "Figured you'd need the energy for today."

Bear squinted at the container. "Strawberry, really?"

"Don't start," I said with a warning look.

Bear muttered a thanks under his breath, took the yogurt, and slunk back to his bed, leaving the door open just wide enough for me to see...

"Gracie," Cole said breathlessly, like he was surprised to see me. Which I guess was fair since this was *his* hotel room after all. But then again, Bear was *my* brother. Of course I'd be there at some point to check in on him.

He was leaning against the doorframe to the bathroom eyeing me, his hair a rumpled mess, and his t-shirt slightly wrinkled.

His eyes found mine, and I greedily took them in for a second, forgetting how to think straight.

Even if I can't have him, I can at least enjoy him while I have him. Right?
Right?

"I, uh—" I held up the cup of coffee, suddenly hyperaware of how awkward I was being. "I brought this too. Black, two creamers on the side. If you want it, that is."

His lips quirked into a small, crooked smile. "You remembered."

I shrugged, hoping to shake off the blush creeping up my face. "I... had an extra."

Cole reached out to take the cup, his fingers brushing mine briefly. The contact made my stomach dip, and if I hadn't been blushing before, I definitely was now.

"Thanks," he said in a lower than usual voice.

I cleared my throat, breaking apart to put some much-needed distance between us. "We're leaving in twenty."

The drive to Utah State University was pretty uneventful.

Emma stared out her window for most of it, her phone silent for once, but her face pinched, as if she were lost in ugly thought.

Bear was looking out the window, Airpods in, for an entirely *different* reason: because he was tired and didn't want anyone else to notice. I always did, though.

And Cole... well, let's just say, that relationship was confusing as ever.

When we pulled into the parking lot, I think *that's* when it hit me.

There was a mess of cars, vans, and buses everywhere. Even the sidewalks were crowded with students milling around in matching FFA jackets or scrubs.

This is real now. No turning back.

Inside the conference center, the chaos only intensified. The main hall was massive and filled with rows of booths and registration tables.

"Alright, we're gonna go check in," Cole said just loud enough for me to hear him over the crowd as he glanced between Bear and Emma. Then back at me. "You good here?"

I had to stop myself from immediately asking them (well, mostly him) to stay because at that point, I was starting to freak out a little.

But instead, I plastered on the brightest smile (that Cole saw right through, unfortunately) and nodded. *You're a big girl, Gracie. You can handle yourself.*

"We'll be right back, I promise. Just wait right here," he said after a beat.

Saying that probably shouldn't have made me forget all the reasons as to why we couldn't work, or about all the things actually keeping us apart.

But call me delusional, or crazy, or *whatever* because suddenly, being here didn't feel so overwhelming anymore.

I mean, don't get me wrong, I was still shaking in my boots, but now... I was counting on him to come back. To *stay* back.

At least for now.

*Maybe I **can** get through today.*

"Maybe next time, Gracie should check in for *all* of us, instead of just herself..." Bear grumbled as they disappeared into the crowd.

By the way, that was an honest mistake as the president of the team. I was so used to checking in by myself and for myself *only*, that I'd forgotten to do the same for everyone else yesterday too.

Anyways...

I let myself wander toward the edge of the conference room, and for a second, I just stood there in the middle of it, absorbing it all.

This was it—the moment I'd been waiting for, practicing for, *obsessing* over for months.

No, scratch that. *Years*.

I took a deep breath, letting the adrenaline steady me. I couldn't mess this up. Not for me, not for my team.

Suddenly, I hit something solid.

"Oh my gosh!" I stumbled back, my binder slipping from my hands as I tried to steady myself. Papers tumbled onto the floor. "I'm so sorry!" I blurted, scrambling to pick the mess up.

The object I'd just run into: a girl around my age, crouched down to help, a relaxed smile tugging at her lips. "No worries," she said, handing me a few papers. "I wasn't looking where I was going either. You travel heavy, huh?"

I let out a small, nervous laugh, taking the pages from her. "I just like to be prepared... for everything."

"Your arms must hate you," she grinned, handing me the last of the fallen sheets.

"*Ha*," I said, tucking the papers back into my binder. "Strength training is on Wednesdays if you want to join. I'm Gracie, by the way."

"Mikayla," she replied, brushing off her hands as she stood. "Nice to meet you. But also, just a tip—this whole thing? It's not life or death. Sometimes you just have to wing it and see what happens. No stress, got it?"

Yeah freaking right... "I don't really do 'winging it'."

"Fair enough," Mikayla replied with a shrug, pulling her dirty blonde hair into a messy, haphazard bun. "But you know," she added, tilting her head, "sometimes people get so caught up in being perfect that they forget to enjoy the moment. Just saying."

I crossed my arms, clutching the binder tight against my chest. "I don't think caring about doing well means you're not enjoying it. You can do both."

"Totally," Mikayla said, holding her hands up in mock surrender. "Don't get me wrong, it's cool to care. I just think sometimes people take this stuff way too seriously. Like, sure, you prep and practice, but it's not like anyone's career is riding on this, right? It's just for fun."

I almost wanted to laugh at the insanity of that statement. *Be so for real with me right now, girlfriend.* "You are aware that some of us put a lot of time and effort into being here, right?"

She shrugged again. "*Obviously.* And that's great for them. I mean it. But I'm here for the experience, not to stress myself out. It's just one competition, right?"

"I—"

"Oh, listen. I gotta run, but it was nice to meet you, Gracie. Good luck out there."

"Nice to meet you too," I mumbled, not really meaning it as she turned to walk away.

Could someone *really* be that selfish to act as a placeholder for a person who actually *wanted* to be here?

And she was wrong. This *was* life or death.

Because if it wasn't, I would've spent three years of my life on nothing. I'd always just have been "Bear's sister" or the family screw-up.

No.

This mattered. *I* mattered. I *had* to.

If Mikayla wanted to just "have fun," that was her problem. This was too important to me to let her get in my head.

Eventually, the event organizers corralled us into a large lecture hall with rows of desks stretching as far back as the eye could see, each spaced out to prevent cheating.

The first part of the competition was a multiple-choice quiz.

We were separated from our teammates, scattered throughout the room like puzzle pieces that didn't quite fit together.

I ended up near the front, close enough to see the sharp frown lines of the proctor's scowl as he handed out the papers. "Remember," he said stiffly, "you're on your own here. No talking, no sharing answers. You've got forty-five minutes."

I gripped my pencil, heart pounding in my chest, destined to forget everything I'd ever learned based on the way he was acting.

But the second I read the first question, relief washed over me.

A cow's gestation period—it was so basic I almost laughed.

My pencil moved across the page before I had time to second-guess myself.

The next question was just as easy. And the one after that. And the one after *that* one. *I can't believe how simple this is. Maybe I'll even be the first person to ever get one hundred percent on this stupid test.*

I was flying through the questions, one after another, barely pausing.

Halfway down the page, I couldn't help but grin. *If the rest of the competition goes like this, I've got this in the bag.*

When I reached the last page, I paused for a second to glance up at the clock behind me, expecting to see *at least* thirty minutes left.

But as I looked that way, my eyes caught on something else—or rather, *someone* else a few rows back.

Cole.

Just as I was noting the way his hair was falling over his eyes (cue the fireman delusion again), as if on cue, he glanced up. *At me.*

And that bastard smiled.

Before I could even process what had happened, I quickly whipped my head back to my own paper, my heart doing a somersault in my chest. But it was too late. I was already a goner.

The next question in front of me was straightforward enough: Canine nutrition, something I should've been able to answer in my sleep. But the words were suddenly swimming in front of my eyes.

I wasn't sure if it was because of Cole or the insurmountable amount of pressure I was putting myself under, but I. Didn't. Know. The. Answer.

The internal clock in my mind (along with the one on the wall) were basically sending out flares to my nervous system.

I knew finishing the test was important. In fact, it was *detrimental* if I wanted to actually place, but...

"Five-minute warning," the proctor barked suddenly.

Panic slammed into me like a freight train.

Where had all the time gone?

Somehow, I finished the rest of the page and flipped the packet over (because Heaven forbid someone cheat off my *wrong answers*), only to find an entire back page of unanswered questions staring right back at me.

Oh no. No, no, no.

My pencil flew across the page as I guessed on almost every question.

"Time's up," the proctor called.

I set my pencil down, my whole body feeling physically ill.

The grin I'd been wearing earlier was long gone, replaced by the sinking realization that I'd just blown it.

All because of a *smile*.

But maybe I could make up for it in the next round. I wasn't out of the running just yet.

Think positive here, Gracie.

We were herded into a dimly lit lab for the identification section.

Microscopes lined the tables, each set up with samples we needed to identify—bacteria, parasites, plant cells... stuff like that.

The good news? With everyone broken into even smaller groups, Cole wasn't anywhere in sight, and I could finally get my head back in the game.

I still felt a little shaky from earlier, but this was my thing. The nitty-gritty science stuff, the hands-on work... I was good at this, right?

Wrong.

I made the mistake of scanning the room again, attempting to find Bear and make sure he wasn't dead somewhere (I joked about that, but it was actually a legitimate fear of mine).

But instead, my eyes snagged on Mikayla.

She was at her microscope, head propped on one hand like she was watching paint dry. With the other, she was doodling what looked like a very lifelike penis on her worksheet.

Damn her. Of *course* she wasn't worried.

She must've had a career path or rich husband already lined up for her because there was no way someone could care *that* little about being here.

I turned back to my station and glanced at the first slide: a wriggling mass of bacteria.

I continued to stare into the microscope, waiting for the right answer to click into place, but it didn't, because *of course* it didn't.

Not with the way my day was going.

Unfortunately, the more I thought about it, the fuzzier everything got.

Bacillus subtilis? No—wait. Maybe it was *E. coli*.

I scratched out my first answer and wrote another. Then scratched that out, too.

"Focus," I muttered under my breath.

The second slide wasn't much better. Or the third.

Mikayla's smug little smirk had officially been burned into my mind.

By the time I got to my last station, my nerves were shot and my frustration level was at an all-time high. I looked into the microscope at a tangle of plant cells, really only to keep up appearances, because let's be real: my mind had proven itself to be pretty damn useless at that point.

I scribbled something down, barely sure if it was right or if I'd just made up a word and moved on just as the proctor called time.

The practicum was my last chance to pull myself together.

The assignment was simple (that's how they all started, didn't they?): restrain a dog and administer an antibiotic injection. I'd done this a hundred times before.

But my hands wouldn't stop shaking from more than failing sixty-six percent of this competition as I approached the (very unlucky) dog.

Obviously, it sensed my nerves, and its body stiffened immediately.

"Easy, there," I murmured, more to myself than the dog.

The instructor's eyes on me made me physically want to vomit, which *probably* wouldn't help me win this in the long run, so I took a deep breath and tried to steady myself.

Eventually, I managed to get the needle ready, but as I moved closer, the dog let out a soft whimper.

My split-second hesitation was all it took for it to violently jerk its head away from me.

I felt my cheeks start to burn as I fumbled to regain control.

Somehow, I *did* finally manage to get the injection done, but it was clumsy and forced, and not at all how I'd practiced it a million times before.

I stepped back from the table.

That's it. I'm a failure.

But before I could even fully fucking lament in it, Mikayla stepped up to the station beside mine, flashing a confident grin at the instructor as she restrained her dog easily.

When she finished, the whole room practically applauded.

Would it be a felony if I punched this girl right now? It hadn't been with Cole...

Of course, some might've said I was turning over a new leaf, so that was why I let it slide. Not without double-birding her as she left the room, though.

As early afternoon turned to night, the auditorium buzzed with noise, every seat crammed full with rows of tangled backpacks and elbows.

It should've felt more exciting, but if my performance was any indication, this announcement was about to suck balls.

I slouched down in my chair, arms crossed tight, trying not to look at anyone—*especially* not Cole. He'd just try to give me comfort I didn't deserve.

"Relax, Gracie," Bear said from my other side. "You're making *me* nervous."

I didn't even look at him. "Good," I muttered, crossing my arms even tighter like an angry, little kid.

Emma sat on the other side of him, picking at her nails, her knee bouncing a million miles an hour. "I forgot how much I hated this part," she muttered.

I agreed with her but didn't say anything. I *couldn't*. I had too much going on in my brain to add what I was going to do about Emma to the mix.

"Gracie," Cole said after a minute. "It's not over yet. We haven't even heard the results."

I almost gave in to that.

But right then, I realized that if I responded to him or even *looked* at him, I'd probably start crying.

I was tired, I was hungry, I was... slightly homicidal to a girl named Mikayla... I *wanted* to cry, but I was supposed to be the strong one. I was supposed to *win*.

So instead, I said nothing to him either.

Eventually, the announcer finally walked on stage, shuffling papers and tapping the mic, as if we didn't already want to strangle him for dragging this whole thing out.

"Thank you for your patience, everyone," he started. My heart immediately lodged itself in my throat.

The names were rattled off in rapid fire. Tenth place. Ninth place. Eighth place.

We weren't in the bottom three. That was good, right?

Except all I could think about was, *I don't have a great feeling about this.*

That's when it happened.

"Seventh place goes to... Hillview High!"

My heart dropped. *Crap.*

"*Seventh*?" I echoed in disbelief.

Bear leaned closer, nudging me. "Hey, that's not bad. Top ten!"

"Top ten isn't winning!" I snapped, louder than I meant to.

My cheeks reddened as the applause died down *just* in time for people to hear my little outburst.

Heads turned my direction, but I couldn't even *begin* to care.

This was supposed to be my thing, the one thing I was good at. My first year as president, and I messed it all up.

I could feel my team's eyes on me too, probably racking their brains with what they felt like were obligatory words of comfort, like: *oh, we'll get 'em next time* or *the only thing that matters is that we had fun,* but I *hadn't* had fun.

The only thing that mattered was winning, and I'd lost.

"I'll be back," I muttered, my voice probably drowned out by the places of teams that actually mattered.

I shoved out of my chair before anyone could stop me, and before I knew it, I was outside.

The cool night air hit my face like a splash of icy water, and I slid down the first brick wall I came to, letting the rough surface bite into my palms.

We had failed... no. *I* had failed.

After a while of staring out into the inky darkness, it occurred to me then that I probably needed to head back soon. Just in case someone thought I'd gotten kidnapped or something... if they'd even noticed I was gone, that is.

But I couldn't bring myself to get up off the ground.

The distant sound of footsteps suddenly caught my attention, and my back went ramrod straight as I tried to adjust myself so that I looked *somewhat* presentable.

I quickly wiped away the stupid tears that had fallen off my face with the back of my hand and glanced up in time to see Mikayla and the rest of her groupies approaching.

Oh, great. I bet she's about to brag about her win.

But she proved me wrong. Guess I was just wrong about *everything* today, huh? "Hey! Congrats on seventh place, girl!" she said cheerfully.

I managed a weak smile. At least she wasn't going to be a bitch about it. But I'd still *lost*, hadn't I?

Was I supposed to feel happy about a pity compliment?

"Seventh place is a joke. But *you* on the other hand... third place," I gestured to the bronze medal around her and her team's necks. "That's an accomplishment."

Mikayla shrugged nonchalantly, "Eh, it's whatever."

I let out a frustrated sigh. *Could this girl just not be herself for five seconds?* "How can you just not give a damn like that?"

She grinned, like she was letting me in on a little secret. "Once you've done this for a couple of years, you realize that there are no damns to be given. The *real* fun comes after hours."

"Excuse me?"

"After the results come in, we throw this absolute banger party back at the hotel. *Oh my gosh*, you should totally come!"

I scoffed, wrinkling my nose. "I don't know. I'm not really a... party girl."

A beat passed between us. Then Mikayla shrugged again. "Suit yourself."

As luck (or irony) would have it, that was the *exact* moment that Cole decided to wander outside, calling my name to anyone who would listen.

*Huh, I guess someone **did** notice that I'd left.*

Although, to be fair, storming out after a very public outburst couldn't exactly be considered *stealthy*.

He hadn't seen me yet, but the thought of facing him when I was at my *lowest* lowest made me want to run out into traffic and get hit by a car (I know, I know. I'm hilarious).

So, without actually thinking about the long-term consequences of my actions, I jogged over to Mikayla and her friends. "Actually, on second thought, a party might be exactly what I need."

She laughed, like she couldn't believe it had taken me so long to figure that out too, and gave my shoulder a tight squeeze, "Good, 'cause it looks like you could use a drink."

And so that was the story of how I found myself getting into her Nissan Altima, smushed between a bunch of people that I'd just met, going to a party that I didn't want to go to, hoping that this would be exactly what I needed to block my entire life out.

Chapter Thirty-One:

Cole

Back in my hotel room, I flipped through the TV channels, trying to drown the loop of frustration and worry in my head.

I ended up landing on some over-the-top Spanish soap opera, catching a few words here and there—*baño*, *amor*, something dramatic about a secret twin (maybe)—but none of it really stuck.

Because let's be honest: my mind was somewhere else, circling the same question over and over: *Where the hell is Gracie?*

She wasn't answering her phone. Not for me, not for Emma, not even for Bear. And I knew her well enough to recognize the pattern. She was avoiding us.

It was classic Gracie, jumping off the deep end into her own mind instead of letting someone (*like me*) help her out of it.

Yes, I knew she could take care of herself, and she told me such... All. The. Damn. Time. But after everything we'd been through, couldn't she just trust me a little? Let me in even *once*?

I threw the remote onto the bed and scrubbed a hand over my face.

I knew I'd screwed up the day of our fight. And probably every day since, especially knowing that I'd made her cry for God knows what reason and still hadn't fixed it yet.

But she wasn't exactly a peach herself either.

Gracie had this way of arguing like she was trying to win a debate, not solve a problem. And it was infuriating and kind of impressive all at once.

And okay, maybe I didn't always have the most *productive* responses when she got like that.

Half the time I wanted to yell at her, and the other half of the time, I just wanted to kiss her until she stopped overthinking everything and realized I wasn't the enemy.

Mostly the latter.

Just as I was about to ignore my better judgment, giving her space be damned, a thud came from outside the door.

I leapt off the bed, trying (and failing) not to trip over Bear's suitcase, and yanked the door open to...

"Gracie?"

She was standing there, swaying slightly. Her cheeks were flushed, and the smell of alcohol hit me immediately.

But she was alive and standing in front of me.

For a second, I didn't know whether to hug her or lose it.

But fuck me if I made that mistake ever again.

I pulled her into my arms.

"Do you wanna build a snowman?" she sang, muffled into my shirt. "I'm here to fulfil my sisterly duties, by the way. Hehe, *duties...*"

Before I could even respond, she pushed past me, drunkenly stumbling further into the room so badly that I had to catch her elbow and steady her.

My frustration flared up all over again.

"Bear's fine," I said, closing the door behind us. "He went to sleep a couple of hours ago. Like *you* should've done. It's *two in the morning*, Gracie. Where the hell have you been?"

She waved a hand, like her being gone so long wasn't a *huge fucking deal*. "I'm fiiiiine." The word stretched out as she swayed slightly. "I was with Mikayla."

"I have absolutely no clue who that is," I replied, stepping in front of her to block her path when she tried to move again. "And I don't care if you were with the King of England. What were you *thinking*? You could've gotten hurt or kidnapped or..."

"Look at you, all sweet and gentleman-y," she said, her grin widening. "But not to worry, Prince Charming, I'm a big girl. I can handle myself."

She leaned forward, a little too far for her unsteady balance, and before I could react, she tipped into me, her weight pressing against my chest.

I caught her instinctively, my arms steadying her before she completely toppled over.

She tilted her head back to look up at me, as her hands snaked up to rest against my chest. And just like that, my stomach did a traitorous dip, like I was free-falling off a cliff.

Her lips curled into the softest, most mischievous smile, like she knew exactly what she was doing to me. "Your heart is going to beat out of your chest if you're not careful, y'know?" she teased, her voice a little breathless.

I swallowed hard, trying to force myself to ignore how close she was, how her fingers curled slightly into the fabric of my t-shirt with desire I'd never seen in her before, or how her brother was *literally* six feet from us, sleeping in the other bed.

"You need to lie down," I said firmly, even though every fiber of my being felt like it was about to give in. "You're drunk, and this is—"

"Wrong?" she guessed with a laugh. "Oh, c'mon, Cole. This is the most right I've felt in a long time."

Her hand came up, her thumb brushing over my lower lip. "I wanna kiss that damn permafrown off your face, Brown. Just like we did a couple weeks ago. That's what I wanna do."

My brain short-circuited then.

That did it: she knew *exactly* what she was doing to me. There was no way she didn't.

"Gracie," I said, my voice rough as my eyes darkened with something I couldn't shove back down—something she was pulling out of me without even trying that hard to.

Thankfully, though, I managed to get a grip over myself and gently caught her wrist, lowering her hand away from my face before I gave in to every stupid impulse screaming in my head.

"You're drunk, Gracie. You're not thinking straight."

"Maybe I'm *finally* thinking straight," she countered, her smirk fading slightly as her eyes zeroed in on my hands holding hers away from me. "For once, I'm saying what I really feel. And I feel like..." she hesitated, vulnerability bleeding into her voice. "*This* is the only thing that makes sense right now."

"Like Bear being sick? Me having to take care of him all the time like I'm his mom or something? That makes no sense. I'm *seventeen*! I never asked for any of that."

I stayed silent, carefully letting go of her wrists.

"And Emma..." her voice cracked, and she quickly looked away. "She's my best friend. At least, I *thought* she was. But she's been keeping this huge, life-changing secret from me, and it's like... why didn't she ever trust me enough to know what was going on? How does *that* make sense?"

I didn't know what to say. I fought the urge to pull her closer and insist that she wasn't as alone as she thought she was. But before I could find the right words, her fingers curled into my shirt again.

"And then there's you," she said softly, her eyes locking on mine. "My sworn enemy. But you're not. I don't hate you. Not even a little bit. And maybe that shouldn't make sense, but it does. Cole, you make sense to me."

"Gracie..." I started, trying to tamp down the feelings firing in my chest so that I'd at *least* be a better sounding board for her. But she didn't let me finish.

"Just kiss me, Cole," she whispered. "Please. I need something to make sense again."

I *wanted* to. Fuck, I probably *needed* to.

Everything in me was screaming just to give in, to close the space between us and give her exactly what she wanted just so it'd make her happy.

But *would* it make her happy? Or was that just the alcohol talking?

With a will that could've moved mountains, I finally stepped back, her fingers slipping from my shirt as I put space between us. "We can't, Gracie."

The way she looked up at me, confusion wetting her eyes, almost broke something inside of me. "You don't want me," she concluded softly.

"No, no. That's not it," I insisted, almost reaching back for her. "I want you. You have no idea how much I want you. But I want you to want me because you mean it. I want you to want me because the thought of me makes you smile, not just tonight but every damn day. I want you to want me when you're sober, when you're *sure*. When I can kiss that beautiful smile of yours and you can remember every single second of it."

She looked down at the floor, her bottom lip still trembling.

Fuck, she was killing me.

I stole a look around the room, my eyes catching on the desk chair in the corner. I dragged it towards my bed, sitting down a safe distance away (for both of us).

"You're going to sleep this off, and then we're gonna talk. For real this time."

She hesitated, glancing at the door. "Maybe I should just..."

"*Gracie*," I said, motioning for her to sit on the bed. "For once in your life, can you please just trust that someone is capable enough to take care of you? I won't let anything bad happen, I promise."

She blinked at me, but didn't say anything. Then, she sighed, curling up on the bed, her back to me.

As the minutes ticked by, though, what started off as an act of frustration turned into even breathing and her eventually falling asleep.

And I stayed there, watching over her like some lovesick idiot, because no matter what happened between us, I couldn't imagine being anywhere else.

March 11th

Gracie

He said that he needed help grabbing something. Promised that it'd only take a couple of minutes and that "digging through the church's storage closet was really a two-person job."

I went along with it because how could I say no?

The first thing I remember after that was darkness.

Then he was throwing me up against the wall.

I tried to scream. Really, I did. But before I could even process what was happening, he clamped his hand over my mouth and started undoing his pants.

My whole nervous system went into flight-or-fight mode. But I was only fourteen, and instead of choosing to do either, my body went numb.

My mind went numb.

I went numb.

After he was done, he left me in there. Alone. Crying. Disgusted with myself. I mattered *that* little to him.

I wasn't really even sure what had just happened to me. But I knew that it was something I never wanted to feel again.

I went to the pastor about it. And he laughed at me.

He *laughed*. Said I was making it all up for attention.

"He's a nice guy, Gracie. Why would he do that to you?"

I didn't tell anyone else about him after that. *Especially* not my parents. Because maybe they were right. Maybe I *did* just have "daddy issues." Maybe I *was* just making it up for attention. Maybe he was just "a nice guy."

He ended up convincing everyone that he could drive me to and from worship team practice after that.

He was "close," he said. It wasn't a "problem," he said.

I didn't want to be a burden, always just sitting there waiting for my mom to remember she had a daughter and come get me. So, I let him.

He drove me there, and he drove me home. He knew where I lived. He knew what he was doing.

It happened two more times.

What nobody ever tells you about rape? It's the shame that follows you afterwards.

Even when you know that there was nothing you could've done differently, even when you know it wasn't your fault, you still feel... disgusting.

You hate yourself.

He promised he wouldn't tell anyone about what had happened. He said that he was doing me a favor, and if the secret got out, everyone would hate me.

And I believed him.

I kept my secret. But he didn't keep his.

Because suddenly, it was all over the school. Suddenly, everyone knew. Suddenly, everyone treated me like a freak, a mistake... and maybe I was.

It was still something that followed me around. All the jokes, all the horrible nicknames, the double life my family knew nothing about, and wouldn't accept even if they *did*.

I still had nightmares about him coming to find me in that stupid tiki mask he always used to wear.

I wasn't safe anymore.

And I should've been.

He had been arrested a couple of months later for raping another girl around my age.

Maybe I could somehow manage to live with what he'd done to me, but I would never forgive myself for being the reason that he'd moved on to her.

I jolted awake, the kind of headache that felt like tiny jackhammers drilling behind my eyes.

My mouth was dry, my skin was clammy, and a cold sweat clung to my body, sticking my hair to my face. I shoved the tangled mess of blankets over me off, looking around me for something familiar to lower my pulse.

The blinds... the carpet... the comforter.

Wait. This isn't my comforter.

Or, I was realizing, my room.

I blinked hard, trying to clear the fog from my brain.

The room was dimly lit, darker than I usually kept it just in case of nightmares. And the grooves in the ceiling that I usually counted to help me fall back asleep were gone.

Panic suddenly began to bubble in my throat as I tried to sit up.

Where the hell am I?

But the pounding in my head stopped me halfway.

There was someone at my side immediately. "Whoa, hey. Easy there. Don't try to move too fast. Can I get you something?"

I flinched instinctively, my arm shooting out before my brain could fully catch up with my body.

And my fist connected with something solid.

"*Shit*—" The figure groaned in pain, recoiling. "What the...? *Gracie!*"

The bedside lamp clicked on, flooding the room with a soft, golden light that I would have appreciated a lot more if it weren't for...

Cole.

He was pinching the bridge of his nose, his face stuck somewhere between a wince and a smirk.

And on closer inspection, I noticed that his brown hair was sticking up at odd angles, his T-shirt was wrinkled, like he'd been up all night.

"Oh my gosh—sorry! Sorry," I blurted, my voice rising in pitch as heat flooded my cheeks. Then, realizing I sounded too much like I cared, I cleared my throat, trying to sound more indifferent. "I mean... *sorry*."

Cole, still holding his nose, let out a low chuckle. "I'm getting the weirdest sense of déjà vu right now."

My face turned a deeper shade of red as the memory of when I punched him the *first* time flashed in my mind.

My first trip to the principal's office...

I quickly glanced away. "You snuck up on me. What was I *supposed* to do?"

"I wasn't sneaking. I was *sitting*. Quietly. Like a normal person." He tilted his head, studying me with amusement dancing in his eyes. "I guess I underestimated how dangerous you are, half-conscious."

"You're lucky I didn't aim lower," I mumbled, pulling the edges of the blanket I'd tossed aside earlier over me defensively.

His grin widened. "Noted. Next time I'm coming over to check on *Hungover Gracie*, I'll announce myself. Maybe bring a shield. You know, just in case."

Before I could stop myself, I snorted out a laugh, (partly from the situation, partly from being in this situation with *him*) which only made my cheeks burn even hotter.

When I stole another look at him, he was looking way too pleased with himself to know he had such an effect on me, so I reached for the nearest pillow, pressing it to my face in an attempt to smother the life out of this... weird lapse in judgement.

A beat between us passed, and Cole fell silent beside me.

My immediate worry was that he'd literally gotten up and left or something. And I mean, who could've blame him, really? I was a mess. He had no obligation to stay.

But as I peeked out from underneath the pillow and saw that he was *still* there? Still watching me with those concerned eyes of his? The anxiety in my chest vaporized, replaced with a kind of... nice, warm feeling instead.

Huh. That's weird.

"Honestly, though," he said, leaning against the bedpost. "How are you feeling?"

I blinked, attempting to push down my feelings. "Uh... fine. Just... headachy."

Because what was I *supposed* to say? Thanks for being here? Thanks for letting me use your room? Please... stay?

"Is that the technical term?" he joked.

I stuck my tongue out at him, just as zombie butterflies started resurrecting in my stomach. "Shut up, Cole."

He laughed, and the sound filled the room in a way that made it feel cozier. *Safer.*

"So... um," I started after a minute of silence. "What *am* I doing in your hotel room exactly?"

He raised an eyebrow. "Damn, Gracie. You make it sound like we..."

"*Don't* finish that," I said, squeezing my eyes shut.

I didn't have to remember everything from last night to know that I'd definitely said or done something stupid. Especially since I had ended up in *the* Cole Brown's bed, of all places.

I mean, I guess I should've been more grateful it was *that* and not some drug-riddled street corner. Although, I think the old me would've much rather preferred the latter...

"Relax. Nothing happened," he chuckled quickly. "Not for lack of interesting commentary on your part, though."

I groaned, throwing the pillow back over my head. "Please stop talking."

He let out another laugh, lifting the pillow off my face with an almost boyish grin. "I'm starting to think you don't handle compliments well," he teased.

But as I looked closer at him, I realized that even though he was joking, his eyes were soft, *searching*, as if asking permission—not just to keep the pillow pulled away, but to stay close, to *keep* teasing, to exist in this space between us.

He wasn't just looking at me; he was looking *into* me, checking to see if this was okay, if this was something I wanted as much as him.

But there was still a part of me that wondered if giving into that want, if putting into words what was happening between us, would end up doing more harm than good. And that freaked me out because I didn't want this to end...

I didn't want *us* to end.

So, instead, I straightened myself on the bed, hugging my knees to my chest as I looked anywhere but him. Because it was easier that way. That's what I told myself, at least.

That's when I noticed Bear shift slightly in the other bed, looking so small that he might've just disappeared into the blankets altogether if I looked away for too long.

Cole must've caught the change in my expression because his face softened even more. "He's fine," he said, his voice quiet. "Didn't wake up once."

I nodded, my eyes back on Bear's tiny frame as it rose and fell steadily. But before I could stop it, guilt threaded through me like barbed wire.

I should've been with him. Not out doing... well, what I *was* doing.

You mean getting drunk and embarrassing yourself in front of everyone? You're selfish. That's all you'll ever be.

It was a hard pill to swallow, but it was the truth. How was I supposed to be the one taking care of him when I couldn't even keep my own life together? Bear deserved better than me.

"Gracie?"

I blinked, whipping my head toward him like I'd been caught doing something I shouldn't—or I guess *thinking* something I shouldn't.

Cole's brow was furrowed, concern etched into every line of his face, and my cheeks flushed.

"You okay?"

"Yeah, fine," I said, quickly rushing to change the subject. "But wait. If I slept in your bed last night, where did you..."

Suddenly, my eyes fell back to the chair he'd been sitting on. A pillow and blanket were crumpled and shoved haphazardly on the ground. Which only meant one thing...

"You slept *there*?" I asked, narrowing my eyes at him.

He shrugged. "It wasn't so bad."

"You didn't have to do that."

His lips twitched, the corner of his mouth lifting into a half-smile like it was every day he was faced with the dilemma of giving a drunk girl his bed. "What was I supposed to do, Gracie? Leave you in the hallway?"

I opened my mouth to protest, but something in his tone kept me from arguing. Instead, I bit my lip, softening as I gave him a once-over.

"Thank you," I said finally, my voice quieter.

His eyebrows lifted slightly. "For what?"

"For being decent."

His grin faded, instantly replaced by something more serious. He leaned forward slightly, resting his elbows on his knees as he looked *into* me again.

"Gracie..." he started, his voice trailing off. "You don't have to thank me for that."

"*Yes*, I do." I said, averting his gaze as if he could see the lump forming in my throat. "Not everyone would've. So... thank you."

His jaw tightened at that. "That's just basic human decency, Gracie." he said after a minute. "That's the bare minimum."

"Not everyone thinks so."

His smile was entirely gone now, replaced by something darker. "Has that... Has that happened to you before? Where someone wasn't 'decent' to you?"

I swallowed hard.

Here it was. The truth coming out anyway.

In middle school, things were easier. He hated me, I hated him. He called me a freak for what happened, and now... what if I told him the second time around and his reaction was just as bad?

Or worse, because I actually *wanted* him to stay now? I...

"Gracie," he said softly, taking my silence as answer enough. "You don't deserve that. Not from anyone. Not ever."

Okay. *That* surprised me.

And suddenly, I was crying.

"Hey," he murmured, lifting my chin gently with his thumb. "Look at me."

I tried to fight it. It was probably better for both of us this way. But something about the way he said it, (like it was a plea, not a demand) made me give in.

He doubled down. "You deserve better than that. And not just because it's the right thing. You deserve better because you're... you."

If only he knew who *I* was... or at least, the person he used to *think* I was.

This whole thing with Cole had started as some kind of social experiment. Ride the wave of "friendship," reap all the rewards until he remembered who he was.

But now, feelings were involved. Feelings that I didn't exactly understand, but I *wanted* them to last. Was that selfish of me?

"You deserve people who see that," he continued, his voice breaking slightly. "Who respect you... no. Who *cherish* you. Every day."

Cole reached out, wiping a tear from my cheek away with his thumb. "Gracie," he whispered, "You deserve the world. You deserve to believe that."

And in that moment, I let myself believe in the fantasy that the girl always got the guy.

I let myself believe that I could lie and cheat and manipulate myself into getting a happy ending.

And I told myself I could learn to be better because I wanted to be someone who deserved the way he looked at me.

Besides, this was just a small, innocent crush. What's the worst that could happen?

Chapter Thirty-Two:

MARCH 12TH

S he was different.

She'd been that way since we had gotten back from our competition. Actually, scratch that—since I'd walked in on her dad flinging her across their living room.

I stabbed my fork into the soggy cafeteria meal in front of me, the prongs bending slightly under the force. The texture of the fish stick was mushy and lukewarm, but I swallowed a bite anyway.

Two tables over, Emma sat at the center of a group, her hands moving animatedly as she told some exaggerated version of our trip home.

Her storytelling had never been a problem before. She'd always had a knack for it. Even *I* found myself on the edge of my seat, waiting to hear how we'd survived the van breaking down in the middle of nowhere.

Which was weird, considering I had been on the damn trip.

The van "breaking down" was *news to me,* and a generous interpretation.

The truth? Forty-five minutes out from the school parking lot, the check engine light came on, and Bear had muttered something dramatic about not wanting to die stranded on the side of the road in "the shit-mobile."

We laughed, ignored it, and kept driving—end of story.

Well *apparently not.* Because now, she was spinning this elaborate tale about smoke billowing from the hood, Cole heroically flagging down a passing trucker, and all of us scavenging for snacks like we were in some post-apocalyptic movie.

And people were *eating it up.*

"And there we were," she said, her voice dropping into a suspenseful whisper. "Cole's standing there, waving his arms around like one of those inflatable balloon men outside of car lots. I'm digging through the glove box for an extra car battery—which, by the way, we *didn't* have, thank you, Mrs. Nolan..."

I tried to smile, like I wasn't too busy noticing how every time she laughed, it sounded a little too forced.

Like I hadn't picked up on the way her smile always seemed to fall just a second too soon. Like I hadn't realized that she was leaning on these stories like a crutch—each one perfectly captivating, perfectly rehearsed... little white lies that stacked up into something bigger. Something shinier.

Until she didn't know *what* to believe.

It was funny—I'd never noticed how good she was at it until *the incident.* But now, I noticed *everything.* And I wasn't sure if I could play pretend with her anymore.

My nails bit into the palm of my hand as I shifted in my seat, trying to keep myself from going there and blowing the lid on the little "adventure" we'd had yesterday.

Just smile and nod, Gracie. Smile and nod. Lunch is only forty-five minutes, anyway. Be a good friend and let her have this.

But that's when I saw it.

When she reached up to tuck a strand of hair behind her ear, the fabric of her sleeve shifted just enough to reveal a shadowy bruise beneath.

My stomach flipped.

Before I could call her out on it and say: *see? This is clearly a problem*, one of the other girls beat me to it.

"Emma, what happened to your wrist?"

She didn't miss a beat. Her lips curved into a sheepish grin as she held up her arm like it was no big deal. "Oh, this?" she laughed lightly, shaking her head. "You won't believe it—I tripped over my dog yesterday. He's getting *so big*. He's like a furry wrecking ball now."

The table broke into another fit of laughter.

But *my* blood boiled.

She didn't own a dog. She hadn't had a pet since she was eight. And it was a cat. It had run away, or maybe it had died; *I didn't know*.

All I knew was that she was lying to impress a bunch of loser assholes, to get them to like "her." And more importantly, she was lying to her best fucking friend, telling her that her dad wasn't abusing her when he was.

It was a lie.

She was a *liar*.

My fingers curled tighter into fists under the table, fighting to keep it together and not blow up her whole life over something I didn't really understand.

She kept talking like nothing was wrong, but it *was*.

Her dad was *abusing* her.

This wasn't a one-time thing; this was an every*day* thing. And she couldn't keep convincing me otherwise anymore.

"I wear long sleeves so people don't think he's abusing me." Liar.

"Gracie?"

I blinked, snapping back to reality as Cole slid into the seat next to me, balancing his tray of food in one hand.

He glanced at me, his brow furrowed just slightly. "You okay?"

And then there was this thing I had with Cole...

I didn't deserve someone like him. Maybe the old version. Maybe when he was a jerk. But not now.

Not when I was clearly using him for a past he couldn't remember hating me in. Not when Emma was *right there*, making up random stories to hide how much pain she was clearly in. Not when I *knew* and hadn't done anything about it.

I bet Cole would've jumped right in to save her because that's the kind of guy he is now.

But I wasn't a hero.

You're selfish, Gracie. You don't deserve him, or her, or to be happy.

"Stop for a second, please..." I muttered, instinctively tugging at the ends of my hair.

You don't deserve any of it—not when your best friend is hurting. Not when you're sitting here watching her suffer and doing nothing.

I bet you're even happy that her own __father__ is abusing her. You've always been jealous that she has him when you have...

"I said, stop!"

The words burst out before I could stop them. A few heads even turned our way.

Heat surged into my face as Cole's expression shifted from confused to serious.

"Gracie? What's going on?" he asked carefully, like he was trying to steady me before I could break into a million pieces.

Maybe breaking would've been easier.

Without thinking, I pushed back from the table.

All I knew was that I needed space.

I didn't want his concern. I didn't want his pity.

Not when there was someone more important to be worrying about right now.

Emma—my best. fucking. friend.

"I'm fine," I muttered, my gaze darting away from his. "It's nothing."

Great. Her secret's becoming mine too...

Cole pursed his lips. "Doesn't sound like nothing."

I can't tell him. He can't know. I promised her I wouldn't say anything, didn't I? I'm being a good friend by keeping her secret.

"Well, it *is*, okay? Just... drop it. It's not your problem."

Because it's my best friend's problem instead.

"You don't get to decide that."

This was *bad*. Really bad. I couldn't even tell him about *my* "secret," let alone Emma's.

I know in a roundabout way, that meant I didn't trust him, but if he'd just let me handle it myself, everything would be okay again.

Then he wouldn't get his memory back, then he wouldn't hate me...

"You don't understand—"

"Then *make* me understand," he insisted, standing up to meet me where I was.

Usually, I was the kind of girl who refused to back down from something like that, but all him towering over me was doing was reminding me of the fun, little "episode" in the barn.

It's okay, it's okay, it's okay.

"You think I don't notice when something's wrong? I notice, Gracie. I *always* notice."

"I'm not having this conversation right now." I said, backing up a step.

"Then don't," he replied, reaching for me. "Just sit down. Eat something. We don't even have to talk."

"I can't," I whispered, guiltily moving away from his touch. "You don't understand."

"Gracie, what's going on? Where are you—"

"I have to go." I muttered, snatching my bag off the ground.

I didn't have the words to fix this. *Any* of it. Not when my best friend was hurting. Not when my little brother was dying of some incurable disease. Not when my parents were never home. Not when I was just using Cole...

Selfish, selfish, selfish. That's all I'll ever be.

Without looking back, I pushed through the cafeteria doors, my hands gripping my bag strap so tightly my knuckles turned white.

I couldn't sit there anymore. Couldn't pretend everything was fine when it wasn't. Not with Emma. Not with Bear. Not with Cole. Not with me.

Because I wasn't just failing them—I was failing myself, too.

March 13th

The long, dark hallway expands before me. Only the faint, yellow glow of a single lightbulb lights my path.

The air lingers over my face like a wet cloth, and I struggle to breathe through the thick of it.

I press forward, determined to find an exit, but the hallway morphs into a total bleak abyss, and suddenly, I can't see a thing.

I frantically reach for the wall beside me.

Or at least, I think it's a wall.

My breathing is labored now as I sink to my knees and squeeze my eyes shut wishing for a way out.

Or a light.

*Something, **anything**.*

But when I open them again, the darkness has only consumed me more.

Adrenaline now pumps through my veins, and I start to shake.

An ominous red light fills the hallway, and I see him... the monster living with my best friend.

Over her cold, lifeless body.

Blood trickles from her skull. Slowly at first. But then, the earth begins to shake like a tsunami.

I brace myself for impact.

The warm, sticky, bright red liquid begins to spew from the walls.

I scramble to my feet, blood coming from everywhere. Every crack. Every crevasse. There is no escape.

I tried to scream, but no words form.

"You should've done something while you had the chance, Gracie!" I hear Emma's voice say.

417

But it doesn't come from her corpse. It comes from the walls, from him, from the floor beneath me...

The sound goes off like a siren, everywhere and nowhere all at once.

"I'm sorry." I silently cried, "I'm so sorry."

I close my eyes one last time.

And then...

Nothing.

The room felt suffocating, as if someone were sitting on my chest, taunting me with air I couldn't have.

My eyes shot open, and for a split second, I couldn't tell where I was. My hands fisted into the sheets as I blinked, letting the shadows of the room come into focus.

My bed, my fan shaking overhead... *my room.*

I was here. I was safe. I was okay. It was only a dream.

But the minute I closed my eyes again, the image roared back to life.

Emma's limp body, the blood pooling around her, the horrible, twisted grin of the man who did it... a sharp sob escaped my lips before I could stop it.

I pressed my palms to my eyes, willing the tears not to fall.

It wasn't real. It wasn't real.

But the worst part was knowing it *could* be.

"You should've done something, Gracie."

I shoved the blankets off and sat upright, clutching my knees to my chest as my breath came in short, ragged bursts.

No matter how hard I tried, I couldn't escape the image of her lying there like that.

Emma's bruised wrist flashed in my mind right then.

I tripped over my dog yesterday.

Lies, lies, lies.

I swung my legs over the edge of the bed and cradled my head in my hands. *What am I even supposed to do?*

My immediate thought was to tell someone what was going on. Maybe they could help in ways I couldn't.

But Emma had *asked* me not to say anything.

What if she hated me for spilling her secret? What if it ruined our friendship?

I'd told myself since I'd walked in on her and her dad that what happened in their house wasn't my business. That by avoiding the situation, it would just... go away. And it had—at least for me.

Because *I* didn't have to live with it.

I didn't have to wear long sleeves in the summer to cover up bruises. I didn't have to lie, or make up stories, or pretend everything was fine when it wasn't.

But Emma did.

Emma had to live with it every single day—trapped in a house with a man who should have protected her.

He was *supposed* to be her dad. He was supposed to love her.

I'd convinced myself that it wasn't my cross to bear—it was hers.

But wasn't that the problem?

Everyone who saw the signs, everyone who knew, had just... stepped aside and continued to let it happen.

And now I was one of them.

Her *best* friend.

I squeezed my eyes shut again, biting down on my lip until I tasted metal.

I want it to stop. All of it.

But there was only one way to do it.

My eyes slowly fluttered open as the realization dawned on me.

Nobody had come to save me when I'd needed it most. But that didn't mean Emma had to go through the same thing.

Maybe she'd hate me. Maybe she'd never forgive me. But I *had* to do this.

She was my best friend, and I cared about her. So much so that it hurt.

I couldn't let fear stop me from doing the right thing.

With shaking hands, I reached for my phone, the screen casting a dim light in the dark room.

My fingers hovered over the keypad, shaking so badly I could barely type.

Before I knew it, the phone was ringing.

My heart thundered in my ears, magnifying the fear that this could all go horribly, horribly wrong.

I could lose my best friend.

You'll lose her either way if you sit here and do nothing.

That's when the call connected.

"Hello, this is Child Protective Services. How may I help you?"

I swallowed hard. "I..." my voice cracked. This was it. There was no turning back after this. "I need to report something."

The silence stretched long after, and I almost wanted to hang up. To pretend I hadn't said anything. To convince myself that I was wrong, that maybe it wasn't as bad as I thought it was.

But I couldn't unsee the bruises, couldn't unhear her dad yelling at her like that. I *couldn't* do it. Not anymore.

I forced myself to speak again, pushing past the lump in my throat.

This wasn't about me. This was about Emma. She deserved to not be scared in her own home. She *deserved* that.

I couldn't stand by and hope that somebody else would say something.

Without meaning to, I sniffled, and when I reached up, my fingers brushed against my cheek, coming away wet.

Oh. I was crying.

The voice on the other end of the line shifted, growing even gentler as she asked questions, like she could sense how terrified I was about this whole situation without me having to say a word.

I didn't know how, but it worked, and my chest loosened just enough for me to let out a shaky breath.

"Okay, sweetie," the operator said finally. "If you hear anything else, please don't hesitate to reach out. And take it easy, alright?"

"Okay." I whispered, "Thank you."

The call ended, and I sat there, phone still pressed to my ear, long after the line went dead.

The quiet was deafening, but the ache in my chest felt different now. It wasn't gone by any means, but it was softer now at least. *I did the right thing*.

I didn't know what came next. Or if Emma would ever forgive me. Or if I could even forgive *myself* for butting in the middle of this whole thing.

But I knew one thing for sure:

Caring about someone sometimes meant making the hardest call of your life. And sometimes, it meant being the one to fight for them when they couldn't.

Chapter Thirty-Three:

Emma

"*Emma Daniels, would you please come down to the office? Emma Daniels, please come down to the office.*"

I froze mid-thought, my pencil hovering over the last problem on my math test.

What's this for?

Every pair of eyes in the classroom fell on me, but I didn't dare meet them.

Instead, I stared at the numbers on my test that were starting to slant as if ignoring the intercom would make it all go away. As if there was *another* Emma Daniels somewhere in the building.

There wasn't. I knew there wasn't.

I forced myself to bubble in the last answer, my hands shaking as I slid the test onto my teacher's desk.

She gave me a small, tight-lipped smile that made heat rush to my face.

Sympathy. That was never a good sign.

The hallway felt longer than usual.

Every step felt like it would be my last one, like my legs would just cave out on me.

It was probably nothing. Maybe they just needed something signed. Or maybe they were telling me I'd gotten one of the scholarships that I'd applied for.

Because I *knew* it wasn't my dad trying to sneak me out of class for a daddy/daughter date.

When pigs could fly, maybe.

I turned a corner and passed a teacher, who gave me the kind of look you give a kid whose goldfish just died.

My chest tightened.

Did everyone know something I didn't?

Maybe they finally found out about the monster you are. The monster your dad's been protecting everyone from.

I swallowed hard, trying to ignore the voice in my head, but nevertheless, it got to me. It always did.

By the time I'd reached the office, I felt like I was officially going to be sick.

The receptionist glanced up from her computer and smiled softly, like she knew exactly why I was there. That made *one* of us.

But before I could say a word, she stood like she was giving me her condolences.

"Come with me, hon," she said, her voice too sweet for it to be *just* a school thing.

Which only meant, whatever this was, it was bad. It was *really* bad.

My feet moved, but my brain suddenly felt disconnected, like I was floating outside myself.

She led me down the hall to the counseling center, and that's when the world narrowed.

*What is **happening** right now?*

"Mr. Bailey will be out in just a moment," she said, motioning toward a chair outside the office. "Let me know if I can get anything, okay, sweetheart?"

Before I could respond and say that she could get me *the heck out of here*, she disappeared back down the hall, leaving me alone with my spiraling thoughts.

I sat there, clutching my backpack strap with my sweaty palms, and stared at the floor. Because what *else* could I do?

I was doomed.

It was over.

I was almost sure I knew what this was for now.

And what could I even say to get out of it? How was I supposed to deny the scars, or the cuts, or the bruises?

I couldn't.

This was it.

The second I walked into that office, my life would be blown up. It was kind of like Schrödinger's cat experiment.

I was simultaneously dead and alive at the same time. Well, maybe more dead than alive because if my dad found out...

When he found out, it'd be my fault. It'd be *all* my fault.

Because who was I kidding? My dad was going to kill me.

They were going to take away our house, put me in foster care, send him to jail... everything would fall apart because of me.

I ruined our lives.

And there was nowhere to run.

Gracie

I knew I should've been in class, but what was the point? Today had been fucked from the start.

I hadn't talked to Cole since I'd walked out on him yesterday.

Before (as in pre-amnesia Cole and I), we'd go through these spurts of not talking, and honestly, back then, I enjoyed not hearing from him. It gave me space to think, to let me breathe, to keep on loathing him on my own terms.

But now... it was different. He was different.

We were different.

And yet, I was still the same.

In the back of my mind, I knew that the logical thing to do *was* to end "things" with him, to make him hate me, so that his leaving could be under *my* control. After all, he'd remember who I really was eventually. I was just speeding up the inevitable.

Yet here I was, like some obsessive stalker.

I hadn't even meant to pass his English class—at least, that's what I told myself, anyway.

But I guess my feet had other plans, like they were some kind of magnet pulling me toward what I couldn't have.

The door was open just a crack, so I leaned against the wall, arms crossed, trying to look like I belonged just in case someone walked by.

From my angle, I could barely see him, but it was still enough to get my "fix."

He was at his desk, hunched over his computer, typing furiously.

His brow was furrowed in concentration, his lips pressed into a determined line, and I had to bite my cheek to stop a giggle from slipping out.

That was his "game face," the same one he wore during football practice—*not* that I'd snuck into see him practice ever... okay, fine. Maybe I had. Sue me.

Suddenly, though, he paused for a second, his hands hovering over the keyboard as he looked up from his desk.

His head tilted slightly, gaze sweeping the room like he sensed something was off.

I ducked back behind the doorframe, pressing myself back up against the wall so he wouldn't accidentally see me.

What am I even doing?

I wasn't supposed to be here—lurking, spying... whatever the hell this was.

My heart pounded in my chest, louder than it had any right to be.

I shouldn't be here.

Somehow, I found the will to push off the wall and walk back to my *own* class as quickly as possible.

Cole was fine, or at least, he *would* be. He'd get over me ruining everything, and he'd move on with his life. He didn't need me.

But maybe I needed him...

My hands clenched into fists, nails pressing crescents into my palms.

I hated how much I wanted him. I hated that I still cared.

Because I *did* care. About him, about Emma, about Bear, about all of it. And caring was exhausting.

Bear was another story. Or maybe the same one—just a different chapter in this dumpster fire of a week.

My parents, who had apparently finally remembered that they had kids, had swooped in out of nowhere and decided they were going to start "parenting" again.

Except their version of parenting was a joke.

They weren't fixing anything that mattered—like Bear's IVIG infusions that were *still* overdue.

Nope, they were too busy wrapping him up in metaphorical bubble wrap. No hanging out with friends. No screen time after eight. No sugar.

Meanwhile, the important stuff? The stuff that actually kept him alive? That was still on hold.

I'd been the one keeping it all together. *I'd* made his smoothies since he wasn't able to eat normal things, *I'd* carried his backpack when he couldn't lift it, *I'd* made sure he took his meds on time.

And now they had the audacity to waltz in with their "rules" and "precautions" like they even knew what was going on in their own damn son's life?

And then there was Emma.

I'd called CPS. I'd done the thing. The big, terrible, life-ruining thing. Because someone had to. Because the bruises weren't going to stop on their own. Because I cared about her, even if I knew deep down that she'd never see it that way.

But what if it only made things worse? What if they kept her with him and he... killed her? Or what if they put her in a foster home that was just as bad?

That's when the intercom crackled to life.

"Emma Daniels, would you please come down to the office? Emma Daniels, please come down to the office."

The world tilted.

No, no, no. Not now. Not like this.

I hadn't meant to literally out her in front of the whole school. She really *was* going to hate me for this, wasn't she?

I backed against another wall, my breath caught in my throat.

A door opened down the hall, and there she was.

Her backpack was slung over one shoulder, and her face pale and hollow, like she already knew her life was about to implode.

She walked right past me.

She didn't even see me.

She just walked past like I was nothing. Like a stranger.

And maybe that's all I was now. Because I felt like I'd betrayed her in the worst possible way.

March 17th

Emma

The days all blurred together, like one long, miserable rerun of a show I hated.

Strangers filed in and out of the house, probing every part of my life. They wore polite smiles, asked the same questions over and over, like they were reading from a script they didn't really understand.

And through it all, my dad stayed eerily silent.

You know how they *say it's the quiet ones that you have to worry about*? Well, I was. *Worried*, that was.

Sure, he'd shaved. He'd even started wearing clean shirts and buying groceries again, like he used to when Mom was alive.

Anyone else might've thought he was turning over a new leaf, but I knew better. Because I *knew* that the second CPS left, he was going to kill me.

And this time, I wasn't sure if that was in the literal sense or not.

I hadn't talked to Gracie since the secret had gotten out, but I *knew* she was the one who had blabbed it to the world.

She'd tried to play the hero and lost.

Because the truth was, statistically, people like me *didn't* get out of these kinds of situations. Because apparently, the State doesn't *actually* want to do anything about it—that's too much work for them.

So instead, after they poke and prod and tell your parent how terrible they are, they shake their hand and just go on their merry, little way.

Yes, you heard that right. They leave you with your kid... the kid that spilled your secret. And unless you have somewhere else to go, there's *nowhere* to go but down.

So, there it was. I was no statistic beater. In fact, I was probably more of a dead girl.

But it was okay. I could make it out of this. I just needed to put on my game day face and be brave.

I needed to pretend like my best friend was a total liar, and that my dad wasn't a monster.

Easy, right?

I was in the zone, prepped and ready for battle, when they sat me down again—another couch, another overly cheerful stranger who probably thought they could save me. *Little did she know...*

"How would you describe your dad?" she asked, like it'd bring on some new revelation... like I'd admit to *anything*.

I'd answered the question more times than I could count, but if saying it one more time meant they'd leave me alone, I was happy to go along with it.

"He's great," I said simply. "Best dad there is."

Her pen scratched against the notepad. Then, she glanced up, clearly waiting for something more.

After about a minute of dead silence, "And does he abuse you?"

"No."

She wanted me to rat him out, I knew she did. But I just couldn't do it. I couldn't let them take away the only family I had left in the world over something stupid my friend said.

At that point, the plan to wait until I turned eighteen to move out had completely crashed and burned. And as much as I loved my dad (or maybe just the idea of him; I didn't know anymore), I knew he'd never let this go.

I had a little cash saved, enough to maybe get a place in town if I needed it. But even with that, I knew everything was going to be different now.

I could accept who my dad was, even if it hurt. But I still wanted the life other girls got—the *normal* stuff.

Him driving me to college, or walking me down the aisle someday, or meeting his grandkids...

But none of that was going to happen now, not after this.

He cared too much about his reputation, and I'd just ruined it.

"What's that on your arm?"

The question caught me off guard, and I looked down with a sinking feeling in my chest to see the faint, dark mark I'd forgotten to cover up—the scar from his belt.

It was the one I'd gotten after Gracie had walked in on us after our practice for the FFA competition.

"Ran into a door," I said quickly, pulling my sleeve down.

"Big door, don't you think?"

"It... was."

She leaned forward, letting out a soft sigh. "Emma, does your dad abuse you?"

"*It's not abuse!*" The words tore out of me before I could stop them. I shot up from the couch so fast it scraped against the floor, my whole body shaking as heat rose in my chest like it might burn me from the inside out. "Why can't you just leave it alone? *Leave me alone!*"

Her eyes widened, but I didn't care.

"You don't get it! Because he's *my* dad, not yours! He's *all* I have! And if he's mad at me, it's because I deserve it!" My voice broke, and my vision blurred with tears I refused to wipe away. "*I mess up*! I make him angry! It's my fault! It's always my fault!"

"Emma," she said softly, reaching toward me.

"*No!* Don't touch me!" I snapped, stepping back, arms wrapped tight around myself. "You think you can just sit here, write in your little notebook, and fix this? You don't know anything about me! You don't know what will happen when you leave! You don't know what I'll have to deal with when this is over!"

A sob ripped out of my throat. "He's all I have left," I choked out, quieter now, my knees threatening to buckle. "Please don't take him away. I'm sorry. Let me fix this. *Please*."

She was quiet for a long moment. Then, finally, she cleared her throat. "Emma, it's normal to be reprimanded for bad behavior. What's not normal is being beaten for it."

"You don't understand..."

A tear slipped down my cheek before I could stop it.

"No, honey. I don't think *you* understand. He shouldn't be hitting you."

"Leave me alone," I whispered. "Don't pretend like you care."

Chapter Thirty-Four:

G racie

 I hadn't left my room since ruining Emma's life.

And the fact that *she* hadn't been at school either was enough for me to know... I was the worst friend ever.

Cole had sent a few texts over the past couple of days too. Ones like, *"Are you okay?"* or *"Just checking in."* But even those had stopped after a while.

It felt like every bridge I'd built was burning, and I was too tired to do anything but *watch* it happen.

My thumb scrolled aimlessly through social media, but I wasn't really seeing anything. It was just... noise. Something to fill the silence.

Eventually, I found myself digging through old photos on Instagram.

My finger hovered over one of Emma and me from a couple of summers back, frosting smeared across our grins.

We'd tried baking cookies from scratch, and half the dough ended up on the floor. It'd been somewhat of a total disaster, but also one of the best days of my life.

Another photo popped up—me and Emma at the eighth grade talent show, scream-singing to "I'm Gonna Be (500 Miles)" using the fakest Scottish accents imaginable.

We hadn't won by a long shot, but The Proclaimer gods had still been made proud that day.

Back then, everything was so simple. No fights. No terrible parents... Just two best friends who thought the world would always stay like that.

Buzz.

A notification.

For a split second, I let myself hope it was Emma. It was stupid, but there it was anyway.

It wasn't her.

Obviously.

A lump formed in my throat, and I dropped my phone onto the bed, rolling onto my back to stare up at the ceiling. *I just want things to go back to normal.*

But nothing would ever be normal again, would it?

My life had ended the moment I'd been raped.

Life was never going to "get better" after Bear had gotten sick. Or when my parents up and abandoned me.

And every day after that was just the universe laughing at me for trying to exist... even *trying* to be "normal" after "normal" had been ripped away from me.

Mom and Dad didn't even *care* about what had happened to me. Not that I'd told them, but shouldn't they have noticed? Shouldn't they have seen how I'd stopped talking, how I wasn't *me* anymore?

But no, they were too busy with Bear, too wrapped up in their own world to notice their daughter drowning right in front of them.

It wasn't fair. None of it was fair.

Suddenly, the front door creaked open, and the smell of pizza drifted in. "Dinner!" Dad called.

Wow, that's a first: I don't have to make dinner for everyone by myself this time.

I dragged myself out of bed, forcing my legs to move. *I just have to make it through the rest of this night. Then I can go back to hiding in my room.*

So, with a deep breath, I pushed everything down, steeling myself for another night of pretending to play the part of the perfect daughter... at least one more time.

Dinner was exactly what I'd expected it to be: about as fun as pulling teeth.

My parents sat across from me, each pretending like the other didn't exist. *Perks of being divorced, I guess.*

But that just meant Bear became the shining topic of conversation instead.

"How's your muscle strength been lately, honey?" Mom asked him.

"It's fine," he mumbled, not looking up from his plate.

"Are you sure?" she pressed, tilting her head. "What about your legs? Any weakness there?"

He shrugged, cutting his pizza into uneven bite-sized pieces. "Yep. Fine."

"*Fine* isn't good enough, Bear," she said, her voice tightening. "If you're feeling off, we need to tell Dr. Patel."

Dad jumped in before my brother could even respond. "He's been fine. He's on a new medication. It's going great."

I picked at the edge of my paper napkin, trying my hardest to bite my tongue.

If my parents knew *anything* about their son, they'd know that Bear *wasn't* on any new medication. He'd been using Pyridostigmine on and off for the past couple of months, but after the last time it had left him throwing up for three days, I'd started slowly throwing the pills away instead of letting him take them.

Now, we were just relying on his IVIG infusions—which we were *still* late on because of Bear's stupid doctor.

But I stayed quiet.

"Richard, I'm serious," Mom snapped. "You have to be consistent with Bear's physical therapy. You can't just medicate him and call it quits because you're too lazy to take care of him."

Dad scoffed, throwing his napkin down onto the table. "Don't you lecture me, *Diane*. I've been handling things just fine without you swooping in with your Chicago advice."

"That *Chicago advice* is the only reason there's still a roof over our heads," she shot back.

"Oh, now we're an *our*? I didn't think we were an *our* anymore after you served me *divorce papers*."

My grip on my own napkin tightened, the material crumpling under my fingers.

"Because you were sleeping with another woman!"

"I was not sleeping with—"

"STOP!"

The words tore out of me before I realized I'd stood up, my chair screeching against the floor.

Both of them turned to me, like they'd forgotten I was even there.

"You're both acting *insane*," I exclaimed. "All you ever do is fight. You think that helps anyone? You think this is helping Bear?"

"*Gracie*—" Mom started.

"*No*. Don't '*Gracie*' me. You don't get to act like you're the victim here. *Neither* of you do. You're both so busy trying to prove who's the better parent that you've actually forgotten how to fucking parent!"

"That's not true," Dad argued, standing up now too.

"Oh, really?" I snapped. "When was the last time either of you asked me how *I* was doing? Do you even know me anymore? Or are you so focused on Bear and your little power struggle that I don't exist to you?"

"Gracie, of course you exist to us—"

"No, I don't!" I yelled, tears stinging my eyes. "You don't even *know* me. You don't care about me. You've *never* cared about me. You only care about winning this stupid little competition you have with each other."

"That's not fair," Mom started.

"*Fair*?" I laughed bitterly. "You wanna talk about fair? What's fair about me being the one to hold everything together while you two actively try to rip it apart? What's fair about me having to grow up overnight because Bear got sick and you decided I didn't need parents anymore? You don't even *know* why I keep people at arm's length, do you?"

They were silent, their faces pale.

"It's because of you!" I screamed, my voice breaking. "Because to you, I'm just some girl with daddy issues!"

437

"I have *never* said that to you..." Dad stammered, reaching out to me like that could fix anything.

I ripped my arm from him like he'd burned me. "Oh, really? *Elizabeth Smart.* Does that ring a bell?"

He raised an eyebrow, confusion flickering across his face.

"Four years ago. You and mom. That special they did on TV about Elizabeth Smart," I said, dryly.

"The girl who was abducted in Utah?" Mom asked, standing *herself*. "What does that have to do with this? How do you even know about her?"

"Abducted. Tortured. *Raped.*"

Mom's face blanched. "You were supposed to be in bed. Why were you up?"

"You said she had *daddy issues*!" I screamed. "How could you say that about her? About anyone?"

"Gracie, where is this all coming from?" Dad asked, his tone caught somewhere between defensive and bewildered.

"You have no idea what I've gone through to keep this family together," I said, voice trembling. "No idea how many hoops I had to jump through to shield you from the disgusting disappointment that is your daughter. All for you to sit there and say that she. Had. Daddy. Issues."

"I'm not feeling well," Bear mumbled under his breath.

I whipped my head back to him, anger boiling over before I could stop myself. "This is *not* the time, Bear. *Geez.* Can you shut up for just five seconds of your life? Or is that too hard for you too? You can't walk, you can't eat actual food, you can't..."

Mom gasped. "Gracie Abigail Lewis!"

"*What*? Are you mad that I'm telling your precious son the truth? That your *daddy issues* daughter is contaminating him?"

Bear pushed back his chair and stood, wobbling slightly but holding onto the table for balance. "I'm going to bed," he muttered.

"Oh, no, don't worry," I snapped, walking backwards to the front door just so I could continue to glare at them as I yanked my coat off one of the wall hooks. "I'll just leave. That's what you want anyways, isn't it?"

I scoffed when no one answered. "Sorry I couldn't be good enough for you. My bad. I'll just go so you can have that perfect little family you've always wanted, and—"

A thud cut me off mid-sentence.

Bear.

He was now on the floor, his legs splayed awkwardly underneath him like a puppet with its strings cut.

The coat slipped from my hands. "Bear?"

It only took a split second of standing there like that before my legs got the memo, and I took off in his direction, sliding on my knees as I shook his shoulder violently.

"Bear, *please*! Wake up!"

Mom was already on the phone, her voice hysterical as she rattled off our address to the 911 operator.

Dad knelt beside me, his hands hovering over Bear like he didn't know what to do.

"Stay with me, Bear," I begged as tears blurred my vision. "You're okay. You're gonna be okay."

His lips parted, but no sound came out.

"Help is on the way, baby," Mom said, her voice breaking as she dropped the phone and crawled to Bear's other side.

We sat on the floor like that—all three of us holding onto Bear as we waited for the ambulance to come.

Together at last, but at what cost?
God, please don't take him from me.

Chapter Thirty-Five:

H ospitals are loud in the quietest kinds of ways.

The steady hum of fluorescent lights. The shuffle of hurried feet. The sound of doors opening and closing, but never the door I was watching.

Please don't take him from me.

It'd been three hours since Bear had collapsed. Three hours since the paramedics had carried him out. Three hours since a nurse took Mom and Dad back to see him and told me to stay put.

I hadn't sat down once.

I'd tried pacing, but I was too nauseous to move around for very long, so I leaned against the wall instead, arms crossed, nails digging into my elbows like I could keep myself from crying.

News flash: it didn't work. I was a sobbing disaster, and my mind playing Worst-Case-Scenario Roulette wasn't helping.

Maybe I was overreacting. Maybe they'd walk out any second now and tell me it was nothing. A little dehydration, a bad day, or some horrible prank they'd pulled on me to teach me a lesson, and we'd all laugh about it later when we were home together again.

If we were home together again.

Why. Couldn't. I. Stop. Shaking?

Maybe it's because this is your fault, Gracie.

I finally sank into one of the uncomfortable plastic chairs against the wall, continuing to stare at the closed double doors as if I could open them with the sheer will of my mind.

My stomach churned like broken glass, every breath scraping its way out of my lungs as I replayed the scene over and over again.

"...can you shut up for just five seconds of your life? Or is that too hard for you too?"

I hadn't meant it. Really, I didn't. If I could go back, I'd say everything differently. Or maybe I wouldn't even say anything at all.

I bit my lip so hard I tasted blood, but I didn't let up.

I deserved it. I deserved to be in pain.

Please don't let him die. Please don't let him die...

The hallway had been quiet for so long that I'd kind of gotten used to it. So when the starting lines to *This Cowboy's Hat* by Chris LeDoux suddenly started echoing off the tiles, my head jerked up in curiosity.

A group rounded the corner, laughing a little too loudly for people who were literally in the hospital right then.

One of the guys, probably mid-twenties or something, was leaning against another dude, his face a mess of bruises and cuts.

But weirdly enough, he wasn't focused on any of that. His eyes were glued to the girl next to him.

She was the one playing the song, singing along off-key.

Social anxiety must hate to see her coming.

He watched her like she was the only person in the world, and his face cracked into a crooked smile—the kind that could make you forget about... I don't know, a shattered leg or whatever was clearly wrong with him.

I should've looked away. I should've kept my eyes glued to the ugly, cracked tiles under my feet and minded my own damn business.

But the song wouldn't let me.

Because Cole loves that song.

He used to blast it every day at work, windows down, volume cranked all the way up (before *and* after his accident—ironic, huh?).

I hated that song, which, of course, made him love it all the more. He'd shoot me a sadistic grin and yell, "Sing along, Gracie!" like I would *ever*.

Thinking about it now made my lips twitch, just for a second, at the memory of him. Even the parts that made me want to strangle him sometimes.

But the smile disappeared just as quickly when I realized...

I missed him.

Not in an oh-I-haven't-seen-you-in-a-while missed him. But in the kind of way that made you feel like a part of yourself had been ripped out.

I thought I was doing him a favor by pushing him away, and maybe I still was. But as it turned out, I needed to be selfish *one* more time... for my sanity, at least.

I didn't even realize I'd pulled out my phone until it was in my hand, my thumb hovering over his name.

Calling him was bad—for *both* of us. Besides, I'd spent my whole life being my own savior. I didn't need him.

But before I could stop myself, my thumb hit the screen.

It didn't even ring once.

"Gracie?"

I swallowed, trying to keep my voice even. "Hey."

"*Hey*," he echoed, and I swore I heard the tiniest of smiles in his voice. "I haven't heard from you in—"

"I'm at the hospital."

"Shit. What happened?" The smile vanished from his voice instantly, and I hated myself for being the reason for it.

Maybe talking to him is a bad idea...

"It's Bear," I forced out quietly before I could take the coward's way out and just hang up on him altogether. "There was a lot of yelling... mostly from my end, and then he just passed out, and they won't let me see him, and..."

My voice broke before I could finish.

Why couldn't I just hold myself together for *five freaking seconds*? I **had** to. It was my fault we were in this mess to begin with.

I was selfish. I was the problem. I was the reason I had no friends. I was the reason my brother might...

Die.

"Gracie, take a deep breath for me."

"I *can't*, though—"

"You can," he cut in. "Just one. Come on."

I pressed the heel of my hand against my forehead, trying to shove the tears back down. "I hate you, y'know? You never listen to me. I said I *can't*."

"You don't hate me, Gracie."

"*Yes*, I do," I shot back, but even I was starting to hear how weak it sounded.

444

"You and I both know you don't mean that," he murmured softly, and I swear I could hear that stupid little smirk sneaking back into his voice.

I choked out a bitter laugh. "You're so full of yourself."

"And yet, you called me anyway."

Silence stretched between us for half a second, but finally, I broke, letting out a shaky breath. "I didn't know who else to call."

"You know what?" he said suddenly, "I'm coming to you. I'll be there in twenty minutes."

I blinked. "You don't even know which hospital—"

"Doesn't matter," he said, firmly. "I'll find you."

And honestly? I didn't doubt it for a second.

Cole

It was easy to find her.

Gracie always stood out in a crowd—even when she wasn't trying to.

Ok, *especially* when she wasn't trying to.

She was pacing at the end of the hall, her hair pulled back in a messy braid, a navy Yale sweatshirt slipping off one shoulder when the elevator doors opened to her floor.

She looked up right then like she somehow *knew* I was there, and before I could even react, she was running toward me, crashing into my arms, and gripping my jacket like it was the only thing holding her upright.

Instinct kicked in, and I pulled her close, holding on like I could keep the outside world from touching her.

Her head buried into my chest, and suddenly, I didn't care who was watching. I didn't care about anything except the fact that she was here. With me.

And you know what? She could yell and scream and push me as hard as she wanted, but I'd still be here.

Always.

"Cole, you make sense to me..."

I pressed my chin to the top of her head, whispering, "I'm here, Gracie. I'm right here."

And I wasn't going anywhere.

Gracie

I must've fallen asleep on Cole's shoulder at some point in the waiting room.

I didn't mean to. I'd told myself I wouldn't—that I *couldn't*. But at some point, exhaustion won, and my head drifted against him.

He didn't move, though. Not once. He just let me stay there, safe like that for a little while.

But the next thing I knew, he was nudging me awake.

"Gracie," he murmured, his breath warm on my cheek. "Hey. The doctor's here."

I blinked groggily, the lights overhead burning into my retinas.

Waking up to that was almost as bad as being hungover. And it certainly felt like it—that I was living in some alcohol-induced nightmare I couldn't really wake up from.

"You can see your brother now," the doctor said, nodding toward the hallway.

Somehow, I forced myself to stand, and without thinking, I reached for Cole's hand.

He didn't let go.

The walk to Bear's room felt like wading through molasses, and every step came with a new wave of dread as my mind cycled through every possibility.

Why were they bringing me to see him? Did that mean he was better? *Worse*?

He had to be fine. I had to believe that I'd walk in there, and he'd roll his eyes at me and tell me to stop worrying so much. I had to believe that I'd get the chance to apologize for earlier. That he'd even forgive me.

But the second I stepped inside, all that hope crumbled.

Because instead of him being up, he was lying in a hospital bed, completely motionless as tubes snaked across his body and machines beeped softly in the background.

The only saving grace was that the window behind him was open slightly, so he must've been coherent enough at one point to request it (that was his thing every time we visited the hospital: open a window to "let the light in" so it felt more like home).

"We're keeping him in a medically induced coma," the doctor explained, his voice sounding underwater, muffled beneath the same blue moonlight that washed over my brother's face from the window. "We need to run some more tests to determine the cause of the collapse and ensure there's no further damage."

All I could do was nod.

"We'll need consent to proceed with the additional tests, and seeing as your parents have stepped out for now, I'll just need you to sign..."

He held out a pen.

I blinked, resetting my brain enough to acknowledge the object in his hand, but for some reason, I couldn't do anything more than that.

"I'm not over eighteen," I muttered, finally finding the words.

The doctor frowned slightly. "Sorry, what was th—"

"I said *I'm not over eighteen*!" The words scraped against my throat as I threw my hands up in pure frustration. "I'm not an adult! I'm not—"

The anger boiled over, and I switched gears in record time. "Where are they? Where are my parents?" I snapped. "Why would they leave him alone? Why the *hell* would they—"

"Gracie."

One word. One word was all it took to shut me up.

Cole stepped closer, closing the gap I'd managed to put between us.

His eyes locked onto mine, and just like that, the fire burned out. Like it'd be okay. Like we'd figure it out.

Like there *was* a 'we' to figure it out.

The doctor, who I'd honestly forgotten was even there in the all of two seconds I was looking at Cole, cleared his throat uncomfortably as he glanced between us. "I don't know where your parents went, but I can assure you they're likely—"

"Yeah, we'll get to that," Cole interrupted, his hand lifting to stop the doctor mid-sentence. He wasn't rude about it, but you could tell he wasn't leaving any room for negotiation. His eyes never left mine. "Can we have a minute?"

The doctor hesitated, unsure if he should push back. But then he gave Cole another look and seemed to think better of it. "Of course. I'll step out," he muttered, shuffling awkwardly toward the door.

I didn't realize I was shaking until Cole's hand slid to the small of my back.

"Come on," he murmured, "Let's take a breather, okay?"

I didn't resist when he guided me out of the room, his hand staying firm on my back, like he was silently reassuring me that he wasn't about to let go anytime soon.

By the time we reached the end of the hallway, my chest felt like it might burst.

Through the tall windows in front of us, I could see the parking lot stretch out beyond the glass, cars shimmering under the glow of street-lights.

I stared out at it, wishing I could disappear into the darkness, become one of the shadows and just escape.

Escape to a reality where my brother wasn't sick, I wasn't a freak, my parents actually wanted to be a part of this family...

Cole's hand dropped from my back then as he took a step away, giving me space.

And that's when everything inside me broke.

"What the *absolute hell* is wrong with them?" I shouted, my voice ricocheting off the bare walls before I could rein myself in. "How could they just *leave*? He could die in there, and they just... what? Decided to take a coffee break or something? Do they even *care*?"

Cole stayed silent.

"And why does the responsibility always fall on me?" I continued, my voice cracking as the tears threatened to spill. "I'm *seventeen*! I'm not supposed to be the one figuring this all out. I shouldn't have to sign papers or make decisions or—" My words caught, breaking into a choked sob.

"My whole childhood's... gone," I whispered. "I didn't get to be a kid. I didn't get a choice. It's just... gone. And Bear—he's all I have. What if I lose him too? What if he..." My throat closed up, and I couldn't finish my sentence, couldn't say the word *die* again. "I can't. I can't keep doing this. I'm *scared*."

The admission left me hollow, and I almost didn't want to look back into Cole's eyes, because then he'd know.

He'd know how vulnerable I was, how *broken* I was.

Was I even ready for that?

But then I felt him step closer, and his arms wrapped around me, pulling me into him.

It wasn't the kind of hug meant to stop the crying or make me pull myself together. It was the kind of hug that said, *Break. Fall apart if you need to. I've got you. I promise.*

"I'm right here, Gracie," he said softly, his breath brushing against my temple.

For a minute, I stood stiff in his embrace, like my body didn't know how to accept it. I didn't deserve it. I didn't deserve *him*.

But maybe I could let myself think I did for just a second longer...

I buried my face in his chest.

That's when the tears came harder, soaking his shirt. But he didn't pull away. His hand moved in slow, soothing circles on my back, as his chin rested lightly on top of my head.

"I just want it to stop hurting."

He pulled back just slightly, his eyes searching mine as if to ask: *How can I help you right now?*

And then, before I could second-guess myself, I closed the distance between us and pressed my lips to his.

You. *I want you right now.*

It wasn't soft or tentative. It was raw and desperate—a way to drown out the ache clawing at my chest.

My fingers curled into the fabric of his shirt, holding onto him like he was the only solid thing in my crumbling world.

He froze only for a millisecond before kissing me right back.

At first, it was slow, as if he were letting me set the pace. But when I didn't pull away, he melted into me completely.

His hand cradled my face, his thumb brushing against my cheek as the kiss deepened. He guided me back until my shoulders met the wall.

Our lips moved together with urgency as my hands found their way into his hair, and I clung to him, pouring everything I couldn't say out loud into that kiss.

When he pulled back, his forehead rested against mine, his breath warm and unsteady against my lips.

"Gracie," he murmured suddenly, "I'm in love with you."

Wait. What?

The words slammed into me, and I spun around, stumbling back and breaking out of his arms. "What did you just say?"

No, no, no, no. This can't be happening right now.

"I love you," he said again, softer this time, but just as sure.

His eyes searched mine like he was expecting to uncover the same kind of feeling in mine. But it *wasn't* there. It *couldn't* be there.

I don't even know what love is.

"No," was all I could say.

His brow furrowed. "No?"

"No. You *can't* love me," I said, my voice rising as I shook my head furiously, as if that could undo what he'd just said. "You don't know what you're saying. You don't even *know* me."

"Gracie—"

"Stop!" My pulse thundered in my ears as I stepped back again like I could physically outrun this. "You don't understand. You don't... you don't even remember what's happened between us. If you did, you wouldn't—" My voice cracked, the words splintering like glass in my throat.

Don't cry, don't cry, don't cry.

This was never supposed to happen...

"Wouldn't what? Wouldn't love you? Is that what you're saying?"

"Yes!" Because it was the truth, wasn't it? Even if it felt like ripping my chest open to admit it. "If you remembered who I really am, you wouldn't even *like* me, let alone love me."

I was using him.

If pre-amnesia Cole were here (if he could only see us now), he'd lose his damn mind. He'd laugh. He'd yell. He'd *hate* me.

And he had every right to.

I was a horrible, selfish person for even *thinking* we could be anything but enemies.

"Gracie, what are you talking about? I know *exactly* who you are—"

'No, you *don't*!" I insisted. "You *think* you do, but you don't. Because the real me? The one you forgot? That girl is a loser. You *hated* her. Please, just trust me. You don't love me. Go home, get some sleep. You'll feel differently soon. Hell, maybe even tomorrow."

I turned to take my own advice and walk away, but before I could take another step, his hand caught my wrist, spinning me back around.

"We are *having* this conversation, Gracie," he said firmly. "Not tomorrow, not next week. *Now.*"

I yanked my arm back, my chest heaving as I glared at him. "You don't get it," I said. "I'm trying to protect you."

"Protect me from *what*?"

"From *me*, you moron."

"Gracie, what the hell are you talking about?"

"Why does this matter so much to you anyway? You're the one who—"

I stopped, face paling, just as *his* eyes darkened. "I'm the one who *what*?" *Shit...*

I could fight telling him, like I had been doing for months, but what was the point? We were here. This was happening. No more hiding the truth.

I was going to lose him anyway.

I let out a breath. *Here goes nothing...* "You're the one who told everyone I was hooking up with a college guy."

Confusion flicked across his face immediately. "Wait, what do you—"

I wasn't done. "But it wasn't a rumor, *okay*?! It wasn't a rumor, because it was real. But I didn't 'hook up' with anyone, Cole. He *raped* me."

His face shifted as the hallway fell deathly silent—concern giving way to confusion, then slowly morphing into a horrible, dawning realization.

"You were... crying. I made you cry." he said finally.

I laughed dryly. "You've made me cry a million times, Cole. That's why you can't love me. We just don't work." My body continued to shake as I went back to the past I hated revisiting. "And y'know what? You told the whole fucking school about it! I don't know how you even found out, but you turned the worst thing that's ever happened to me into a *joke*."

453

His hand dragged through his hair, his expression crumpling with guilt. "Gracie, I had no idea. I had a memory about doing something to make you cry... I just had no idea it was *that*. I—"

"Does that make it any better?" I sobbed, cutting him off again. "Do you think that changes anything? What if it had been your little sister? What if someone had done that to her? How would you feel?"

"I would feel *terrible*, okay?" he burst out, his voice rising to match mine. "I was a stupid-ass kid, okay? Is that what you want me to say? I'm sorry. I am *so sorry*, Gracie. But I'm not that person anymore."

"But I still *am* that person! That's what I can't get you to understand. This is my life! My life—where everyone knows me now as the hormonal middle school whore. Where people literally call me *Slutty* to my face. *This* is the real me, Cole." My voice wavered as the tears finally spilled over. "So, no. You don't love me. You're falling for some version of me that doesn't exist. You should hate me. You *would* hate me if you remembered everything."

Cole's jaw tightened, but he didn't step back. "I remember enough to know that you are *not* broken, Gracie. Say what you want about me, but don't you dare say that about yourself. Ever again. And just so we're clear, if you think I would hate you because of some fucked-up thing some grown ass man did to you—"

"Cole, stop—"

"*No*," he interrupted, his voice rising. "Let me finish. I don't hate you. I could *never* hate you. Why can't you see that?"

"Because nothing about my life is normal!" My voice had risen to the point of being nearly a scream. "My brother is in the hospital, my parents are never around, and I was *raped*. I don't get to have a normal crush or a normal life or a normal *anything*. Just. Go. Home. Forget about this. About *me*. It's better this way."

But he didn't move. He stood there, his eyes dark with determination, refusing to leave, refusing to give in.

"You still haven't given me a good reason as to why I shouldn't love you."

I scoffed, like the reasoning was so completely obvious. "Because..." but nothing else came.

And that's when my heart started racing, pounding so hard in my chest I could hear it in my ears.

Because he wasn't leaving.

I couldn't get him to leave.

He's too close, he's too close.

I want this to stop.

He's not listening to me.

"Gracie, please," he said softly, taking another step closer. "You're not alone anymore. You don't have to push me away. I'm right here—"

I took a step back, using my hands as a barrier between us. "You don't get it. You don't know what it's like to live with *this*... every day. You don't know what it's like to ruin everything you touch."

"That's not true. You don't ruin anything."

Just back up for a second...

"You don't know that! You don't remember!" I shot back.

My chest felt like it was caving in, my breath coming faster now as the walls closed in on me. *Space. Now. Right now.*

"You think you know me, but you don't. You don't know what it's like to live in a house where no one cares enough to notice that you're not okay. You don't know what it's like to walk into a school and have everyone look at you like you're *disgusting*."

455

He stepped closer, reaching out for me. "Gracie, I..."

"Just because you don't have a dad to disappoint anymore doesn't mean *I* don't." I blurted out suddenly, hands protecting my chest.

I hadn't realized it before, but somehow, I'd managed to back myself straight into a corner by the vending machines, as the palms of his hands were placed just above my head, caging me in...

Just like he had a couple of months ago in the barn.

I met his eyes just in time to see his face hardening as he yanked his hands away from the wall and away from me like I had burned him.

Guilt overtook me instantly. *Selfish Gracie. You break everything you touch.*

A beat passed between us, and then... "That's low," he said quietly. "Even for you."

"Cole, wait. I didn't mean—" But it was too late.

"Good news, Gracie," he said, his voice clipped as he stepped further away. "You finally got what you wanted. I'll leave you alone."

Before I could beg him to stay or even explain why I was so fucked up in the first place, the sound of his footsteps were echoing down the hallway.

And I just stood there. Shaking uncontrollably until he disappeared around the dimly lit corner.

*What the **hell** did I just do?*

I didn't mean it. Not at all. Especially since I knew how much his dad meant to him.

I just... I just needed space. A second to think. To *breathe*. Away from him being so close.

But instead, I'd said the one thing I couldn't take back.

I'd hurt *another* person I cared about with my big, stupid mouth.

I'd pushed until he left... and maybe for good.

At the realization, my knees buckled, and I sank to the floor. A guttural sob tore through me, like it was being dragged out from the deepest parts of me.

I knew I didn't deserve to cry. Not after what I'd done. But I did anyway.

We were never meant to last as long as we did.

He's better off without me.

But even still, I didn't want it to end like this. I didn't want it to *end*.

"I didn't mean it," I whispered to the empty space, my voice cracking. "I didn't mean it."

But it didn't matter. He wasn't there to hear it.

A fresh wave of guilt crashed over me, and I buried my face in my hands as fresh tears continued to spill over.

I didn't want him to leave. Not forever, anyway. I just didn't know how to let him stay.

Not without ruining it. Like I always did.

Cole

I gripped the steering wheel so hard that I was surprised it didn't just snap in half, breaking like everything else these days.

The empty stretch of highway blurred past me, but it barely registered. My mind was stuck on Gracie still.

What the hell was her problem, anyways? I'd tried to be patient and understanding with her, even when she lashed out for *no reason*.

I'd given up my old friends, left behind the "guy I used to be," and tried like hell to prove I was someone she could count on.

I'd changed my whole damn life for her, thinking that maybe, just maybe, one of these days, she'd finally let me in.

But *no*. Because nothing about my fucked-up life could ever be that simple. Every time we took one step forward, we took three steps back.

My chest burned, and I slammed my hand against the steering wheel, trying to force the anger away.

The sting shot up my arm, but I welcomed it—*needed* it. The pain was better than *this*.

I hit it again, harder this time just for good measure, and the horn blared for a second. Good. Let it scream for me.

It wasn't fair. *None* of this was fair.

She kept dragging up all this shit from a past I couldn't remember like it was my responsibility to change it. But how could I fix something I didn't even know I'd broken?

The speedometer continued to climb as I pressed harder on the gas, the engine roaring under the strain. But I didn't care. Let it break. Let it *all* break.

I slammed the wheel again, harder this time, and a sick, twisted sense of satisfaction rolled through me.

The pain felt good—*so fucking good*.

I was tired. Tired of trying to be what she needed, tired of bending over backwards to prove myself to someone who clearly didn't give a damn.

I should've walked away, but I. Kept. Coming. Back.

She wasn't going to let me into her life no matter *what* I did, so why keep trying?

And I guess that's what pissed me off the most. The fact that I couldn't just give up on her and leave.

I felt like I was losing my mind.

It was madness. It was torture.

Because at the end of the day, I wasn't ready to let her go. She was infuriating, she was intoxicating, she was *everything* to me.

But how long could I keep this up, really?

The truck's engine roared louder as my foot pressed harder on the gas, but I couldn't hear it over the rush of blood in my ears.

*If she could see that I'm on her side **just this once**, we wouldn't be in this situation. I don't deserve to be treated like this. Especially by her. Especially when...*

Then it hit me.

Like a freight train slamming into me at full speed.

It started with a blinding white light piercing through my vision.

I let out a groan as my head snapped back involuntarily, one hand clutching at my temple as the truck swerved.

I barely managed to pull over onto the shoulder before a flood of images, sounds, and emotions started to assault me.

"I hate you, Dad!"

"I love you, son. I'll see you when I get back."

Dad never broke his promises. Not once.

But sometimes, I wished he'd been more specific because the next time we saw each other, he was lying in a casket... at his funeral.

I gritted my teeth as the memories kept coming.

They weren't gentle. They didn't give me time to adjust.

They *stormed* through me like a hurricane, ripping everything apart from the inside out.

Middle school. Gracie.

She was there standing in the school parking lot, laughing with her parents and brother. They were so wrapped up in their own little world, so oblivious to what reality actually looked like.

My dad was gone, and there she was, with her perfect, shiny, happy family.

Jealously and anger twisted inside me like a hot knife slicing into my stomach.

I hated her back then for what she had... for what *I'd* lost.

And now, I had even *more* reason to hate her.

For stringing me along, for letting me follow her around the school like a damn puppy, so stupidly in love with her that I couldn't think straight.

She knew what she was doing. She *had* to know.

And she'd let me do this to myself.

She'd let me fall for her, let me think there was a chance, only to tear it away like it meant nothing.

Like *I* meant nothing.

Like this was all just some big game to her.

The memories kept coming, faster now, overlapping, merging into one chaotic mess that I couldn't even begin to untangle.

The throbbing in my head reached full force, and I let out a strangled yell, my hands clutching at my hair as if I could pull the images out of my skull.

And then, just as it was all getting to be too much, it stopped.

The memories went quiet.

The *world* went quiet.

I remembered now.

I remembered *everything*.

Welcome back, me.

Chapter Thirty-Six:

G racie

Somehow, I pulled myself up off the hospital floor.

My legs still felt like jelly, but I managed to stumble forward anyways, wiping at my face with the back of my sleeve.

The hallway smothered me on the way back to my brother's room, but I kept moving. I *had* to. For Bear. For myself. For some shred of hope that things would get better.

I pushed open his door, attempting to accept the faint hum of machines that greeted me instead of his voice as the new normal.

It was weird how peaceful he looked. Bear wasn't *supposed* to be like that. He was supposed to be moving, teasing me... making a sarcastic comment or two...

"What am I ever going to do about you?" I sniffled softly, trying to smile as I pulled a chair closer to his bed and sank into it.

He didn't respond, obviously. But in my head, I could almost hear his voice, dry and poorly timed as ever. *"Well, you know me. I like to keep things interesting."*

I let out a shaky laugh as I leaned forward, tracing the fitted sheet with my pointer finger as I tried to keep my voice steady. "You could've warned me this was going to happen, you jerk,"

I paused, glancing at his still face. "I've been mad at you before, but this? This takes the cake. You're supposed to be invincible, y'know? But now I'm sitting here, talking to your comatose body like a crazy person."

I bit my lip, the lump in my throat growing harder to swallow. "I'm scared, okay? Scared that you won't wake up. Scared that you will, but nothing will ever be the same. You're all I have, Bear. I *need* you."

The silence stretched between us, and for a second, I just sat there, my hand brushing against his cold one. "I know you'd probably tell me to shut up. That I'm being dramatic and overthinking everything like always. And you're probably right."

I exhaled, letting out another shuddery breath as I dug my nails into my palms until crescent moons began to form. "Speaking of me overthinking things, there's something else I should tell you..."

I looked at him again, like I expected him to roll his eyes and tell me to get on with it. "Cole told me he loved me," I admitted quietly. Maybe if I said it out loud enough times, it'd actually register... or I'd actually believe it. Or I'd feel like I deserved it more. "And I told him to leave. Because that's what I do. I ruin things. I use people. I use *him.*"

"You're an idiot." Bear would've said. I knew he would've.

"I know," I said, the tears finally spilling over. "But it's more than that. Love isn't supposed to feel safe for me. It isn't even something I thought I could feel. And I know that's a cop-out answer, but..."

I paused, swallowing hard as I stared at the monitors beside his bed. "But Cole... he's different. He's not like the guy from the worship team. He's not Mom or Dad. He's a genuinely good guy... but he's put in all this work to be better, and I haven't. How can I say I deserve a happy ending? One with... *him*, even?"

I sighed, letting the truth wash over me. "Because if I'm being completely honest with myself, I think... I think I love him too, Bear," I whispered, the words terrifying and exhilarating all at once.

"And it's not like in the movies or books, where everything's perfect and easy. It's messy and scary and makes me feel like I'm opening myself up to getting hurt. But I *love* him. I just don't know how to let him in. It's like... every time someone gets too close, I freak out and expect it to all go horribly wrong."

*"If you spend your whole life afraid of what could happen, you'll miss your opportunity. At some point, you have to realize that he made his choice to love you. You didn't tell him to do that, you didn't hold a gun to his head. **You didn't use him**. Give yourself some grace. Let yourself be happy."*

"When did you get so insightful?" I teased, my vision starting to blur as I grabbed onto Bear's hand, holding onto it for dear life.

After what had happened... with *him*, the guy from the worship team, I'd thought that I didn't deserve to be happy. Because in my mind, people like me didn't get happy endings. Bad things didn't happen to good people, did they?

But now, sitting here, looking around this room, knowing that I was safe, I had a whole new perspective. I'd done the impossible.

I'd survived.

The knowledge wasn't some magical cure, and it definitely wasn't the key to instantly erasing all the pain. But it was *something*. It was a start. It was a *beginning*.

For so long, I'd blamed God for letting it happen to me. I'd told myself that if I couldn't trust Him to protect me, I couldn't trust *anyone*.

So, I pushed people away.

I hurt them before they could hurt me.

But looking at the bigger picture, I understood now... God hadn't ruined my life. He hadn't abandoned me. Maybe I just saw what I wanted to believe—that I was alone, that I wasn't worth saving, that I was nothing more than the shattered remains of the girl I used to be.

But if that were true, then why was I still here?

I hadn't been left behind. I hadn't been forgotten. I'd been given a chance. A do-over. A *restart*. And y'know what? I *wanted* to be happy again. I wanted to feel like I deserved it.

Because I did.

I didn't know why I was raped. I probably never would. But maybe that was okay. Maybe I didn't need to have all the answers to start living again. Because for the first time, I was realizing that I didn't have to keep punishing myself for what had happened.

It wasn't my fault.

It wasn't my fault at all.

My past didn't define me. *I* defined me. And only I could decide who I was or wasn't.

I was a survivor, not a disgrace.

There was nothing wrong with me.

I could accept help.

I could accept love.

I could accept God.

All it took was one small leap of faith.

And maybe, I was finally ready to make that jump.

March 19ᵗʰ

I love him. You hear that, world?

I'm. In. Love. With. Cole. Brown.

And I needed to tell him.

I hadn't seen him all day. He wasn't at work, or in class, or randomly walking down the hall... which wasn't technically like him, but I guess I understood if he was avoiding me. I kind of deserved it.

But that was just what was going to make telling him how I felt even better—he was going to be so happy I felt the same way.

When the lunch bell rang, I grabbed my bag and made my way into the cafeteria, set on the sole purpose of finding Cole.

The noise of overlapping conversations and trays banging against the tables filled the air, as my heart pounded faster and faster, louder and louder until I was sure even if he *wasn't* at school today, he could hear it.

Please be here. Please understand. Please...

And then, I saw him.

Full-on manspreading on top of one of the lunch tables with Dylan and the rest of his loser friends.

I let out a little laugh at that.

*Poor Cole. I can't stand **seeing** those guys, let alone being surrounded by them.*

Good news, though, I could just cut into their conversation and save him. Maybe throw in a couple of well-deserved and very underhanded comments at Dylan before pulling Cole away to tell him how I felt.

It'd be perfect.

"Cole!" I called out as I started walking towards him. Just as he started laughing (actually laughing) at something Dylan said.

What the hell?

Our eyes met for just a second, and I could've sworn his expression softened a bit as he opened his mouth to... *invite me over to them?* But just as suddenly, he stiffened, *stopped* laughing, and broke eye contact with me.

I tried to swallow the lump in my throat but kept walking toward him—even though every fiber in my being was telling me not to.

He deserves to be a little mad at me. I can be the one to grovel for once. Right?

"Hey, Cole, can I talk to you... *alone* for a minute?"

He stared at me, his expression uncharacteristically unreadable, then tilted his head slightly. "What do you want, Gracie?" His tone wasn't outright mean, but it was sharp enough to hurt a little.

"Please?" I asked again, trying to meet his gaze as he shared a look with Dylan as if to ask *Can you believe this chick right now?*

Oh, great. This is so much more worse than I thought.

"Ohhh, Cole's in trouble," Dylan grinned, just as one of the other guys was snickering.

I felt my cheeks burn with embarrassment. *It's official. I'm in my own personal hell.*

Cole's jaw tightened as the silence between us stretched. But after a long minute, he decided to have mercy on what shreds of my social life remained and exhaled loudly to the table.

"I'll be back," he said, but not before joining in laughter at a joke Dylan, the *king of the assholes* made about one of the freshmen walking by.

We stopped near the door at the edge of the cafeteria, and I let a beat pass (mostly so I could stop myself from crying like a loser) before turning to face him.

Maybe it's not as bad as I think it...

But giving him a once-over, I noticed that his body language was completely closed. And he almost looked... bored to be here?

His eyes were back on Dylan's table.

I think I want to die.

"I couldn't say it last night," I blurted out before I could change my mind. "But that doesn't mean I don't feel it. I love you too, Cole."

His arms tightened across his chest, but his expression didn't change. "You *love* me?"

"I do." I took a breath, forcing myself to keep going even though I felt like I was five seconds from vomiting. *You can be mad at me, just don't stay mad at me forever.*

"I think... I think I've loved you for a while now, but I was too scared to admit that to myself. I'm so sorry for everything. I treated you like shit, and you have every right to be mad. But I want to fix it. I know what I want now, and that's *you*. Always."

For a second, I could've sworn I saw his shoulders soften a little like he might actually hear me out. But then, like a door slamming shut, it was gone, replaced by total indifference all over again.

He cleared his throat. "I got my memories back, Gracie. I know what you were doing."

Wait, what? Oh crap.

I opened my mouth, desperate to try to explain myself, but he didn't give me the chance.

"You let me follow you around this stupid school, embarrassing the hell out of myself because I thought I had feelings for you..."

My stomach plummeted then. "You *thought* you had feelings for me?" I repeated quietly, the words burning a hole through me.

"*Yes,*" he answered, shaking his head like he couldn't believe it had taken that long to realize it. "We're Cole and Gracie. We hate each other. And you know what?" he narrowed his eyes at me. "I bet this whole thing was like Christmas morning to you. You finally got what you wanted. You made me look like an idiot in front of everyone."

"Wait, no. I—"

"So, congratu-fucking-lations. You won. Is that what you wanted to hear? You made me think that someone like you could ever fall for a monster like me. Let's just go back to our own lives now, alright? I've got football, you've got..." he gestured toward me.

You know it's FFA. I wanted to say. But he didn't. Maybe because remembering hurt too much. "...your thing. You played the long game. You got me back for what I did to you in middle school. See you around, I guess."

"Cole, please just—"

He didn't let me finish. Instead, he turned and walked back to his friends, leaving me standing there all alone in the cafeteria.

My chest hollowed as the reality of what had just happened sank in.

We were Gracie and Cole.

We were supposed to hate each other.

His feelings for me weren't real.

I'd just lost him. For good.

Chapter Thirty-Seven:

MARCH 22ND

C ole

Hillview High was the same as always. The hallways were still crowded and noisy, the cafeteria still smelled like day-old pizza, I had my old table back, my old *friends* back, I could walk into a room and people respected me for just being there...

But it all felt different now.

Or maybe *I* was different now.

I did what I was supposed to do: I squared my shoulders, plastered a smirk on my face and acted like nothing was bothering me. But something *was* bothering me, and I wasn't sure why.

The guys were cracking raunchy *your mom* jokes while they shoved each other around, and normally, I'd be right there with them, soaking it in, playing the part. But now, it felt like I *was* playing a part.

My stupid brain kept paralleling Gracie and my team, comparing what used to be and what *should* be.

All I knew was that if I were with Gracie, we would be getting ready to head to our next classes instead of actively trying to ditch fourth period.

She never liked you. She was just getting back at you for always being a dick for her. Why can't you just see that?

Maybe because there was a part of me that didn't want that to be true.

Max glanced at me out of the corner of his eye, his brow furrowed just slightly, like he was trying to gauge what version of me he was dealing with today.

Ever since I'd gotten my memories back, he'd been watching me like I was a bomb about to go off. And I guess I couldn't blame him—I *felt* like a bomb about to go off half the time, for no reason other than everything just feeling... different.

I should've been grateful to have my old life back. Coach had even felt so bad about the whole accident thing that he'd offered to let me be captain again next year.

But deep down, I think I knew that if I had the choice, if I could go back and lose my memory all over again, I'd do it happily.

I'd go back to being blissfully unaware of my past, *especially with Gracie*, so I could keep loving her—even if she didn't give two flying shits about me.

And how fucked up was that?

We were getting close to her locker now, and my pulse picked up instinctively.

There she was: her dark hair falling over her shoulders as she filed through her notebooks.

She hadn't seen me yet. I could've kept walking (I *should've* kept walking), but something rooted me in place.

Because I still wanted to see her.

Even if it was just from a distance.

Unfortunately, Dylan noticed her too, ruining the moment.

"Would you look who it is!" he said, elbowing me as a grin crept up his face.

My jaw clenched before I could stop it. Something about the way he looked at her (*at Gracie*) pissed me off. Like she was just another girl to tease or whatever the hell Dylan did.

Let's get one thing straight: she was *not* just another girl.

No.

She was the girl who argued with me about the littlest damn things, the girl who infuriated me beyond what should've been humanly reasonable... the girl who used to hum along to the radio without realizing it, who was so beautiful it almost hurt...

And even if we weren't talking, even if she hated my guts (*and I was supposed to hate hers too*), she wasn't for Dylan or anyone else to even *look* at.

Possessive? Maybe. But she was supposed to be mine—mine to annoy, mine to tease, mine to...

Don't finish that thought.

"Relax, dude," Max muttered beside me, nodding at the way my hands had tightened into fists without me even realizing.

"I *am* relaxed," I shot back, quickly shaking the tension from my arms.

Dylan was still grinning. "C'mon, Cole. Don't tell me all that fake dating has gone to your head. Isn't she supposed to be your mortal enemy or something?"

He nudged me again, and it took every ounce of self-control I had not to shove him into the nearest locker.

"She's not—" I started, but then I caught myself.

The guys were all watching now, waiting for me to deliver the entertainment of fighting with her to them on a silver platter.

*Why am I even defending her? We're **supposed** to fight. It's who we are.*

I let out a breath and forced a smirk, hoping it looked more natural than it felt. "She's nothing. You're right."

The words tasted like ash in my mouth.

"Watch and learn, boys," I muttered, straightening my jacket.

The guys' muffled laughter trailed behind me as I made my way toward her locker.

She was still standing with her back to me, her head tilted slightly as she shoved a stack of books back into her bag to flip through a blue one.

"I usually tell people blue because that's easier for them to remember. But it's not just one color. It's... the sunset. My favorite color is the sunset..."

I swallowed down the lump in my throat. This was going to be shit, wasn't it?

I had to figure out a way pull myself together. And to do it, I had to force myself to forget the past few months with her—no matter how much it killed me to.

But let's be real. If it hadn't been for the team still watching me, I would've tucked my tail between my legs and left right then.

Instead, I leaned against the locker beside hers, making sure the metal clanged loudly so she'd notice I was there. She flinched (just slightly), but it was enough to make my stomach twist violently.

I hated that. Hated that we were back to square one again... or maybe we were *always* there, and I had just been too blind to notice.

Right. Because she was just playing me the whole time.

"Hey, Gracie," I drawled, forcing my voice to sound casual. "How's my least favorite person doing today?"

Her fingers tightened on the notebook, the paper crumpling beneath her grip. She didn't look at me.

"Not today, Cole. Please." Her voice was steady but not small. No, Gracie was *never* small. "I'm not in the mood."

It wasn't the comeback I'd expected—or wanted.

We were *Cole and Gracie.* We were *supposed* to fight, supposed to yell, supposed to go for the jugular until one of us came out victorious. Then, we'd reset the game board and try again.

But besides her tone, this wasn't normal... like a lot of things these days.

What the hell had post-accident me done over the past couple of months?

Not that I didn't remember, because I *did.* But it just felt like I was living in the twilight zone. Gracie wasn't fighting back; I was *feeling* things for her. Dylan was more annoying than usual...?

No. Forget it. Everything was fine. Dylan was chill, and Gracie was in there somewhere. I just had to get back in the groove.

"Oh, come on." I pressed, angling toward her, "What's the matter? Still upset that your little plan didn't work until after we graduated high school? Could you imagine what a shitty year that would've been for me? Me chasing after you, thinking one day you'd actually love me back? Guess that's on me, though... thinking you were even capable of it, that is."

I was hoping by saying that, although *saying* it scraped my insides like broken glass, she'd put us back on the right track. Whip around and shove me or even throw her damn notebook at me. Something, *anything* for it to make sense to really hate her again.

Because right now? I couldn't. I couldn't fucking hate her for lying about wanting to be around me for months after the accident, and I didn't know why.

Maybe because I know I've done way worse.

Instead, she slid the notebook into her bag, pulling her locker door closed, and finally turned to face me.

Her expression wasn't angry. It wasn't *anything*, really.

"I hope someday, you realize that I meant what I said," she said quietly.

Then, she turned, disappearing into the crowded hallway.

I seethed as I watched her go.

Why the hell was she still on that? She'd *won* the war. So, why was she still pretending like she cared?

Like she had *ever* cared?

The guys around me were laughing again, slapping me on the back like I'd done something incredible, but it felt hollow.

Max shot me a look, one that told me he saw more than I'd wanted him to. He raised an eyebrow at me. "You good, man?"

"Yeah," I lied, shrugging him off. "I'm fine."

"You sure?"

"I have to get to class." I blurted out to no one in particular.

"Since when do you go to class...?" Dylan called after me as I stormed off.

The others kept up their conversation, already talking about next season, the party this weekend... all things that used to matter to me too.

But my thoughts kept drifting back to Gracie's expression, and to the way she'd looked at me like she was seeing through all of it.

Gracie

I went home and cried after that. Because even though I knew I shouldn't have, I still loved him.

Chapter Thirty-Eight:

MARCH 27TH

C ole

"Well, well, well. Would you look what the cat dragged in?"

I turned slowly to face him. *Dylan.*

We'd been hanging out a lot lately... maybe because falling back into my old life was a hell of a lot easier than admitting that I might've been wrong about everything to begin with.

Because who was I really? The quarterback from some nowhere town in Utah? The problem child hailed up on a pedestal I didn't deserve?

Was that even a life I could build anything on? Or was I trying to walk the same line my dad had just because it worked for him?

*But **did** it work for him?*

I thought back to that day. The day he was supposed to come home.

Mom setting the table. My sister toddling through the sprinklers in the backyard. Me, sulking on the couch, still mad that he wanted me to go camping with him for Labor Day instead of waterskiing with my friends...

For so long, I'd *decided* his feelings for him. That he had this esteemed football career and then threw it all away for a wife and kids.

That was the story *I* knew.

But what if *he* didn't think that way?

What if he'd thanked his lucky stars every day that he got to build a life with the woman he loved? That he got to turn a house into a home?

Even with the yelling. Or the fights. Even when I didn't make it easy for him, he would've still picked us. Every time.

Life didn't end when football did. Not for him.

So what if I had gotten it wrong? What if the way I remembered him wasn't the full picture?

There was a reason people still talked about him. A reason why he was Max's "second dad."

Not because he was a great athlete. But because he was a great *man*.

I'd had the chance to be like that too, and I'd fucked it all up. Because I'd been too wrapped up in my own ego and couldn't see a good thing when it was right in front of me.

Losing my memory had given me a chance to redo my life from the inside out. It'd given me a chance to do better, and I'd only seen it as a problem.

But who's to say that was what it even was? Even *if* all Gracie was doing by talking to me was getting back at me for everything I'd done to her.

If you were wrong about your dad, are you wrong about how Gracie feels too?

Was that right? Was I deciding her feelings for her?

"Cole?"

477

My head snapped back to Dylan. "Oh. Hey, man. Didn't see you there."

He clicked his tongue like I'd disappointed him. "You're not daydreaming about her again, are you? Trust me, you're better off."

But it wasn't just about Gracie.

It was *everything*.

How was I supposed to go back to who I was, knowing everything I knew now?

Because I wasn't pre-amnesia Cole anymore.

But I wasn't just the guy who'd forgotten everything either.

So, who the hell *was* I?

Dylan scanned the cafeteria when I didn't answer him. "I know what'll cheer you up..." He grinned, pointing suddenly. "*There*! Gandork. He's legit wearing elf ears right now. Go say something."

"I don't know..."

He scoffed, pushing past me. "*Fine*. I'll get you started then. Hey, Gandork!"

Garrett looked up from the conversation he was having with the chess club, instantly flushing red.

He then slunk back into his chair, where seconds earlier he'd been proudly showing off the elf costume I guessed he'd made. (We'd started talking in English class after I apologized to him, and he'd mentioned wanting to go into costume design after graduation, so the outfit made sense.)

"Nu-uh-uh. Not so fast, elf boy," Dylan sneered, grabbing Garrett's arm tight enough to make it turn pink.

Garrett gave me a look as if to ask me what *I* was doing.

Hell if I knew either.

You should say something...

478

I cleared my throat in warning, but there wasn't much else I could do. *Was* there?

"You know, Gandork," Dylan continued. "I'm really curious. Does your cape match your underwear? Maybe we should find out..."

As I stood behind him in *complete* silence, Max's voice echoed in my head: *"Fear might get people to follow you, but it'll never make them trust you."*

And then... I stepped aside—both metaphorically and physically.

Away from Dylan. Away from my past. Away from being just 'the quarterback.' Away from the person I used to be.

Because I wanted to be different.

No. I *was* different.

Getting my memory back didn't erase the last few months of my life. The Cole I was before and the Cole I am now could coexist. I *could* do better.

For my dad. For the life I was starting to rebuild. For *myself*.

This was it. This was where I finally chose better. Because I remembered my past. And I knew where my future was heading.

"Get your hands off him now."

Dylan gave me a look over his shoulder. "Excuse me?"

"I won't repeat myself again. Hands off. *Now.*"

At that point, a crowd had gathered. Dylan looked around us all and laughed like he couldn't believe it. "Very funny, Brown. You almost had me for a second there."

I stepped forward and yanked his hand off Garrett. *No, I'm not kidding.*

His face paled suddenly. "Cole?"

"I appreciate you keeping my spot warm for me until I remembered who I was. But your services are no longer needed. Because you know what

Dylan? I *do* remember who I am, and it's not someone who puts up with this kind of bullshit."

"Wait... we were just having fun."

I laughed dryly. "Yeah? Well, the time for fun is over. And if I *ever* hear that you're 'having fun' like this again, I'm gonna kick your ass."

I turned to Garrett then. "Come on, let's go."

For a second, he looked between the two of us in shock. But slowly, a shy smile grew on his face as he glanced at his friends.

"Can everyone else come too? I've been meaning to teach you this new game I picked up, and we'll need them for it..." he cleared his throat quickly, "That is, if you want to."

My mouth lifted at the corners. "Absolutely. C'mon, gang."

I could feel Dylan's eyes burning a hole into my back as we started walking away.

"Why the hell are you doing this, Cole?" he called out to me.

I turned around to face him one last time. "Because being the bully isn't who I am anymore." Then I clapped Garrett on the back. "You ready?"

His grin widened. "Ready."

And we walked away from my past together.

For good this time.

Chapter Thirty-Nine:

APRIL 19TH

G racie

Before I knew it, March had ended, and so much had happened.

After Emma's entire life had blown up (because of me), CPS did a little digging into her family tree and discovered that she actually had a grandmother living in New Hampshire.

One thing led to another, and *bam*! She was on a plane heading across the country, while her dad rotted in jail.

As for Cole, he'd slipped back into his old life pretty easily. I'd even heard rumors that he was set to reclaim his spot as captain of the football team in the fall.

It was like the past couple of months had never happened. Well... mostly.

Anyone with half a brain could see he was different now. He started taking classes more seriously, started *studying*... There were even a few times when I would walk into the library to find him already there working on his math homework or something.

But the biggest difference was... he was nicer now.

He was a better friend to Max, and I'd even seen him step in when some underclassmen were getting harassed by Dylan and his groupies.

The old Cole might've laughed along, but this one didn't. He'd just stand up and say something to shut Dylan up instantly. Then, he'd make sure the kid was okay before walking away like it was no big deal. Like he was some kind of freaking hero.

I'd catch him staring at me in the hallway too sometimes, like he was working up the courage to say something. He'd even tried once. But I'd just shaken my head and walked away.

Because truthfully, I wasn't ready for what we had to be over.

Maybe he was right. Maybe we were just too different. Maybe we were always destined to hate each other. But I *couldn't* hate him. So I stayed away and let myself keep the good memories we had together instead.

Speaking of good, though, Bear was awake (thank God).

I couldn't even begin to explain what it'd felt like to hear his voice again. Or to watch him roll his eyes when I stole his pudding cups from the hospital tray. And every time there was a hockey game on, I'd drag my homework to his room, and we'd watch it on his tablet together.

And even my *parents* were trying more.

The other night, my dad came home *early* and asked how my day had been. I was so caught off guard at first, all I could do was stare at him in complete shock. But then we talked, *really* talked, about school and everything in between. And for once, I didn't feel like invisible.

We weren't a normal family by any means, and I didn't think we ever would be. But it was a start.

As for me... I was caught somewhere between the mess.

Junior year had been a whirlwind of moments that forced me to face parts of myself I'd spent years running from. It hadn't been easy, but it'd been worth it.

I'd found my way back to God.

Not in some big, dramatic way, but in the little things: the quiet of the morning, the warmth of the sun through my window, the way music sometimes felt like it was speaking directly to me.

I'd even started going to church again—not *that* church, and not back on a worship team. I wasn't ready for that, and maybe I never would be. But I was learning that was okay.

Faith wasn't about having all the answers. Sometimes, it was just about believing there was still more *life* to live.

And to give, too.

Because now I knew what happened to me wasn't my fault.

I was a *survivor* (that was something I called myself now, by the way).

Not because it erased the pain, but because it recognized my strength.

And with the school year winding down, I knew it was finally time to use that strength to move forward.

But first, I needed to say goodbye.

The drive to West Canyon Park felt longer than I remembered, like the road itself was stretching to give me more time to rethink what I was about to do.

But I didn't turn around. I didn't run from it. Not this time.

The gravel crunched under my tires as I pulled into the clearing, and my hands tightened around the wheel. I hadn't been back since... well, everything that'd happened with Cole.

But the memories were still here, waiting for me. Even before I stepped out, I could feel them pressing in from every direction...

This was it—the place where I'd first fallen in love.

It was funny. I'd been so sure that I wasn't someone who *could* fall in love that I'd ignored all the signs of it happening. But now, I realized... that was what love felt like. *Him*.

And even though he was gone to me for all intents and purposes, we would always have the memories.

Especially of that night.

I climbed out of the car, my heartbeat loud in my ears.

The clearing by the lake looked exactly the same, like time hadn't touched it at all.

The same massive oak tree stood tall near the water's edge, its branches dipping low, and for a second, I could almost see him standing there, hands shoved in his pockets, shyly grinning at me just before he pulled me into his arms to dance.

I let out a slow breath and pulled my notebook from my bag, flipping to the letter I'd written and rewritten about a million times.

It wasn't just a goodbye to Cole—it was a goodbye to the part of me that stayed stuck in this place, clinging to something I knew I couldn't have anymore.

I sat on a smooth boulder near the water and quickly scribbled out one last line. After a minute, I folded the letter carefully, smoothing out the creases before standing and heading for the bridge that stretched over the lake.

I used to love this spot—mostly because it reminded me of him. Now, it was something else. A crossroads. A moment I couldn't take back once I let go.

My fingers shook slightly as I held the letter over the edge.

I didn't *want* to let it go. I didn't want the parts of Gracie and Cole that I'd come to love to end.

All the late-night confessions, the Christmas food fights, that feeling when someone *finally* takes the time to understand you—not who you portray on the outside, but who you *are* on the inside...

But at the same time, letting go wasn't about forgetting. It wasn't about pretending something had never mattered. It was about making peace with the fact that it had.

There would always be a part of me that wanted to keep walking down memory lane just to run into him.

But not today.

I kissed the edge of the envelope softly, and then, before I could talk myself out of it, I let go.

The letter drifted down, catching the golden light of the setting sun before it hit the water with a quiet ripple. The ink bled almost instantly, softening the words into something unreadable.

I stood there for a long time, watching the ripples, along with my letter, until they faded into the stillness of the lake.

Cole

I'd told myself I wasn't going to do this.

For the past hour, I'd been pacing up and down the hospital halls. Not in the main ones either—no, I'd stuck to the quieter parts, the ones where nobody would notice me walking back and forth, pretending like I had a reason to be there.

Or maybe I was just trying to talk myself out of it altogether.

It was stupid. *I* was stupid. Who's to say she would even be there? Or that she'd even want to see me?

I shoved my hands in my jean pockets as my eyes kept darting down the hall, looking for any sign of her—dark hair, oversized glasses, that determined walk she had when she was on a mission. But nothing.

This wasn't even the first time I'd done this.

I'd seen her a couple of times at school—just long enough to catch her in the hallway before she ducked into class or went the other way.

She hadn't wanted to talk to me since the hallway incident. I got it. I deserved that. But that didn't make it any easier.

Maybe I should've just left. She'd probably see me and think, *What in the actual hell is he doing here?*

But my feet didn't get the memo, and I kept going, desperate to see *her*.

When I'd finally managed to find Bear's room (they'd moved him since the last time I was here), I stopped, leaning awkwardly against the doorframe, peering inside.

Gracie wasn't there, *damn my luck*, but her parents were, sitting next to Bear, who looked pale but was awake.

Relief flooded me for a second.

But it was quickly drowned by a wave of guilt.

Bear being awake was *huge*. It was the kind of thing Gracie would have told me about before... everything.

She would've called or texted me in all caps or with way too many emojis. And I would have enjoyed every fucking second of it.

But I hadn't been there for her when she needed me most.

I hadn't been there for her at all.

Maybe I was right. Maybe she *was* only trying to get back at me for always being a jerk to her... *by being your friend, dumbass?*

And see that's where I lost that battle. Because if she *had* just been using me, would we really have gotten to know each other like we had?

"I hope someday you realize I meant what I said..."

"Cole?"

I looked up from the wall I'd just zoned out on to find three pairs of eyes directly on me.

I hadn't ever met Gracie's parents before, and I was sure Bear wasn't going to vouch for me, so for all they knew, I was just some deranged psychopath looking for their daughter.

"What are you doing here?" Bear asked from his bed.

"I just, uh... wanted to check in," I mumbled, my hands going deeper into my pockets as I stepped inside. *Smooth. Real smooth.* "You holding up okay?"

"Yeah. Just tired."

The silence that followed was uncomfortable enough to make me regret staying at all.

I glanced around the room like Gracie would somehow materialize out of thin air, but all it did was remind me how out of place I was.

What was I even doing here anyways? Trying to apologize for the past month? In front of Gracie's *family*? In a *hospital*?

It sounded like a better plan in my head.

After what felt like an eternity of staring at me, Gracie's dad turned his attention back to Ms. Lewis. "Did you see that thing on the news? Some girl claiming sexual assault. Talk about daddy issues." He chuckled then like it was some kind of joke.

That's when it hit me. Just how fucking disgusting hearing that sentence come out of someone's mouth was.

It threw me back to middle school, and it was only then that it clicked...

I had no right to start the rumor that Gracie had slept with someone back then, and I *especially* had no right to hate her after she decided to finally fight back.

If the past couple of months had taught me anything, it was that the woman was a saint.

Because for her to help me navigate life again after the accident, not because she had to, but because she *wanted* to, especially after everything I had done to her? That showed just how fucking incredible of a person she was.

She was the first person in my life to show me that I mattered more than my past. And you know what? I took it back. She was never "pretending to be my friend." She really *was* my friend, and I'd let my pride and ego get in the way because I was too stubborn to accept it, to accept *her*.

I cleared my throat slowly.

Gracie didn't need me fighting her battles for her. Hell, she'd probably be pissed if I even *tried* to fight them for her, but I had to say it.

"Just so we're clear? That girl on the news? You don't know her. You don't know what happened to her, or how hard it probably was for her to say something to someone. You have no idea what girls like her have to go through. Or what your *own daughter* has had to go through. So, maybe you should think before you speak."

The room went silent.

Gracie's mom stared at me, wide-mouthed, her eyes darting to Mr. Lewis like she couldn't believe some random guy had walked into her son's hospital room and called him out like that.

Bear just grinned at me from his bed, as if he were impressed, and Mr. Lewis... he just sat there, stunned into silence.

Good. I hope he replayed every word over and over in his head until they crushed him.

"Where is she?" I asked suddenly.

I was going to make this right with her. No matter what it took. It'd be her choice to forgive me or not now.

Gracie's mom blinked at me. "Who? Gracie?"

"Yes, *Gracie*."

She shared a look with Mr. Lewis. "She stepped out for a minute. Why?"

I didn't answer. Because I didn't care what else they had to say. I realized then that I knew exactly where she was.

I spun on my heel, my feet moving before my brain had fully caught up with it.

My heart slammed into my ribs as I sprinted down the hallway and out the hospital doors. The cool evening air hit my face like a wake-up call, but it had nothing on the wake-up call I'd gotten in that room.

Because now, I *finally* got it.

I finally understood why it was so hard for her to trust people. Why me pushing her buttons had never helped. And even why her telling me she loved me wasn't "some thing." It was a *huge* fucking deal.

It wasn't something she'd just say because I did. She'd waited—waited until she really felt it. Because she hadn't planned on falling for me. She'd fallen for the person I'd become.

And I could be that person again.

I *wanted* to be that person again.

I fumbled with my car keys, throwing myself into the driver's seat like my life depended on it.

Because it did.

I'd probably have to explain to Gracie later why her dad was so weird around me. Hell, I'd probably never get invited to a family dinner after what had just happened in the hospital. But I'd defend her again in a heartbeat.

Because I *loved* her.

I didn't even care if she never forgave me. I just needed her to know she wasn't alone anymore.

The wheels squealed as I pressed my foot to the gas and pulled out of the parking lot.

I was coming.

And no matter how long it took, I was hers, and I'd spend the rest of my life proving it to her.

My truck screeched to a halt in the gravel lot, the tires spitting up dust like the world was on fire, and it sure as hell felt like it.

My heart hammered so hard that I could feel it in my throat as I threw open the door and ran, my boots pounding against the ground.

And then I saw her.

Gracie.

She was standing on that stupid old bridge, her figure outlined by the fiery orange of the sunset.

For a second, time stopped, and all I could see was her. Ethereal. Perfect. Like the kind of moment you'd spend the rest of your life trying to hold onto.

But that's when reality hit.

Leaning over the railing, on a bridge with all the stability of a dollar-store lawn chair, in the middle of nowhere, completely alone...

I mean, who was I kidding? I'd tried to do the same thing for less.

But I had to hand it to her. The girl could make a bad decision look poetic.

Dude, not the time—right.

My body moved on instinct, quickly closing the distance, and before I knew it, my arms were around her waist.

I pulled her back so hard from the ledge that we both stumbled, but I didn't care. She wasn't going anywhere. Not on my watch.

She whipped around, anger firing off like flares in her eyes, but all I cared about was that she was still here.

Still breathing. Still Gracie.

"*What the hell, Cole?*" she yelled, shoving me off her.

"I thought you were gonna jump!" I fired back, my voice louder than I meant for it to be. "Are you *insane*?"

"Are *you* insane? Why would you even think that?"

"I don't know!" My hands raked through my hair, my chest heaving as I struggled to fight the adrenaline coursing through my veins. "Because I'm losing my mind, okay? Because after everything, the thought of losing you—"

I cut myself off, swallowing hard.

She rolled her eyes, but her expression softened. "Don't flatter yourself, Cole. If I was going to end it all, it'd take more than you to push me there."

"Oh, *real mature*, Princess." I shot back, the nickname slipping out before I could stop it.

Her lips parted, as if she were about to argue some more, but she stopped herself. "You haven't called me that in a while," she said, her voice quieter, almost like she missed it.

Not as much as I missed her.

I didn't mean to smile, but there it was, pulling at my lips. "You're still my princess, Gracie. Always have been."

She looked up at me, like she didn't know whether to roll her eyes or cry, and for a second, I thought she might do both.

I took a step closer, still watching her.

Her eyes darted across my face like she was trying to figure me out, trying to decide if I was here to stay. There was something in the way her cheeks flushed (a soft, rosy pink that I'd been hopelessly obsessed with for months) that damn near undid me.

And then, almost at the exact same time, we both said it.

"I'm sorry."

Her eyes widened for half a second, and I couldn't tell if she was surprised I said it or surprised that *she* did.

"I didn't mean it," she said quietly, looking away. "What I said about your dad, about you... I was wrong, and I shouldn't have pushed you away like that. You were just trying to help, and I'm sorry. I understand why you can't..." she swallowed, like the words physically hurt to say, "love me."

My stomach dropped. "Is that what you think this is? That I don't love you?"

"I mean..." she started, "Yeah. We're 'Gracie and Cole.' We hate each other, right?"

I let the words sink in for a beat, but not before I slowly reached for her hand.

She flinched slightly, her brows furrowing like she wasn't sure what to make of me, but then she let her fingers entwine with mine.

"You're right. We're Gracie and Cole. We get on each other's nerves, we're both stubborn as hell... on paper, we shouldn't work. But we do." I exhaled a shaky breath, trying to find the right words. "Losing my memory was probably the best thing that ever happened to me because it gave me a second chance... with *you*. And I'd lose it all again if it meant I got to find you every time."

Her eyes glistened, and she let out a soft, almost disbelieving laugh as I lifted her hand to my lips and kissed it. "You're such a sap."

"Only for you," I murmured.

I didn't wait another second to lean down and kiss her for real.

She melted into me, her free hand gripping the front of my shirt like she didn't want to let go. I didn't want to either.

When I finally pulled back, just enough to catch my breath, her cheeks were even more flushed, her lips slightly swollen, and she looked so damn beautiful it hurt.

"Now," I said, a smirk tugging at my lips as I brushed a strand of hair away from her face, "let's get off this bridge before we actually fall in."

She laughed, smacking my chest lightly, leaning into me as we walked back, hand in hand.

And for the first time in a long time, I believed in happy endings.

Chapter Fourty:

May 26th

"Took me long enough to come out here, Dad," I muttered, standing in front of his grave, having no idea where to even start.

The headstone was weathered but well taken care of. Clearly, there was no shortage of people who loved him.

But I'd never been one of the people to come out here and see him.

It'd always felt... too hard.

Though, something had changed for me in the last couple of months. I *needed* to be here right now. I needed to talk to him.

I knelt down, brushing a few stray leaves off the base of the stone. "It's been a while. Guess that one's on me, huh?"

A shaky breath escaped me as I looked up at the sky for a minute. The clouds were shifting in the late afternoon light.

"The past couple of months have been a wild ride. Like, *wild* wild. You probably wouldn't even believe half of it."

A smile tugged at the corner of my mouth. "I lost my memory. Forgot everything—my name, my life... all of it. But honestly? It ended up being the best thing that could've ever happened to me. It made me fix a lot of stuff I didn't even realize was broken."

A lump formed in my throat, and I swallowed hard. "I've apologized to a lot of people recently. But, uh... there's one person I haven't made up with yet. *You.*"

"I'm sorry, Dad," I said, my voice breaking just a little. "For being a jerk. For pushing you away. For not wanting to go on those camping trips with you. I thought I had all the time in the world, and then... I didn't. I didn't realize how much I'd miss you until you were gone."

I rubbed my fingers through the grass at the base of his grave, trying to hold myself together. "You were the best damn dad there was, and I'm forever grateful for the time I got to spend with you."

The words hung in the air, and I let my eyes drift to the headstone, the neat, clean letters carved into stone—a name I shared.

A memory came to mind—the one I'd gotten before the rest had come back to me. Fishing with him, the mist rising off the lake. The pride in his voice when I reeled in the biggest trout of my life, the belly laughter when we accidentally fell into the water...

"I'd give anything for one more camping trip," I whispered. "One more weekend to just talk. To not rush through the time I had like it didn't matter. I wish I could tell you how much those trips actually meant to me."

I took a deep breath, letting the silence settle over me. But for the first time in a while, it didn't feel suffocating. It felt... peaceful. Like he was listening. Like he understood.

From a distance, I heard the car horn. Max, probably. He and Gracie were waiting for me, probably wondering what was taking so long.

I glanced over my shoulder. "Just a minute!" I called, grinning.

I turned back to the headstone. "I have to go, Dad. Tonight's a big night for me. I'm asking Gracie to be my girlfriend."

I chuckled at the thought. If you would've told me a year ago that I'd be head over heels in love with the girl I thought I hated, I would've called you crazy. "You'd like her. She's spunky. Keeps me in check. And you and I both know I need that."

The horn honked again, longer this time, and I laughed, rolling my eyes.

"By the way," I added, "Chloe's doing okay. She's gotten into the trumpet recently, which has been... fun." I laughed, shaking my head. "Who am I kidding? It's awful. She's so bad it rattles the windows, but she's determined. I bet you're laughing your ass off up there watching us suffer through it."

One last thing.

I reached into my bag and pulled out one of Dad's old camping lanterns, the one he'd always insisted on bringing for good luck, even if it barely worked anymore.

We'd found it while we were cleaning the closet in Mom's office, and she'd let me have it. But I got the feeling it was better kept with Dad.

I set it carefully at the base of his headstone, letting my fingers stay for just a second longer. "I'm looking forward to going on one of our camping trips again someday," I said quietly.

The horn blared for a third time, and I stood up, brushing off my jeans.

As I turned to leave, something caught my eye—a sudden flash of movement.

An owl swooped down, landing on the tree branch above me and my dad. It tilted its head, looking at me for just a minute before taking off again, disappearing into the sky.

My breath caught in my throat.

Because somehow, I knew it was him. He'd been looking out for me all along.

Love you too, Dad.

With that, I turned and jogged back to the car, taking a deep breath to steady myself.

I barely had time to buckle myself into the passenger seat before Gracie was leaning forward and kissing me, her lips soft and warm against mine. "Took you long enough," she teased.

Max smirked from the driver's seat, slapping me on the back. "Let's go, gang. We've got a party to crash."

As the car pulled away from the cemetery, I glanced back one last time. The lantern sat steady at the base of his headstone, gleaming faintly in the fading light.

I'd see him again. Someday soon.

But not too soon, I thought, smiling as Gracie reached for my hand.

There was still so much more to live for.

Acknowledgements

It's hard to believe that *Forget Me Not* started out as an idea I had while sitting on my brother's bedroom floor. It was spring break of my seventh grade year, and I thought... what better way to deal with the boredom than to write a book? Little did I know that this story would follow me through first kisses, high school graduation, go all the way with me to Arizona and then back to Utah for college, and survive love, loss, and everything in between.

So before I get started thanking anyone, I need to thank thirteen-year-old me who was born a dreamer and believed in this story even when I didn't. We did it!!

But my dreams of getting this book out into the universe would have never been possible without these people helping along the way:

I'm sending the MOST love to my beta readers (AKA, my unpaid family and friends): Damien Candelaria, Al Hollis, my mom, dad, Mimi, and Grandpa—you guys absolutely rock.

Also, thank you SO MUCH to my editors, Yoanna, Leilani, and Emily Lisa T. for taking my little manuscript and turning it into something truly amazing.

Lastly, to anyone who has a past that they think disqualifies them from love, this story is for you. Remember that you are not too broken for remembering, and you are NOT too weak for hurting.

Healing doesn't always mean forgetting; sometimes it means carrying the memory and choosing love anyway.

Thank you, thank you, THANK YOU for picking up this book and giving it a chance. Love you lots!

xoxo,

Savannah

Savannah Sheets has been telling stories for as long as she can remember. When she was little, she'd line up the letter magnets on her refrigerator door, inventing far-off places filled with princesses and princes—even going as far as to start writing them down just so her mom would never run out of things to read to her and her younger brother.

Somewhere between the gibberish and scribbles, she fell in love with the way words could make people feel something. That same love for understanding others led her to studying criminal justice, where she hopes to keep telling stories that matter—both on and off the page.

Follow her journey on Instagram @savannah_sheets to stay up to date on her latest projects and adventures!

www.ingramcontent.com/pod-product-compliance
Lightning Source LLC
Chambersburg PA
CBHW010646100726
47901CB00009B/2450